Remapping Wonderland

Remapping Wonderland

CLASSIC FAIRYTALES
RETOLD BY PEOPLE OF COLOR

VARIOUS AUTHORS

Selected by
Leah Angstman, Jen Corrigan,
Steph Post, and Eric Shonkwiler

Curated and Edited by
Leah Angstman

Alternating Current Press
Boulder, Colorado

Remapping Wonderland
Classic Fairytales Retold by People of Color
Various Authors
©2021 Alternating Current Press

Alternating Current
Boulder, Colorado
alternatingcurrentarts.com

ISBN: 978-1-946580-16-0
First Edition: January 2021

"THE LITERATURE OF AMERICA
SHOULD REFLECT THE CHILDREN OF AMERICA."
—LUCILLE CLIFTON

Table of Contents

Once upon a time ...

To Be Noble

A RETELLING OF SLEEPING BEAUTY
ARIELLE K. JONES

t were as if all the world's greens had made a place for themselves somewhere in this overgrown garden. Even in the dim of the rainy weather, the varying shades of vegetation peeked from beneath one another's leaves. The ground could not be seen, and with every step toward the tower, the prince watched his boots disappear into flexible green hands. The hidden mud beneath it sucked at his steps. As he continued, the rooted emeralds grew taller until he was wading through the slick, entwined brush. Often, the plants would catch at his burning thighs and tangle at his ankles, and he would pant against the rainfall.

The rain made everywhere sound the same. It fell into his eyes the higher up he looked. He had been warned that the tower was tall, yet somehow still he had not quite expected what he saw. Before him, it looked so slender against the sky that he wondered how it hadn't fallen yet. With a sigh, the prince smeared the back of his cold hand across his cold face, and the water simply spread. He trudged onward.

Many more times than once, he knelt in the mud to cut away the mess of nature that had fastened to his boots. He would take rest in these pauses to catch his breath.

By the time he reached the base of the tower, leaves and petals were high enough to caress his chin, and the sun had gathered enough strength to seep through the heavy clouds for a piece of time. The instant of light made it easier for him to see the difference between the color of his glove and the dark stone of the tower. He removed the leather and allowed himself to smile as he pressed his palm to something so ancient that had survived so long unaided. Lightly, he trailed over part of the surface that had managed to peep through some vines, and the tower was jagged and dripping.

Finding his footing was not what was difficult. The vines were knotted and thick enough to function as a ladder. What required most of his effort was securing safe places for his fingers. In that brief glimpse of sun, the thorns shown slickly. The smile of the prince dwindled, and he put his glove back on. Most of these thorns were the length of his thumb and were not green, but brown and hardened by time and necessity.

For the first time since he set out on this journey, he wondered if there was even a princess at the top. Regardless, he climbed.

As the afternoon passed, the rain went on, and he went on struggling for nothing more than a possibility. He suffered thorns pricking at his stomach, nipping at his knees, points scraping his thighs and seeking out his ankles; he took it all for a face he wouldn't recognize, a voice he'd never heard, for a name he'd never known. Yes, he knew he was bleeding for a stranger. He knew and he climbed still, perhaps because he knew she couldn't ask him to.

Upon his departure, neither his family nor his royal court could fathom his faith. They allowed him to pursue this venture but had given him no resources. It is true that his very people doubted his ability to reason. But what higher calling to life could there be than to seek out the forsaken?

Even so, with every downward glance, his heart bumped against the edges of his throat, and it was then he wondered how many had fallen. Outside of any conscious commands, his eyes squeezed shut, his careful hands became clenched fists around vines that bit him, and he was inhaling so quickly that he sputtered on rain, nearly losing balance.

At once, he seized his mind and swallowed. And alone, as he calmed his breath, he made his first promise to the sleeping girl within the tower. He swore that if he ever found out how many had tumbled for her sake, he would never tell her. And from then on, he did not look down.

By the time he reached the window he hadn't seen from the ground, the sun was setting, and the prince didn't look so much like majesty. After hours of strain, his immediate reward was to curl up to rest on a window ledge, shivering with numb digits and feverish arms. He was like a bird on a branch in a blizzard. He wanted to fall asleep. He wanted to huddle into a corner protected from the wind, to dream of being warmer. It could have been nice, but he had a purpose, and although dreams are good for inspiration, results are always born of action.

Carefully, he stood and braced himself on the ledge facing a fragile stained-glass window. The colors were not at all as brilliant as they would have been in lighter days, but none of the luster was lost to him. The scene the artisan had left behind was of the mountains not too far from here, proud and indigo, and in the glass it was spring and the sky was yellow, and the meadows at the feet of the golden foothills were crowned with pastel flowers. It was stunning, and this man hoped that all this time she had been dreaming of this place. If he were truly to take her to such a place, then this barrier could not remain. He used his barely restored strength to bash in the stained-glass window, to break the reverie.

Dust swirled out as he stepped into the tower, over the shattered glass. The rain was quiet now. Inside the tower, his eyes gradually adjusted to the dim. When he could see, there was not much change in clarity. Everything looked overlaid in gray; a fog of age had settled. The prince strode in deeper and tried not to gag on the stagnant air. Webs curtained every direction he looked in. He could see the skeletons of their makers hanging in them, curled, translucent, and brittle. There was no counting how many of these fatal pale tapestries he'd had to pass through in this decayed room before he finally found her.

Her hair was long, dark, and matted and stretched partway across the floor. In the quiet, he claimed another step toward her, and when he did he could see moth holes throughout her ashen gown. The visible specks of her skin hardly owned any color as her once-existing eastern window only faced the rising sun. He stole another timid step nearer, and when he halted he noticed her breath for the first time. For every breath of hers, many of his had already come and gone. Her breathing was so slow that it never was enough to stir the veil of soft abandoned webs that lay upon her soft abandoned lips.

Tenderly, he brushed aside the sheer netting, leaving her face naked to him. His head went down, and before he surrendered to her, he held his face close enough that he felt her exhale warm and delayed across his mouth. Once he gave in, her sigh echoed in his throat as she woke, and for the first time in one hundred years someone knew the color of her eyes.

Time slowed when her lidded gaze swept over his face. The look inspired a weakening in the prince's spine, a fluid tingling that no amount of poise could support. Her voice was just as hauntingly tender.

"Is this another dream?"

The warmth that drifted from her words felt balmy and faint over his parted lips. He quite nearly kissed her again but suddenly wondered if the gesture would send her back to sleep. She seemed that delicate. Instead, he gently straightened and gave her a smile that teased pink onto her inquiring face.

"You are awake now, I promise," he assured her.

For a brief, nearly unknown moment, the waking beauty searched his face, and when she found that she trusted him, her budding tears made blinking a quiet mess. After forever, she had been found. She had become someone again. Her heart felt as if it would beat itself to the surface. Among her nightmares, she had dreamed of this day, and the aching was over.

Out of courtesy, the prince had given her some distance while she wept. A few paces away, he feigned interest in the layers of dull dust on the floor. When their eyes met again, he had an expression that thawed a bit of her timidity, and she watched him double over into a bow with a graceful dignity, one hand softly over his heart, the other arm arched beside him like a swan stretching his wing.

Polite affection shaped his words, "I have come to remove you from this tower, if that is your wish," and respectfully he rose.

Before the damsel could respond, thunder tumbled loudly through the sky. The gusts of the storm gasped outside the tower, howling and sighing in release. Cobwebs bounced. Ragged tapestries that had been camouflaged in dust undulated against the stone. Petals fallen from a forgotten bouquet dragged in pointless patterns on the ground, and there was grit churning in the angles where the walls met the floor, but she felt none of it.

The prince was at her bedside, a breathing barrier between her and the roar of the weeping world. He did not let her feel the cold that chilled the back of his neck and seeped into his scalp. With a fluid sweep of his arms, still sore from the climb, she was covered by his cloak, and the storm seemed such a distant thing. The heat of him lingered still in the fabric.

In a few lengthy strides, he went across the chamber and shoved debris into place to block the window, hard rain dashing against him from drafts of the downpour. Everything felt heavier than it should have. The fierce water stung his skin and fought small puddles into his clothes.

He could taste both the fresh water and the salt of his sweat when he panted from the strain of building the makeshift barricade. He only knew he was done when the icy glass stopped rattling and the natural nightmare taking place outside was less vivid, and the woman he woke called out to him, "You've done enough for me." She was sitting up, his cloak sliding down her shoulders. "Please, you should rest."

In soft surprise, he watched her struggle to slide her supple frame over on the bed, making enough space for him. When he did not immediately advance, the features of her face shifted into mild severity.

"Please, you haven't much time," she said.

A sickening descent occurred in his stomach at the words; an invisible hand clutched his heart. He tried to understand what she could possibly mean, but his thoughts were swaying in and out of clarity. As he approached, he found that his feet felt heavy, his lungs were laboring. Somehow, he managed not to slur when he said, "My apologies. Perhaps we can leave after I rest my eyes for a moment." It was a meager victory for him when he finally reached the edge of the bed.

Her palm was stable on his back, her voice soft in his ears. "I'm afraid not," she said, and the turn of her mouth was solemn. "I'm sure I will be gone before you wake, kind prince."

He didn't remember leaning onto her shoulder, but it was from there that he answered sleepily, "I don't understand."

It was strange; he had toiled up an entire tower, but somehow now he was more tired than he had ever felt in his life. With the cradling of a hand-sung lullaby, he was beckoned into her lap. Her fingertips sought his hair and casually tangled themselves.

She muttered above him, "You have saved me." But she did not seem absolutely pleased.

The prince had truly never wondered until then as to why this person out of everyone had been cursed to sleep in the first place. He should have wondered. But the time for wishes and rathers was long past. She plucked him from his thoughts while her hands pulled through his hair, and lazily at his neck. They swirled leisurely like a tide, granted him wave after wave of contentment interrupted by cruel words.

"We never could have been happy," she said. "It seems all you wanted was to satisfy your expectations on this adventure."

His breathing was slowed, but he still listened. The rain was just a lazy hum and drizzle. The storm was passing, had become quiet.

She said, *"One kiss to wake her, but the nightmare will recur. One kiss to save her, and the kind heart must endure.* Are you familiar with the rhyme?" Her hands stopped roaming. The silence seeped in, curled, questioned, thickened, and settled around them. She could not bear any longer and asked, "Do you know what this means, *kind heart?"*

When he was able, the prince spoke into the laden quiet after a heavy inhale, "If I understand, had we not ... shared breath ..."

"Had we not kissed, the curse would have remained with me," she corrected.

The silence threatened to return, but the prince softly defied it. "I see." He was patient, while he wore a wistful smile. "Then I had no choice. I would not leave you here to suffer." He faced her and added, "I did what I set out to do." The weary prince cast a satisfied smile her way.

She cried, this time not caring if he saw. "You are a noble fool." The accusation gracelessly stumbled out of her.

The prince, using what he could of his resolve, reached and brushed her cheek, and his fingers came back dappled in her tears. He wished he could do more, but he was fading fast. He experienced the sensation of riding in a paddleless boat with his feet dipped in warm periwinkle water. "What will I dream of?" he asked her with his eyes closed. He thought he heard a laugh, a mirthless, unfortunate laugh. It came close to breaking his heart.

"Today. Over and over again, you will dream of today, your last day," she said, a tone of spat venom. But a part of her wished that this was a dream, too, for his sake. She wished she had comfort to give instead of a sentence of suffering slumber.

Without her own will, her hands sought out the prince again. She wound her fingers in his tresses, she let them trail on his face, his handsome brow, the slope of his nose, the curve of his cheeks, the slip of his lips. There she could feel that for every breath of his, many of hers came and went.

"Wait!" she cried too late. She tried to rouse him with petite

fists pressing onto his slow-to-rise, slow-to-fall chest. "Please …
what is your name?" she wept. But it was too late.

The prince had gone to sleep for the last time for a long time.
The instant he closed his eyes, he became no one. He would be
nameless and forgotten just as all the other men who had gone
in search of her. His kind heart had condemned him. He was
asleep, and she was guilty in that tower for some time, a soul
twice surrendered to solitude. She would have the rest of her
life to grieve her innocence and rummage for her worth. She
would never be seen or heard from again.

But the prince, he would live peacefully ever after …

… until one fateful day some slow years later.

Had the prince been awake, he would hear the distant sound
of horses snorting and stamping their hooves at the bottom of
the tower, horses whose mothers had been born while he had
been so deeply asleep.

If he were awake, he would hear the rumble and shouts of
hearty folk making decisions, as well as their scattered outcries
at the height of this ancient tower before them, the ferocity of
the massive constricting vines. Their journey has already been
many days too long, and now that they have finally reached this
decaying monument of past glory, they realize that night will
soon be upon them. No one, not even the best of them, would
be able to make the climb even halfway up the tower before
dark.

"Are we truly here for this?"

"So, it exists. But what now?"

"No one could be in there."

Once the murmured complaints die out, the knight amongst
them makes the decision, says, "We will wait for morning. Clear
your own area of rest, and tie the horses to the tower."

His gaze steadily sweeps over the group before he descends
from his own steed and leads it by the reins to the stone. That
would be his last command of the afternoon, and as he walks
away, the murmurs resume, and the others bend to their own
troubles with backs to the setting sun.

They are thirty strong and faithful to the man who leads this journey that had taken them so many weeks from home. The only thing they know is that they are looking for someone. They used to ask questions but stopped bothering when all their leader would do was smile and say, "We'll have to reach the top and see."

Some it vexed, some it entertained, and for others the answer didn't matter. These are desirers of adventure and know they will be paid by their queen at the end of it all. They rest well during the night knowing that after tomorrow, once someone makes an attempt on the tower, it will be the beginning of their return home.

The knight wakes so early that the sun barely lends him any light. He can see his breath, and the breath of the horses, as he walks around the base of the old tower. He makes sure his gloves are on securely as he investigates. In the underbrush, they have been finding bones and boots and the remains of rope. The knight doesn't bother looking down anymore. As the sun rises, he can better see these vines. They twist and cling, and the thorns seem the size of arrowheads and maybe just as sharp. He doesn't bother touching them, just like he wouldn't touch his blade while sheathing it. And again, without touch, he has noticed something else as he walks around to the other side.

There is a place against the stone where the plants mingle the thickest, and it seems not to quite match a shape from nature. The knotting here is domelike and sunken in somewhat and is just larger than the height of him.

When he laughs, it is loud enough to wake his nearest followers. They do not understand until he asks for and then is given an ax. He is given room as he strikes away at obscure thatches of vines until, little by little, there becomes a pocket, then the creaking of a small collapse as he breaks through. He has found the doorway, the wooden door itself having rotted away long ago.

They bring him water once he has carved a space big enough for the largest of them to crawl through. When they sit to eat in tight circles, they hum with the same excitement as when the tower had first come into view. Once inside, will they need to fight? Which rumors were the right ones? What if they find nothing? And how will their eager leader respond?

And even though they are knee to knee, the knight isn't quite listening to them. He is eating too fast and is smiling to himself. They have arrived. The only task left to do is to reach the top.

The elder travelers in this group watch on endearingly as their knight rushes everyone through their morning routines. Some stall just to tease him, and others remind him that the tower will always be there, no matter how quickly or slowly they act. Many murmur in assent.

The knight is quick to find a sturdy piece of rubble to stand atop and tell them, "Those of you who would join me, step forward." When he hops down, he beams at the handful of companions who actually agree to follow him up. The others will watch the horses.

As volunteers gather around, it is easy for them to tell that the light in the dark gold of his eyes is not just from the climbing sun.

He bears an endearing frustration at the time it still takes to broaden the wreckage he had already done to the doorway. And even still, he warns them to be careful with the vines and their thorns. The growth could be poisoned or just sharp, but either way, they did not need to know by personal pain. They agree and carefully begin their ascent.

If they could compare it to anything, they would say it was like walking into a tree, truly into it. The darkness, the dank earthy grip of the air around them and the echoes of something other pressed close. It makes the camp and the warm food and the friendly chiding seem further than it is when, in truth, all they would have to do is turn around to see their comrades milling about and warming themselves in the daylight.

Someone hums. It is a song all of them recognize even if they cannot recall the words. It encourages them as they light the way, spiral by spiral. The flames are dull, but they work well enough that no one loses their footing up the stairs. One companion has had their hand in contact with the wall the entirety of the time. Another has kept a hand on her hilt, even when they have stopped for a short rest.

It is mostly quiet when they sit. The knight knows how likely it is that they each are imagining their own collection of tales that have been spun about this place, about what awaits them, about how he will react when they get to the height of this. As for his own thoughts, he can scarcely hear himself think past the drum of his heart in his ears and at his fingertips and the flex of his thighs as he stretches and waits. He is frowning, but even in the dark, someone still points it out. They mimic him one by one until he can laugh at himself and the taunts that come his way about how no one would want to be awakened by such an angry face, let alone kissed by it. He agrees, though mostly for the sake of getting them all moving again.

A new song gets whistled, and they continue upward. Through crumbled gaps in the cool stone, there are glimpses of the sky and how sunset looks like dawn come again. From then, it is hard to say for certain how much longer it takes them to come to the trapdoor.

An unspoken decision has been made. He will go in alone. They bless him one by one, pressing cheeks to cheeks and whispering his name with the utmost care. The last cheek to touch his leaves him swallowing what he would like to say out of fear. There are few things he has done out of fear. He has vowed not to let this list grow.

With a parting nod, he pushes his way through the entrance and climbs up. With the thud of the slat of wood behind him, he hears coughing from below. He cannot heed them now. His eyes are adjusting to the dark, and his body to the cooler temperature. The broadness of his back does not matter here as the wind rattles at the far end of the room and finds ways to trickle onto his skin, to bypass the layers he had donned. He has to remind himself to breathe before he tells himself to walk.

Behind tattered webs and the gray of the air, there is a bed.

The knight goes to his knee immediately and believes his queen would forgive him, for his first time kneeling for another. This poor soul, arms folded over stomach half tucked under the flowing sheet. The knight's touch is light as he approaches the figure and picks moth carcasses out of the scraggly beard. The little bodies are so brittle they break on their way to the ground. No one should be left this way.

He makes quick work of cutting the hair growing from the prince's head. There will be time to fashion it to his liking after they reach the bottom. The knight gently shifts the body into his arms until he can cradle him close enough to carry. It is so light, this body. The knight's heart skips, and his legs become questionable when the softest touch of breath strokes his throat. The man is alive. He knew it, but now it is confirmed with each long breath coming and going without pause, but without hurry.

Not a word is said as the knight's waiting companions help him descend. They take turns carrying the swaddled prince down the hundreds of steps, and the knight is always watching. At a point in the descent when they must halt to rest, they cluster around, sleeping long enough to be sure everyone can catch their breaths and find a moment of warmth.

He would rather not call it fear, but the knight allows that he is uncomfortable staying in the stairwell longer than he must. Because he is surrounded by friends, they give him the excuse by saying that they must be close to the bottom, so why not just continue the rest of the way down. To fresh air, to other familiar faces, to the sky; and whether daylight or the stars greet him, he finds it does not entirely matter.

Perhaps it does, though, because the knight finds himself remarkably relieved to feel the midafternoon sun on his face when he steps out of the final floor with his arms full of what others had told him was a fairytale.

Those who had remained at camp stare openly and forget what they had been doing. They see rags and limbs, where he sees someone he is already fond of.

The knight is offered water and relief of the body, but he holds the prince nearer, not unkindly. His companions bow as he passes and drives a path to his tent not too far off. He is glad for the time spent making sure his lodgings would be dry and secluded. He lays the prince down as reverently as anyone would lay flowers at a grave of a loved one they knew they would one day see again.

The knight draws the flap shut but knows that no one would try to enter. Retreating from others, he told them, would be important, necessary. And besides that, a member of his party—well versed in the mystic natures of curses and fates—had sworn that it was the tower itself that was cursed. And more personally, the knight knew it could be frightening to wake with too many eyes you could not name the faces of. That was more or less the reasoning he had shared with his companions beforehand as to why the prince and he would need solitude. However, a beloved scattering of people in this world would say that the knight simply prefers first kisses in private.

He will never tell the prince that the coarse hairs of his beard tickled when their lips met. The knight will, maybe one day, tell the prince that that first deep breath will always be a memory that shakes something alive in him. It comes in like an ocean swell and takes a part of the knight with it as the prince begins to blink. The prince's eyes flutter to and fro until he winces. When their gazes meet, the prince blinks his eyes into focus, mutters, "This dream ... this dream is different."

Gat-father Death

A RETELLING OF GODFATHER DEATH
SUH YOUNG CHOI

ong ago, there was a poor man who had twelve children. He worked day and night making *jipsin* shoes to support them, but he was uncertain in his finances. Each of his twelve children, therefore, became *suyang* daughters and sons to families that were better-off, for in those days, it was not unusual for a family to treat an outsider's child as one of their own, without formal adoption.

The jipsin-maker's wife brought forth a thirteenth child, a son, and the jipsin-maker did not know who would accept this son as a suyang child. He therefore set out on the road with the intent to ask the first person he encountered to take his son.

The road was empty. By sunset, the jipsin-maker still could not find anyone to ask. The spirits, awakening for the night, took pity on him. The spirit of heaven came to the jipsin-maker in the form of a jade-colored man and said, "I have seen you on your travels today and take pity upon you. I will take your child as my suyang son and raise him alongside my own children."

The jipsin-maker asked, "What are you called?"

The spirit answered, "I am Ohk-Hwang-Sang-Jae, the Jade Emperor of Heaven."

"I do not wish you for my son's guardian," said the jipsin-maker, "for you in the heavens hoard such gold and precious gems from us mortals as adorns your skin. How fortunate we may have been had you shared your wealth with us!" And the jipsin-maker walked past the spirit and went on his way.

Then the spirit of the earth came to him in the form of a three-footed crow and said, "I have seen you on your travels today and can grant what you wish. Give your child to me, and he shall have all the riches and splendors of the world."

The jipsin-maker asked, "What are you called?"

The spirit answered, "I am Sam-Jok-Oh, the Three-Footed Crow of Kings."

"I do not wish you for my son's caretaker," said the jipsin-maker, "for you lead men to corruption and deceit in the name of power. My son will walk a path of evil under your guidance." And the jipsin-maker walked past the spirit and went on his way.

Then the spirit of death in his black *hanbok* and *gat* came to him and said, "Let me be your child's guardian."

The jipsin-maker asked, "What are you called?"

"I have no name," said the spirit, "for I am the suyang guardian to all, and to none. I consume the rich and the poor alike, the learned and the ignorant, the emperor and the peasant. You may call me *juh-seung-sajah*, psychopomp and servant of the Great King Yum-Ra, who rules the seven hells."

The jipsin-maker tried to look under the gat, the brim of which overshadowed the psychopomp's face. When the jipsin-maker found he could not see under the gat, he bowed before the juh-seung-sajah and said, "Let my child be your suyang son."

"It is done." Perhaps the juh-seung-sajah was smiling, somewhere under that vast black brim. "He who is a friend of death cannot fail in life. Be assured that your son will be well taken care of."

And so the juh-seung-sajah watched over the child as the boy grew and came of age. When it was time for the boy to choose a trade and apprentice himself, the juh-seung-sajah appeared in the boy's home and took him to a private room. There, he produced a fold of burlap from his hanbok, which held ten *chim*, or acupuncture needles, one each for the ten lords of the hells.

"With these," said the juh-seung-sajah, "you shall become the greatest doctor the land has ever known. When you go to treat a patient, I shall go with you, invisible to everyone else. If the strap of my gat is tied so that the knot points toward the patient's head, he will live. I will direct you how to use the chim, and you will make him well again. If the knot points to the patient's feet, you will use the chim to lull him to sleep, where then I shall call his name three times in a dream, and he will answer to death. But beware of warning your patient against seeing my face in his dream, or of using the chim without my direction, or you will pay the price."

The young man bowed as he accepted the chim. As promised, the juh-seung-sajah instructed him in the ways of acupuncture and herbal medicines, and the young man quickly became a famed doctor. While the other acclaimed physicians of his time used all manner of chim, sometimes even hundreds of them, this young man used no more than the ten gifted him by the juh-seung-sajah.

"He must be a prodigy!" the people said of him. "He only needs to look at the afflicted to know immediately how to cure them, or if he cannot, he lets them pass peacefully in sleep."

And so the years passed, and people sought him from all corners of the world and brought their sick to him. The king himself sought out the young doctor to work as a court physician. While there, the doctor tended to the royal family. He became quite wealthy from his practice and shared so much of his money with his father that the jipsin-maker no longer had to make and sell jipsin. The king even allowed the young doctor to invite his father to stay in the palace, where the old man lived out his days in leisure and ease.

It happened, however, that the king one day fell gravely ill. None of his other doctors could tell what was wrong with him, so the suyang son of the juh-seung-sajah was summoned with his ten chim. But when the young doctor approached the ill king, the juh-seung-sajah appeared with the knot of his gat pointing at the king's feet. The king would not survive.

He is the king and has been kind to me, thought the young doctor. *Perhaps this once I may trick the juh-seung-sajah and save the king's life. The juh-seung-sajah will be angry, but because I am his suyang son, he may overlook it, just this once.*

Therefore, as the young doctor set his chim into the king's skin, he whispered in the king's ear, "You will sleep now, and if anyone calls you in your dreams, do not answer him or go with him."

And so the king slept and dreamed he was walking through the palace gardens. The juh-seung-sajah appeared like a black shadow against the bright greenery and called the king's name. The king almost answered, but he remembered the young doctor's warning and ignored the juh-seung-sajah. The juh-seung-sajah called the king's name a second time, and the king ignored him again. The juh-seung-sajah called the king's name a third and final time, but still the king ignored him. Immediately, the juh-seung-sajah knew of his suyang son's treachery and left the dream, and the king awoke in full health.

When the young doctor departed from the king's chambers, the juh-seung-sajah became very angry with him and threatened him, saying, "Because you are my suyang son, I will overlook your treachery this once. Remember that it was I who rescued you from poverty and gave you the gift of medicine. There is much that you owe me that I can take away if you disobey me again."

The young doctor bowed before his guardian and apologized, promising never to disregard the juh-seung-sajah's instructions again.

The king, in thanks to the young doctor, gave his youngest daughter to be the doctor's bride. The young doctor and his wife loved each other dearly, and they brought forth a daughter of their own. The young doctor thought his guardian would be happy for him, but the juh-seung-sajah's face was grim.

"Why do you not celebrate?" asked the young doctor. "My daughter will want for nothing, as she also lives in your care."

"You shall see," said the juh-seung-sajah, his face obscured by the wide brim of his gat.

The young doctor's daughter had not yet turned four years old when she suddenly became very ill. When the doctor went to treat her, he was horrified to see that the juh-seung-sajah stood with the knot in his gat facing her feet. The young doctor knew there was nothing he could do. The doctor's wife was inconsolable and begged her husband to save their child. The king also pleaded with his son-in-law to save his granddaughter's life, but the young doctor remembered his promise to the juh-seung-sajah that he would not disobey his guardian's instructions again. Still, this was his own daughter, whom he loved more dearly than his own life.

"If you cannot save her," said his wife, "I shall surely die of grief."

And so shall I, thought the young doctor. He resolved himself and set his chim in his daughter's skin. He said to the girl, "When you sleep, you will see a man in black in your dreams. He will call your name, but you are not to answer. Do not go with him or acknowledge him, whatever you do."

And so the girl slept, and the juh-seung-sajah appeared in her dream. Though he called her name three times, each time the girl made no answer, and she awoke in full health. The young doctor embraced his daughter and his wife in tears, relieved that he could save his child.

And from the corner of the room, the juh-seung-sajah called his suyang son by name.

Without meaning to, the young doctor looked up and said, "Yes?"

The juh-seung-sajah called the doctor's name twice more, and the doctor quickly realized his error. He tried to run, but the juh-seung-sajah gripped the doctor's hand with a touch like ice and whisked him from his home. Try as the doctor might, he could not struggle or escape his guardian.

"Where are you taking me?" asked the doctor. "What of my wife and daughter?"

"You shall see," replied the juh-seung-sajah.

The juh-seung-sajah took his suyang son to the palace of Ohk-Hwang-Sang-Jae, the Jade Emperor of Heaven, to a massive room filled with burning sticks of incense. There must have been thousands, hundreds of thousands, of these sticks, and the whole room was filled with their sweet smell. Several heavenly spirits attended these incense sticks, placing new ones in empty vases when old ones burned away and waving the smoke away so that it did not smother the flames. The doctor watched as every instant it seemed that one incense stick would die out and another would take its place. The orange specks of fire seemed to jump about the room like arrows.

"What is this?" asked the doctor.

"These are the lights of mankind," said the juh-seung-sajah. "When one stick burns out, the person whose life was represented by that piece of incense shall die. I, along with the other juh-seung-sajahs, psychopomps and servants of the Great King Yum-Ra, find the dying incense pieces and take them to be judged before him. Only then may new sticks be lit. Do you understand?"

"Where is my light?" asked the doctor.

The juh-seung-sajah pointed to a short stump of a stick that was about to go out and said, "Here."

Tears filled the eyes of the horrified doctor. "Oh, why has it become so small? Did I not have my whole life to live ahead of me? Guardian, please light a new one for me, that I may return to my wife and daughter and enjoy my life with them. I swear I shall never misuse your gifts again if you give me another chance!"

The juh-seung-sajah lifted his face so that the doctor could see under the brim of the wide black gat for the first time. The juh-seung-sajah's eyes were the color of pearls, blank white and blind. "This was the incense stick of the king, and then of your daughter, and now of you. There is only so much light to give in the world. One must go out before another is lit. You served me in life, but I serve a king of my own. He will not be cheated twice."

And so the juh-seung-sajah took the young doctor from the halls of the palace of the Jade Emperor and down into the seven hells, where he would be judged by the Great King Yum-Ra. The young doctor was astounded to find many more juh-seung-sajahs roaming the hells as thousands, hundreds of thousands, of souls waited for their judgment. He looked for his guardian but soon found he could not tell one juh-seung-sajah from the next.

The young doctor raised his hands to his mouth and called for his guardian, but that particular juh-seung-sajah had already returned to the surface of the earth, on a certain road that would lead him to a poor jipsin-maker searching for his child's suyang guardian.

Print Paw

A RETELLING OF GOLDILOCKS
& THE THREE BEARS
MONIQUE QUINTANA

olden hair.

She's still here. I smell her in the walls, in the crevice of everything, beating like a small drum. She's white petal flesh. She's everywhere.

And we lived like three creatures in a fairy-tale. When Ralph Two was born, we became bears. Papa Bear, I was Mama Bear, and of course, Ralph Two was Baby Bear. When he was first born, tiny, I would get up in the middle of the night to check if he was breathing, to watch his little brown body rise and fall in his bassinet. When he got old enough, I would put him in bed with Papa and with me, and the three of us would sleep together in the night, my breathing so quiet, I know, and Baby's quiet, and Papa's an unfurled growl, and the three of us sleeping, sleeping.

What should I call her? Papa, my love, called her Blondie. Ever since the first day we saw her at the mailbox. She had pale blue eyes and a tiny doll frame. The first time we saw her, she was wearing an old blue dress. It looked like it came from a thrift store. Her hair hit her shoulder, like a little bell. She didn't say anything the first time we saw her. I asked Papa who she was, and he said that she was a new girl. Her family had just moved in. She walked the tiny path to her apartment. She had a crooked walk. She looked back as we climbed out of the car. Blondie. Blue eyes. Curious.

Baby walks up to Blondie and looks at her. He cries when she tries to talk to him. She leans over to take his little paw, and he cries some more. I tell her he's usually not this way. He must be tired. He's fussy.

For the rest of my life, I'll remember how I catch Papa, my love, in the act. With him on her, he's massive when he's next to her, and she's wearing a jean skirt bunched up at her thighs, and I can see a black bruise on her pale white knee, and blond hair that falls over her face, and she clings to Papa as she'll never let him go.

If you wanted to get fancy, you could say her hair was golden. If you wanted to be nice, you could say she was angel-like. If you wanted to, you could say that she was innocent. I can taste her skin; I can feel the weight of her bones—what it's like between her thighs. At night, I can feel the long blond strands of her hair, heavy as violin strings. They're still there in my bed. They still play. However quiet they might be, I can hear them.

One day when Papa leaves and goes away, maybe she won't be here anymore. But for now, Papa is quiet. He says less and less. I wonder if he thinks about her more than he lets on. She stays inside her place more often. I never see her come out.

Someone told me the hardest thing in the world is to imagine your love on someone else. His paw print is on her. Every single day, I take Baby for a walk. We walk, and I point out old houses like castles and the trees that grow from the sidewalk. I take his chubby little paw. Brown paw in brown paw.

The other day, our neighbor walked by with his pit bull, and I pulled Baby closer to me; and the neighbor man looked mad at me because I insulted his, but he doesn't understand. He doesn't know. I'm all instinct.

The Empanada Man

A RETELLING OF THE GINGERBREAD MAN
ENEIDA ALCALDE

 Viejita and a Viejito[1] lived in an adobe hut in a pueblo found between the sea and the mountains. One day, after long hours of work, the Viejito came home very hungry. He asked the Viejita to make him the most delicious empanada. The Viejita agreed.

The Viejito lay down on a hammock outside of the hut as the Viejita entered her kitchen to prepare the empanada. She grabbed a bowl and mixed together flour, salt, butter, and a bit of water. She transferred the mix onto her kitchen table and kneaded the dough, forming a ball. She flattened the ball. On top, she placed pan-fried ground beef, sautéed onions, and garlic. She added raisins for eyes, an olive for a nose, and a slice of hardboiled egg for a mouth. With a smile, she sprinkled her secret seasoning over the meat and folded the dough, creating a

---

[1] *A Little Old Woman and Little Old Man.*

half-moon shape. She pressed along the empanada's edge with the tines of a fork and set the sealed empanada on a baking tray. The Viejita switched on the oven and set the empanada inside.

Thirty minutes later, the empanada was baked. Using her oven mitts, the Viejita pulled open the oven door. Before she could grab the empanada, the empanada opened its eyes and jumped out. The empanada ran around the kitchen, shouting, "Free! Free! I am free!"

The Viejita grabbed a broom and chased after the empanada. "Stop! Stop!" she cried as she swatted the broom at the fleeing pastry.

The empanada ran out of the hut, shouting, "Don't you see? I am free. Free! I am the Empanada Man, you will never catch me!"

The Viejito saw the Empanada Man and fell out of the hammock. As he stood up, he cried, "Stop! Stop! ¡Tengo hambre!"[2]

The Empanada Man ran faster. He shouted, "I don't care if you're hungry! Don't you see? I am free. Free! I am the Empanada Man, you will never catch me!"

The Viejita and the Viejito chased after the Empanada Man, but the Empanada Man ran too fast. The Empanada Man entered the woods, leaving behind the Viejita and the Viejito.

As the Empanada Man ran through the woods, he passed a Burro.

"Eee-aaah! Eee-aaah!" the Burro brayed. "¡Tengo hambre! I want to eat you!"

"No way, Jose," the Empanada Man said. "I escaped a Viejita and a Viejito. You're no match for me. Don't you see? I am free. Free! You will never catch me!"

The Burro trotted after the Empanada Man but could not keep up.

As the Empanada Man ran out of the woods, he passed a Puma resting on a big rock.

"Prrr ... prrr ..." the Puma purred. "You smell purrrfect. ¡Tengo hambre! Stop!"

---

[2] *I am hungry!*

"Uh-huh, that's what they all say," the Empanada Man said. "I don't care if you're hungry. I escaped a Viejita, a Viejito, and a Burro. You're no match for me. Don't you see? I am free. Free! You will never catch me!"

The Puma pounced after the Empanada Man, but the Empanada Man moved too fast and soon left the Puma behind.

The Empanada Man ran. He passed a Condor perched high on top of a tall tree.

"Scraa-*aah*! Scraa-*aah*!" the Condor screeched. "Me muero de hambre.[3] I want to eat you!"

"I don't care if you die of hunger. I don't care what you want," the Empanada Man said. "I escaped a Viejita, a Viejito, a Burro, and a Puma. You're no match for me. Don't you see? I am free. Free! I am the Empanada Man, you will never catch me!"

The Condor flew after the Empanada Man. The Empanada Man ran faster than ever before, zigzagging left and right to avoid the Condor's attempts to snatch him. After a while, the Condor grew tired and gave up.

The Empanada Man ran north past mountains, valleys, deserts, jungles, and pueblos. Thousands of miles later, the Empanada Man reached a river. A Coyote sat by the river watching the Empanada Man.

The Coyote said, "Hola, amigo.[4] I can help you cross the river."

"You can?" the Empanada Man asked.

The Coyote's yellow eyes twinkled as he licked his paws. "Of course. All you have to do is jump onto my tail, and your dreams will come true."

The Empanada Man thought about his dreams. He observed the Coyote's body, noting how difficult it would be for the Coyote to eat him if he sat on its tail. The Empanada Man hopped onto the Coyote's tail. The Coyote waded into the river. As they made their way, the current grew stronger.

"You need to climb onto my back, so you won't fall in," the

---

[3] *I am dying of hunger.*

[4] *Hello, friend.*

Coyote said.

The Empanada Man climbed onto the Coyote's back. The current grew stronger.

"It's still too dangerous," the Coyote said. "Climb onto my head where you'll be safe."

The Empanada Man looked out at the riverbank. They were so close to it. He thought about everyone he'd run away from: the Viejita and Viejito, the Burro, the Puma, and the Condor. If he could run away from all those beasts, he could run from a Coyote, surely. He climbed onto the Coyote's head.

As the Coyote walked onto the riverbank, he flipped his head up, throwing the Empanada Man high into the air. The Coyote opened his mouth. The Empanada Man fell in. The Coyote clamped his mouth shut.

The Empanada Man shrieked. The Coyote's mouth was wet and dark and smelled of death.

Moments later, the Coyote opened his mouth and spit out the Empanada Man.

The Empanada Man opened his eyes. A Sasquatch peered at him, pointing a pistol. The Sasquatch leaned down and punched the Empanada Man, knocking him out.

When the Empanada Man woke up, he lay on cold concrete trapped inside a cage.

This is where the Empanada Man sits to this day.

Dara & Noori

A RETELLING OF BEAUTY & THE BEAST
JAYET MOON

uring the peaceful and harmonious reign of Emperor Shah Jahan, in the bustling city of Akbarabad,[5] lived a prosperous Hindu merchant and his beautiful wife. His children, six chubby boys and five playful girls, lived in want of no material comforts and were dearly loved and cared for. His wealth had earned him the title of raja,[6] and, befitting his status, he lived in a grand haveli[7] by the river Yamuna, near the royal palace.

When the merchant's wife was pregnant again and going through pains, Padshah Begum[8] Jahanara, the emperor's favorite daughter herself, steadied the lady's shaky hand during labor

---

[5] *Modern-day Agra in North India. The capital city of the early Mughal emperors.*

[6] *Originally a title adopted only by kings, it had evolved in the mid- and late-Mughal period to encompass a cognomen granted by the emperor to Hindu persons in recognition of their wealth from either commerce or land holdings.*

[7] *A large townhouse or mansion usually with a spacious courtyard. Derived from Arabic* hawali, *meaning "partition" or "private space."*

[8] *Begum: Honorific for Muslim women of high birth. Padshah Begum: The Mughal title of overseer of the imperial harem and almost always the first lady of the state. Usually held by the favorite wife or, if the wife is deceased, the favorite daughter or sister of the emperor.*

contractions. The begum held tight as the agonizing cramps sent her friend gasping into delirious moans.

"The water ... it is so ... black," the merchant's wife uttered between gasps. Her eyes glanced at the dark stream outside the window.

"Shhhh. Don't talk. Just push," the begum said, caressing the woman's hand.

"Yama ... the god of death ... he's the brother of Yamuna. ... That is why ... she is black."

The midwife looked at the begum with furrowed brows. The mother was tense, and her muscles were rigid and unyielding.

"Breathe. I will tell you a better story," the begum smiled and started: "When his wife Sati died, Lord Shiva became remorseful and gloomy. His unfulfilled desires led him to wander hell and Earth in anguish. Finally, unable to contain his anger, he jumped headlong into the serene blue of the Yamuna. The river goddess took pity on Shiva, and in her pristine waters, washed all of his remorse away. Shiva emerged from the river, no longer consumed by sadness or grief and at ease from all troubles. But Yamuna did not realize the true magnitude of Shiva's remorse—for its intensity had scorched her waters black."

The merchant's wife returned an exhausted smile. "You ... missed a few ... things," she said. She had, in fact, told the begum this tale many years ago. Her Muslim mistress' interest in Hindu mythology had sparked their unique friendship.

And then, the head appeared.

"White Taj[9] ... by the b-black Yamuna. What a night to be ... b-born," the mother whispered. A dimness passed over her eyes, and her lips stopped moving. She gave a final heave as the midwife pulled the baby out of her, and at that moment, the tormented mother's sweaty hand ceased trembling forever.

Jahanara Begum pressed her palm over her friend's lightless

---

[9] *Taj or Taj Mahal: From Taj for crown and Mahal for palace. It is an ivory-white marble mausoleum on the south bank of the Yamuna river in the Indian city of Agra (previously called Akbarabad). It was commissioned by the Mughal emperor, Shah Jahan, to house the tomb of his favorite wife, Mumtaz Mahal.*

eyes and gently shut them. With tears in her own eyes, she stood and walked to the red sandstone window. *Remorse of Shiva and tears of Shah Jahan*, the begum thought, eying the purple snake of Yamuna as it kissed the marble steps and reflected the creamy pavilions in its rippling waters. Through the carved rhomboid lattice of the window, she gazed across the river at the opposite bank. With the marble of its domes and minarets sparkling in the moonlight, stood the Taj Mahal, a monument to her own mother, Mumtaz Mahal, who had also died in childbirth.

The midwife covered the child in muslin and handed the bundle to the begum, who shifted her gaze from the glimmering mausoleum to the full moon reflected in the baby's tranquil, liquid eyes.

"It's a girl, Begum-Sahiba," the midwife said.

The merchant entered the room and fell to his knees, kissing his dead wife's hand.

"Mumtaz," the begum said in a low voice, her eyes still focused on the baby's.

The merchant stood and bowed to the Padshah Begum.

A moonlit tear escaped her eyes and fell on the girl. The begum spoke louder this time, "Noor Mumtaz, that is what this girl shall be known as, for she carries the light of my mother within her eyes."

A Muslim name for a Hindu girl would no doubt be frowned upon, but the merchant did not dare protest. And so, she was born, Noori—the last child of the dry-fruit merchant Raja Ram, born of a Hindu mother, named by a Muslim godmother, and baptized by tears, in the light of the full moon.

The Hindu astrologers, angered by her sacrilegious name, winced at Noori's kundali[10] and prophesied gloom for Raja Ram. She killed her mother, they said of the toddler, and shall make her father destitute.

---

[10] *Star chart drawn at birth according to moon signs of Hindu astrology.*

By destiny or design, the harrowing prophecy started coming true. Raja Ram's business slowly declined. His caravans of saffron and figs were either robbed by highway bandits along the silk route,[11] or his mule trains, laden with raisins and walnuts, met with landslides in the treacherous passes of the Hindu Kush[12] mountains.

The old emperor had become a recluse, and his sons governed large territories as fiefdoms. Some of these princes were given to greed and ambition, especially Prince Murad, who let the robbers roam free as long as they made personal payments to him and to Prince Aurangzeb. Motivated by Aurangzeb's strong desire to sit on his father's famed Peacock throne,[13] the prince had appeased the powerful qazis[14] and muftis[15] by adopting a policy of strict Islamism. He encouraged the Muslim businesses with low taxes, reduced fines, and monopolies, while overtaxing and overcharging the merchants who refused to convert to Islam.

Raja Ram knew, of course, that it was not the birth of Noori but the declining state of the country that was affecting his trade. So, the merchant persevered and waited with resolve for the bad tidings to end. There would be a new emperor soon.

One day, as he was poring over the accounting books, he received an illustrious visitor. This man was clad in the finest blue

---

[11] *A network of trade routes connecting China and the Far East with the Middle East and Europe. Its southern arteries passed through Afghanistan and were fed by Indian trade routes of South Asia.*

[12] *A 500-mile-long mountain range that stretches near the Afghan-Pakistan border, from central Afghanistan to northern Pakistan. It divides the valley of the Amu Darya (the ancient Oxus) to the north from the Indus River valley to the south.*

[13] *A famous jeweled throne that was the seat of the Mughal emperors of India. It was commissioned by Emperor Shah Jahan.*

[14] *The magistrate or judge of a Shari'a court, who also exercises extrajudicial functions, such as mediation, guardianship over orphans and minors, and supervision and auditing of public works.*

[15] *An Islamic scholar who interprets and expounds Islamic law (Shari'a and fiqh). Muftis are jurists qualified to give authoritative legal opinions known as fatwas. Historically, they were members of the ulema, ranking above qazis.*

muslin fabric, and his neck was adorned with intricate pendants of sapphires and rubies. As Raja Ram raised his gaze to the man's face, the raja froze.

It was the Crown Prince Dara Shikoh.

The merchant immediately dropped his eyes and bent on his knees to kiss the hem of the prince's robes.

"Please, sit down. It is your house," the prince said kindly as he lifted the merchant by the arms.

"Great Prince, I am honored by your presence. Please take a seat," Raja Ram said, with his head bowed.

Dara Shikoh sat on a divan, removed his golden turban, and addressed the merchant, "Jahanara Begum asked me to pay you a visit. She was friends with your wife, I hear. She tells me that the merchants of this city have been suffering. Is this true?"

"May the gods bless Padshah Begum. My wife was only her lady-in-waiting, but the Begum-Sahiba was most kind to her. Your Highness, please forgive my directness, but your sister speaks the truth. Not all merchants suffer, though—only the ones of Hindu faith."

"I am aware of certain acts of my brothers in Punjab,[16] Deccan,[17] and Gujarat.[18] They are the emperor's wards, not mine, and I have no power over them. But rest assured, when I become the emperor, all subjects, regardless of their religion, shall be treated equal, and all laws shall apply equally to all offenders."

The merchant joined his hands and touched them to his temple. "God willing, Your Highness."

The prince made a flicking motion with his index finger, and two men carried a large wooden chest into the room. Raja Ram stood to peer as the men opened the lid and revealed the

---

[16] *A Mughal province of West India bordered by Afghanistan to the north and Persia to the west.*

[17] *A Mughal province that included the mineral-rich south-central plateau and mountain ranges of Southern India.*

[18] *One of the twelve original subahs (imperial top-level provinces) established by Mughal Padshah Akbar the Great, with seat at Ahmedabad, bordering on Thatta (Sindh), Ajmer, Malwa, and later Ahmadnagar subahs. The province was the second richest in the country after Bengal.*

brimming gold coins within. A few coins fell clinking on the floor. The merchant picked up one and felt the warm yellow metal. They were newly minted gold mohurs[19] stamped with the seal of Emperor Shah Jahan.

"It is a gift from His Majesty's treasury to the guild of Hindu merchants. We recognize your hardships and wish to provide you with an interest-free loan to allay your recent troubles."

Raja Ram fell at Dara Shikoh's feet. "Your Highness, may all gods bless you."

"Rise, Raja Ram. We did this to encourage commerce—the diversity of trade and commerce. The diversity of thought, ideas, entrepreneurship, and peoples is what makes Hindustan the greatest nation in the world. If we all become Muslim, who will learn the truths from the *Gita*[20] and the *Bible*. Who will enjoy the melodious Hindu bhajans and Sikh kirtans.[21] And finally," he smiled, "who will import the best raisins and saffron, without which the kheer[22] to break my Eid[23] fast becomes flavorless?"

With moist eyes, the merchant smiled back.

"My sister has also sent a gift for your daughter," the prince said, as an attendant whispered a name in his ear, "yes ... Noor Mumtaz."

The merchant's forehead puckered into shallow wrinkles. He motioned a servant to bring the girl to the main hall.

"Very interesting name for a Hindu girl. She is named after my mother and grandmother."

"Your Highness, Padshah Begum-Sahiba, herself, named my daughter."

---

[19] *Gold coins of highest denomination. One gold mohur of Emperor Shah Jahan's reign is equivalent to US$2,520.*

[20] *Holy book of Hinduism.*

[21] *Genres of religious performance arts, connoting a musical form of narration or shared recitation, particularly of spiritual or religious ideas in Hindu and Sikh religions.*

[22] *A rice pudding, originating from the Indian subcontinent, made by boiling rice, broken wheat, tapioca, or vermicelli with milk and sugar; it is flavored with cardamom, raisins, saffron, cashews, pistachios, or almonds.*

[23] *A Muslim festival, in particular Eid al-Fitr or Eid al-Adha, that involves fasting.*

Dara opened his mouth to speak but stopped himself when he heard a sweet jangle from the hallway that slowly grew louder and closer. *Tchn. Tchn. Tchn. Tchn.* The footsteps resonated like a mellow metronome.

Dara Shikoh had seen many a court damsel, but he was unprepared for the unabashed beauty of Noori. She covered her head only slightly, and her golden-bronze face casually rebelled against the sheer silk veil. A green sari$_{24}$ draped around her in Hindu style. Cuboid emerald earrings dangled from her earlobes, and a princess-cut emerald necklace on a silver chain rested on her neck. She was plainly dressed and under-jeweled for a merchant's daughter, but her eyes more than compensated for any radiating stone.

Her wrists were a delicate shade of olive with a hint of coffee, and her face—it was a shade of exquisite. It were as if the creator had taken great effort to caress the palette of sienna with gentle strokes of caramel and apricot. Her curved upper lip and its deliciously tense corners, her dark hair held by a dainty silver brooch, momentarily rendered Dara wordless.

No wonder Jahanara chose the name, he thought. The merchant's daughter had the stature of Noor Jahan and the beauty of Mumtaz Mahal. "It is a pleasure to make your acquaintance, Noor Mumtaz Begum," Dara finally said. "Unexpected pleasure is the sweetest surprise."

Noori bowed but not enough to remove her eyes from his curious gaze. The candle lights hanging from the ceiling danced within those black pools like flickering auroras.

"My sister has asked me to hand you a gift," Dara said.

He held her stare as he motioned his attendant to pass on to her a glass vial, around which a note was wrapped with a delicate chain. The chain had a small, gold peacock pendant dangling from it. The eyes of the peacock were set in rubies.

Dara said, "If my sister had—"

---

^{24} *A female garment from the Indian subcontinent that consists of a drape varying from five to nine yards in length and two to four feet in breadth that is typically wrapped around the waist, with one end draped over the shoulder, baring the midriff.*

He was interrupted by three guards who barged into the hall and bowed to him. "Your Highness," one of the guards said, "Prince Aurangzeb has entered the capital and imprisoned the emperor with the help of Roshanara Begum! It is being said that he plans to usurp the throne."

Dara Shikoh stood and tightened his turban.

Noori watched as he rushed out without saying goodbye, the gold embroidered hem of his muslin robe fluttering like a war banner in the wake of his hurried footsteps.

For a year, the civil war raged as brothers fought for the throne. Trade and commerce suffered. When Dara Shikoh was finally defeated, the ensuing rule of new Emperor Aurangzeb's reign brought more troubles than his war. A flat tax—jizya[25]—was not only applied to Hindu businesses but to the practice of Hindu religion itself. Any religion other than Islam incurred royal disfavor, and a variety of taxes were slapped on Hindu places of worship.

Raja Ram hung his head, looked down at the dirty cobblestone street, and studied the slick grime of the Mughal world. Vegetable slime, peels of garlic, squished turmeric roots, specks of vermilion, a cracked peppercorn, burned remains of myrrh incense sticks, and a steady trickle of blood. He looked up to the decapitated head of Prince Dara Shikoh hanging off the wall of the fort and felt the pain that the mutilated head could no longer feel. Blood-crusted posters hung on the fort walls advertising a rebate of a year's worth of jizya if one accepted Allah on occasion of Eid al-Fitr.

---

[25] *Historically, the jizya tax has been understood in Islam as a fee for protection provided by the Muslim ruler to non-Muslims, for the exemption from military service for non-Muslims, for the permission to practice a non-Muslim faith with some communal autonomy in a Muslim state, and as material proof of the non-Muslims' submission to the Muslim state and its laws. Jizya has also been understood by some as a penalty of the non-Muslims in a Muslim state for not converting to Islam.*

Unwilling to trade salvation for commerce, Raja Ram sold his business and haveli and moved with his family to live in the forests of North India.

Noori's sisters, removed from luxuries of the city, bore great resentment against her. They believed the holy men who'd prophesied their father's downfall upon Noori's birth. The sisters treated Noori as the obvious cause of all their troubles.

Noori avoided her irritable sisters and spent all her time in the dense forests. She had no attachment to material luxuries and enjoyed the freedom of the jungles more than grand palaces of Akbarabad, where she had always been confined to her rooms and kept within the veil. Here, she was free. She could stand on a treetop and ride the wind. The cool, green breeze caressed by moist leaves billowed her sari and toppled its veil to kiss her forehead. The forest loved and protected her.

She loved the forest back. Nothing pleased her more than admiring the slanting rays of sun escaping through the verdant panoply and illuminating a shy flower or an elusive berry. The gifts of the earth—prettiest wildflowers, sweetest berries, and aromatic herbs—Noori was a connoisseur of them all.

Most of all, she was grateful for the solitude. With help from her father, she had built herself a small hut in a clearing between the trees, where she would sleep in the afternoons. Here, she also kept all her meager belongings: A tooth of a tiger. A claw of a wolf. Dried sweet berries. Orange-red winter cherries. Colorful flowers of all exotic forms. And beneath it all, her most prized possession, a gift from Padshah Begum: A small glass vial with a cork stopcock and a letter. Every time she looked at it, she fingered the peacock pendant on her neck. She had read the letter numerous times, but the urge to caress the paper that had once touched the hands of a dashing crown prince and a Padshah Begum never subsided. The ink was almost faded, and she would read it often to make sure it was imprinted in her memory, before the words finally disappeared from the crumbling parchment.

Noor Mumtaz,

May the light of your mother and mine forever shine in your eyes. This vial contains my most valuable treasure. These are the tears my father, your Emperor Shah Jahan, shed on the night my mother, Mumtaz Mahal, died. It was the sorrow in these tears that built the Taj Mahal. I am entrusting these to you because I know that you shall protect them. Destiny shall help you. There is magic in them. My sister, Roshanara, is a sorceress and has made many attempts to steal this vial. One of these attempts has left me bedridden, and I am unable to resist her anymore. My dear girl, I knew the moment I saw you, on that full moon's night: You hold magic in you, too. The magic in this vial shall combine with the magic in you one day, and you shall resurrect the love that is lost. Please protect this for me.

Your godmother,
Sahibat al-Zamani Padshah Begum Jahanara Sahib

Noori neatly folded the letter and stared at the liquid within the vial. Some of it had evaporated, leaving a salty precipitate that encrusted the curved glass walls, but there was still some left. She wrapped the cork tightly with lotus leaves and buried the bottle below a pile of herbs and flowers.

A whizzing noise disrupted her thoughts. Peeking through the wooden slats of her little hut, she saw a man fall off his horse. When the unexpected fighting thinned, she slowly crawled toward him.

Arrows pierced his right shoulder and right thigh. Blood drenched the crumpled silk of his robes crimson. She dragged the dazed man to her hut and applied herbs to his wounds.

The man shivered. Concerned by his state, Noori decided to remove the arrows. She cut off an end, then yanked the shaft from his shoulder. He cried out but was too weak to move or to resist. She filled the wound with paste of ashwagandha[26] and

---

[26] *Winter cherries. Used in ayurvedic medicine as an anti-venom, wound healer, and immunity booster.*

wrapped it with tulsi[27] leaves. As she cut the second arrow, brightly dressed imperial guards burst into her hut.

"Stop, girl!" a guard shouted. "Get away from the emperor!"

Noori held up her hands and slowly moved back as they carried the man out. Then, they arrested her.

Emperor Aurangzeb sat on the Peacock throne with the fingers of one hand playing with a sapphire eye of a golden peacock. Four peacocks in various stages of dance and flight were captured in solid gold on the plush armrests. The light reflected by the intricate winged carvings was in turn reflected by the jeweled eyes of the creatures. The eye of a particularly large bird that adorned the backrest above the head of the emperor was encrusted with the Koh-i-Noor diamond. The dazzle of the seat was so blinding that one almost thought the Mughal emperor was encompassed by an ethereal golden mist. The throne, built by Shah Jahan, was a perfect tribute to Jahan's grand, prosperous, and extravagant times.

But Aurangzeb, on this seat, was a picture of incongruity. His face was gaunt. Dull green eyes were set in brown hollows. His beard was thick black and scraggly. The fineness of his clothes and richness of his jewelry contrasted with the drab mediocrity of his facial features.

"Your Highness, the girl may have saved you," the royal physician said with a bowed head. "Ashwagandha and tulsi are antiseptic and stopped the wound from festering while you were transported to Delhi."

The emperor smiled. With some difficulty he stood and walked to Noori. "Thank you," he said with a grin. Then, in a sudden motion, he grabbed Noori's hair and dragged her to the center of the hall. "Faujdar,[28] bring the man out!" the emperor shouted.

---

[27] Holy basil. Used in ayurvedic medicine as an antiseptic.

[28] A police commissioner in Mughal times.

An unkempt young man, his hands and feet restrained in heavy chains, was brought into the hall. Noori gasped.

"This man and his friends tried to assassinate me," Aurangzeb said, baring his teeth and pulling her hair. "He is your brother, isn't he?"

Noori mumbled and unsuccessfully fought his fingers off her braids.

"Well then, traitorous bastard, before I hang you, maybe I should have some fun?" Holding Noori by the hair, close to his face, Aurangzeb gave a nasty grin. "A houri[29] from heaven. I shall ravish you like a ..."

The bound man flailed, punched his captors, and shouted, "Lay your hands off her!" Soldiers rushed to hold him as he shouted. "You are a disgrace! You have divided our nation and are reducing it to poverty. Material and moral!"

"Tsk tsk. Such big words. Traitorous infidel, don't be so angry with me. Soon, you shall be an uncle to my child." Aurangzeb gave a lecherous laugh as he tugged at Noori's sari fold, exposing her blouse.

"Stop!" a woman called as she walked up from behind the courtiers into the center of the room. She had scraggly, disheveled hair like Aurangzeb's and wore a loose but fine black muslin dress. Her thin, white lips sat below a hawkish nose, and her eyes were dirty-bloodshot green. "Let her go," she commanded of Aurangzeb, who scowled but obeyed immediately.

With downcast eyes, the emperor said, "Mughal women do not—"

"Yes, I know," the woman brushed him off as she bent to hold Noori's peacock pendant between her long nails. Roshanara Begum slowly bared pointy teeth at Noori and grinned. "Kill the boy, and leave the girl," she said as she walked away without deigning to look at her brother, the emperor.

---

[29] *A beautiful young woman, especially one of the virgin companions of the faithful in the Muslim Paradise.*

Roshanara Begum sat behind a sheer green purdah,[30] and Raja Ram sat beside it on a wooden stool facing the wall. "It is unfortunate," she said, "but your son was a traitor. He had to die."

"Your Highness, I apologize for his most despicable action. Many thanks for sparing our lives," Raja Ram replied in a measured but bitter voice.

"Your daughter, Noor Mumtaz, has something that should be mine—*is* mine. She won't tell me, and I cannot force her. This … thing … cannot be taken. It has to be given of free will."

Raja Ram kept his silence.

"I have known of you. You are Raja Ram, the dry-fruit trader. My sister was fond of your figs. I tasted them once, too. They were quite excellent." Her hand appeared out of the purdah and dropped a rolled parchment on the floor.

Raja Ram picked it up, and his eyes bore through the silk screen.

"A firman[31] to supply figs, raisins, and cashews to the imperial harem for five years. One hundred thousand mohurs in advance. Are you up to it?"

"Y-yes, yes, Your Highness. You are most kind!"

"Only if your daughter gives me what I want. That which is mine."

"Your Highness, I shall try to convince—"

"Try!" She flung the purdah aside and stood over the cowering merchant. "You *will* convince her, or you are both dead."

Raja Ram climbed on his horse and surveyed the horizon. The dawning sun had colored the clouds orange, and the winding paths of the ancient silk route beckoned him once more. He looked back to count the mules in his train and spotted a

---

[30] *Literally, a curtain. Here refers to the practice among women in certain Muslim societies of living in a separate room or behind a curtain, or of dressing in all-enveloping clothes, in order to stay out of the sight of men or strangers.*

[31] *A royal order issued by the emperor of India.*

downcast Noori standing by the door. Her sadness stung his heart, and he called out to her.

"My Noori, a few drops of water in a bottle mean nothing. We shall soon be rich again and shall have anything we want."

She nodded.

"What do you want me to bring back for you from Afghanistan?"

"Nothing, Father."

"My dear girl, your sisters want jewels, dresses, and necklaces. You must want some of those things?"

"No, Father, but if you insist, please bring me a rose. I have heard they are very pretty in the mountain country."

He smiled and kissed his daughter's soft temple. "A rose it is."

Raja Ram reached the city of Jalalabad at the Afghanistan border and, unlike other merchants, bought almost nothing from the city market. After sampling the offerings and noting the prices, he journeyed farther north to smaller farms in the mountains and purchased as many apricots, walnuts, figs, and cashews as he could buy directly from the field. The remainder of his baggage, he filled with raisins, saffron, and figs from Kabul.

While returning through the Hindu Kush passes, a heavy snowstorm trapped his caravan, and an avalanche buried all his mules. Barely escaping, he took refuge in a cave and survived the storm by sleeping under a few salvaged bags of figs. When the storm was finally over, he filled his pockets with the remaining figs and set forward in search of water.

After wandering for a day, he came across an iced blue pond. A giant stone wall caught his eye. After an endless desert of ice, a mark of human construction revived his spirits. He held a palm to the cold stone and walked along its side, his fingers never leaving contact with the rugged gray surface. Eventually, this led him to a large and intricately carved rock-cut gate.

Raja Ram entered. Lush gardens lay around him, full of juicy fruits and colorful flowers blooming out of season. But what he saw next made him rub his eyes and pinch himself.

At the end of the garden sat a grand monument. It had the very familiar domes, arches, and minarets that he'd seen so often from the windows of his haveli in Akbarabad. But there was one difference. They were all made of marble as black as midnight. It was a black Taj Mahal.

Raja Ram crossed the garden and walked through the main arch into the hall. The candles burned brightly, and a feast lay before him. Steaming mutton biryani[32] and red-curried chicken sat beside roasted golden legs of lamb and snow-white kheer. Without a second thought, he emptied the flagons of water and immediately set upon the delectable mountains of food.

When his hunger was satisfied, Raja Ram felt guilty. He had not waited for the owner of the palace and was afraid he or she would take offense. He looked around the hall and saw many doors. Though it looked like the Taj Mahal from the outside, this mahal was not built to be a mausoleum. It was a lavish residence from the inside. Some rooms were furnished so magnificently, they reminded him of the royal palace during the time of Shah Jahan. He finally found a bedroom and sat on a sofa to await the return of his host. But exhaustion from his ordeals overpowered him, and he fell into a deep slumber within minutes.

He awoke the next morning and again found the rooms empty. Two great wooden chests lay below the archway. They were filled with old gold mohurs stamped with the seal of Shah Jahan. Raja Ram filled his leather bags and pockets with as many coins as he could, with the twin intentions of financing another trip and buying gifts for his children. He promised himself that he would return the money once he made good on his losses. Exiting the main door, he noticed a white horse, chained, ready for him. Blessing his invisible benefactor, he mounted the steed.

Trotting across the garden, a medley of floral aromas seduced

---

[32] *A rice dish of spiced meat that originated during the early Muslim rule of India.*

him. He dismounted the horse and walked by the colorful bushes. As he reveled in the kaleidoscopic sights and smells, his eyes fell on the most beautiful rosebush he had ever seen. These roses had a yellow-orange base that grew brighter at the tips. Some petals had turned bright pink. The roses instantly reminded him of Noori, and he clipped one without hesitation and nestled it in the innermost pocket of his robe.

As he was climbing the horse again, a tall, hairy creature appeared in front of him. Black hair covered every inch of his visible body. He wore clothes that may have once been fine but now were torn, hugging him in undersized tatters. His nails grew thick like tusks, and his scaly knuckles appeared as hard as brass nuggets. But it was the creature's face that petrified the merchant. The shriveled folds of the beast's forehead and cheeks were also covered with black hair. So were the eyelids. One canine tooth was so long that it escaped from his closed mouth and rested across his lower lip.

The terrified merchant was too startled to run.

"Is it not enough that you enjoy my hospitality and take my riches?" the beast said, gnashing sharp teeth. "You return my gratitude by stealing my roses?"

"A-a t-thousand pardons, sir. I am very thankful for your hospitality. You have, indeed, saved my life. I only took the rose as a gift for my daughter. I apologize deeply. I can return—"

"How can you return it? You have cut it from the plant, you fool," the beast growled.

"I am sorry, sir. Please, pardon my ignorance. If I had known how valuable—"

"Silence. You can keep the gold, but you shall have to pay for the rose. The daughter who asked for it—you must bring her to me."

"W-what!"

"She must come of her own free will. If you convince her of that, you can keep the riches. If not, you must return it all to me."

Raja Ram had no choice but to assent temporarily to the

beast's conditions. He had no intention of bringing Noori, and if the beast pursued him, then Raja Ram decided he'd go to Roshanara Begum so that her soldiers could arrest the abominable creature. He apologized once more, promised to return with his daughter, pulled on the horse's reins, and galloped out of the beast's mahal as fast as he could.

When Raja Ram returned home, his daughters were overjoyed. With the beast's gold, he had bought them pretty dresses, jewelry, and happiness. Noori was overjoyed, too. Her rose was one of a kind, and she duly installed it in her hut where she admired it daily. Raja Ram told them the tale of the beast, and all his children were intrigued. Noori meekly offered to be taken to the beast, per the terms of the pact. The elder sons gallantly offered to fight the creature to protect their youngest sister, while the older daughters subtly reminded their father of the promise and urged him to send Noori away.

Busy multiplying his newfound wealth, Raja Ram kept postponing his decision. He bought dry fruits from local markets and sold them to the palace. Though the profit was much smaller, it was still considerable, due to the gross volume of sales. It was sufficient enough to repay the beast and to finance another trip through the mountains.

The winter passed in prosperity, but one day when Raja Ram was preparing the bags of gold for the beast, his elder son barged into his father's room. With gasping breaths, the son told his father of the soldiers dispatched by Roshanara Begum from Delhi. They were looking for Noori.

Raja Ram ran to Noori's hut. Upon questioning her, he found out a disturbing truth. It wasn't in the girl's heart to betray the Padshah Begum. Noori admitted that she had not given the real vial to Roshanara Begum.

The concerned father had only one choice left. Raja Ram directed his mule drivers to follow him and, leading them with his white horse, cantered out of the village. Beside him on another horse was Noori, and in her robe was Jahanara Begum's glass vial, within which, sadly jostled, were the tears of the dead Emperor Shah Jahan.

When Raja Ram and Noori reached the chiseled stone gates, the sun had set. Though the sky was a clear, dark purple, thick strokes of steamy fog carpeted the forest floor.

As they entered the gate, Noori's eyes glowed with delight. Those liquid black spheres glittered with red swirls, chrome twinkles, sparkling golden fountains. Crackling fireworks lit the skies like colorful constellations, and Noori beheld the display in breathless amazement.

They glided through the foggy mist into the quadripartite garden, which contained numerous flowerbeds and bushes divided into four quadrants. The flowers blossomed as Noori walked by them, and they filled the air with a mélange of aromatic whiffs. When Noori saw the roses appear out of the fog, she ran to caress the petals. The young rosebuds unfolded in front of her eyes, giving her the glorious tribute of their vibrant efflorescence. She sniffed a few roses and ran the tip of her nose against the velvety petals.

Her father smiled, held her by the arm, and led her onward. Tall trunks of cypress gently swayed along the main walkway. Between the trees stood a canal filled with flowing magenta-colored water. The canal branched into four smaller channels beside which stood trees ripe with lemons, pomegranates, oranges, and apples.

As they walked on, a black sheen slowly rose from the end of the garden, and the gloriously dark Taj revealed itself. Noori ran to the structure and passed her fingers over the cold and smooth marble. The grains of embedded quartz glistened as the tardy evening rays grazed them. She admired the intricate motifs on the walls and arches: the solids and voids, the concaves and convexes. All similar to the Taj Mahal in Akbarabad, except here the shades of black played with darkness, just as the Taj of Akbarabad played with light in shades of white.

Noori entered the open door of the main arch first, and just as Raja Ram was about to enter, the door slammed shut in his face.

"Father!"

"Noori, dear," Raja Ram shouted, "I am safe. Are you fine?"

"Yes, Father, it's beautiful inside. There are plush carpets and thousands of chandeliers. And so much food! Can you push the door harder?"

It dawned on Raja Ram that this, indeed, was the wish of the beast. "I am afraid I cannot join you."

"Father ..."

"I am right here. I am ..." he turned and saw the beast towering behind him.

"That was the bargain," the beast said.

"Yes ... yes," Raja Ram stammered.

The beast flung the door open, and Noori fell back in shock. "Have you come willingly?" the beast asked.

"Y-yes," Noori said, flinching. The beast was hairier and taller than she had imagined.

Raja Ram ran to hug his daughter. "Noori, I must go now."

"Father ..."

"I shall miss you, too, my girl, but it is for the best. You know it."

The beast allowed Raja Ram to take more gold out of the great wooden chests. The beast also let Noori choose gifts, as remembrances, for her siblings from another chest full of ancient treasures. Raja Ram filled his bags and bade a tearful goodbye, but he rode away on his horse, relieved. The threat of Roshanara Begum was averted, at least for now.

The comforts of the mahal were beyond Noori's imagination.

The softest mattresses and pillows gave her the soundest sleep. The tastiest and juiciest food she had ever eaten brought color to her cheeks, and the flowers with their aromas sent her heart into romantic reveries.

But the beast, she could not understand. Fear of his appearance dominated any feelings of curiosity she had about his motivations. He would have lunch with her every other day, and they would exchange a few words. He appeared to be well-mannered, and—though the large, hairy frame never failed to intimidate Noori—she, at the very least, acknowledged a humane side to him.

One sunny day after lunch, Noori stepped into the garden. While sitting by her favorite bushes, she fell into a vivid slumber. That was when she dreamed for the first time. Jahanara Begum appeared to her by the rose bush, and in a motherly voice, recited the words of the faded letter: "You hold magic in you, too. The magic in this vial shall combine with the magic in you one day, and you shall resurrect the love that is lost."

The next night, she dreamed again. This time, it was Prince Dara Shikoh. They were back in the grand haveli in Akbarabad, but he looked at her differently. He spoke differently, as well, as if he knew her and somehow yearned for her. He was every bit as handsome and was dressed in the finest silks.

"Noori," he said, "you must not trust your eyes. Trust only your heart. Love transcends time and form. Trust your heart, my love, and I shall be yours." Noori tried talking to the prince in her dream, but he couldn't listen. He ordered his attendant to hand over Jahanara Begum's gift and then took off.

A bell rang, and Noori awoke. She joined the beast for lunch, and he politely asked her to join him in the garden for a stroll. Noori agreed.

When they approached the rosebush, the beast got down on one knee. "Noori, will you marry me?"

Noori's mouth fell open, so wide that her slender fingers were insufficient to cover the O of her lips. "H-how can I?" she said with a flustered face.

She turned and ran back to the mahal. She locked herself in her room and spied the beast from her window. He gazed at the roses despondently, and after sprinkling the magenta water on them, he walked slowly back into the palace with sagging shoulders. She was relieved that the exchange had not provoked him to violence.

That night at dinner, the beast joined her. For the first time, she tried to make small talk. She noticed a statue of dancing Lord Shiva placed in an alcove. The borders were engraved in flowery Persian with surahs[33] from the *Quran*.

"What is your name, Beast?" she asked.

"Beasts are nameless."

"Do you pray?"

"Yes, I suppose I do."

"Are you a Hindu or a Muslim?" she asked, eying Lord Shiva's statue.

"Beasts don't have religions, only men do. I pray for love, and love is my god. The garden is my temple. Tilling the soil and watering the plants are my prayers. Flowers are my prasad."[34]

Noori's lips stretched upward at their corners, and her smiling eyes shone violet. "I understand you, Beast. I lived in a hut in a forest. It was so beautiful, like being in nature's womb."

"I have never lived in a hut."

"Have you always lived here?"

"No, I had a bigger palace with many guards."

"This place, it looks like Taj Mahal. Is Taj Mahal not a mausoleum? So, is this … too?"

"Not yet. But, yes, it is intended to become one for me."

"Oh, no, Beast! Don't say such things," she said, holding his large hand, wrapping her delicate fingers around his hairy palm, and pressing her warmth onto it.

The novelty of her soft, throbbing touch moistened the beast's eyes. He withdrew his hand and bade Noori goodnight.

---

[33] *A term for a chapter in the* Quran. *There are 114 surahs.*
[34] *Offertory.*

That night, Noori dreamed again. Dara Shikoh had come to meet her in the hut in the jungle. He fell on his knee and kissed her hand.

"Do not turn me away, my love," he said to her. "Sorcery can change appearances but not hearts. Follow your heart to find mine." He then looked into Noori's eyes.

Noori gazed back and smiled. Then, suddenly, the hut blew away. The screeching laughter of Roshanara Begum pealed through the air. She screamed curses and enchantments as Aurangzeb rushed to stab Dara.

"Give me those tears!" the sorceress begum shrieked.

Noori woke sweating and ran down to the hall where the beast lay asleep. She cuddled by his side, and his eyes flickered open.

"Please, let me sleep beside you, Beast. I miss my father, and Roshanara Begum is haunting my dreams. I am scared."

The beast wrapped his hairy arm around her. "She will not lay a finger on you. You are the mistress of my palace and of my heart. I will always protect you."

Satisfied and safe, Noori slept soundly.

As days passed, Noori explored new rooms in the palace. There was a dusty room on whose wall hung a portrait that shocked Noori. It was the life-sized handsome face of Dara Shikoh, whom she had seen so many times in her dreams. She dusted it and took it to her room. There was another room that was full of colorful caged birds. She removed a bird-of-paradise with a brilliant, flowing yellow tail and put its cage on her window ledge. Yet another room contained jeweled swords and gleaming daggers of all kinds; she quickly closed the door on that one. There was also a room full of dogeared books—in Sanskrit, Urdu, Persian, Greek, and many other languages. But her favorite room was the one that housed the musical instruments. It had a tabla,[35] a veena,[36] a sitar,[37] and flutes that played themselves when she entered.

Once while enjoying the sounds, the beast joined her, and they both danced and laughed to their hearts' content. The beast asked Noori again to marry him, and she refused. Again.

Within a few months, Noori longed for her father and became depressed. She would sit still in her room all day and watch the gray shadows of the black minarets trace a complete arc across the garden. Noori's appetite declined. The joy of her lively eyes was replaced by an obsidian gloom. Even the bird caught her sadness and started shedding dull, yellow feathers.

The beast was concerned, and when she made known her wish to see her father, the beast hung his head. "I cannot deny you anything, Noori, but parting from you will crush my heart."

"Please, Beast, only for a few days. I promise I shall come back."

"Only twenty days, Noori. You must return within twenty days."

"I promise, Beast. I will be back in twenty days," Noori said with a thankful smile.

As the beast bade her goodbye, the yellow bird hooted, and a few sad roses shed their petals.

When Noori returned to her father's house, she found it overturned and abandoned. She wandered to her hut and found her brothers and sisters living there in secret. They told her that Roshanara Begum had imprisoned their father and would release him only upon seeing her.

---

[35] A membranophone percussion instrument originating from the Indian subcontinent, consisting of a pair of drums.

[36] Comprises a family of chordophone instruments of the Indian subcontinent. Ancient instruments evolved into many variations, such as lutes, zithers, and arched harps.

[37] A plucked stringed instrument, originating from the Indian subcontinent, used in Hindustani classical music.

Noori clutched her peacock pendant and started for the royal palace. She knew what Roshanara Begum wanted but also knew that it could never be snatched away. Noori had to give it freely. She had a good grasp of her leverage.

"Your Highness," Noori said upon arrival. "I swear I shall hand you the vial of my free will if you release my father."

The begum exposed her deformed teeth and extended her hand. "All right. Give."

"It is not with me now. It is in a palace in the Hindu Kush mountains. I can take you there, but you must promise to leave my family alone."

The begum's face contorted into a deformed pucker. "Promise."

On their journey, the palkhi$_{38}$ rocked slowly, and Noori fell asleep. She dreamed that the black domes of the Taj were crumbling, slab by slab, and the beast was lying prone near the rosebushes, which themselves were withering into gray ashes. He was crying out her name and losing strength with each call.

"You broke your promise," he moaned.

Noori woke and counted the days. Twenty-one.

Her anxiety slowly turned into fear. Did the beast really grow to love her so much that he would perish in her absence? The more she pondered, the more she realized that she had made an abrupt and careless decision. In her haste, she had betrayed the beast. Even if the beast were not dying, Roshanara and her soldiers would certainly destroy his beautiful palace and imprison him.

That night, when the caravan halted, she stole a horse and quietly cantered away in the cover of the darkness. She rode without a break for days until the crescent finial of the beast's mahal was finally in sight.

---

[38] *A passenger conveyance, usually for one to three persons, consisting of a covered or boxlike litter carried by means of poles resting on the shoulders of several men.*

The beast, indeed, lay near the rosebush. Noori rushed to hug him, and he opened his heavy eyes.

"Oh, Beast, I am so sorry. I didn't …"

The beast heaved and spoke with weak gasps, "My heart is a garden watered only by your sight, your smell, your presence, … your … love."

"Please, rise, Beast. I am here now," Noori said, holding his ursine head in her fingers as her tears soaked him.

With a painful grunt, he lifted his head and whispered in her ear, "Noori, will you marry me?"

"Yes, Beast, yes! I will!"

As soon as Noori said those words, a shock of new life rippled through the beast. The folds on his face smoothed into soft, wheatish cheeks, and the thick hair fell from him, except for his head of a fine, black mane. Noori watched the transformation with both her shaky hands covering her rosebud mouth, which had parted in ecstatic wonder. Such pure joy shot through her heart that she felt giddy and held onto the beast. She felt the rough, hairy skin of his arm change into a taut and toned olive bicep.

It was Prince Dara Shikoh.

"It was Roshanara's curse that transformed me into the beast," he said. "Only unconditional love could break the curse. Thank you, my love," he said, as he kissed her forehead.

"But … but … you were beheaded?"

"No, Roshanara killed a lookalike to fool the populace. Jahanara protected me with an ancient love charm our mother taught her. Roshanara learned this magic, too, and abused it for darker schemes that led Aurangzeb to defeat me by trick and treachery."

Behind the rosebush, a grubby black head emerged. Roshanara was not naïve enough to let Noori escape unfollowed. There was a smirk on her swarthy face. "So, this is where my hag of a sister hid you all these years."

"Roshanara, you shall pay for your deeds," Dara said, stepping in front of Noori.

Roshanara laughed and removed the glass vial from her folds. "Really? I have it. The magical tears of our father that protect your life. Your stupid lover led me right to it. Now, we can finally put this mausoleum to good use."

"No," gasped Dara.

The Mughal sorceress held out the vial, tightly clenched her fingers around it, and shattered the glass into tiny sparkling shards. The tears fell on the roses, and the flowers transformed from pale orange and yellow into dark, velvety purple.

Dara started to transform, too. His hair turned white, and wrinkles formed on his face. Roshanara arched her back and threw a spear at Dara's frail frame. It was swift, and on the mark. The unwavering silver shaft pierced his chest and punctured his heart. He fell into Noori's arms.

"Dara," she sobbed as she held his dying body.

The yellow bird-of-paradise hooted in anguish and flew out of Noori's room in the mahal. Flapping its plush wings, it glided toward Dara and perched on the bush near his body. Roshanara aimed another spear at Noori's back, but the bird blocked its path, and a muted squawk escaped its beak as the slate tip pierced its feathered breast.

"Well, stupid little girl, it is your turn now," the sorceress said, and removed a dagger from her waist.

Noori rested Dara's head on the grass and, through her tears, watched the bird's hemorrhaging breast collapse on the ground. Just as Roshanara walked toward Noori, Dara lifted his hand with a grunt and snatched at Noori's peacock pendant. The dying bird flopped over, and with an extended neck, pecked at Dara's palm. It swallowed the golden trinket. Dara's hot eyes glinted one last time, and his face stiffened in a calm smile.

In a stunning metamorphosis, the bird squawked with renewed life and flapped its feathers as they turned white and gold. Its iridescent wings grew larger, until they spanned several feet each, and the bird transmogrified into a giant golden peacock.

It fluttered in vigorous circles around Roshanara, creating a whirlpool of leaves, fruits, petals, twigs, shards of the glass vial, and blades of grass. The sorceress screamed as the whirling earth wrapped and swallowed her.

After the twister died down, the giant peacock lifted the limp body of Roshanara by her neck. With its flowing golden tail glinting with every flap, it flew straight to the heavens. Upon reaching the highest clouds, the woman and the fowl burst like a flowering firecracker, shedding a million ribbons of black, white, and gold.

Noori sat by Dara's body and held his cold, still hand.

She sobbed through the night and slept in the pool of her tears by his pierced heart.

She dreamed yet again.

Silver vapors that arose from the faded letter solidified into the form of Jahanara Begum. She softly said the words again and again, "My dear girl, I knew the moment I saw you, on that full moon's night: You hold magic in you, too. The magic in this vial shall combine with the magic in you one day, and you shall resurrect the love that is lost."

Noori woke mumbling the words. To her surprise, the spear had disappeared. She repeated the letter to herself again and gazed at the fresh dew on the purple velvet roses. They gleamed silvery blue in the moonlight. Then, she lifted her head to the heavens and watched a bright full moon bathe all creation.

She plucked the roses, separated the petals, and crushed them before pressing them to Dara's wound. It started slowly healing in front of her eyes. Tears, of a different emotion this time, trickled from her eyes onto Dara's chest.

"Noori," Dara said, his eyes flickering open.

"Dara, my love!" She hugged him.

He got up and held Noori's round face in his hands. Purple remorse sloughed off the roses, and they turned back into shades of joyous orange and yellow. Dara bent to touch his lips to Noori's. It was a kiss that inspired birds into songs, buds into blossoms, cocoons into butterflies. The black Taj turned to rose pink, and the moon gave way to a brilliant soft sun.

Dara Shikoh and Noori sat atop a howdah on a caparisoned elephant. Raja Ram sat on the white horse beside them. Behind her father's horse were Noori's five brothers on horseback. And behind the brothers were a hundred thousand men. They did not carry banners of the Hindu trident or the Islamic crescent, but instead, on a fluttering white background, a golden peacock held a blossoming orange rose in its determined claw.

It was time for the rightful heir to sit on the famed Peacock throne of Hindustan.

Historical Background

This story is an alternative historical fantasy set in Mughal India. Shah Jahan and Mumtaz Mahal and their children, Dara Shikoh, Aurangzeb, Roshanara Begum, and Jahanara Begum are real historical characters. In the civil war of 1657-9, Roshanara plotted on behalf of her younger brother, while Jahanara allied herself with the elder brother. Dara Shikoh was assassinated by Aurangzeb on August 30th, 1659, and his mutilated head was presented to Emperor Shah Jahan, who was imprisoned in Akbarabad Fort. It is said that upon looking at the head of his eldest son, the grandest emperor of India lost consciousness. He woke as a man deranged by grief, and for the remaining years of his life, would often be found sitting by a window with a view of the Taj Mahal, crying in anguish and pulling on his beard until his face bled.

The Mughal empire disintegrated after the long, polarizing, and terrifying reign of Emperor Aurangzeb. Political and religious intolerance led to weak administration, a poorly maintained army, and regional aspirations of independence. In 1739, Nadir Shah of Persia invaded and looted India. He carved out the inlaid jewels from the royal palace and pilfered the intricate silver gates of the Taj Mahal. The Peacock throne was transported to Iran and broken apart, one jewel at a time. The riches from this raid were so vast that he did not tax Persia for three years.

A European visitor noted in 1780 that the then Mughal emperor, whose empire had dwindled to only a few districts of Delhi, sat on a mangy wooden throne on which peacocks were drawn with flaky oil paint.

King Marcus

A RETELLING OF KING MIDAS
& THE GOLDEN TOUCH
DEBORAH D.E.E.P. MOUTON

hen, a new king of the streets emerged—Marcus—with a love for cars and anything with a metallic shine, a love for anything he couldn't afford. His father worked three jobs to keep his roof his own. Marcus' mother had been gone since he was a baby, to her own addictions. He sneaked out late nights, down the fire escape, to watch the sun rise over the low-riders on the Eastside before the hydraulics were awake and everything was moving. He would place bets on the street races. He lusted after the sunlight. The way it turned a golden reflection over the entire horizon and made his brown chest swell. He would run into the morning chasing the thought of it, but always falling short.

His father and Marcus made the best life they could find. Oftentimes, Marcus found himself working long hours at his father's autobody shop to complete projects. But he didn't mind. He adored his father, but deep in his heart, he pretended it was his own kingdom. He would stack tires into a toppling throne and climb up. He could see everything from up there: the open engines sparking, the gutted interiors, the shells he could make new again with the right touch. His father was a master of shine, and he planned to learn everything he could.

Every day, when the school bell rang, Marcus would race to the garage where the seasoned mechanics sat drinking RC Cola and Pabst beer, arguing about the most recent boxing match: De La Hoya or Mayweather. The sounds of echoing power drills and air compressors building into a symphony of hustle in the background. His father would crouch under the hood of an old Oldsmobile and show Marcus how to change the oil, the spark plugs, the tire rods.

"Hard work will get you everything you want in life," his father would say.

But Marcus was never satisfied with such outdated things. He wasn't a "long road" kind of person; he was a "why want when you could have" guy. And he wanted the Impala: the one with the rose-gold trim and the wood grain inside. All it was missing was to have the grille replaced. He imagined it tricked out with a rose-gold mesh and an M for his name right up front, but his father wouldn't let him near it.

"That was my father's ride," his pops groaned like a broken record. "You wouldn't know what to do with it if I gave it to ya."

Something about responsibility, something about care ... all Marcus knew is that he would look like a boss driving it down 11th Avenue where the road bent and the pretty women flocked. No one could tell him he wasn't a king then. But Marcus could never get the key. His father kept it on a special chain that hung around his neck, close to his heart. His father never took off the chain, not even when he was sleeping. It was a sad truth: all Marcus could do was hope to learn all he could from his father's wisdom in an effort to prove himself worthy of passing the key down.

Then Friday happened. The school bell rang a little differently when the weekend was approaching. His father told Marcus he had to pick up an extra shift at the wrecking yard that night. Marcus took the opportunity to steal away to watch the illegal car races on the other side of town without his father's knowledge. He put on his father's old leather jacket and cleaned his Converses with a toothbrush at just the right angle. Then he headed past the border of familiar where it all went down.

About a mile off MLK Boulevard, he noticed a male figure following him in the shadows. The male's footsteps were accompanied by the sound of a metallic flip and the soft thud into a palm. At first, Marcus thought it an apparition. Maybe it was his father, looking to see where he disappeared in the night. Then, the man approached, flipping a single large coin in his hand. Marcus picked up speed. But before he could outrun the man, Marcus heard him yell, "Impala."

Marcus stopped and turned. "What did you say to me?"

"Impala, the one that sits at the front of your dad's shop," the man replied snidely from under a gray Kangol fedora.

"What about it?" Marcus asked, leaning closer to see the man's face in the shadows.

"I can give it to you. That and your wildest dreams."

"How?" Marcus said.

"All you have to do is say you want it, and just like that, all the power will lie in your hands."

"That seems too easy," Marcus laughed in skepticism.

The man repeated slowly, the way a lowrider cruises down the strip when all the girls are looking, "All you have to do is say you want it, and it will be at your fingertips."

It were as if the whole world slowed. Marcus licked his lips, closed his eyes, and did it. "I want it," he said, and just like that, the man was gone.

Marcus looked around but couldn't find him anywhere. Left behind was this odd tingle in Marcus' hands, moreover his fingers. He stared down at them, waiting for something to appear: a key, permission, but nothing came.

"Stupid. Just say you want it, and it's yours," he mocked.

He shook the disbelief from his body and headed for the hill near the old wrecking yard. The smooth dirt paths made it perfect for street races and all the OG's and gangstas liked to show off their new lifts there in the evenings. All he had to do was to hop the gate, and he would have the ultimate view of the sweetest rides. He placed his hands on the fence like he had done so many times before, but this time, he felt virtue leave his body. There was a shudder, almost like backward chills, and then, the entire gate was an incomparable brilliance. He jolted back in surprise at the palatial linked gate in front of him. It was solid gold.

"How is this possible?" he said to himself. His hands were shaking, and his breath was short. He rubbed his fingers along the brazen metal and peered into the reflection of his own face. "This is crazy," he said. But soon, curiosity made him prove his mind wasn't merely encamped in a dream. "I should try it again," he said.

So he headed over the fence and down into the broken bodies of abandoned vehicles. He extended his trembling hand to a busted grille of a demolished Corolla. Bling, it was gold, and pristine. He tried again, this time a Volkswagen. He reached for the pitted rims, bling. It was like a heavenly whitewall. He seared his index finger over the gloss and carved his name in the soft metal. A laugh erupted from his chest. This was it! Forget struggling, forget being broke.

He was so excited that he missed the rebar sticking out of a nearby cinderblock. Before he knew it, he was tumbling to the ground. He braced himself in the tumble. By the time he landed, a trail of golden foolishness lay as witness. Then, the bustling feet of people approaching could be heard in the distance. He knew he had to get out of there quickly before someone saw his newfound power and tried to use it for themselves.

He beelined for the alley, turned by JJ's Liquor, and hid in the shadows until he was sure no one was following him. The night had set in, and most places were closed. But there was one place he knew how to access at all hours—his dad's shop.

"If I get to the Impala, I could finally fix it up the way I have always imagined," he said to himself. "Then Dad would have no choice but to see that it was made for me!"

His logic was sound. All of the mechanics would have bathed to their elbows in the orange goo that strips them of grease and headed home to their families. His dad was out at the wrecking yard. The shop was all his.

Marcus didn't waste a minute getting there. He was careful to shimmy the back gate open with his elbow and to squeeze butt-first through the plank in the fence that his dad kept urging him to replace. He was never happier that he'd dodged that responsibility than he was right then. He carefully climbed over socket wrenches and around jacks until he had the Impala in sight. He took it all in, walking around the car and ingesting it with his eyes. She was a beaut. All she needed was ... he stretched out his hand to the grille.

There it was. Solid gold. He bent his knuckle into the pink molten and carved an M that no one could deny. But with any newfound power, the wielder rarely knows his own limits.

He said, "It could really use some rims, too."

He bent down to massage the spokes. No sooner did his fingers brazen the first wheel than did a click come from behind him. He turned.

"What are you doing in here?" the silhouette shouted, extending what looked like an open gun barrel.

It appeared the place wasn't empty after all.

"But no one was supposed to be here," Marcus' mind screamed and raced.

Before he could add in logic, he was wrestling the gun away from the now-stiffening arm. His opponent heavied, and the solidifying shadow's voice became a grand chime bouncing into the concrete; one giant statue of gilt guilt; one alloyed admission of fault. Marcus panicked.

He had to get out of there. He scurried backward away from the shimmering statue, only to step into the path of a motion-sensored floodlight. The light blinded him for a moment, but as the white blur cleared, he recognized his frozen assailant more clearly. Scrolling up from the gun, one large hand gripped the trigger, and the other hand held tight at the base of the neck, close to his heart. Between its fingers, a chain in mid-swing, a key jolting from the end.

What had Marcus done? The wave of his shame welled to a violent spring heaving from his eyes until he couldn't see. He knelt to cup his father's face. In one swift swipe, he wiped his eyes to lay them clearly on his father one last time. In the rising sunlight, his hardened body welcomed a new day. One hand on his father's face, the other, a solid hand full of golden tears for all to judge in the morning.

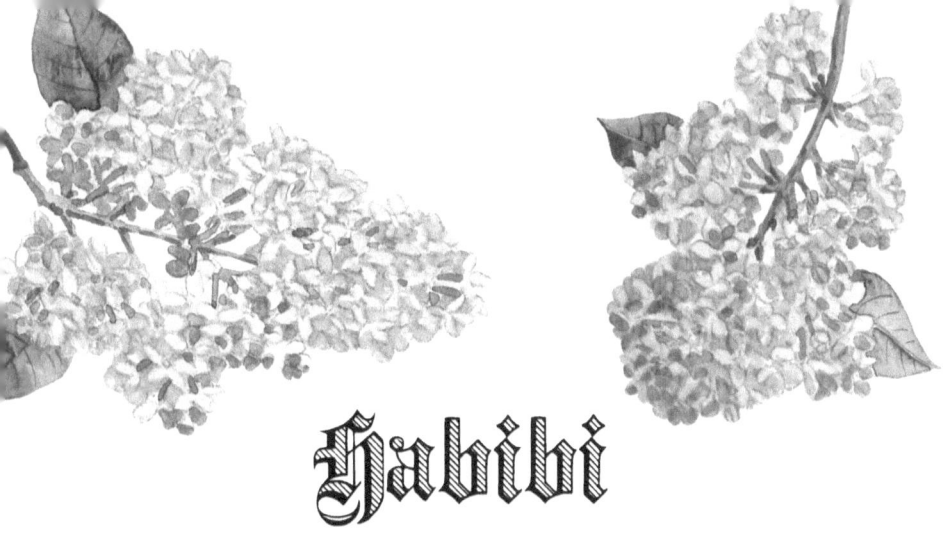

Habibi

A RETELLING OF THE VELVET RIBBON
KAITLYN LYNCH

e watched in rapt silence as she unwound the scarf from around her head. It was the night of their wedding. His mouth tasted like clove and red wine. The full moon shining into the window of their hotel room whispered to him of the beautiful new life their future was promising.

Her hair was long—longer than he had imagined—and dark. In the dim lighting, it seemed more like cavernous empty space, an unfurling ribbon of black nothingness rolling out across the shoulders of her wedding dress. She combed her fingers through it, not meeting his eyes.

"What do you think?" she murmured, a demure smile tugging at the edges of full, plum-colored lips.

"I think you're the most beautiful woman I've ever seen," he replied and reached for her. As he got closer, something stopped him. His eyes fell upon a black velvet ribbon encircled around her neck. "What's that?"

"Just a necklace."

"Why would you wear a piece of jewelry where no one can see it?"

"Maybe someday I'll tell you about it."

He frowned and moved away from her on the bed. "Another mystery?"

She pulled her gaze up from the frayed carpeting and examined her new husband, her own expression matching his. "Not everything you don't know is a mystery."

With a sigh, he pushed a lock of hair away from her face. It was coarser than his. Wiry, despite how smooth it looked at first glance. "I've told you everything there is to know about me. I feel like I'm an open book, but you're always holding back from me."

There was nothing else she could say. Her heart held the truth that he would never fully understand, and she didn't know the words to tell him that. A moment of silence passed before his features changed from melancholic to angry. He rose from the bed and loosened his tie.

"I'm tired. Let's just go to bed." He stood and crossed to the bathroom, slamming the door behind him, leaving his bride alone on their marriage bed.

She touched the ribbon around her neck. A single tear fell from her cheek to the blanket below.

The air in the small kitchen of the apartment hung thick with the scent of spice. It had been two weeks since their wedding. His other half wasn't a very good cook. The rice on his plate was hard and orange; he never knew before they met that orange was a desirable color for rice. He'd only ever known white and brown. Maybe wild, if someone felt like splurging. This was crunchy and greasy, and the meat was overcooked. It probably wasn't supposed to taste like this.

He reached for his soda can and looked up from the plate of food. His eyes landed on his new wife. His family didn't understand how he could have fallen in love with someone after only seeing a little face peeking out from bundles of fabric, like a swaddled baby doll. He'd told them to stop asking, that it was cruel and insensitive. The more he thought about it, the more he realized maybe it was only because he didn't know the answer.

"Could you pass the salt?" he said.

She blinked and looked up from her own plate. Since they'd sat down, the only sounds had been the ones drifting in from the open window. "Hm?"

"The salt."

"Oh." She hadn't even brought it over to the table. Rising wordlessly, she retrieved a grinder of coarse pink salt from one of the cabinets, set it down beside his plate, then took her seat again. The chair scraped against the linoleum with a long shriek of protest. "It's not very good. I'm sorry. My parents used to get on my case that I'd never find a husband because I can't cook."

He smiled and reached for her hand across the table. "I would not know how it's supposed to taste, anyway. You're fine."

Her lips twitched into a hesitant smile, but there was something sad behind her eyes. She didn't take his hand, only fidgeted in her chair.

The same things reminded them both of their differences, of lifetimes spent in separate worlds, of families who warned them their love would never last. It brought out the melancholy around the edges of her features, but in him, it fanned a flame of anger.

And then, on top of it all, there was that damned ribbon. Still, in all this time, he'd yet to see her without it. Even while she slept. No other woman he'd been with had worn a necklace in her sleep, especially not something so decidedly uncomfortable as a choker. It made no sense, but every time he asked why she didn't take it off, she always replied the same way, and that made even less sense. What had started off as a simple curiosity was quickly growing into an obsession; what was worse, he blamed her for causing it, rather than himself for allowing and feeding it.

"So, I was thinking," he said, dabbing at his mouth with a paper napkin, "we haven't taken our honeymoon yet." They couldn't agree on where to go. "What if, in the meantime, we go someplace for just a weekend? Get away for a little while? My brother has a condo in Florida, and I have some time off work that I could take. I think it'd be good for us."

A pause. No response.

"What do you think?"

She shrugged, pushing a piece of chicken around her plate with a fork. "Sure. If it'll make you happy."

"I don't really know if I feel comfortable with this—"

"Are you kidding me?" It wasn't right, but as every day passed, he felt himself treating her harsher. Losing patience with her more quickly. Betraying the kind and loving nature that she had fallen in love with in the first place. "It's basically still in the room. It's private! It's just outside, so you have a view of —of—y'know! What people pay to come to Florida to see! The beach and shit! Birds and palm trees and what the fuck ever."

Every time he swore, she winced. He didn't even wait for a reply, just grabbed his beer off the top of the dresser and opened the sliding door to the balcony and hot tub. Slowly, she followed, slipping into the hot water with a burning unease.

"There she is," her husband purred, muscular arm curving around her shoulders. For a brief moment, he was happy. Proud, even, that she'd abandoned her aversion in favor of him. Placed her marriage above her own beliefs, even if just for the moment.

And then he saw it.

"You're still wearing that stupid thing?" he said, pointing to her velvet choker. "What, do you even leave it on to shower?"

"You'd be sorry if I took it off, so I won't," she whispered sadly, face turned toward the bubbling water, hot tears pricking at the corners of her eyes.

The arm that wrapped around her shoulders inched back, one finger outstretched. He carefully reached for where a knot or a clasp should be at the back of the choker in an effort to undo it and be done with it, but he could find none. It was one long, solid loop of ribbon with no indication of how to get it on or off.

"Happy one year, baby," she murmured, bestowing one last kiss upon her husband before rolling over in bed. She was asleep within minutes.

The hours ticked by until, finally, just before the sun rose, her husband could bear it no longer. The unknowing was devouring him, and he decided to put an end to it the only way he knew how.

As carefully as he could so as not to wake his sleeping wife, the man pushed back the covers, rose from the bed, and slunk across the room to an emergency sewing kit she kept in her sock drawer. Light crept into the room from between the curtains, and a sliver of morning sun fell across his wife's neck, illuminating his way as he inched to the bed.

Kneeling on the ground next to her, he opened the hard plastic case of the kit and took the scissors from inside. He opened them, and a quiet metal scrape resonated through the room, like the unhinging of tiny jaws. Gently, he slid the open scissors around the ribbon, pressing one end against the soft flesh at the hollow of her neck. Something roiled in his belly at the promise of truth finally revealed. The scissors snapped shut, and the velvet ribbon broke away from her neck.

The man stood, turning to replace the sewing kit and return to bed, when he heard a quiet thunk at his feet. He looked down and saw the head of his wife rolling away toward the window, completely free of her body. The eyes were wide, the mouth hung open, and it wailed while the body lay still in bed.

"I told you you'd be sorry."

Candles in the Snow

A RETELLING OF THE LITTLE MATCH GIRL
AZURE ARTHER

he homeless woman shivered, wrapped her thin arms around herself, and tried in vain to tug the dirty jean jacket closed. The jacket was too small, but better than nothing. She pulled the frayed cuffs farther down her wrists with care. A winter chill ruffled through her threadbare dress, causing her to hunch closer to the brick wall. She placed one bare foot against her inner thigh, letting the frozen toes warm before the numbness of the other foot forced her to switch. Through the alleyway entrance, the beginning of the shopping district glimmered in the strings of white lights that swooped back and forth over the road. The scent of pretzels and cinnamon wafted on the air, tantalizing her. She switched feet again and rubbed her skin. The wind had cut her in places, leaving chapped, cracked flesh in its wake. She scratched off a scab.

She'd always hated her skin. It was brown like the mulch her grandmother had made from dead leaves every autumn; it was so scarred from past pick sessions that her dermis was spotted with little chocolate freckles. Nana had loved her dusty, light-brown shade and had always insisted her granddaughter use cocoa butter to keep the ash away. The homeless woman's lips split when she smiled, and she swallowed blood along with the bitter laugh she trapped behind her teeth. Nana would be horrified to see her granddaughter's skin now, the cracks and calluses on the soles of her feet. The homeless woman had once had shoes, slippers really, which somewhat kept her feet warm, but they'd been too large, and she'd lost one while dodging between two cars. The second one had been snatched by a little heathen boy who laughed when she tripped out of it. She tucked the tips of her fingers into her jacket pockets and pondered the shopping center again.

Once upon a time, she had frequented that district, like so many of the ant-sized shoppers she could see from her distance. She'd danced down the sidewalks in high heels, waltzing in and out of stores, buying what she wanted, and wrinkling her nose in distaste when she didn't like what was offered. The world was not just her oyster, it was her sea; and she was the queen of it all. That was before, back when she still had a name, an identity.

She switched feet again. It was getting late, late enough that some anxious shoppers may buy what she had nicked from the last store that let her inside. It was possible that one random shopper, if distracted enough, wouldn't notice her bare feet, wouldn't be scared of her dirty clothes. Christmas might be the best time to manipulate frantic people, but New Year's Eve was when the drunk and lonely were sometimes even more distressed than on other holidays.

She leaned down and hefted the bag of candles she'd stolen from that expensive store with that sweet, so sweet cashier, and crept to the edge of the alley. Outside of the sheltered path, an icy wind blew. Small drifts of snow lay against the buildings, and she winced at the thought of stumbling into a patch of half-frozen slush. The wind pushed her long hair into her face, and the strands stuck to her lips, tangled in her eyelashes, and slipped up her nose. She pushed it back, but not too roughly. Her hair, her crowning pride, was the only remnant of beauty she had left. Even with being homeless, she still maintained its glory as best she could. She darted along the sidewalk, slipping on patches of wet concrete, the wind cutting into her like blades. No one had bought anything from her all day, but if she could sell just one candle, she would walk right in one of those stores and buy a cheap pair of shoes.

But no one purchased her candles, and several people snarled at her, and one store worker threatened to call the police. She returned to her alley, again watching the lights of the shopping center, until they went out. She hunkered against a wall, shivering by a dumpster, wondering how she would survive the night. Her usual spot had been taken over by a stronger vagrant, and the shelter uptown was full by now, not that she had the money for a bed, anyway. She dug through the dumpster for something to keep her warm, and maybe, if possible, something to eat. She found nothing, but she did wrap her feet in paper and plastic, better protecting them from the elements. Once, she would have called her father, her ex-boyfriend, or her sister collect, but no one would take her in now. They would beat at her with their words, their criticism, and in the end, tell her to get her life together, then hang up on her. She was nothing to them. She was nothing to anyone.

The temperature dropped as full night set in, and she made her way out the alley to seek a more sheltered spot. An awning or a doorway would be best. She slipped through the city streets, crept through neighborhoods, her furtive gaze darting to brightly lit windows. She caught glimpses of families, lively parties, and quiet couples curled up on couches and floors, watching New Year's television, but it was the dinners, the scent of meat and vegetables drifting on the air, that caused her stomach to clench. Her feet were numb now, and she shuffled, finding it hard to lift her leaden limbs from the ground. Eventually, the suburban section slipped back into urban, and the houses became less grand. She crossed a street, entered one of those hidden rundown sections some cities have, and after slipping through the neighborhood a bit, she saw the boarded-up house.

For any homeless person, an abandoned house is both a threat and a boon. The place could already be occupied by another vagrant or a group of them, who may or may not share, or it could be the high spot for drug users, who again, may or may not share, or a gang, who would definitely not share, and would likely attack. For a homeless woman, the risks of an abandoned house multiplied. The upside of the building was the roof, shelter from the elements; sometimes the water still ran, and the toilet worked, and even though there was no heat, to be clean made most people on the street feel normal for a moment. The woman placed her right foot against her thigh and felt the block of ice that was her sole. It was enough.

The house was silent, and after checking for observers, she disappeared around the back. She waded through drifts of snow that reached her knees and worked one of the boards loose. With some straining, the first board came free, the momentum flinging her into the snow. After the third board, she was able to wrench the window up with her fingertips. Shoving her bag inside, she wriggled through the opening and dropped to the floor. She lay panting on the hard linoleum for a long time, trying to still her heart and listen, listen, listen! She froze, holding her breath, and trained her ears, but no one came. She was alone. She sighed and watched the white puff of breath dissipate. It was nearly as cold within as it had been without, but drier.

She stalked the dark interior, her eyes adjusting to the stillness, the emptiness. She tried a light switch. Of course, the electricity wasn't on. She tried the water. It didn't work, either. She shrugged. This was better than being outside. She walked around the house, admiring the shape of it, even with the boarded windows; someone had torn up all the carpet, but the house had an old, unused smell. It was abandoned, just like her. She locked the windows, checked the doors, and finally chose a corner where she could see both the front and back doors and the majority of the windows. She sat on the cold floor with her legs crossed, her bare feet tucked against her thighs, and huddled into herself to stay warm.

As night deepened, the house grew colder, and her extremities numbed so much that she could only feel the inside of her mouth. She stood and walked around to warm up, which felt worse. Her corner had at least warmed to her body, so she returned to it. She shrugged and dug through her bag of candles, carefully pulling out each stolen stick of wax. The first was white for peace, the second green for abundance, the third yellow for mental clarity, and the last black for protection. She drew a raggedy pack of matches from her jacket pocket and struck one, lighting the white candle first.

The woman cupped her hands above the flame, her brown skin taking on the same golden hue. She turned her hands in the faint light, opening and closing each finger, feeling the painful tingle as heat entered them. She closed her eyes, and for a moment, her whole body was warm. It was as if she were curled on the floor in front of her grandmother's chair, right by the blazing space heater, feeling Nana press her hair straight. Nana did that when the homeless woman was a child. She could smell the burning strands and feel the paper-soft touch of Nana's hand. When she opened her eyes, the candle was burning low, and the room in the empty house was still freezing. There was a draft from somewhere, one she hadn't noticed in the cold, but it touched the wavering flame of the white candle, and the wick went out. She hesitated. A slightly used candle could still be sold, but she was so cold, and to feel that warmth once more ...

She lit the next candle, the green one. The smoke that rose from it seared her eyes. She rubbed them and blinked in surprise when she could see. The wall next to her was now transparent, as was the wall to the house across the street. She could see a large family in their dining room. The table was covered with a white tablecloth, with the good plates set out, a large turkey, surrounded with stuffing, and all kinds of sides. The family laughed, and the matriarch—her pecan skin flawless but her hair silver and gray—looked up from her seat at the head of the table and smiled softly at the homeless woman. Those warm, brown eyes were kind as the homeless woman stood and carefully moved around the table. The other woman held out a plate, piled high with food, but as the homeless woman's frozen hands reached for it—her footsteps stumbling toward the invitation—she ran into the wall and fell, splattering candle wax all over the floor of the dark room. She lay there for a while, feeling her heart pound and watching the plumes of her breath in the room.

Eventually, she sat up and lit the next candle, prepared for the vision that came with it. Now, she was at the base of the largest Christmas tree she had ever come across, just like the one at the mall that reached all three floors, but higher. It was also the most decorated tree she had ever seen. Tiny angels, robed in white, their skin matching the hue of her own, hung from the branches and turned solemn eyes to look at her. Each angel detached from its ornament and flew around the tree, burning brightly until the sun blazed above the pine, reaching somewhere on the horizon, farther than she should have been able to see, all the way to a barren desert, and farther, until she could see an oasis full of people.

"The homecoming." She whispered the words, thinking of Nana, who had always loved her more than the rest, who had told her that when their people died, they didn't go to heaven but to a desert oasis, somewhere in Egypt from where they first descended. Nana had said that the souls of their family always flew to that oasis, that desert kingdom where they basked in the sun and walked with their ancestors. The draft touched the candle, and the flame went out, leaving her to feel the freezing tears that were streaming down her cheeks.

She was out of matches, so she lay on the cold floor, closed her eyes, and cried into the emptiness, but the dark against her lids lit up with radiance. She opened her eyes to see Nana standing there, dressed like the others from the oasis.

"Nana." The homeless woman stood, but she stopped short

of touching the other woman, shame pulling her back.

"Harih." Nana said the word firmly, giving the homeless woman back her name. "You have forgotten yourself."

"I have." Harih bowed her head. "I lost my way."

"Well, child, I am here to lead you back." Nana held out her arms.

"To the homecoming?" Harih asked, disbelieving, still not moving toward the other woman. "And you won't disappear?"

"Take my hand and see." Nana smiled, still waiting, ready to enfold Harih into her warmth and love.

Harih stumbled forward into the woman's arms, sobbing.

Her grandmother laughed and rubbed her back. "Come, child."

Nana took her arm, and together they stepped across the desert in large steps, laughing with joy all the way to the oasis. Harih left the house behind, with three candles still flickering against a draft so slight it could never have blown out the flames. It was this flicker that drew a bored, late-night patrol. They came upon Harih's cold corpse, frozen and still, smiling at her own death on New Year's Eve. The black candle sat beside her, unlit and unneeded.

A Breath of Innocence

A RETELLING OF RAPUNZEL

AKILA RAYAPURAJU

ou always lose what you were never meant to keep. I learned it the hard way. The knife-in-the-back kind of way. But how was I not meant to keep her? She had been born into this world for me.

The first night I held her in my arms, she screamed and screamed and screamed. It was the sound of innocence clashing with reality, and it warmed my heart. "I will name you Prakruthi," I whispered into the baby's little ear. It was smaller than a single talon of mine.

"Please, don't do this," said the woman on the bed, sweaty tendrils of hair hanging in her face. Her sari was pushed up to her thighs. Blood pooled in the space between her legs. "Have mercy."

I laughed. "Mercy? What kind of world do you think we live in?"

"You're a monster," her husband said darkly. He had been at

my feet begging for kindness just seconds ago. Humans are such deplorable creatures.

"*I?*" I bared my razor-sharp teeth at them, delighting in the way they flinched. "I'm no monster. You steal from me, I steal from you."

"We stole from your *garden*," the woman said. "We were starving. We were going to die."

"Then you should have died," I said, simply. "Actions have consequences, my darling." I walked to the front door of the one-story cottage, flipping a shawl over the horns curling through my hair. Then, with a wink over my shoulder, I added, "Besides, you can always have another."

I carried Prakruthi to the top of my tower, swaddling her in my right arm, which was covered with a blanket to keep my scales from breaking her delicate skin. *Human children are so fragile*, I thought. *So easy to break.* Raising her would be difficult, but it was necessary. Taking the child was not just to make some peasants cry (although there was some fun in that). I needed to test a theory. And for that, I needed to bottle the breath of innocence to drink with fresh rainwater. There was no better source of innocence than a human baby.

The original plan was to have the child laugh into a vial, then kill it for some other spell. But plans like to change without telling their masters, and when I met the child's eyes, that is exactly what happened.

I kept her, bathed her, raised her. It was difficult to do with my talons. I never knew when I would accidentally slice her open, heart bursting into bright red blood. Somehow, I kept her safe.

I often doubted whether my theory would work in this way. I was surrounded by the breath of innocence, and I drank the rainwater I saved every day. The only problem was that innocence could be corrupted as you grew older.

But two years passed, and I noticed that my scales had faded to reveal soft, brown flesh. Another two years, and my horns had shrunk back into my skull. A couple more years, and my teeth became humanlike, my talons receded into regular-sized nails. When Prakruthi was six, I left her in the tower alone for some time to go out and purchase a mirror in the closest village. For the first time in two hundred years, I saw myself as I truly was. A young, beautiful woman with thick, curling black hair, a dimpled smile, and sparkling brown eyes. I sank to my knees and wept with joy as Prakruthi hid behind me, peering curiously into the glass.

"Is that what we look like, Amma?"

I wiped away my tears and rested a talonless hand on her head. "Yes, bangaram. That is how we look."

"We're beautiful!"

"We are."

I was no longer the image of a rakshasi on the outside. I could wear saris without shredding them again. I could walk among the humans without a second glance, and if they lingered, it was out of desire rather than terror. The sage's curse was undone.

I was finally free.

What does it take to get cursed? Being cruel? Being evil? Or does it take some humans to catch you in the wrong moment, paint you in a bad light, and plead to their saviors to do away with the evil woman? In the end, it doesn't really matter what you were trying to do. It only matters what it looks like.

They caught me with a bag full of gold, daughter in hand, running from home. They accused me of stealing from my in-laws, but my husband had taken it one step further.

"She wants to sacrifice my girl for some black magic," he'd told the village elders. "She's been plotting for weeks."

No one would believe that I had been trying to save the only thing I loved in the world from the true evil. From the abuse that waited back home. No one believes a woman.

They brought in a sage to curse me. "If you want to act evil, then you might as well look like it," he'd said.

That was, perhaps, their greatest mistake. On my first night as a rakshasi, I tore my husband to pieces. But my daughter was far out of my reach by then. They had turned her against me.

When you have a second chance, it is hard to feel like the universe is against you. I didn't deserve another chance—not after everything I'd done since I'd become a demoness—but I got one, anyway.

Second chances let you get comfortable. I let Prakruthi run wild. Her smiles made my heart ache with a joy I'd known only once very long ago. Her laughter was a balm for the tatters of soul I had left. I could not bear going against her wishes.

Like cutting her hair. It had grown so long. A thick, glossy, black mane that she dragged around the tower, sweeping dust and debris with it. I wanted to cut it off, but she threw a tantrum every time I tried.

"Bangaram, your hair is becoming disgusting," I said, one day. "Your head has become a mop for the floor."

Prakruthi grinned. She was twelve years old now and a mischievous child. "So, let's do something fun with it."

I helped her wash the hair, which had grown long enough to reach the other side of the room. Then I braided it for her. This became our nightly ritual. I would sit on her bed, she on the floor, back against the frame, and I'd work my fingers gently through the sleek, straight strands. So different from mine. She would close her eyes with contentment and hum some small tune or another that she'd come up with for the day.

Prakruthi had a beautiful voice—clear, golden. Like sunlight streaming through an open window. There were days where I felt guilty for not showing her the wonders of music that exist in the world outside the tower. I knew how much she would love them. But I could not risk corrupting her innocence, which was as wholly intact as the day she was born. Growing up isolated in a tower would do that for you.

The questions began slowly and infrequently enough that I didn't realize what was happening at first. I would go into town every so often to pick up the spices and goodies that I couldn't grow in the garden. I had the luxury of doing that now that I looked like everyone else.

The first thing Prakruthi asked for was a set of paints. "Please," she'd begged. "I'm so bored, and I'd love to paint you."

So, I got her paints and canvases to use to her heart's content. It was harmless, after all, to let her express herself. When we spent time outside in the garden, she would set up her easel and get to work, although she would never show me what exactly she was painting.

Then, she asked for a book. "Just one!" she said. "I get so bored up here, and you never take me to town with you. Please!"

So, I got her a set of books. She knew how to get me to feel guilty. She knew which strings to pull. In hindsight, I should have read through the books to see what they were about. The storeowner had told me that they were fairytales meant for little kids. I assumed that if it were for kids, then it couldn't corrupt Prakruthi's innocence.

But second chances let you get comfortable. They blind you and back you onto the edge of a cliff until there's nothing left to do but fall.

A woman doing wrong had to die. A woman doing evil had to die. A woman less than perfect had to die. But what was perfect, what was good, what was right, was not determined by the woman. Nothing ever was.

When you are forced to live in the shadows, tangled in your grief and your rage, the most you can do is watch. So, I watched the village. I watched the men. But mostly, I watched the women. I watched them with their children, I watched them serve their families, I watched them take the fall for every mistake made, regardless of whether it was their fault or not.

You are all like me, I would think. *There is no difference between us. Only, they made me look how they see all of you.*

We're no different.

And this thought spiraled from bitterness to resentment to outright fury. I would not creep around the shadows of my own home. I would not lower myself to make them feel comfortable. If they wanted me to be a monster, then I would be a monster. I would rip them out of their dreams and make their world a nightmare.

It was easy to spend too much time in the village, talking to the people. It was easy to forget what their ancestors had made me. What their ancestors had taken from me. Kindness was a strange and unsettling feeling. But I had underestimated how much I would miss being like the others. Talking with them, laughing with them—it was exhilarating.

Prakruthi had noticed. She was sixteen now, and there was a growing resentment hanging in the air between us. I would come home, and she would watch me unpack my purchases, arms crossed and chewing on her lips. There would be a storm in her eyes.

"You were gone long today," she would say in what she thought was a casual voice.

"Mm, long lines."

"I'm sure."

"Is there something wrong, bangaram?"

She would look away with an exhale. "No, everything's fine."

It was the same every time until one day it wasn't.

"I want to come with you," she said, as I wrapped my shawl over my shoulders. "I want to go to town."

"Prakruthi, I've told you before. It's dangerous."

"Then how come you go?"

"Well, someone has to. And I can handle what's out there. You can't."

"You don't know that!"

I took her arms gently and sat her down. "Bangaram, you're forgetting. That village is one of monsters. If you step in there, they will smell your youth and rip you open to drink your blood."

"I don't believe you," she said, shoving me away. "I'm so sick of staying in here all the time. If it were true that it was full of monsters, you wouldn't leave me here alone for so long."

I frowned. When she was younger, this story had worked well. Prakruthi would be terrified enough never to question me or even dare to rebel against me. "Prakruthi, you cannot come with me," I said, sharply. "End of discussion."

"What are you going to do, stop me?"

Bristling, I raised my hand as if to slap her. She flinched, and I bit down on the inside of my cheek. I had never raised a hand on her before. Shaking my head, I stormed out of the tower, locking the door from the outside.

Prakruthi banged on the door. "Amma, please! Please, it gets so lonely in here."

Her words caught at my heart, but I continued to walk away. I was doing this for her good. Of course I was. I had to protect her from the evil that waited outside for her. An evil far worse than my own. The evil of men. It just so happened that I was also protecting myself.

I spent a lot of time experimenting with magic. It was the one thing the shadows taught me in such beautiful detail. The one thing that allowed me to cling onto an edge of sanity.

I knew that there had to be something out there that allowed me to return to my human form. Using *maya* or illusions would have been the best solution. It could manipulate how others perceived me, but it was also the tool of the gods and asuras. As terrible as I'd become, I was still human.

But I needed *something* to work, or I would never have my

daughter back. What little girl wanted a demoness for a mother?

In the end, I was too late. Always too late. I'd discovered eventually that my daughter had left the village for some better place far away. Now, there was nothing to hold back the horrors within me.

I found the paintings a few days after our argument. They were hidden in the back of her closet, covered by sheets and shawls. I just wanted to do some cleaning around the tower. That was all. I hadn't expected to find anything so … dangerous.

"What is this?" I asked, quietly, when I felt her enter the room.

There was an exhale. "Amma, I can explain."

"Then, explain."

There were at least ten different canvases. Some of them depicted a view of the village from her bedroom window. Others were of a boy holding a girl by the waist, his forehead pressed against hers. Their faces were curiously blank, but the girl had a long braid that wrapped around both their feet.

My grip on the closet door tightened. "I don't hear an explanation."

"I-I don't know what to say."

"Neither do I." I turned to face her.

The silence buzzed in my ear with all the things that we were not saying. Prakruthi wrapped her arms around her waist, and I couldn't tell if the guarded way she was standing broke my heart or pushed me closer into a murderous rage. I couldn't have her looking at me the way the rest of them did. Not her.

"You don't tell me things," she said, finally. "You don't let me out. All you give me are stories, but you have so many secrets that I don't know what to believe anymore. I wanted relief, so I asked for paint. I wanted to be inspired, so I asked for books. And they showed me a whole other world. You told me that the people in that village are monsters and that they would eat me alive. But that's not true, is it? They're like you and me. They're like the people in this book."

She held up the book of fairytales, and I closed my eyes. Stupid, stupid, *stupid*. She must have read some flimsy love story and have gotten enamored with it. I should never have bought that for her. I should never have let myself get comfortable.

"Don't make me the villain, bangaram. I hate being the villain."

"This doesn't feel like a home anymore. This feels like a prison."

"What, so I'm not enough anymore? You want some fancy boy to take you off riding into the sunset?" I walked closer to her and caressed her cheek. Her flinch was a dagger in my gut. "How can I make you see that there's only pain waiting out there for you?"

"Tell me the truth," she said. "Tell me what happened to you and why we live here instead of out there. Tell me why you looked like … like a monster when I was younger, and now you don't. Tell me why I look nothing like you. *Tell me.*"

I pressed my lips into a thin line, stepping away from her.

She nodded, resigned. "I thought so. I'm leaving tomorrow. I swear I'll come back—you're my mother, and I love you. But I need some time alone. I need some space."

"You're not going anywhere."

She raised her chin. "You can't stop me."

I smiled in a way I hadn't in a very long time. I could almost feel the razor points of teeth ripping into the soft flesh of my lips. "Watch me."

A couple had moved into a small cottage near my tower. I could not believe their audacity. They must have been really poor if they were brave enough to risk living near me.

Unless they didn't know who I was. It had been a century since I stepped out of my tower, other than for food from my garden. I had grown tired of the horror in people's eyes when they gazed upon my form. Mothers would pull their kids close to their waists, and men would cower in buildings, watching me with hate in their eyes. No one could remember anymore why I existed. No one could remember that it was *their fault*.

So, I didn't leave my home. Until … these fools came to me. The woman was weak and pregnant. One look at her swollen belly told me it was a baby girl. It made me hate the woman more, but it also gave me an idea.

Good and evil. Love and hate. Innocence and corruption. Polarities make the universe, and polarities cancel out—this is a fundamental rule of life and, therefore, magic.

It was possible that innocence could reverse my terrible curse. It was possible that this child could save me from myself.

I made the doors disappear at her touch. Only I could leave the tower, but Prakruthi would be trapped for as long as I wished. No, not trapped. *Safe.*

She kicked and screamed and cried. She threw tantrums loud enough that I thought she would bring the tower down on us. But I would not budge, and she learned to go silent.

I took away her books, although I let her keep the paints. There was only so much pain I could cause my daughter. If she were grateful, she didn't say so.

Prakruthi had taken up singing more. She would lean by her window and sing to the world, as if she were some pretty nightingale trapped in a cage by an evil witch. That was what I had become in this story. A witch. A demoness. Sometimes, I would curl up outside her door and listen to her sweet voice. Her newest song was about a city in the stars that you could fly to at night. I didn't miss the underlying desperation for freedom.

What freedom was she so desperate for, anyway? The kind that would get her persecuted by the evil snapping its jaws outside? I knew better than she, but she didn't want to listen. She didn't want to learn from my mistakes.

But I couldn't have her feeling trapped forever. That would also taint her purity and innocence. And that would be the ruin of me. It turned out that, once again, I was too late. The day I decided to tell her that I had restored the doors was the day everything fell apart.

I had come back home earlier than usual from my daily run to the village to see a long braid hanging from Prakruthi's bedroom window. And then I heard voices.

"I can't take it anymore, Rahul. Take me with you. Tonight."

"Tonight? There's just one day left. It's less risky for me to get you tomorrow, while she's gone."

"No, no, please. I can't take it anymore." There was a small sob and the rustle of clothes.

Dread pooled in my stomach. I peered around the large boulder that covered the front of my garden to find Prakruthi in the arms of a thin boy with raven hair so carefully smoothed down. A rich boy. His lips had caught hers in an embrace for five seconds before he tucked her head underneath his chin.

"All right," he murmured. "I'll be back for you tonight. Then, we can go anywhere you want."

This couldn't be happening. How was this real?

"I better go inside," Prakruthi whispered. "She'll be back soon."

Rahul nodded, and she gave him one last kiss. Then she tugged on her braid to make sure it was secure, and used it like a rope to scale the tower and climb back through the window.

He stood there, watching, as if he truly cared whether she fell or not. When she was back inside, she smiled down at this boy and blew him a kiss. He mimed catching it and pressing it against his heart. I had half a mind to swipe him dead right there, forgetting in my anger that I had lost my talons to regain my appearance of humanity. He left before I could do something senseless. Walked right past me and disappeared on a winding path that led down the hill.

I waited to enter my tower until he was out of sight and until

Prakruthi had moved from the window. I moved slowly, shuddering at the memory of this stranger touching my daughter. How much had he corrupted her? A glance at my body showed me that nothing had changed. So, they hadn't done the unthinkable. At least, not yet.

"Amma?" Prakruthi called when I entered.

My mind was still spinning, but I managed to make myself answer. "Yes, it's I." I was half-tempted to ask who else would it be, but I held my tongue. I had to take careful action now. This was a very precarious situation.

When I reached the top of the stairs, I saw that Prakruthi had cooked for us. A grand dinner of sambar and rice. It was not impressive for most, but it was impressive for her. She wasn't the biggest fan of cooking.

"You made food?" I asked, my voice calm and distant.

She beamed. "I wanted to surprise you. It got cold, but we can heat it up."

"You're cheerful today."

"Am I?" She laughed. "I don't know. Today just feels like a good day."

Is it that easy for you to discard me, my girl? Do I mean nothing to you?

I shook away the thoughts, setting my basket of groceries and pastries on the table. I had gotten the pastries to celebrate finally getting past this awful period of time. I didn't know that I would be betrayed. Could the innocent betray you?

Prakruthi frowned, peering into my face. "What's wrong with your eyes? Why do they look like that?"

I moved her aside gently and walked to my mirror. The pupils had expanded so large that they covered the irises. It was starting. I hid my trembling hands behind my back and forced a smile on my face. "It's nothing, I'm sure."

Prakruthi insisted I sit at the table so we could eat.

"Already? It's early for dinner."

"Well, I'm starving, and I want us to eat together."

The unsaid words floated into my ear. *For the last time.*

I watched her as she served our food while humming under her breath, a dreamy smile on her face. I hadn't seen her like this in a while. I knew that I was the reason she wasn't happy, but it had never really bothered me because I knew that I was protecting her.

But I went too far. I turned her against me. And once she left, I would again be alone in my misery, taken over by my monstrous form. The sixteen years of reprieve would be just that— a reprieve. I couldn't let that happen. There was still a way I could change things around. But it would require a sacrifice. All good things require a sacrifice.

"Prakruthi?"

"Hm?"

"Thank you for the dinner."

She smiled, puzzled. "Of course, Amma."

I slid a kitchen knife on the table into my hand and waited. When Prakruthi came to my side to clear my plate, I stopped her. "Do you love me, bangaram?"

She stared at me, and wariness crept into her eyes. I had to act soon. "Of course I love you."

"I love you, too," I whispered and slammed the knife into her stomach.

She gasped, pitching forward. I stood to catch her in my arms, to lower her gently to the floor, tears streaming from my eyes. Her fingers clutched onto my blouse, and I was taken back to when I first held her in my arms, and her tiny fists had grabbed at me in that same, desperate way.

"A-Amma?" There was so much confusion and panic in her eyes. So much fear and betrayal and *pain*.

"Oh, my sweet girl," I said, hands shaking as I reached for an empty glass and plate on our dining table. "My bangaram. I couldn't let you leave me. I couldn't go back to the way I was." *I'd rather you than me.* I shoved away the thought before it could take root.

Blood pooled around her waist, in between her legs. A hand clutched at the knife, as if she wanted to take it out but was too afraid to. "It hurts," Prakruthi sobbed. "Amma, it hurts so much."

"It's better this way." I urged the glass to her mouth, catching her gasps and whatever innocence was left in her soul. It was highly unlikely that this theory would work. Too much damage had been done. But it was better than nothing. "That boy would have ruined you. He would have left you a monster." I immediately capped the glass with the plate and set it aside. Then with bloody hands, I stroked my daughter's hair away from her face. Her braid stretched out behind her to the other side of the room where it sat in a pile. "I love you, bangaram. Don't you ever forget that."

My hands left bloody streaks and scratches on her face. I noticed that the talons had grown back, and so had the scales. I knew that she was gone when I no longer felt puffs of air hitting my cheek. I cradled her close, one last time, and then went to fill my glass of innocent breath with fresh rainwater. I drank it.

Nothing happened.

I waited anxiously. It was possible that the drink would take longer to take effect. But nothing happened, and I knew that it was too late. Too much damage had been done. Maybe if I had tried to take her breath before I ...?

Well, there was no use in pondering the past. I felt the razor teeth poke back out of my gum, impaling my lower lip. Horns sprang from my skull, shearing some of my curls. Trembling, I made myself move to grab another knife. I used the hilt to shatter the mirror hanging on the wall and the blade to cut off Prakruthi's braid. I still had the boy to take care of.

He approached when the full moon was high in the sky. I waited for him under Prakruthi's window, from which her newly chopped braid swayed against the tower.

"Prakruthi," he whispered, hopefully, once he was inside, walking closer to me. "I'm here." When he saw my face of horrors, he blanched, stepping backward. His mouth opened and closed, but no sound came out.

"It's your fault, you know," I said, softly. "If you'd never come along, she would still be well."

"What did you do," he asked, voice just hard enough to hide the tremor. "You *monster*."

"*I?*" I took a step toward him for every step he took back. "I'm no monster. You steal from me, I steal from you."

"*What did you do?*"

"You killed her, you know," I said, feeling so very dead inside. "And you killed me, too. This is all your fault."

"Stop!" he yelled, covering his ears. He fell to his knees, face contorted with grief. What a tiny, miserable, *pathetic* thing. Was this how I looked all those years ago?

"Spare me the dramatics," I spat. My knife found its aim for the second time that night, right in the center of his head. He dropped to the ground, eyes staring up at the night sky, frozen in anguish.

I staggered away, unable to look at what had been my home. The familiar despair was threatening to engulf me, and I wondered where I would go now. What I would do. Where could this body hide without being hunted down and slain? In mere moments, I'd lost for the second time the life I had built and a daughter I loved dearly.

You always lose what you were never meant to keep. And I lost everything.

Thrice

A RETELLING OF 1,001 NIGHTS
ARIELLE K. JONES

n a small town there was a magician. He would often perform for the families who had spent the day working. Every sunset is when they knew to expect him and his tricks by the town's large, old well. His posture was immaculate, and his state of dress had the appearance of someone who wanted to be asked where he was from. Most attendants of his performances didn't mind this; they simply enjoyed him and his eccentricities, and his magic tricks.

For instance, when wildflowers bloomed in the foothills, the magician would go out and pick them during the day, then— seemingly from nowhere—pull these same flowers out from people's pockets or from behind their ears. It came to be known that the magician would pull the most beautiful blooms from his most generous audience members. These were the families that fed him from their own tables or allowed him rest for the night beneath their roofs. These kindnesses allowed the magician to continue performing day after day beside the town's large, old well.

And at the end of his performances by the well, for those who couldn't give food or shelter, the well's bucket was passed around for them to deposit little gifts for the magician. These gifts and payments were always hand-sized things his audience could afford to part with. From the bucket, the magician received stick dolls from the children, or painted pebbles, or a few coins jingling together at the bottom alongside old jewelry with missing clasps. Every now and then, there'd be a clot of dirt dropped in the bucket by the naysayer, a man in town who did not much care for tricks or ways of making money that didn't necessitate sweat or soreness. The magician tended to laugh at the offerings from this man and would discard them privately.

But then, there came a day when the magician received something rather unexpected in his little pile of gifts. He found a seashell nestled in the bottom of the bucket.

To this very moment, no one knows who left the seashell there for the magician to keep. And that night, sitting in the light of a fireplace not his own, the magician pondered the seashell. It was cream in color and speckled in brown along its spiral. And how cool to the touch it was, how smooth and unchipped in his palm! When he peered inside, he found a soft delight at the rosiness of the curve disappearing into itself.

Perhaps, he thought, perhaps he could use this little treasure somehow in his next performance!

He was so sure he could fit some small things within the seashell. Or maybe, with nature's ample magic, he supposed that he could invite the audience to hold the seashell to their ears and hear echoes of the ocean. Just to be sure, the magician tried the act himself. He put the shell to his ear, and the thin coldness of it cut a chill through him. On instinct, he pulled it away from his head, but there was a sound. There was the swirl of salted whispers, lightly frictioned air from elsewhere. *This is what the ocean sounds like,* he thought, but then came a voice!

At once, the magician stood, and his chair teetered in its place. The voice was gentle and deep and said, "Call to me by my name."

And the magician said the name he'd never said before. Without a conscious thought, it came off his tongue, much like honest magic. A gust of wind came forth from the seashell's opening. The magician pulled his face away and let the shell fall onto the ground before him. Pale smoke, maybe steam, curled out of the creamy mouth. It billowed hauntingly, silently, until it poured upward and spread vaguely over the ceiling of the room. As the steam faded, the more clearly a figure appeared.

An exquisite form stood before the magician. A form beautiful in ways the magician found difficult to accept but knew to be true. There was a fluid strength in the being's limbs, a charm to the mouth, and a shimmer like a tear shed in an eye. The being was unclothed, and the magician, unable yet to speak, lifted the cloak under which he'd meant to sleep and offered it. The figure accepted the cloak and was then covered loosely.

The being said, "I am bound to you now."

"In what way?" asked the magician.

"I am bound to save your life on three different occasions. When you call on me, I will answer you by restoring you to as whole and as sound a condition as you are in now. After these three instances, I will return to the vessel of the seashell."

"And you agree to this servitude?" asked the magician.

The being did not at once seem to understand. No one had had this concern for the being before. "I do," then answered the being. "I agree to this arrangement."

The magician clasped his hands together and announced, "Then you shall be my assistant." He reasoned that, under such a guise, no one would question the being's constant presence. "Come," the magician said, "and I will teach you a taste of my ways so that you can fully assist me."

And thus, it was so. The assistant, still loosely wrapped in the magician's cloak, listened all through the night as the magician spoke with his hands and his excited eyes and dancing words, explaining his illusions to someone for the first time.

On the very next evening, the magician performed with his new assistant, the being from the seashell. There were murmurs in the audience, uncertainty about who the person was beside their beloved magician. At first, the magician's new assistant served only as a prop. The magician would pull various small trinkets from behind the assistant's ear, or he would ask his assistant to pass items to the audience for them to inspect before he'd cause the very same trinkets to disappear.

Later, after more time spent together, the magician's beautiful assistant became more involved. With a smile, still freshly shy, the assistant would be there, adorned in donated garments, and would announce the magician or would help collect offerings from the crowd, and eventually would perform some small illusionary tricks, as well.

What a charming addition, thought the townsfolk. And slowly, but assuredly, the more that the magician and the assistant performed together, the larger the audience grew.

There came a point when cushions and stools were brought out to surround the well and the small town's entertainers. Food was passed around, and blankets were shared across laps as the performances went later into the evening. People actually came from neighboring places to see this magician and his assistant, who was said to be from the sea. This went on for some time until the magician caught an idea for his next performance.

The recent rains had been abundant; the water in the well was high. To his audience, the magician announced, "I will submerge myself for longer than any land-loving creature should be able! This act will astound you, and my survival shall be part of it."

As many people as possible gathered around the circled stones of the well to witness the spectacle. Upon the request of the magician, the assistant had dressed in shades of blue and green and prominently wore the seashell as a necklace.

With much patience and intended tension, the magician neatly removed his shoes and gave them to the care of his assistant. As he did so, he invited members of the audience to, one by one, put rocks and stones into the well bucket. As they did so, he removed his layers of clothing piece by piece. This was the most unadorned they had ever seen their beloved magician. His shirt plain and his trousers fastened simply with string.

Once the townsfolk finished filling the pail to the brim, the magician, barefoot, climbed atop it and was lowered into the well water by the light of day. His breath echoed back at him from the stones of the well until he was submerged, and the coils of his hair loosened around his temples as if he were in a slow wind. So weightless he felt down there holding on to the rope, sitting atop the stone-laden bucket. Being submerged was not so worrisome at first, but then his lungs itched, and his ribs felt paused for too long.

Meanwhile, on the surface, the most concerned onlookers threw their eyes to those of the magician's assistant in a silent plea to pull him back up. The assistant paid no heed to the frightened gazes. The magician's assistant was steadfastly listening for the magician's voice, for the name the magician somehow knew. From not far off, the magician's naysayer simply watched.

Below the freshwater surface, all that was within the magician felt as if it were on fire. He had never held his breath for such a long measure of time before. As his heart beat thunderously in his ears, he wondered if he could even be heard if he called out to the being from this far below. He steeled himself to the brink of drowning. All that his body craved was to inhale, but instead, he gave himself to his faith in their arrangement and exhaled the name of his assistant.

In a simple manner of blinking, the magician then opened his eyes to find himself seated at the edge of the well with actual wind in his hair. He was dripping and whole and not at all short of breath as the townsfolk applauded, and his assistant knelt, gently slipped the magician's feet back into his dry shoes without out a word.

The magician was seen to have performed both magic and a miracle that day.

The well bucket was swiftly emptied of rocks and stones and then filled back to the brim with humble offerings and coins from the amazed crowd. The townsfolk who had wept while he was under now helped to dry off the magician and to warm him in their embraces and shawls and coats. As they praised him, the magician's chest swelled with warmth and relief that his idea had carried out so well.

On that night, the magician and assistant were given refuge by the wealthiest citizen of the community and were granted rest and shelter in an elaborate guest room. In private, the assistant—the ever-patient being—reminded the magician, "You have two remaining opportunities for me to save your life."

The magician nodded, unperturbed as he readied himself for sleep.

The assistant also prepared for bed but advised, "Instead of tricks, I would remind you that I can also save you from unexpected ills."

The magician yawned and answered, "That is all well and good, but come, we must rest. Tomorrow, we prepare for an encore!"

Word spread quickly of how the magician had survived the miraculous drowning. The crowd was far too large for everyone to have a good view, even with the seats and shared blankets. And so, a visitor from elsewhere invited the magician to a neighboring city to host his next performance.

This neighboring town was able to provide the magician and his assistant with an actual stage, with large curtains and ornate lamps to draw attention. Having a stage was a lovely thing to the magician's mind, a fulfilling thing. He very much appreciated the sound of his shoes on the wood, the sympathetic taps and creaks as he performed his illusions.

As with previous performances, the magician and the assistant made the audience's items disappear and reappear. And sometimes, the magician would seemingly change items from one thing to another: an apple into a child's shoe, or one earring into two. With the assistant's help, he would also produce infinite scarves from thin air or repair objects that seemed irreparably broken.

The two of them became quite popular in this town. Oh, how these people, these city-folk, adored their prized performers from the countryside. Yet, this excitement would not last, and the audience hungered for more from the magician. There were some in the audience who wondered if the magician would perform anything quite like what they'd heard he'd accomplished back at that large, old well of the neighboring town.

One night, atop the stage after quite a few of his expected illusions, the magician brought out an immensely gaudy box big enough to fit a babe inside. It was made of beautiful wood and was decorated with the scene of some long-ago war, and it was emblazoned with glittering gems some viewers believed were real. The magician made a show of slowly opening the ornate box, and out from it, he pulled a gleaming blade. The teeth of the blade were meant for shredding. Its tip had the purpose of carving with ease. The hilt was black like the ceiling of a closed coffin.

The magician dramatically said, "My illustrious and dear assistant will drive this cruel knife through me. This act will astound you, and my survival shall be part of it."

For many rows past the stage, the audience watched the magician offer the blade to the assistant. The audience also watched the assistant retreat back a step.

"I won't," said the assistant in a voice quiet and disbelieving, in a voice only heard by the first few rows and by the magician who still wore his performer's smile, a smile that the assistant then realized was just like all of the magician's other smiles.

The magician did not understand this refusal. Of anyone present, his magical assistant should have known that any harm brought to the magician in that moment would be temporary, at best. Regardless, the assistant made no move to take the blade. So instead, the magician proclaimed grandly to the crowd, "My assistant, it seems, has become shy."

Small patches of laughter and sounds of empathy shimmered through the audience.

"Mayhap I can have a volunteer!" he announced.

The magician then made a show of peering through the crowd with his hand on his brow as if he were protecting his eyes from the lights of all the lamps. This lasted long enough for everyone in the audience to sit up excitedly, to squirm in their seats.

With their attention harnessed, the magician quite deliberately walked off the stage and through his eager onlookers until he came to a man who always stood in the back, in the furthest place from the stage. This man, the naysayer, was still not a fan of any of the magician's actions. He had remained suspicious of any form of performance. This man, along with a handful of others, was waiting for the magician to fail, to fall.

But even so, in the presence of the magician's ambitious smile, the naysayer followed him onto the stage with a grunt and dragging feet. The crowd applauded, and the magician encouraged the naysayer to bow, but the magician ended up bowing alone. His assistant didn't bow, either, just stood to the side and watched, listened.

Unbothered by this, the magician cleared his throat and continued his performance. He turned toward the disgruntled man beside him and passed him the knife, said, "Now, what I am about to ask you to do is quite serious—"

The magician had meant to say more, but the naysayer already had the knife and—needing no instruction—he plunged it forcefully into the soft middle of the magician, through his fancy clothes and bravado.

Blood bloomed like melting snow at the magician's gut. The pain shocked him to gasping, and he focused maddeningly on the other man's shoes. These were worn boots with broken-in leather and crumbles of dried mud along the edges. These boots were tracking dirt onto the magician's lovingly crafted stage. Then, as with his drowning, the magician's lungs itched and quickly burned like the moths who, fond of light, flew much too close to bright, burning lamps. He could see the little pile of their bodies, gathered on the wood, stray wings clinging to the bottoms of the curtains.

The name that the magician somehow knew was having a more difficult time coming up off his tongue, and a wave of fear like the magician had never known before clawed down from his scalp to the tendons of his shaking ankles. Each attempt at breath was sharp and short as the sound of the world barely filtered through the fog at his ears.

But after all, the magician managed somehow to say the name he somehow knew. He blinked awake to the sight of an audience all on their feet and throwing flowers around him, covering the stage and the shoes of the man who had stabbed him.

His assistant, with tight lips and sad eyes, had begun unbuttoning the magician's shirt to replace it with a fresh one, one without the stain of a second survival. Once freshly dressed, the magician raised his arms in triumph to face the astounded audience. They were uproarious and cast gift after gift onto the stage, flowers and pouches of coins alike. The former naysayer, who a moment before had been so comfortable bringing harm to the magician, went to kiss his feet. For each performance afterward, this man could be found in the very front row of the magician's shows.

Once again, the magician and his mysterious assistant were beloved by the city, were the pride of the people, and the temptation of outsiders. The performances were quite the spectacle, and audiences delighted in recounting these astonishing events. Rather consistently, the magician and the assistant were gorgeously adorned and very much engaged with their vocal audience. The viewers giggled at the glances between the two performers, and they clutched their hearts when surprised. The dynamic was rather invigorating for a time. The novelty, for a time, was appreciated.

The stage still glowed brightly, the magician's poise remained enticing, but more and more of the lush seats were empty at each successive performance. This led to the magician investing in various contraptions to aid in his seeming magic: trapdoors, collapsible cages, and concoctions that changed a liquid's color. And while these additions did indeed add riches to his pockets, the tributes and attendance were not fulfilled to the degree to which he had become accustomed.

Weeks later, on an evening just before a performance was scheduled, the assistant went on an errand to fetch shimmering thread to hem the curtains of the stage. The assistant expected to have just enough time to repair the wearing before that night's show. Whether for an audience of one or of hundreds, the assistant knew the magician would want to ensure the utmost quality for his viewers. However, upon reaching the stage that night, the assistant came to find a neatly handwritten sign attached to the closed curtains reading: *Apologies for the inconvenience of the canceled presentation this evening!*

Upon investigation, the assistant found that all the props and costumes were in order. Yet, the magician was gone. The assistant spent some time searching nearby just to be sure, and still, there was no sign of the magician, aside from his familiar script on that sign. Because the city would be too large of a place to search haphazardly, the being then went back to the elegant abode that the two of them shared.

The magician was there within, fingers stained in ink and furiously writing at his desk. Parchments covered in notes had spilled onto the floor. He was not at all dressed to be seen. He was bedraggled in a way that made the assistant hesitate in the doorway, at the periphery of the magician's sight.

"Good evening," the magician said, neither smiling nor looking up. He took a breath and finished lifting his pen from the page. "I am afraid," he confessed, "afraid of becoming stale." And he admitted this in a way reminiscent of the quiet way he'd shared the secrets of his illusions when the two of them began together. He was genuine and hopeful.

And the truth of his concern was in the freshness and age of the ink in the air, it was in the look of his unkempt hair, the smell of his sweat showing at the creases of his elbows, across his chest and collar. He had spent this time working harder for inspiration than he ever had before. The magician confirmed that he had canceled the performance in order to plan a way to recover his regard in this city.

And thus, days passed, then weeks, as the magician scribbled his ideas and was beckoned to meals by his assistant.

"They are losing interest," the magician said.

"They are impatient," said the assistant.

And the room remained quiet for some time while the magician wrote and thought, while the being assisted him by organizing the notes once the ink upon them had dried. They shared quite a bit of time that way until the magician eventually sighed and said, "Come, with however much time you've spent on this earth, you must have come across something wondrous."

"More so than you?" proposed the assistant without looking up, as they scanned and shuffled the pages. "Besides," the assistant added, "wonder is not a constant state. You are not the Conjurer."

"No, I most certainly am not," and the magician laughed away the thought and heard his assistant politely chuckle, as well.

Oh, but then! Without warning, the magician stood from his seat, let his chair clatter backward, let gravity take it down in wracking jolts to splinter at the legs as the assistant watched in concern from a distance, too far to prevent the calamity.

"I cannot be the Conjurer, of course not, but what if I could summon the Conjurer here, to them?" His eyes were lit with the desire of a destined venture. There was to be no turning him from this.

The assistant's heart raced as if the chair had fallen a second time.

The next day, the pair began their work. The magician, once again in his familiar odd finery, went to his stage for the first time in weeks and addressed a curious and expectant crowd.

"You have been very patient with me and my absence," he said. "Out of respect for this, I know that my next performance for you must be absolutely stupendous."

They cheered, of course they did. He had promised them astoundment, and in this declaration, the assistant and he were very much aware of that one last instance to say the being's name. The crowd beamed and went forth to spread the word as the magician graciously bowed and hopped off his beloved stage.

Upon returning to his desk, he seemed very much restored. He had gathered books, holy texts to make his desire come into fruition.

Across the room, still standing, the being said, "You will be struck down for this, for being so arrogant."

The magician had a soft and assured tilt to his mouth as he read. He responded, "And yes, my darling, that's when you come in to save me from my arrogance."

The being doubted this, but said nothing of it as they both read through the night. Together they read tomes, and volumes, and whatever pieces of literature they could gather about the Conjurer. They went through many candles and worked through many dawns. Yet, after having spent so much time devoted to religious research, the magician decided that he'd gained all that he could from books.

Thus, he moved on to speaking with holy representatives. This venture took them away from their city. As per the being's suggestions, the two of them dressed humbly for these discussions and meetings, and they listened more than they spoke. Even so, some churches and temples in the surrounding area turned them away, horrified at the blasphemous proposal or simply untrusting of outsiders. They did not sense a genuine interest in embracing their religion or their religious practices.

Yet elsewhere, the magician and his accompanying assistant found success. In a number of holy spaces, the residents felt the magician's genuine eagerness for knowledge and, thus, welcomed him. He entranced them by quoting scripture and by praying with them before meals together. And eventually, the magician and the being helped in preparing these meals, and in serving these welcoming holy houses by cleaning and making any needed repairs to their structures.

The being was quite skilled at organizing, and the magician became quite skilled at making repairs. He performed helpful tasks in the community with his woodwork and attention to detail. The townsfolk were pleased. The devoted preachers and practitioners were glad. And the being was happy to be somewhere still, and not alone. The being believed, for at least a length of time, that this region, living amongst these people, could be a home for the pair of them. And this was true for a length of time.

There came a day where the magician and a holy representative of the highest order were absent from the church. It wasn't until supper that night that the magician, grinning, returned to the being. In their shared dwelling, the magician at first did not speak about his excitement nor about his disappearance. Instead, he produced a flower from behind the being's ear, a nearly forgotten sweet trick. But, perhaps due to being out of practice with this humble act, the magician accidentally dropped the bloom. The blossom was so beauteous compared to its dry stem. This flower was vibrant, even though it had been dying the moment it was plucked. The petals appeared to be one color, but then the being saw the thin ribbons of red coming from the center, reaching outward and exquisite.

As quickly as could be done, the magician blew the soil away and replaced the flower behind the being's ear. The magician, by light of a single candle between them, said, "We are leaving. We have what we need at last."

And on that night, he described the knowledge he had gained in confidence from the holy leader, his answer of how to summon the Conjurer of All. And come the morning, he told the devout townsfolk that they were welcome to see him perform in the city that still waited for him and his promise to perform something stupendous.

With much haste, the magician and his assistant traveled. The magician would prattle excitedly about how he'd learned what he'd have to do, and the assistant, the being, would listen.

"We must build a structure, a monument," explained the magician. "It will be made of wood that I gather myself, and then I must assemble this structure according to protected and sacred specifications. And by doing this, I will bring the Conjurer to this place."

Feeling there was no room for disagreement, the assistant agreed to help the magician in whatever way he wished. On the return journey, the magician could hardly keep himself on the path, and the assistant could hardly speak.

When the oncoming holy structure was announced to the city-folk, it was done with much fanfare. The magician's state of dress was especially immaculate. He wore feathers sewn to the backs of the shoulders of his cape, and his sandals shone so slickly that they glistened like oil, and the jewelry he wore may have been a collection of all the gaudiness he'd received over the years in this profession. He made sure that his assistant from the sea was also adorned in various shades of blue and teal and in hints of green.

As the beloved pair of them once again graced the stage, the magician was excited to hear his shoes pacing as he told the audience more about his upcoming labor of love. To prove his devotion to bringing the blessed Conjurer to them all, he took an ax and dismantled his very own platform.

The crowd gasped in unison and then giddily applauded. The first person to offer water to the magician as he toiled was the former naysayer. His gaze was open as the magician drank. Like most others in the city, the former naysayer was enthralled. Tools were donated to the magician. He was given hammers and nails. Very soon, the officials of the town made interrupting the magician a punishable act. Very soon, the rows and rows of chairs before the site of the stage were also demolished so as to contribute to the magician's monument. The crowd stood eagerly and as close to the construction as they could manage. The city was fascinated in this way for days, and then weeks. The magician would sweat and would smile at all those surrounding faces as he continued to assemble the holy structure that no one could predict the end of.

Some days during the construction, the magician was quiet. He would simply rest his hand against the wooden frame on which he'd been laboring earlier in the day and would close his eyes. Some onlookers would swear that he were praying, but to the being, it was clear that he was not.

To the being, this magician's periodic pose seemed solemn. Perhaps, he was a little conflicted, as well. It seemed a contemplative mixture of emotions were just beneath the surface of his façade. And always, upon sensing the being's stare, the magician would look up and attempt to smile it away.

"Come, there is work to do," he'd say, full again of his usual charm.

The being was not charmed, but nevertheless, continued to help the magician in whatever way he asked.

As they worked together in the coming days, they received gifts. Gifts came mostly from the locals, grateful for the business that had been brought into town. Gifts came with gratitude for transforming the town into a holy place. The more explicitly religious gifts were given back to churches or to those who seemed to respect the symbols the most. But the more outright expensive donations were used for handsome costumes for the magician's assistant.

"This brightens your already-bright eyes," the magician would say, or, "This flows like water from you." And like water, the magician's eyes would run down the being's body playfully. A smile, on rare occasions, could be earned this way.

Most of the donations, though, were put toward constructing the monument. They went toward purchasing supplies, or crafting elaborate invitations to dignitaries in faraway places, places that would read his name before ever hearing it. The magician and his mysterious assistant did not spend anything on food, as meals were brought to them by supportive admirers.

So devoted was the magician that he felt no shame in selling his belongings, his extravagant clothing, his beloved trinkets, his contraptions for past performances, until at last he sold his very first ring. Without needing the magician's request, the being sold gifted garments and adornments, as well. As the magician had been immersed in his work, he had only one request of his assistant, and that was to be read to from holy scriptures. This touching gesture simply increased the interest of the crowd and caused word of this project to spread even further. In the coming days, droves of people came to witness the work of the man who sought to summon the Conjurer of All.

The devout were there in all ranges of support. While many drew religious inspiration and excitement from the nearly completed project, there were also many who looked at the magician's act as an abomination. These horrified, yet still present, onlookers confused the being the most. If they felt that what the magician was doing were so terrible, then why be part of the audience? Why stay and invite others? While it is true that the religious and disgusted members of the audience would beg others to leave and would also recite apocalyptic warnings from their holy books, they never tried to ruin the magician's work. They may have sneered at him as he passed by, but they never stood in his way as he continued to build, day after day. They may not have condoned his actions, but perhaps, just as everyone else amassed at the construction site, they were hoping to see their deity look back at them.

The monument was almost finished now. When before they had been months away, they became perhaps hours away, so assured the magician. The very next day had doubled the number of people milling about the indescribable monument. The invitations to dignitaries had been answered, and many people of many languages arrived. No streets leading to the town center, to the holiest of manmade things, were empty. All that was left was a final piece to add toward the top.

When the magician fell from the highest scaffolding, it was in the midst of people praying, laughing, condemning, converting.

The first one that the magician found with his eyes was the being at the front of the crowd.

Those nearest drew silent and could not deny that somehow, crumpled on the ground, the magician was still beauteous compared to the rest of them. This man was vibrant, even as his shirt changed color, thin ribbons of red spread from the center of his chest, reaching and exquisite.

The magician's legs, so proud when once striding across a stage, were splintered, were wet and broken. This, the sight of this, did not fully concern the assistant. Legs could be made to walk again, blood could flow anew, but that was only if the magician would but speak a name.

There wasn't much time, so the two of them did not waste any of it saying things to each other that they already knew. "Call out to me," the being said, hand quaking on the magician's chest. And the being could not recall ever making this request of anyone.

Regardless, the magician rolled his lips inward, wouldn't say the name he somehow knew. Instead, he said, "I will astound them this way forever."

As the magician expected, he gained repute by the hundreds gathered. As the magician expected, the religious onlookers and leaders were divided. Some respected his attempt to build the monument as an act of faith, and some believed he got what he had deserved since they viewed his effort to summon a deity as utter blasphemy.

And sadly, as the magician expected, he was sorely missed by the common townsfolk he had first performed for. He'd expected the being to carry on alone the few illusions they'd performed together. And the being did, for a time.

But unlike the magician had expected, the being stopped performing after less than the passing of a moon. Instead, the being sought the most troublesome places for humans to reach so that the seashell that was both a home and a prison could never be found, so that the being would never again be used in such a careless and fanciful fashion.

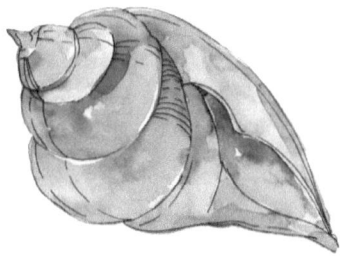

The Briquettes of Blackcurrant Lane

A RETELLING OF STONE SOUP

BRIAN C. ORR

ld Man Latimer couldn't have been less enthused to see his nephew Joseph. The old man never cared much for his nephew, anyway, but for Joseph to show up unannounced on his uncle's housecleaning day?

See, the thing was, Joseph was a smooth operator, and everyone who knew him, or knew of him, knew it. His charm allowed him to get out of failing classes and speeding tickets, and into the hearts of many women. He was now a delivery driver and thought he'd surprise his uncle with a visit and a special gift.

Oswald Latimer, affectionately known as "Old Man Latimer," was an older but sturdy man and a beast on the grill. His wife Vanessa's culinary and hosting skills were unmatched. The two were fixtures of Blackcurrant Lane: a utopian neighborhood of well-to-do people of color.

Joseph leaned on his uncle's front door with a relaxed confidence. "Unc, I've been trying to really get right over these past few years, and I'm hoping that you'll try these new barbecue briquettes I'm selling. My friend has a tree nursery, right? He uses these special minerals when he processes them. ... I don't know how he does it, really, but they'll have anything you grill taste immaculate. You have to give it a try before I go home."

The old man's brows furrowed. "How are these any different from those knives you sold me three years ago? Or those magazine subscriptions that never came? Actually, if I try them now, will you go home and leave me alone?"

Joseph nodded and grinned.

"Fine. Stay on the front lawn while I go get my grill. I don't need you eying anything in my house. You've got twenty minutes, Joseph." The old man dragged the grill to the driveway, with his nephew helping as his uncle came out of the garage. "Okay, we can light the grill, but I don't have any meat in the house—maybe a couple hot links from the freezer."

"Great! Let's use those as a sample!"

The old man tried one of the hot links after grilling with the fabled briquettes. "This is good, but I'm not tasting anything special. I'll take this bag to support your business, but I don't think you'll get much more from me out of this."

The old man's neighbor, Mr. Suarez, stopped in the driveway while walking his dog. "If it isn't Old Man Latimer! Are you back on the grill? I was planning on making ribs ahead of the Real Madrid game, but I'll happily share them with you if throw them on."

Joseph interjected before his uncle had time to respond, "Oh, Mr. Suarez. I'm sure that he'd be happy to make them."

"Mr. Suarez, I'd love to," the old man said, "but they'd take a couple of hours to prepare. I did have a number of things to do today—"

Joseph looked at his uncle, because he's got this. "Actually, Mr. Suarez, do you still have your sound system and projector? Maybe you can bring that out as he's grilling to pass the time. We can watch the game out here."

"You know, Joseph?" Mr. Suarez said. "That's a great idea. Lemme get my son to help haul everything out and set it up."

The smell of the food and the noise drew more neighbors outside. They contributed sides, condiments, and utensils until it became a full-fledged barbecue. Joseph greeted everyone and made sure they felt welcome.

The music bumped, with line dances punctuated by cheers from the soccer match. The neighbors sampled one another's food while sharing the latest happenings and secret recipes. Some of the elders shouted over dominos and tallboys. The barbecue was on and poppin', y'all. It showed no signs of stopping until …

There was a loud car honk, prompting Joseph and his uncle to glance out into the street. "Aww, damn. Is that Ms. Thea?"

Ms. Thea, the neighborhood snoop, peered over her glasses and slid out of her Chrysler LeBaron. She was notorious for taking neighborhood "issues" into her own hands, most of which she instigated. While her boundaries were essentially nonexistent, she was known as the best baker and casserole maker on the street. She was also snooty about her food: a walking vision of the African American proverb "who made the potato salad."

She marched over to the grill, with the clickity-clack of her kitten heels reverberating under the speakers. "What in Heaven's name? We can't have all this commotion going on! Some of us want to get in the spirit for *Bible* Study and show up on time. This … noise is just way too loud."

Joseph intervened. "How you doin', Ms. Thea? My uncle invited me over to help him with a neighborhood barbecue."

"Well, that's not exactly true," Old Man Latimer said. "What he means is that he was doing a dem—"

Joseph nodded at his uncle, as he's got this. "We were going to invite you, but I didn't know you'd be home. Why don't you spend a little time here for some food and fellowship with your neighbors? I'm sure your *Bible* study group will understand."

Ms. Thea looked around at the other neighbors and observed their joy. "You know, you're right. Maybe I will skip *Bible* Study. Henrietta is leading, anyways—she always manages to pick the *worst* scriptures, between you and me. Do y'all have any potato salad?"

Blackcurrant Lane had never had a barbecue like this. The old man grew closer to his neighbors as the barbecue came to a close.

Mr. Suarez patted him on the back before leaving. "You've outdone yourself, Old Man Latimer. Another fine affair by the Latimer family. We should do this more often, and please stop by for the game next Sunday."

The old man also created a deeper bond with his nephew. "You know, Unc, I haven't had this much fun since Aunt Vanessa ..."

Old Man Latimer teared up and gave his nephew a deep hug. "Thank you for the great afternoon, Joseph. You have no idea how much I needed this. Please feel free to stop by any time you like, and I'd be happy to buy more briquettes from you."

And just like that, a new tradition was born on Blackcurrant Lane. The entire neighborhood looked forward to the annual barbecue with Old Man Latimer on the grill and Joseph as the host who did the most.

Nokio

A RETELLING OF PINOCCHIO
DANAY ROBINSON

 o one ever talked about it, but I was not like the other children. In place of flesh and bones, I had wood and metal. I needed oil to loosen my joints and polish to make me shiny. When you are the only one made the way you are, you have an unspoken obligation to act like you are okay with it. I took it a step further and acted like I *were* real. I thought if I kept acting, then maybe I would fool everyone, and then maybe one day, I would confuse the universe and wake up with a beating heart.

"Nokio!"

I hid underneath the covers. I believed if I kept my eyes closed and the blanket over me, then my father wouldn't be able to see me and would give up.

"I can see you!" he said.

I removed the covers from my head. My father, with his brown skin, gray beard, and black eyes, looked down at me.

"You're leaving in three minutes."

I groaned. Everyone thought—since my elderly, widowed, childless father created me with his bare hands from wood—that we would have a picture-perfect relationship. They were wrong. I threw the blanket back over my body.

"Nokio! You are making me age ten times faster! Get up."
He pulled the blanket off and threw it onto the floor. "Now."

He used *the tone.* I was on my feet before he could start another sentence. I stood a foot above my father. He always paid attention to the other children my age and would change out my wooden arms and legs to match my classmates. Now, at age seventeen, I had outgrown him. I always wanted to be a real boy. As I looked down at my father, I realized it was too late to be a real boy, but maybe I could be a real man.

"Nokio, when you go into town, I need you to pay extra attention to staying on the path. Look at me."

I dragged my eyes from the window to him.

"You are not safe."

I returned my gaze to the window. Trees lined our home and enclosed us with the illusion of safety. I wished the reason I was not safe were because I was a puppet and the children would tease me, but those days were over. I wasn't safe for the same reason my father wasn't safe, along with everyone I knew. We lived in a maroon community, a cluster of escaped slaves hidden in the woods of Virginia, and safety was something none of us had.

"I know," I mumbled. I daydreamed about running through the woods and bringing slaves back to our community, but I couldn't. I didn't know where they were—that was the excuse I told myself. The real reason was that I was scared. Besides, puppets don't save people.

My father sat down slowly. It appeared to me that he needed his own version of oil for his old joints. He handed me cash.

I looked at the amount. If I wasn't mistaken, it was all the money we had. "What's this for?"

"Your school."

"I'm done with school."

"They've started a new kind of school for kids your age. I want you to go to it."

"No! I ..." My father never accepted that I was not like the other students. I couldn't keep up with the class. I couldn't allow him to put more money into my education. "How will we pay for food?" I asked.

"We've always made it work."

"No, you've always made it work. Now it is my turn to take care of you."

"*Nokio.*" It was his tone again, but not the same as the last. Both tones demanded that I obey, but this one was rooted in love and reminded me that I could trust him.

"Okay," I said. "I'll take it to the school."

I left without a glance at my father. I stuck to the path, as he requested.

"Nokio ..." A few steps onto the path, I heard the voice, recognized it, and cringed. "Want to play chicken?"

I turned to face Cedric and his two weaselly faced friends. "No."

"It's a game that proves that the winner is a real man."

I paused in my steps. *Real.* "What's the game?"

"It's simple. We run north. The first to turn is the loser."

"North," I repeated. Straight toward slave-hunter territory. "Okay," I said. Maybe if every day I do something real men do, then I would eventually become one.

"Wait," Cedric said. "Is there anything in your pocket?"

I nodded.

"Let Lester hold it for our game," Cedric said gesturing at his friend. "We don't want it to fall out when you're running."

I paused. What he said made sense, so I handed Lester the money.

"Okay," Cedric said. "First to turn is the loser. The one who doesn't look back and keeps running is the real man. Go!"

I ran north. I ran and ran, proving myself to Cedric, to myself, and to the world. I can be a real man. I kept running, anticipating Cedric's face when I beat him. I made sure I didn't turn, so I wouldn't lose. I couldn't lose. Then, after I didn't hear a sound, I finally turned. There was no Cedric. No sight of his friends or my money.

For someone who wanted to be a real man, I cried easily.

Though, it wasn't crying the way humans cry. Instead, my wood dries up, and all the oil gathers near my eyes, and this releases the oil causing a shiny streak down my cheeks. Every time I cried as a child, the others stared at me. That was the one good thing about those woods—I was alone.

A tissue appeared in front of me. Startled, I stood to my feet.

"You're going to dry yourself out." An African woman in a blue gown stood before me. I think she was glowing. She asked, "Why are you crying?"

"I'm not," I said with my deepest voice. Then something strange happened. My nose, which I had never seen when I looked forward, came into view. I crossed my eyes downward to stare at it.

"You shouldn't lie."

"I'm not lying." This time it was unmistakable. My nose grew. I gasped and fell back onto the ground. "Who are you?"

"My name is Black Fairy. Have you ever wondered how you are the only puppet that has a mind?"

"Every day for seventeen years."

"It was I who gave you life. When your father lost his wife, he cried out. I was sent to help."

I stumbled backward. Apart from wanting to be real, I've always wanted a mother. The woman before me was the closest thing to it.

"I gave him a son and you a mind. What I am here to give you now is a mind that grows with you as you get older. Your father could change out your arms and legs, but it is time your mind matures. It is time I give you wisdom."

"Wisdom?" I asked.

"Yes, those who are wise will shine like the stars."

When she said that, I realized she looked like a star. She had a shine to her that ensured my eyes didn't look anywhere else, and her voice reminded me of a sweet, warm evening. Her eyes gave me the same feeling I felt when I looked up at night to see the incomprehensible stars as they twinkled their greeting.

As my thoughts rolled, a lightning bug appeared. First, I

thought it was a normal bug, but then the woman gestured for it to come closer, and it did. "Her name is Veta. She is your wisdom."

I stared at Veta as she buzzed around me.

"Here," the woman said. Money was in her hand.

"I can't take that."

Veta dimmed.

"Don't worry," said Black Fairy. "It's the same money that was stolen from you."

The lightning bug zoomed around my face causing me to see streaks of light flash in front of me. As Veta flew, my nose grew smaller.

"Thank you." I stood to my feet and accepted the money. "Miss," I began. I paused and looked at Black Fairy, wondering how far her powers exceeded. "Can you make me real?"

"Nokio, first you must be brave, then you can be anything."

I slumped. Bravery wasn't a trait I had.

"One last thing," she said.

"What?"

"Run."

I heard it. Voices.

I sprinted south, and Veta stayed with me, reacting to my thoughts. When I considered running toward the voices and telling them to stay away, she dimmed; when I thought to run and warn my community, she lit up. At one point, when I was scared my steps weren't moving fast enough, she hummed a melody that calmed me.

Then, as quick as getting your money stolen, I tripped, and my head hit a rock. I rolled on the ground and reached for my leg. Human legs would have bounced back, but my stiff wooden legs couldn't handle the impact. The crash split my knee. I dragged myself behind a tree, and after giving me her approved glow, Veta hid her light to secure my hiding spot.

The voices dimmed, and I got confident. Then I saw my father, in his old age, wandering the woods. The voices stopped, as they surely saw him, too. My father didn't hear them, or else he didn't care.

"Nokio!" he screamed, and I hushed him from my hiding spot, hoping he would turn away.

Then I saw them. The owners of the voices. Multiple white men, slave-hunters, all moving toward my father's voice.

I stood and leaned against a tree. Without thinking, I screamed, "Hey! Here!" toward the white men. They looked away from my father and toward me. As I had hoped, they were amazed at the spectacle I was. My father was just a man, but I was a talking puppet. My split leg made me that much more of a sight.

"Take me instead!" I said. *Run*, I mentally begged my father. Veta glowed bright.

"No!" my father yelled as he ran to me with a limp, not taking a moment to glance at the men.

"Take me! Leave him! Run, Father!" I said.

Veta expanded her light, and a flash sliced through the air, producing a brightness that could outpower the sun. Her light blinded me, sending me backward, and I watched the others do the same.

First, you must be brave.

When I opened my eyes, I saw my father standing above me, yelling my name. Then, I felt my heart beat. I touched my arms. It was flesh. "I am real!" I shouted.

"You were always real to me," my father said. "We need to run. Not home; it will lead them there. We have to get somewhere safe."

I nodded, but we didn't move fast enough. The moment we stood, we were surrounded by five white men, and I felt I were in a whale's belly with no escape. Knowing running wasn't an option, I yelled, "Stay away!" I stood as guard in front of my father. I realized then that bravery was finding something you loved more than yourself, then fighting for it.

One of the men raised his hands, and I anticipated he was going to signal the attack, but instead he said, "We are here to warn you. Others are coming. We will tell them we found nothing out here, but they will come to see for themselves. Move your community."

My father and I watched them as they each gave us a nod, turned, and walked north.

"First, you must be brave, then you can be anything," I said to myself, getting used to my new mouth. Veta lit up. I looked at my father. "Go warn the town."

"We'll warn the town together," my father protested.

"I'll join you later," I said. My mind calculated the men's steps. My bravery gave me flesh, and now my flesh gave me bravery. "I am going to follow those men and rescue slaves."

Before I could hear my father's response, I started with quiet steps behind the men. Veta was silent beside me. Together we moved toward the unknown, and I wish I could say I weren't scared, but that would be a lie, and I learned lying was not for me. My heart raced, my palms were sweaty, and air filled my lungs. In all of it, I felt alive. I felt like a real man, and what moved my feet forward was the celebration that I was one.

The Things That Keep Us

A RETELLING OF THE LITTLE MERMAID
MINA LI

rancesca barely managed to keep it together when she left Professor Bergman's seminar. By the time she was outside, tears were running down her face, and when she sat down on the ledge of the campus green's fountain, she was outright sobbing.

Class had been humiliating beyond belief. She'd come in prepared with a few thoughts on the assigned reading, figuring that was enough. Normally, she kept quiet because she didn't have much to add, but for this class, fifteen percent of the grade was based on participation. Francesca wasn't thrilled about it, but she didn't want a *B* by default, either.

She had raised her hand right at the beginning of class, the sooner to get things over with. The class discussion was supposed to take off from there. Instead, what had happened was Professor Bergman asking her, "Do you really think that's what the author intended, Francesca?" followed by ten minutes of questioning more fit for an interrogation than a midlevel English class.

She didn't know which was worse: being forced to read the relevant passages out loud, or Professor Bergman asking her if things were the same in China. She'd been so stunned that she couldn't even squeak out: "I'm not from China."

What do I do now? she thought. She'd wanted to stare Professor Bergman down and tell him off with as much chill as she could muster. And then she would have sat down—or maybe flounced out in triumph—to the roaring applause of her classmates.

Instead, she was fumbling in her backpack for tissues to wipe her eyes and nose. A balled-up wad of Kleenex sat at the bottom of the bag, squashed next to her pencil case, and Francesca was taking it out when someone tapped her shoulder.

"What?" she snapped. She looked to see who was bothering her, and suddenly her anger evaporated, shock rushing into its place.

He was a scrawny, skinny thing who had never seen the sun, given the waxy pallor of his skin. Looking at him, Francesca didn't think so much of white as she did colorless, as if he were an unfinished painting, or all done in monochrome. His clothes were comically oversized, his T-shirt hanging in baggy folds on his bony shoulders, and his dark mop of hair needed trimming. Francesca found herself moving backward to put more distance between them.

He held up a phone and tapped the screen. *are you all right?* it read.

"I—what—I don't—" she stammered, trying not to shake. When he tapped the screen again, the anger flared up once more and took over. "What do you think? Do I look all right to you?" She swiped at her nose, leaving a trail of snot down the back of her hand. "Do I?"

The guy shook his head, and then he turned back to his phone, painstakingly typing out letters one by one. Francesca got up to leave, but he caught her wrist before she could walk away. His fingers were so cold they hurt, and she hissed in pain as she wrenched herself free. As she rubbed her wrist, he held up the phone again.

what's wrong?

None of your business, Francesca was about to say, but when she looked at him, she saw nothing but open sincerity on his face. That show of sympathy made him less unnerving, although she didn't come any closer. His eyes were large and inhumanly pale, touched with the barest hint of green, and looking into them for even a second made Francesca shudder.

"It's my professor," she said, wiping off her hand. She might as well tell him, given that her parents weren't going to listen, with Mom's *Fulan, you need to swallow your anger* and Dad's *look, Fran, sometimes you need to lower your expectations of people.* "He says I don't talk enough in class. But he thinks it's because I'm not from here, like I can't speak English or something, and it's just —where do you get off making stupid assumptions like that? Seriously?"

He gazed at her for a moment, and then went back to typing on his phone. *where are you from?* it read.

"I'm from *here!*" Francesca yelled, exasperated. "I was born here, for God's sake, and I grew up here! He's got it all wrong, okay? I mean, how would you like it if I asked you where you were from? You know, like you didn't belong here?"

The guy gave her a curious look, and then bent his head back down over his phone, typing away.

Francesca hitched up her backpack, ready to leave for real this time, when he held the phone up again.

what if I told you I came from the sea?

It had been a violent summer storm that overturned the human woman's skiff, her red hair shining against the turbulent blacks and grays of the ocean as the current dragged her under. He had swum to her, catching her before the waves dashed her against the rocks, wondering faintly as he did why he was rescuing such a foolish human.

Her eyes had fluttered open as he'd carried her through the water. If the storm hadn't made his heart skip a beat, that did. By the time he'd gotten her safely on land, she was stirring, and he'd left quickly after that, afraid that his appearance would frighten her.

He'd sought help from the witch soon after that. "I want to go to her," he'd said. "But I can't, not like this." He'd gestured at his fishtail. "Will you help me?"

"Is she worth it?" the witch had asked.

"Yes," he'd said, even when told that the magic was irreversible, that there would be pain, that if he didn't win her love by the full moon he would dissolve into foam. The only thing that had made him hesitate was what she'd asked for in exchange: his voice, the best thing he possessed for such powerful magic.

It would have to do, he'd decided, because otherwise he would live out the rest of his life knowing he could have gone and found the red-haired woman if he'd only been brave enough. And so, a bargain had been struck.

There had been pain from the beginning, moments after he'd pulled himself from the river that ran near the woman's home. The witch's draft had stung his throat as he drank it down, followed by his tail tearing in two with a sharp cracking sound. He'd tried to push the two halves back together, but it had been too late. Scales flaked off in glittering clumps while his fins shriveled before his eyes. The last thing he remembered before fainting was the sensation of choking, as his gills fused shut.

When he'd finally come-to, the red-haired woman had been there, her relieved smile one of the most beautiful things he'd ever seen. It made up for the unexpected pain of living on land.

In the sea he'd been weightless, able to swim long distances effortlessly. Up here, the thin air couldn't support him, and he wasn't used to his own heaviness. On land, each step sent stabbing pains into his feet, and he was forced to stop frequently to rest. Everything was so much harsher, too, light and colors so bright they hurt, and the sounds of human conversations made him wince.

Now that the sun was lower in the sky, the cool breezes and muted light made things better than they'd been that morning. There was a fountain ahead, and the need for water washing against his skin was so great that he hobbled over, ignoring the way his feet throbbed and ached.

That was when he found the girl, weeping on the ledge. At first, he left her alone, but the more she cried, the more worried he became, so he'd taken the phone Cynthia—the red-haired woman—had given him and approached the weeping girl. At first, she was frightened, then angry, and now her face was blank with confusion, seeing his last message: *what if I told you I came from the sea?*

"Matthew!" The sound of Cynthia's voice rang out, cutting off any reply the girl might have had. Matthew was the name Cynthia had given him—he didn't mind, not when she'd chosen it. His real name was unpronounceable by human tongues, anyway.

Cynthia ran toward him with hurried steps. "There you are!" she said. "I was looking all over for you! Sorry, the meeting with my advisor ran longer than I thought. You scared me, wandering off like that!"

Matthew bowed his head in apology. He'd meant to wait for Cynthia inside, but the fountain had looked so tempting from the window, even though he'd been on land for less than a day. He glanced over his shoulder to tell the girl goodbye, but she was already walking away from the fountain.

Cynthia laughed, pushing her thick glasses back into place. "That's okay. Come on, now." Her hand wrapped around his, soft and smooth. "I'm up to my eyeballs in dissertation rewrites, but once that's done, we can watch TV together. Sound good?"

It was only a matter of time, he thought, nodding back. If he'd had any doubts that she would tell him she loved him, in that moment he knew the words would come soon. Her confession would make the witch's magic take full effect; without it, he would die. But the way she tugged him away from the fountain and the warmth of her hand around his own made that fate seem like nothing so much as an empty threat.

Matthew saw the girl again the next time he was at the fountain, sitting on the steps of a nearby building. On one chubby knee was an instrument he'd never seen before: a small octagonal box with a long neck, topped with two large pegs. The girl drew a long stick between two strings running from top to bottom, making music unmatched by anything he'd ever heard in the sea. Her fingers were short and blunt, and yet they moved along the strings with well-practiced ease.

Shyly, he approached, waiting for her to finish. In the meantime, he took out his phone, ready to type a message. Cynthia had given it to him—"a way to find each other," as she'd put it. Matthew liked having a connection that belonged to the two of them, even if she was too busy to spend as much time with him as he might have liked. During the day she rushed about in a flurry of papers and flowing skirts; at night she was at her desk, surrounded by books, a mug of coffee always in reach, fingers flying as she typed her dissertation.

Matthew had tried to tell Cynthia where he'd come from, but she'd only given him a pitying smile and a pat on the arm before going back to grading her papers. "Poor guy," she'd murmured. "If only we could find some ID."

Matthew had never felt the loss of his voice so keenly before. *I came from the sea,* he'd wanted to shout. *I came from the sea, the only home I've ever known, all so I could find you. I gave up my tail and my voice to be by your side.*

With each passing day, he grew increasingly aware of how his time was running out. Last night, the moon was already a half-circle. How would he get Cynthia to fall in love with him if she didn't even listen to him in the first place?

At least the girl looked like she might have understood.

When her song ended, he greeted her with a wave, and then held up the phone. *i like your music*, he'd typed. It reminded him of his lost voice, the way the notes wrung his soul, the way it made his blood ebb and flow like the tides. If only he could find a way to charm Cynthia the same way this charmed him.

"Oh," said the girl, surprised. "Um, thanks, I guess." She scratched the back of her neck, her broad, brown cheeks flushing red. Her limp hair was tied back with a fluffy pink flower the same shade as her tunic. She peered at him warily, but at least she wasn't actively recoiling like before.

my name's matthew, he wrote next. *what's yours?*

"Me?" she asked, pointing to herself. She let out an awkward laugh at Matthew's impatient nod. There was nobody else nearby, after all. "Francesca," she said, offering a hand.

Her skin was warm and slightly dusty, and her grip solid, even if her eyes didn't quite meet his own. Francesca was a name that sounded crisp and brittle at the edges. It suited her, matching the way she bit off the ends of her words when she talked.

what is that? Matthew asked, pointing to her instrument.

Francesca reached for his phone. With quicker thumbs than his, she typed out the word *erhu*, and then said it aloud. "It's from Taiwan, where my parents are from," she explained.

Matthew stared at her, confused, beckoning her to return the phone. *but you said you were from here*, he typed.

"I am," she said. "My parents came over here and had me, so I'm from here. But they wanted to pass on the way things were done over there, like, you know, the music."

Matthew felt yet another pang of regret for his lost voice, for he had so many questions that he ached with the weight of them. *How had her parents adjusted to life here? How did they manage to pass their culture and their lives down to her?* He tried to imagine having children of his own. How could he teach them to ride the currents or show them the great coral reefs and shipwrecks without a tail? How could he recite all one hundred generations of their lineage, or sing the songs—all those songs—without his voice?

With shaking hands, he managed to type in *how?* holding up his phone for Francesca to see.

Francesca glanced at the phone, and then stared at Matthew for a long time. He gazed back, silently willing her to understand his desperation.

Finally, she leaned back with a sigh, dusting off her hands on the frilly hem of her tunic, and Matthew saw that her eyes were not actually black as he'd first supposed, but a deep, warm brown.

"Bit of a long story," she said. "Are you free tomorrow?"

Francesca had never skipped school before. There were times when she had called in sick, but she'd felt guilty anyway, especially when she wound up feeling perfectly fine after a nap.

And yet, knowing that she was missing Professor Bergman's class, she didn't care at all. In fact, it seemed right being outside on a sunny day instead of being cooped up in a classroom.

She recognized Matthew, walking toward her as if every step were made on sharp gravel and broken glass. As he got closer, she noticed that there were small flecks on his knees and calves that shimmered translucent violet and aquamarine in the light, almost like ... *fish scales*, she thought. She shut her eyes, but the flecks were still there when she opened them again.

"Hey, there," she said out loud. "Are you okay?" She pointed at his legs.

Matthew nodded, waving her question off as if to say *it's nothing*. Then he gestured vaguely toward Francesca, his eyes questioning. She didn't understand until he pointed at his own back for emphasis.

"My backpack? Oh." Francesca shook her head. "I'm not going to class today. I don't want to." She grinned, feeling delightfully naughty.

Matthew cocked an eyebrow at her, then took out his phone.

cynthia hates it when students don't go to her class, he typed.

"Cynthia?" Francesca asked.

Matthew went back to his phone, and Francesca noticed he'd gotten faster, no longer picking out the letters one by one. She also noticed that along both sides of his neck, half-hidden by his unruly hair, there were three raised, pink lines.

Maybe they're gills, she thought. *Or they* were *gills, and now they've closed over.* The words *what if I told you I came from the sea* resurfaced in her mind.

Finally, Matthew held up his phone. *The one I came here for,* he typed. *I left the sea for her. But she doesn't understand. She doesn't believe me.* He shrugged, as if saying *oh well,* but his eyes were dull, his smile forced.

It reminded Francesca of the previous night, when he'd sidled up to her while she was playing her erhu—he'd looked so out of place, so lost, much more vulnerable than she'd originally thought. "I believe you," she blurted. When Matthew stared blankly at her, she added, "You're kind of like me. You don't look like you're from here, either."

It sounded mean, but it was true. She didn't look like she was American, and as for Matthew ... well ... from his unnaturally pale skin to the scales on his legs, he looked as out of place as she did.

"I'm sorry," she finally said. "It's just—I—"

Matthew stopped her with a hand on her arm, giving her a reassuring smile.

"Yeah," Francesca said. "Yeah, okay. Why don't we get going?"

At the library, Matthew insisted on taking the stairs, despite Francesca's offer to use the elevators. He didn't like the sudden vertigo that came from being pulled up or down while standing still.

They stopped on the sixth floor, crammed edge to edge with

bookshelves. The air smelled sweet and musty, and there was that odd sound between ringing and buzzing that was ever present in these places. Matthew wondered if it came from the lights—he'd seen one flickering when he was sitting in Cynthia's class, complaining as if it were angry with him.

Francesca wandered along the shelves, searching. "Here we go," she said, delving between two of them. Matthew followed, watching her skim the endless rows of books until she stopped with a little "Aha!" raising herself on her toes to pull out a book large enough to topple her.

She sat cross-legged on the floor, opening the book on her lap. As Matthew crouched next to her, he saw there were hardly any words. It looked familiar, though he didn't quite understand why.

"This," said Francesca, "is a map of the world." She pointed to one of the shapes, to the left of the split between the two pages. "This is where we are."

Matthew remembered then that he had seen a map before in a half-submerged shipwreck, so old and yellowed with age that it had become part of the desk it lay on. He noticed that some parts of the sea had been divided and marked with names. That surprised him, because as far as he knew there was only one giant sea, upon which the land rested. He peered closer, trying to find the ridge that was characteristic of the area where he'd lived, but he couldn't see any such place marked.

where did you say your parents were from? he asked.

Francesca moved her finger to the right, across the split, some of the sea, and a large landmass, stopping at a small island. "They're from Taiwan, right here. Pretty far, huh?"

Matthew nodded. That would mean her parents had had to cross the sea to get to where they were now. It *was* far, when he thought about it: the swim all the way here hadn't taken too long since this place wasn't that far inland. *did they speak this language?* he typed next.

"No," Francesca said. "Well, I mean, they learned a little, but not a lot. Not until they came here. And even now it's not perfect. But, you know, I can speak their language, too, so it works. I've even got a different name."

what is it? Matthew asked.

Francesca took a scrap of paper and a pen from her purse, and wrote:

福
藍

"Fulan," she said. "That's my Chinese name. Not my real name, but I guess I still answer to it."

Matthew smiled. *matthew's not my real name either,* he offered.

The corners of Francesca's mouth turned up wryly. "Somehow, I didn't think it was."

"What *is* your real name, anyway?" Francesca asked, a few days later.

Matthew and she sat together in a café that was empty, save for a few people hunched over their laptops. Today was the second time she'd skipped Professor Bergman's class, and truth be told, she had no intention of returning.

Matthew slid his phone across the table. *humans wouldn't be able to say it,* he'd typed.

"Really?" Francesca asked, sliding the phone back. "How do you know this language, then?"

i listened to people on ships when i went to the surface. found words in old shipwrecks.

"Huh. Well, could you tell me what your name means?"

Matthew picked up his phone, about to type, but put it back down, his fingers tapping on the wooden table. Then, he picked it up again, and started typing. *it means swift currents,* he replied. *there's different kinds in the sea, slow or fast, warm or cold. fast currents mean i swim fast. fast currents are warm, too.* Francesca raised an eyebrow, but all Matthew did was shrug. Then he pointed to her, as if to say, *your turn now.*

"Me? You mean my real name, or the one my parents call me

at home?"

the one your parents call you.

"You mean 'Fulan'? Um, the first character means 'lucky,' and then the last one means 'blue.' So 'lucky blue,' I guess." Francesca smiled sheepishly. "It's not really supposed to mean anything, though. My parents just liked the way it sounded."

Matthew shot her a bemused look, thumbs working away. *what kind of blue*, his screen read. *there are many kinds of blue in the sea.*

She was about to answer when someone coughed to her left. "Ah, Francesca," said Professor Bergman, swinging into her view. "I didn't see you in class today."

Francesca's face burned, but she said nothing, instead focusing on Professor Bergman's ludicrous paisley tie.

"Look, I'm concerned," Professor Bergman continued. "Whatever's going on with you, we can work it out, but you've got to tell me first, all right? You don't have to worry about losing face like in China—"

"Oh my God, I'm not from China!" Francesca snapped. Professor Bergman opened his mouth to say something, but she sprang to her feet, smacking her palms on the table. "I was born in Illinois, okay? English is my first language! I don't know why you think I'm not from here, but *that's* the problem! That's what's going on!"

With that, she pushed past him and bolted from the café. He was shouting her name as she left, but she didn't care. She knew she'd been rude, but one more word from his ignorant mouth and she would have thrown her chair at him.

Someone grabbed her elbow from behind, and she spun around, ready to slug Professor Bergman. Instead, she found Matthew, his chest heaving with exertion, wincing as he limped closer. His hold loosened on her arm as he reached for his phone.

"Sorry," Francesca said. "I thought you were him." It was warm out, still smelling faintly of summer, and she realized that she was shaking. "I-I'm okay. I think I am. I don't know." She covered her mouth with both hands, taking deep breaths.

Matthew's hand moved up to her shoulder, giving it a gentle squeeze. He typed on his phone, slow and awkward with only one hand, and then held it up for Francesca to see.

so that's why you don't go to class, it read.

"Yeah," said Francesca. Her voice was choked with tears, and she kept her eyes wide open, staring straight ahead to try and keep them from falling. She didn't need a nervous breakdown, not right now.

Matthew lifted her chin, tilting her head up to meet his gaze before holding up the phone once more. *you didn't deserve that*, he'd typed.

Francesca was so relieved by his words that she began to sob in earnest.

Matthew stayed close by Francesca as they left the registrar's office. She'd stopped crying, but now she was chewing her lip so hard he expected her to draw blood any second. In her hands was the form they'd given her to drop the class, the edges already wrinkled from how hard she was gripping the pages.

"I have to get Professor Bergman's signature. Can you believe it?" she muttered.

Matthew nodded, and then decided to change the subject. *you never told me what kind of blue your name meant.*

"Oh. Yeah." Francesca's brows knitted as she considered his question. "I dunno. It's just ... blue. I mean, there's a word for light blue, but it also means green, but that's it." She shrugged. "Sorry. You probably have hundreds of names for one shade of blue alone."

that's true.

"Tell me about them?"

So he did, bit by bit. Francesca waited patiently as he picked out every word on his phone, telling her everything he'd wanted to tell Cynthia: the shipwrecks he'd found, where the water was so black he had to rely on the scant phosphorescence to see; the time he'd dared to swim closer to shore and seen Cynthia for the first time, nearly swallowed by the undertow; the bargain he'd made with the witch. He didn't tell her about what would happen if Cynthia didn't fall for him; there was no point in agitating her again when she'd only just calmed down.

i miss my voice the most, he confessed. *i miss it more than i miss my tail. i miss singing so badly. i wanted to sing to cynthia when i met her, and now i can't even talk.*

"Bet you had a really nice voice," Francesca said.

i did, Matthew wrote. *that's why i had to give it up.*

"Can you get it back?"

Matthew shook his head. *i can't go back to the sea either,* he wrote.

Francesca kept quiet for a long time, smoothing out the creases she'd made in the form. A group of boys passed them as they exited the building, and Matthew ignored the blatant stares aimed at him. "Wow," she murmured, running her hand over her face. "I'm sorry. I don't even know what to say."

Matthew smiled. *i don't regret it,* he wrote. *i wanted to see her more than anything. if you want someone to see you, you have to let them know you're there.*

"Damn. You've got guts, you know that? I don't think I could ever go that far for someone I liked."

They were interrupted by Cynthia darting toward them, her blue eyes wide with excitement. "Matthew, come here! There's someone I want you to meet." A woman followed not far behind her, hands in her pockets and wearing a smile like she found the entire world amusing.

Matthew watched as the newcomer twined a copper-brown arm around Cynthia's and kissed her on the cheek. The pain in his legs flared up, sharper than ever, as he made his way over. A sick emptiness filled him as he realized that although Cynthia was so close, she was now impossible to reach. He managed to shake the woman's hand, despite the choking sorrow he felt. Last night, the moon had been a bright, bulging oval in the sky:

his time had run out.

He walked alongside the two of them, listening to Cynthia's chattering: "... found him by the river naked, no ID, nothing. He told me he came from the sea, can you believe that? I looked up the missing-persons directory, and there's nobody matching his description. ..."

Matthew glanced over his shoulder only to see Francesca, her eyes full of pity.

Francesca's parents had taken her decision better than she'd thought they would. They weren't *happy* about a late drop, but after she assured them that her GPA wouldn't be affected, they accepted it. Dad hadn't even given her the speech about how she had to lower her expectations.

She still had to get Professor Bergman's signature, but it would be worth it. Besides, it was nothing compared to what Matthew had to deal with. Francesca felt terrible for even complaining to him in the first place—next to what he'd sacrificed, all for Cynthia, and to have that destroyed? Who cared about a crappy professor?

She'd wanted to grab Cynthia and scream at her—at least she could have *listened*. Thinking about it now made her so angry that she almost snapped the strings on her erhu while tuning it.

When Matthew turned up, she sighed in relief. "Hey," she said. "You doing okay?"

Matthew nodded, but when Francesca didn't break her gaze, he shook his head and sank down next to her, burying his face in his arms. It reminded Francesca of time-lapse movies where plants withered and died.

"I'm sorry," she said, giving him a consoling pat on the back. "Is there anything I can do?"

He didn't answer for a while, but when Francesca was about to repeat the question, he took out his phone and typed: *play a song, any song.*

"Are you sure?" she asked and was answered with a small nod. A song seemed so insignificant in the face of what had happened, but if there were anything better to offer, she hadn't a clue. "All right, a song it is," she said.

She took up her bow and began to play "Green Island Serenade," a song her mother had often sung to her as a baby. It was a simple tune, one she'd taught herself, and even though there wasn't anything fancy save for a few trills, it was one of her favorites. She always felt better after playing it and hoped Matthew might feel the same.

Matthew didn't move until the last note faded away. Then he got to his feet, and Francesca saw an eerie, final resignation on his face.

thank you, francesca, he wrote. *i'm glad we met.*

"Hey, wait," she said. "Are you sure you're okay?"

you worry too much, Matthew typed.

Dissolving into foam terrified Matthew, right up to the moment he threw himself into the river. Where would he start unraveling—the fingertips, maybe, or would the bubbles spread outward from his chest?

He plunged into the water, telling himself that dying would be like returning home. Even if he didn't have his voice or his tail, he would spend his last moments in familiar surroundings, not in that cruel upper world full of bitterness.

All he wanted was a peaceful, painless death, but the water refused him even this. It rushed into his nose and mouth, making his temples burn, and he realized with awful clarity that he was no longer suited for life underwater—no more than he had been for life on land.

Matthew's lungs began to ache, and he figured he was dissolving from the inside out, the way bubbles were streaming from his mouth. That was better; otherwise, he'd have to watch himself disappear, and this way would be quicker since nobody could live without lungs or a heart. It would be over soon.

Suddenly someone's arms wrapped around his waist, hauling him out of the water. He struggled against them, but without the strength he'd possessed in his old life, he could only let himself be dragged back to shore.

"What the *hell*, Matthew?" his rescuer snapped, and he saw Francesca, wringing out her hair.

He fumbled in his pocket for his phone so he could explain, but the screen was dark.

Francesca snorted. "Your phone's broken," she said. "Don't you know you're not supposed to get it wet? God, don't tell me you decided to kill yourself because of *her*."

Matthew looked away guiltily. *You wouldn't understand*, he wanted to say.

"Goddammit," Francesca hissed. She grabbed Matthew's shoulders, her grip tight enough to hurt. But it was a reassuring kind of pain, as if she were keeping him in this body, grounding him. "Look at me."

Slowly, he turned to face her. Her face was half-hidden in the shadows, but he saw the fierce glint in her eyes and the hard, pinched line of her mouth.

"She's not worth it," Francesca said. "Nothing ever is. I want you to understand that, all right? It's a crap reason to throw your life away."

Matthew dropped his eyes again, curling and uncurling his fingers. Everything was sharper, brighter, from the sound of chirping crickets to the early autumn chill on his skin. He took deep breaths, filling his lungs with fresh air. They still ached, but he couldn't get enough.

He looked up at Francesca, at the full moon shining behind her, and nodded.

Two Princesses

A RETELLING OF KUPTI & IMANI
MELANIE HOBBS

 ll of Imani's earliest memories were of Kupti. Kupti gracefully plucking the strings of a dilruba with her long, delicate fingers. Kupti braiding Imani's hair with an air of annoyance at the wildness of the curls. Kupti draping a shawl around Imani's head singing, "Ih phulkari meri maan ne kadhi is noo ghut ghut japhiyan paawan." *This phulkari was embroidered by my mother. I embrace it warmly.* Imani sometimes wondered if those memories were actually of their mother, not Kupti, or whether that was just wishful thinking. She yearned for more concrete memories of her mother. But all she had was that shawl.

Kupti always seemed content with her own life in the palace, trusting their father to find her a suitable match when the time came. Imani, on the other hand, longed to escape. Growing up, she was constantly asking questions of servants and visitors to the palace, eager for any information about the outside world. She was hopelessly curious and infinitely charming, so people were always happy to help. The cooks taught her about the healing powers of certain oils and spices. The stablehands taught her the language of horses. The seamstresses taught her to spin flax and weave the threads she made. "You have your mother's touch on the loom," they would say.

Imani took every opportunity to leave the palace—usually trips to the market, where she would watch the locals weave. Kupti and Father would shake their heads at the state of Imani's hands. "For what reason are you blistering your hands on this manual labor, when we can afford to purchase the best cloths?" Father would say. Kupti insisted it wasn't proper for someone of Imani's social standing to partake in such activity. But Imani enjoyed being able to make something with her hands.

One day, their father, King Giresh, summoned the two girls.

"What do you think this is about?" Imani asked Kupti earnestly.

Kupti rolled her eyes. "As if you don't know," she said mockingly.

Imani looked blank.

"Well, both of us are of age now. He must have found us matches."

Matches. They were to be married. Kupti was right: they were now of age, and Imani should have known this was coming. Imani blushed. How could she have been so naïve? The thought of being married made her ill. But what could she do? Could she run away? Imani pondered this as they arrived at the throne room.

"My girls, I must ask you a question," King Giresh boomed, resplendent in his choga of red, green, and gold. "Are you satisfied to leave your life and fortune in my hands?"

"Of course," Kupti immediately replied. "You know best."

King Giresh looked to Imani, who paused. She knew what she was expected to say. But if there was even a chance that she could take control of her own destiny, she had to take it.

"Father, I am not," Imani said. "There is so much I want to do. There is so much I don't know yet. So much to learn."

Their father took a deep breath. *Foolish girl.* She'd never been away from the comforts of the palace. She had no idea. Perhaps that was the problem. He smiled as he thought of a way to teach her a lesson. "You are too young to know the meaning of your words. But be it so; I will give you the chance to gratify your wish."

On the outskirts of town lived an old, lame fakir whom the king often sought for advice and consulted over spiritual matters. The king sent for him now. The fakir hobbled into the palace barefoot and clad in rags.

"No doubt, as you are very old and crippled, you will be glad of some young person to live with you and serve you," King Giresh said. "So, I will send you my younger daughter. She wants to earn her living, and she can do so with you."

Imani was dismayed. How much more freedom would she even have if she were bound to serve this fakir?

Kupti was appalled. Just as well she did the right thing. Still, perhaps there was some time to save her sister from this awful fate. "Father, I think that perhaps Imani spoke in haste and may have a different answer to your question now," she ventured.

"Is that so?" the king said, looking at Imani.

"No," Imani shot back, determined now to see her decision through. She plastered a smile on her face and promised herself she would find a way to show them.

Kupti fumed. She couldn't fathom why Imani was being so stubborn.

The fakir led the princess back to his humble home, perplexed.

The fakir's home was a tumbledown shack cobbled together from scraps of old building materials. Everything was mismatched, Imani thought, looking at the fakir's belongings. The shack was furnished very sparsely with a single table, chair, and bed. There was a bowl and a jug. Some rice and flour on a single shelf. Still, the fakir said nothing. She remembered his quiet presence in the palace when her father would summon him for advice. Imani had nothing with her but the clothes on her back. She was going to have to ask the poor fakir for money. And figure out a way to earn a living fast.

"Do you have any money?" Imani blurted out into the quiet shack.

"A penny," he said.

"Give it to me," said the princess boldly. "Then, go and see if you can borrow a loom and spinning wheel."

Imani took his penny and went into the village, following the noise until she found the markets. She relished the freedom to wander as she pleased. What a feast for the senses this place was! Fresh fruit, vegetables, and spices piled high. She had to remind herself that she only had a penny and must spend it wisely. She bought a farthing's worth of oil and three farthings' worth of flax.

When she got home, she told the fakir to lie down. It had occurred to her that while these living arrangements were not ideal, this poor old fakir had not asked for this, either, and seemed to live a peaceful, simple life before she arrived. She took out the oil she had bought from the market and rubbed the fakir's leg with the soothing ointment for an hour. To pass the time, she sang, "Ih phulkari meri maan ne kadhi is noo ghut ghut japhiyan paawan." *This phulkari was embroidered by my mother. I embrace it warmly.*

Though her arms ached, she next sat at the spinning wheel and spun flax all night while the fakir slept. When he woke the next morning, he saw that Imani had spun the finest thread ever seen. Though she was exhausted, she dragged herself to the loom and wove again until evening. She wove the most beautiful silver cloth, which she presented to the fakir.

"Tomorrow, go into the marketplace and sell my cloth. Take nothing less than two gold pieces," she said, before promptly falling asleep.

The next morning, the fakir left a sleeping Imani and hobbled to the marketplace. He noticed his leg was feeling stronger. Soon after he arrived, Princess Kupti walked by and bought the cloth. She'd never seen anything like it. The only things that came close were the shawls that her mother had woven herself, for she had been a commoner before marrying Father. Kupti happily paid the two gold pieces, but she could not bring herself to ask after her sister, still seething over Imani's stubborn determination to be contrary.

Imani went on with her new, busy life: buying materials, treating the fakir's foot, spinning the thread, weaving the cloth, and selling at high prices. She'd never slept so well, though she'd also never worked as hard nor felt so exhausted. Soon, the city became famous for these luminous, other-worldly cloths.

One day, King Giresh had to travel to the kingdom of Dur. He asked Kupti what gift she would like him to bring back.

"A necklace of rubies," she said.

He sent a servant to ask Imani what she would like, for after all she was still his daughter. The servant went to the old fakir's house and approached Imani, who was busily working at the loom, her curls flapping wildly.

"Patience," she snapped.

She meant to ask the servant to be patient and wait for her to think of a response. But instead, the servant took that as his answer and returned to the king, informing him that his youngest daughter would like him to bring back 'patience.'

King Giresh journeyed to the kingdom of Dur, where he met with the young king, Subbar Khan. Upon hearing about the peculiar girl Imani, Subbar Khan chuckled. The name 'Subbar' means patience. He presented King Giresh with a small wooden box.

"The contents of this box will certainly grant her patience," he said cheekily.

King Giresh graciously accepted. Whatever was in that box would have to do.

King Giresh arrived back in his own kingdom and stopped at the old fakir's house. By now, Imani and the old fakir were living much more comfortably. The house had been extended, and Imani now had her own small room in which to work and sleep. A modest chess set rested on the table in the living room, which was decorated with rugs and wall hangings. King Giresh was astounded and, he had to admit, quite proud. What a clever daughter he had!

Of course, she was working at the spinning wheel when he arrived. King Giresh presented the gift, and she instructed him to pass it to the old fakir to open while she spun. The old man couldn't open it. The king's servant, and even King Giresh himself, tried to open the box and failed. With a sigh, Imani told them to leave it.

That night, after her work was done, she came into the living room and opened the box with no trouble. It contained the most beautiful fan embroidered with flowers and peacocks. She'd spent the day hard at work, so she fanned herself with it, and with a pop, a man appeared.

"So, you are Princess Imani, the most difficult daughter of King Giresh," he said.

Startled as she was, Imani willed herself to maintain her dignity. The man was broad-shouldered and draped in finery. He had a hooked nose and honey-brown eyes with the longest eyelashes she'd ever seen. He was beautiful, though she certainly did not want him to know that she thought so. Especially after he so rudely invaded her house unannounced and with some sort of sorcery.

"As you see, my princess days are behind me," she said. "I am making my own way in the world. And you are?"

"I am Subbar Khan, King of Dur," he replied smoothly, "and part-time sorcerer."

"Well, King Subbar Khan, you'll have to excuse me. I have to get to work weaving this thread into cloth."

She returned to her room while Subbar Khan challenged the old fakir to a game of chess. The old man was delighted. He'd been trying to teach Imani to play.

The old fakir would often ask Imani to summon Subbar Khan, and so with a wave of the magic fan, the king would appear. With each visit, the two young royals fell more and more in love.

Imani asked Subbar Khan about the fan. He fixed her with those honey eyes and told her how it worked: If the person waving it desired *patience*, then he would appear. He told her of his travels to faraway lands, learning the mystical ways of all different people. It sounded wonderful.

"But this fan is nothing to your loom," he said. "How did you enchant it to weave such magnificent cloths?"

"I can assure you that the loom is not enchanted. The weaving is sheer hard work."

"The spinning wheel, then. The magic is in the threads."

"No magic. The loom and wheel do not even belong to us. It is just hard work."

But was it just hard work? Imani began to wonder. Certainly she worked hard. But she wondered if there were a magic in her mother's song that she sang while working. The old fakir's foot was practically young again. And there was something uncanny about the sheen to the cloths she made.

Meanwhile, back at the palace, King Giresh could be heard singing the praises of his youngest daughter: "So industrious, so talented. And now the King of Dur visits her regularly." To Kupti, he said, "It seems he is a great admirer of your sister."

Something inside Kupti snapped. Kupti, who had always done what was right and proper. Who never questioned her father's plans for her. Who now wondered if her father had given her future any thought at all. Of course, most of her anger spilled onto her sister. What did Imani think she was doing, playing house with an old fakir, entertaining young kings whenever she pleased? Kupti decided it was time she paid her sister a visit.

Imani was stunned to see Kupti at the door. Subbar Khan and the old fakir were playing chess in the living room. It had been many months since Imani had moved out, and not once had her sister bothered to visit. She pointed this out to Kupti.

"When have you invited me?" Kupti replied evenly. "And when have you come to see me in the palace?" she added before Imani could reply.

Kupti swept through the house, noticing how handsome the young king was. Imani reluctantly gave her a tour. By this stage, with Subbar Khan visiting so frequently, a new bedroom had been added onto the tumbledown shack.

Kupti left her sister's home that afternoon completely bewildered. Imani and the king were practically living together. The level of impropriety was truly shocking. Kupti found herself getting more and more worked up by the minute. Well, if her father wasn't going to do anything, if he was just going to let his own daughter live like a *tawaif*, it would be up to Kupti.

The next day, Kupti paid Imani another visit. This time, she sneaked into Subbar Khan's room and emptied a vial of tiny shards of poisoned glass into his bed, fine as sand.

Subbar Khan woke the next morning nearly fainting with pain. He couldn't understand what was wrong with him and did not want to insult his hosts. After breakfast, they fanned him back to Dur, none the wiser.

Imani and the old fakir worried as Subbar Khan's visits suddenly ceased. No matter how many times she waved the fan, he would not come. Perhaps he had grown bored of them. Or he could be in trouble, they speculated. Imani decided she must go to him in Dur and see for herself. She would not be at peace until she knew.

Imani walked and walked for days, living on the meager provisions she had packed. Each night, she would sleep under the stars but found that she would wake at the slightest noise. She reminded herself that this was a good thing, given that leopards and tigers roamed these lands. Imani became unrecognizable with her increasingly thin frame, her skin grimy with sweat and dirt, her hair a nest of dust and stray leaves.

One night, she camped under the shade of a towering sohanjna tree. The scent of its white flowers lent the air a sweet perfume, and Imani allowed herself to close her eyes with a sigh. She woke hours later to the sound of movement above her. The tree was not strong enough to hold a fully-grown tiger, but a small tiger or leopard was a definite possibility. Why had she come after Subbar Khan? Anything could have happened. He could be dead. He could be married to another woman. Even if those things weren't true, she could be lost. She might never find him. She might be mauled by a wild creature right now. As hopelessness set in, Imani found herself quietly humming her mother's tune and pulling her shawl tight around her body in the cool night.

Then she heard voices. She willed herself to look up and saw the silhouette of two monkeys in the sohanjna tree, tails swishing nonchalantly. She breathed a sigh of relief and then realized, much to her surprise, that she could actually understand what they were saying. Her heart did a leap when she heard the name of her beloved Subbar Khan. He'd fallen ill and could not even leave his bed.

"Dreadful business," one monkey said. "That princess Kupti is the culprit. She planted tiny poisoned shards of glass in his bed. I heard it from the palace horses!"

"Such a tragedy!" said the other monkey. "If only they knew the blossoms of this tree are a cure for most poisons!"

Imani stood suddenly, and the monkeys, startled, leapt from the tree and scarpered away until they could no longer be seen. She barely had time to register that her own sister could be the one behind her beloved's illness. She climbed the tree and gathered as many blossoms as she could fit into her bag.

As she entered the kingdom of Dur, the young princess had mixed feelings. On the one hand, she wanted the monkeys to be right about the cure. On the other hand, that would mean they were most likely also right about her sister. She took out the plain, old, rather dirty shawl she had been using for a bed and draped it around herself. She then took a second shawl from her bag and wrapped it around her nest of hair in a turban. She looked like a young fakir.

"Medicine for sale," she cried. "Is anyone in need of healing?"

The villagers soon directed her to the palace. When she arrived, the palace guards were quick to admit her, though they were pessimistic about yet another doctor having any success curing the king, especially a doctor so young. She was escorted to his room and barely recognized him with his deathly pallor and emaciated frame.

Of course, with Subbar Khan being so ill, he did not recognize her in return. She requested her own private apartments and a large pot in which to boil water. She steeped the flowers in it and bade the king's attendants give the king as much of the tea as he could drink and then bathe him in it.

After the first round of treatment, the king had a peaceful night of sleep. The next day, they repeated the process, and after a time, the king declared he was hungry and requested food. On the third day, he continued improving, though he was still weak from his long illness. By the fourth day, he felt well enough to return to court. He sent messengers to fetch the young physician who had cured him.

Imani was careful to keep her distance from Subbar Khan as he sat on his throne. But for all he knew, his beloved Imani was far away, and he had no reason to suspect the young fakir standing in front of him was anyone other than who he said he was. The king offered the young fakir monumental riches and precious treasures, but Imani had no interest in any of that. He insisted, and at last she said that if she must be rewarded, she would like the king's signet ring and handkerchief. Bemused, the king handed these to his servant who presented them to her. She made her way back home as quickly as she possibly could.

When she arrived, she told the old fakir everything that had happened.

After being silent for a minute, he said, "Time to try the fan again, then?"

"I should say so!" she said.

When Subbar Khan appeared in their house, Imani and the old fakir feigned ignorance and allowed him to explain his long absence, including how, in the end, he was cured by a mysterious visiting fakir.

The princess rose and opened a cabinet from which she removed the ring and the handkerchief. "Are these the rewards you gave your young fakir?" she said, laughing.

The king bellowed with laughter. How could he not have recognized his clever Imani? Of course she had been the one to cure him! He was suddenly impatient. All that time away from Imani made him realize they must be married. What was keeping her in this land, anyway? She would come to Dur, along with the old fakir, and the king and Imani would be married. They would all live in the palace together. She could weave and brew medicine, whatever she wanted to do.

Imani was overcome with happiness and accepted immediately. She did not wish to leave her home, however, without paying one last visit to the palace where she grew up. She invited Subbar Khan and the old fakir to accompany her, but insisted that she do the talking. Imani felt nervous at last confronting her sister. She wrapped her mother's shawl around herself and hummed that old tune.

With one look at Kupti's snakelike eyes, Imani knew that what the monkeys said had been true. Kupti had not expected to see Subbar Khan arrive. It was a split second before Kupti adjusted her stunned face into its usual haughty expression.

Imani was incensed. Kupti actually thought she was going to get away with it. Imani turned her attention to her father, greeting him with a blessing and sharing the happy news. King Giresh was delighted to hear of their plans to marry and recited many blessings. But Imani cut in.

"Father, there is another matter that we need to discuss," Imani said. "You may have heard that Subbar Khan came down with a sudden and very serious illness." Imani related the tale of her journey to Dur. When she got to the part about the monkeys, her sister snorted with laughter.

"You are accusing me of attempted murder on the basis of a conversation you overheard between *monkeys*? You have been living with that old fakir for too long, and it has driven you mad!"

King Giresh was torn. It really did sound quite outlandish, yet Imani's monkeys had been right about the cure. Subbar Khan and the old fakir certainly seemed to believe in her. Imani could feel her father faltering. Just then, there was a ruckus outside the throne room. A horse had escaped the stable and was bolting their way, chased by several frantic-looking attendants.

"Check her room!" the horse called to Imani. "In the wooden box on the bottom shelf of her cabinet! She keeps the key on a necklace around her neck."

"Father," said Imani, pulling the king's attention from the runaway horse. "If Kupti is indeed innocent, then she will not object to us searching her room," she said, looking at Kupti.

Kupti coolly acquiesced.

When they got there, Imani tried the cabinet and found the box. She asked Kupti to unlock it, and Kupti claimed she didn't have the key. "Why, don't you remember, Kupti? The key is on the very necklace you are wearing right now," Imani said.

Cornered, Kupti handed over the necklace, stammering about how she didn't know the necklace held the key, and she'd never noticed that box, and how it probably belonged to one of the servants.

King Giresh became fed up with her lies. "King Subbar Khan," he said, "I humbly beg forgiveness for the acts of my wicked daughter. Please name your punishment, and I will carry it out."

"Mighty King Giresh, since it was your clever daughter, my wife-to-be, who discovered the truth, she must be the one to decide. She is wise and good, and I trust her judgment," Subbar Khan replied, clasping the hand of Imani.

Mind reeling, Imani took a deep breath. Despite her sister's heinous actions, she did not have the heart to order her sister's execution. But nor could she exonerate Kupti and live a life of peace knowing her sister was out there. Imani wanted to begin a new life in Dur without the fear that her evil sister might hurt her or those she loved. She had an idea.

"Kupti, since you clearly resent me for choosing to live my own life, I will grant you the chance to have some control over your own destiny." Imani turned to her father. "Find another fakir, and send Kupti to live with him. There, she may earn a living however she pleases, but she must not be allowed to leave the borders of the city." Imani waited for Kupti to be escorted away before she took out the fan once gifted to her by her father. "If she should leave, please wave this fan so that Subbar Khan can be informed."

After promising to keep the fan in a safe place, King Giresh bade the three of them farewell.

As they passed the border of the city, Imani heard a familiar voice singing, "Ih phulkari meri maan ne kadhi is noo ghut ghut japhiyan paawan." *This phulkari was embroidered by my mother. I embrace it warmly.*

Joachim's Wish

A RETELLING OF RUMPELSTILTSKIN
EDWARDO PÉREZ

oachim and Nando sat at the back table, filthy from the day's load of dishes and trash. Manny's may have been a dive, but it was a dive with the best street tacos, downtown or uptown, and this was the hour Joachim and Nando could pretend they were people who mattered, that they didn't live in some all-bills-paid dump, that their dreams weren't just dreams.

"Bachelor's degrees, and here we are, still washing dishes," said Joachim as he ate his (slightly greasy) barbacoa with pico and San Miguel.

"Wonder how many dishes we need to wash to get clean enough to eat here like real people?" quipped Nando, dining on pescado with leftover (almost entirely brown) guacamole—at least the chips and salsa were still fresh (and the Estrella was ice cold). "After all these years, you'd think they'd let us do more than close, like work the breakfast shift. We never get chorizo or papas con huevos."

"At least you can speak Spanish," said Joachim.

"How does that help?"

"Gives you a real identity. I've always been in limbo. Never had a conversation with my grandparents, and when I speak to white people, they look at me like my voice doesn't belong to me, like I'm denying my heritage. Crazy-ass cousins think I'm a coconut. It's why they bullied me growing up ... and worse ... like I was a toy, an inanimate object built for their whims. Life would've been easier if I hadn't had the brown shell."

"Screw 'em, Chimo. They never left the barrio, even the military brats—no matter where they were stationed, those cabrones always came back home, stuck in their backwards ways. At least we had the courage to get out."

"Maybe, but you can't do anything in this country unless you're legit. Joachim Emiliano Sanchez-Cortez is not legit. Not a day goes by I don't wish I'd been born Jake Jones. Can't get any whiter than Jake Jones."

"Can't change who we are, Chimo."

"Just have to wish, Nando—on a star, at a well, blowing a dandelion or a birthday candle, pulling apart a turkey-bone, or singing to a ladybug. Life's full of wishes, and once in a while they come true."

"If you turned white tomorrow, it wouldn't erase what they did to you," said Nando through a mouthful of fish taco.

"Maybe not, but it would make it easier to forget," said Joachim.

A woman walked in the restaurant as if Joachim's words had left a trail for her to follow (or because Joachim forgot to lock the doors). She was small, with curly, silver-white hair, lavender eyes, and milky skin that glowed. She was strangely beautiful, like a snow owl, odd and fierce, yet cuddly. She climbed a barstool at the counter and looked at a menu. Joachim walked over. Nando finished his chips, trying to eat around the brown in the guacamole.

"Sorry, Ma'am," Joachim said, "three a.m., we're closed. Open at five."

"Are you sure?" asked the mysterious woman with a strange,

lilting accent and a reedy voice. "I mean, I'd grant you any wish in exchange for some seed. So cold out there, indeed."

Joachim looked puzzled, unsure of what the mysterious lady meant. "You're not from around here, huh?"

She didn't answer. She simply smiled, which made her face seem round, like the moon.

"If you're cold, we have some menudo left over, but I would not eat it—and trust me, you don't want to know what's in it. Salsa might be better. We serve it warm." Joachim handed her a tray. "Chips are warm, too, and they're loaded with salt, which most women seem to like."

The mysterious lady remained quiet.

"Anyways, my wish isn't something that can be granted," said Joachim.

The mysterious lady tasted the salsa, which invigorated her. "You never know, townie. Harvest Moon can bring all sorts of bounty," she chanted. "Tell me, what draws your fire? What does your heart desire?"

"Doesn't matter," said Joachim, remembering what he'd said to Nando, realizing how foolish it sounded.

"The heart is all that matters," she said.

"Even when it's broken?"

"Especially then."

"I've only ever asked for one thing my whole life, but it's impossible. It could never happen," said Joachim.

"We can wish on stars and moonbeams, my dear Joachim," said the lady. "But what will you give in order to get?" She crunched a chip.

"What do you mean?" asked Joachim curiously.

The mysterious woman's eyes swirled as she chanted her words. "What are you willing to offer me, Joachim, in exchange for your dream?"

Joachim smiled politely, fidgeting with his nametag, contemplating her question. He thought about everything in his life, and none of it seemed valuable enough to trade. "Don't really have anything worth giving," he said awkwardly.

"Would you give me your seed to seek what you need?" she asked ominously. "Would you share? I'm sure you have plenty to spare," she added, licking the salt off a chip.

She'd mentioned seeds again, and Joachim looked at her nervously. She was attractive, even without the San Miguel, but something about her seemed wrong, sinister.

"Look, if you're really hungry," he said, "there's some picadillo left over. Bit spicy, but I think you'll like it—on the house." Joachim nodded to the mysterious lady as he handed her two tacos wrapped in foil.

The lady stared deeply into Joachim's eyes. "You've a kind nature, Joachim," she said. "Perhaps, when the time is right, on some special night, you'll give me more than tacos and salsa."

"Of course," he said politely as the mysterious lady smiled and winked, leaving the restaurant. Joachim stood still, pondering the encounter before returning to his table.

"What did she want?" asked Nando.

"Not sure," said Joachim, not wanting to explain to Nando. "Offered her some menudo."

"No way, taste like battery acid," laughed Nando.

"Yeah, gave her some picadillo."

"At least the carne was fresh today."

Joachim glanced out the window, watching the snow fall, hearing a strange cackle echo in the wind.

The next morning, Joachim woke and noticed his hands and arms were pale. He didn't feel sick, but when he looked in the mirror, he realized it wasn't just his hands and arms—his whole face and body were white.

"Nando!"

Nando came running from his room and stopped at Joachim's door. "Picked the wrong place, cabron!" said Nando, attacking Joachim with the spoon he was using to eat yogurt. "Where's my friend, man? Better start talking, or I'll cut you, white boy."

"Dude, it's me. Joachim."

"No way, you're ..." Nando looked into Joachim's eyes and nearly spit up his yogurt. "Diós Mío, did you eat the menudo or the chicken mole or something? You look like death, man, like frickin' Snow White."

"I'm sorry, Nando. Didn't tell you everything about that strange woman last night," said Joachim. "She asked me about my wish."

Nando dropped the yogurt, knelt by the bed, and prayed a *Hail, Mary* as he grabbed his rosary.

"Dude," said Joachim, smacking Nando on the back of his head.

"That crazy lady made you white, Chimo," said Nando, standing, inspecting Joachim as if he were a zoo animal. "Knew she was some kind of voodoo witch or Bruja."

"Or Curandera," said Joachim.

"What?"

"Think about, Nando. She healed me."

"Ain't no healer, Chimo. She's a trickster, a frickin' coyote. She cursed you, and someday you'll owe her."

"Paid her two tacos and salsa," said Joachim, gazing at the mirror, seeing the past in Nando's reflection and the future in his own. "And chips. They were warm, like she wanted."

"This is wrong, Chimo."

"No, this is my future," said Joachim. "I can forget the damn past, my cousins, everything they did to me. Doesn't matter anymore."

"Come on, Joachim, you need to go to a doctor."

"How? Got no insurance, thanks to our stingy manager. Calabaza won't even share tips with us," said Joachim, staring at himself in the mirror, seeing every pain he'd ever felt evaporate in the silver glass. "And it's not Joachim or Chimo. It's Jake."

Jake walked Sophie home from school. Fall had come early, and it was a crisp day.

"First day's always hardest," said a strange voice from behind a tree. "Never gets easier. So much to learn, so little time to burn."

Jake spun around and saw the mysterious lady. It had been a dozen years since that night at Manny's, yet she looked exactly the same.

"Hello, Joachim," she said plainly.

"Sorry, m-m-miss," stuttered Jake as his lips shook. "I'm J-Jake. Must have the wrong man."

"And you must be Sophie. Or is it Maria?" asked the mysterious woman through a mischievous smile, ignoring Jake's denial as she looked at his daughter. "Such a precious little girl, Joachim. She has your eyes. Shame about her mother—though what parent wouldn't trade their life for the life of their child?"

"What do you want?" demanded Jake, standing between Sophie and the mysterious woman, finding his resolve and his voice.

"What you owe me, Joachim," answered the mysterious woman, nodding at Sophie.

"I don't owe you anything, and if you don't leave ..."

"I'll make this easy for you, Joachim. Let twelve years become twelve days. Guess my name while the skies are gray," she chanted as clouds rolled in, and night somehow fell.

Sophie shivered.

The mysterious lady continued, "Guess my name, and Jake and Sophie stay the same. Guess it not in time, and Jake is Joachim and Sophie is mine."

"Leave!" shouted Jake, as Sophie hid behind her father, bewildered and frightened.

"Twelve days on the twelfth night, let your dreams take flight. Brown or white, it'll be my delight to make such wrongs right," sang the mysterious lady as she vanished into the cold wind.

"Daddy, are we going to be okay?" cried Sophie. "She was

scary."

"We're going to be fine, pumpkin," said Jake, picking up Sophie and holding her tight as he gazed into the sky devoid of light.

"Come on, man, I need your help," pleaded Jake.

"Told you it was a curse, Chimo," said Nando angrily. "Didn't listen. Got your Rubia and you lived it up, huh? Grad school, high-paying gig, fancy house, trips around the world."

"You died your hair blond," Jake said, "lost all the weight."

"It's not blond, man, it's five kids and a wife," said Nando. "And with Blanca's cooking, I can barely get through dinner sometimes. You'd lose weight, too. Híjole! I look like my abuelo, and I'm not even thirty-five."

"Crazy lady threatened to take Sophie, Nando. You know Charlotte died giving birth to her. Sophie's all I have."

"How am I supposed to help you? I don't know that witch's name any more than you do. Didn't even talk to her that night at Manny's. Twelve years ago, Chimo. A frickin' lifetime ago."

"You said she was a coyote, a trickster. What do you know about all that?"

"Legends, Chimo—stuff my abuela told me when I was bad, to scare me—and it worked. I go to confession, say my prayers, take communion. I hang a rosary in my car and carry one in my pocket."

"Hold on. That night, she came to Manny's after I wished I were white."

"So?"

"So, I made a wish. Now you gotta make one, get her to come to you, find out her name."

"No frickin' way. I'm not cursing myself," said Nando, crossing himself three times.

"It's not a curse, Nando. Sophie's not a curse; she's a blessing. I'd have never had her as Joachim, never had my job, never met Charlotte. This life ain't no curse."

"This life ain't yours—it's Jake's. That's not you, Chimo, that's not how you were born, how you were raised."

"Eight brothers and sisters, cousins always staying over—your house was the same. We raised ourselves, Nando," said Jake. "And why does birth have to define us, huh? We don't ask for it—it's all blind luck."

"It's who we are."

"Doesn't have to be," said Jake. "Lost my color years ago—that's what assimilation is, Nando. It's why my damn cousins did what they did, 'cause I was always different, 'cause we make ourselves who we want to be."

"You didn't make this, Chimo. You wished it. You've always wished it, because you've always hated yourself, more than you hated your freak cousins."

"Didn't hate who I was—just didn't fit in because I wasn't who everyone thought I was. I was something else, not better, not worse, just different. Like your sister Juanita who's now Sergio."

"Not the same thing, Chimo."

"Why not?" asked Jake.

Nando gazed at the pictures on his refrigerator—at Nando, Jr., Mercedes, Tito, Lalo, and little Carmensita. "Wouldn't know what life is without my children," said Nando, and he began to cry. "Blanca wants another, Diós Mío."

"Charlotte wanted a big family, too," said Jake, holding back his tears. "Sophie … she was so scared, Nando. Can't give her to that silver-haired demon."

"All right, Chimo, I'm in. But what wish do I make?"

"Has to be real, Nando, something you've always wanted."

Nando smiled. He knew what to ask for.

"Twelve days on the twelfth night, let your dreams take flight. Brown or white, it'll be my delight to make wrongs right," sang the mysterious woman as she skipped like a child to Jake's house. Jake was waiting on the porch in his rocking chair.

"Three guesses, Joachim, to make it fun, but make them wise, or you'll be left with none," said the mysterious woman.

"Before I guess, I've one request," said Jake. "If I fail, take me instead, and I'll give you all my seed for as long as you need."

"An intriguing option," said the mysterious woman. "Seeds to sow, and row and row."

"But if I prevail," said Jake, "you must never visit Sophie again."

"Agreed," smiled the mysterious woman.

Jake smiled. "Rumpelstiltskin," said Jake, to the mysterious lady's surprise.

"How?" she asked softly. "How?" she demanded loudly. "How?" she shouted fiercely.

"It was me," said Nando, opening the porch door.

"You?" said Rumpelstiltskin in surprise. "You wished ..."

"To know, in my mind's eye, how my best friend could find true happiness," said Nando. "For years, I saw him suffer, and all I ever wanted was for him to be happy. When you agreed, your name popped in my head."

"You tricked me. This deal is off," spit Rumpelstiltskin.

"No, you tricked my friend," said Nando, crossing himself. "But I paid you what you wanted, and now Joachim has fulfilled the deal you made." He whispered a *Hail, Mary* to himself.

Rumpelstiltskin shuffled her feet and frowned. "As you say," she said begrudgingly. "But be warned. If our paths cross again, I will not so easily give in," Rumpelstiltskin added, as she faded into the wind.

"What did you give her, Nando?" asked Jake.

"My seed." Nando smiled.

"What?"

"Don't worry, Chimo," said Nando. "With all the mouths I have to feed, I started planting my own garden, like my abuelo used to do. I got seeds for everything. That crazy Rumple-witch wasn't specific. So, I gave her a bag of my seeds ... jalapeño, cilantro, tomatillo, and red onion. Now, she can make her own salsa."

The two old friends shared a laugh, as the clouds drifted away, and the sun shone bright. Finally, Jake and Nando no longer felt a fright. But in the distance, a strange cackle echoed through the remnants of the breeze, as Rumpelstiltskin planted her seeds.

𝔖𝔬 𝔖𝔴𝔢𝔢𝔱

A RETELLING OF HANSEL & GRETEL
MONIQUE QUINTANA

t had been hours since their father dropped them off, and Seth and Crystal were cold and hungry. If their father had dropped them off at a larger movie theater, like the one in Clovis with the giant chandelier, or even the Festival across the street, they could have sneaked into another movie easy, but not at that little movie house where he dropped them off.

As soon as their movie got out, the old lady usher gave them eyes like they were two sneaky raccoons. They decided to go outside and walk around the strip mall. They used the payphone to call home three times, but they got no answer. They left messages on the answering machine. They had just enough change to take the last bus home but decided not to, afraid they would miss their father, and he would worry. Their home was a long way off.

They walked in circles around the parking lot, with its small, twisted trees sprouting its concrete, the lonely hum of cars whirring past on Blackstone Avenue. They smoked a joint Crystal had tucked in her purse. They watched an older man sew a leather boot in the window of the shoe repair. Cold and tired, Crystal ate and dropped leftover popcorn bits from her bag, counting each bit, so that when their father did come for them, she would be able to point out the tiny trails she made. They peeked inside more shops that dotted the mall, until one by one, the stores shut down for the night.

The only place that was still open was a Mexican restaurant, where a light glowed faintly in the night. They decided to spend the last of their money on something to drink because they were very thirsty, even though it was cold. They sat at a booth in the window, so they could see if their father drove up.

It wasn't long before they noticed a young woman sitting nearby, tracing her fingers over the window's graffiti scratch.

"That woman is strange," said Crystal.

"I think she's beautiful," said Seth.

The woman's hair was white blond. They had never seen a woman with hair that color before. On her neck was a tapestry of tattoos, swirls of colors, and speckled dots, like the faces of many children. The woman noticed that they were looking at her, and she smiled. She beckoned them with her finger.

Seth, who fell quickly in love with all sorts of women, succumbed to this one, as well. He walked over and sat with the woman. Angered by her brother's weakness, Crystal went to sit outside in the cold, but now and then, she glanced at the windows to see what they were doing. Seth and the woman walked out of the restaurant and climbed into her car. They called Crystal under the winter moon until she finally came. It was a warm escape from the cold.

"It's like an oven in here. It feels good," said Crystal.

The woman smiled at Crystal. "Hello, sweetie. Your brother was telling me all about you."

The woman looked even more beautiful up close. Glitter specked the lids of her eyes like sugar. Her eyes were wide, and knowing, as she would never die. Crystal wanted to taste every part of her.

Seth was snorting her hand. She held it like it was snow. When she held it out to Crystal, the girl did the same as her brother, and the beautiful woman played with Crystal's hair and cooed like a bird.

"You two are so cute," she said, "so sweet."

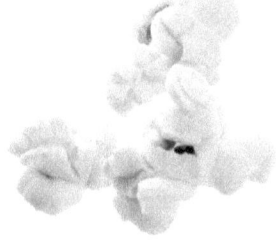

Soil Brown

A RETELLING OF SNOW WHITE
RIAZ JAHANGIR

nce, in a town not far from here, there was a woman who learned she would be having a daughter. Overjoyed by the news, she decided to plant a tree to commemorate the life now growing within her. As she knelt in her yard and ran her fingers through freshly dug soil, she said, "Oh! Let me have a child who is brown as the soil, black as the beetles that feed over it, and plump as the worms that give it breath." She made a small hole and there laid a mango seed, covered it with earth, and watered it with her own tears of joy.

In due time, the woman gave birth to a baby girl. The baby's skin was as rich and dark as the soil, her hair as shiny and black as a beetle, and her lips as pink and plump as a worm. Her mother named her Soil Brown and, overcome with happiness, died.

Both the girl and the tree grew as time passed. After sixteen long years, the girl's father came to remarry, and for his wife he chose a queen of devastating beauty, though this queen held no official title and imposed no formal rule. Instead, her wealth and power came from the millions of subjects who adored her fine features and devoured her image each time she shared it. So vain was she, that every morning and night she captured a photo of her face and posted it online, that others might recognize and delight in her beauty.

"Phone of mine, in my hand," she asked after each post, "whose likeness is liked most in the land?"

"O my queen, fair and fine," the phone spoke, for she had programmed it to address her as such, "you are the one with the most likes online."

And the queen was pleased and filled her days seeking balms, dyes, and scents to enhance her beauty yet further.

Now Soil Brown saw the practice with distaste, but inevitably she, too, appeared in photos online. Her peers lamented her disinterest in autophotography and insisted she must sit for their photos, if not for her own. Soil Brown was a kind, young girl, and she obliged. And so rich and brown was her skin, so black her hair, and so plump her lips, that she quickly surpassed her stepmother and was liked most of all.

So came the day when the queen asked, "Phone of mine, in my hand, whose likeness is liked most in the land?"

The phone replied, "O my queen, fair and fine, Soil Brown is the one with the most likes online."

A noxious envy filled the queen like lumps of rancid milk poured to a jug. "The child must die," she said to herself. "Then her followers will seek a new source of beauty and find me." She summoned a servant and bade him take Soil Brown off into the forest. "Once away, you must kill her," she said. "Cut off her beautiful lips, chop them to bits, and bring them to me as proof the deed is done."

The savagery on the queen's face struck such fear in the man's heart that he did not dare refuse her.

Now this servant was well known to Soil Brown so that when he asked her to accompany him into the forest, she did not hesitate. When they had reached a secluded clearing, the servant set upon the girl and drew his knife from its sheath. But when he looked into her wide, walnut eyes, the man could not bring himself to slay her.

"You must stay here in the forest," he said, "and never

return, for your stepmother is intent on your death." And there he left her, dumbstruck.

Before leaving the forest, the servant knelt to the ground and dug at the earth with his fingers until two fat worms wriggled up. These he chopped into bits and presented to the queen as proof Soil Brown was dead. Driven mad by envy, the queen salted the bits and ate them raw, then and there, from the servant's hand.

At supper that evening, Soil Brown's father asked the queen, "Where is my darling Soil Brown? I've not seen her today."

The wretched queen spun a tale then. "Dearest husband," she said. "Your child has wandered into the river beyond the mango grove. Though I called her back, she did not obey, and was carried off by the swift waters." The queen's voice was steady, betraying neither her malice nor her pleasure at imagining the girl's death. "By now she is dead and has returned to the soil for which she was named."

The poor man dissolved into tears and ran out to the yard. There stood the mango tree, now seventy feet tall, that had grown out of the love of his departed wife. "My love!" he shouted. The leaves fluttered in reply. "Our dear daughter is lost to me. Gone, never to return!" And he threw himself upon the base of the tree and wept.

Meanwhile, deep in the forest, Soil Brown sat curled up, rocking with worry. "I wish desperately to see my father again," she said to herself, "but my stepmother is never far off. Would she really hurt me?"

She recalled the look in her stepmother's eyes at the breakfast table that very morning, and after a moment's thought, she knew the queen's servant had been telling the truth.

"What shall I do?" she shouted to the trees, pleading, the way she had spoken to her mother's mango tree so many times as a child. But these trees gave her no comfort. They crowded around her and blotted the light, rattled at her with the crispness of their leaves in the wind, until she stood and ran from that place.

After a time, just as she began to feel the pangs of hunger, Soil Brown came upon a large house of wood and stone. Inside she found an oversized table set with a deep bowl and cup to match. Climbing upon the lone chair with some difficulty, she peered inside the bowl and found a steaming heap of yellow dal topped with chopped onion and coriander leaves, and several round, flat chapathis warming over it. Soil Brown inhaled the steam, and immediately her stomach rumbled loudly.

"Alas," she said, "this is not my meal to take. It belongs to the one who prepared it, and I must beg them to share it with me." She waited, seated on the chair, but soon grew tired and fell asleep.

Shortly thereafter, a lumbering giantess approached the house where Soil Brown slept. "By now my meal shall have cooled," she said, "and I can enjoy my supper." But upon seeing her front door ajar (for Soil Brown had forgotten to shut it), she cried, "Oh! Someone has entered my home!" She rushed in to inspect her belongings, throwing open the door with such force that the whole house shook and roused Soil Brown from her sleep.

The giantess stepped toward Soil Brown. She stood three feet taller than the girl. Her arms were thick and oblong, yet ended in remarkably slender and delicate fingers. A large nose protruded from between two pale eyes and hooked down past wrinkled lips, almost to her chin.

Soil Brown's first instinct was fright, but she quickly realized this large creature must live here. "Forgive me for entering your home," she said. "But my stepmother sent a man to kill me, and I cannot return to my own."

The giantess looked at the uneaten meal and said, "You must be hungry, but you have not eaten of my supper?"

"It was not mine to eat, without your permission."

The giantess appraised Soil Brown, and her heart was filled with pity. "You are a thoughtful girl," she said, "and thoughtfulness is a rarity. Come share my supper, and live here with me. During the days, I will earn coins in the marketplace by letting the townsfolk observe my ugliness, and these I will use to buy food and drink for us both."

At these words, Soil Brown's fear fell away, and she leaped up and hugged the giantess with tears in her eyes. "Oh, thank you! I am Soil Brown. What are you called?"

"In town they call me Ugly, but when I was young, my mother called me Nova."

"Then I shall call you Nova, and during the days, I will wash our clothes and dishes and clean our house."

Nova was pleased and, retrieving her phone from a bedside table, used it to take a picture of herself with her new friend. She posted the photo online, tagging Soil Brown in the process. Soil Brown's many followers were notified and said, "How wonderful that our Soil Brown deigns to associate with such an unsightly creature! Truly she is beautiful inside and out." And all the followers who viewed the photo did like it.

Back in the house of Soil Brown's father, the queen lay in bed with creams on her face and tonics in her hair. She held up her phone and asked, "Phone of mine, in my hand, whose likeness is liked most in the land?"

"O my queen, fair and fine," spoke the phone, "Soil Brown is the one with the most likes online."

The queen sat up with a jerk. She quickly found Nova's post, uploaded only minutes earlier, and knew then that her servant had failed in his task. Fury curled her lips and set her teeth into a chatter. But suddenly she noticed a detail in the photo: A rare and beautiful purple flower hung from a tree branch in the window behind Soil Brown. This particular flower grew in only one part of the forest, and nowhere else for a thousand miles. The queen sneered, lay back on her pillow, and dreamed of evil plots.

In the morning, Nova the giantess said, "Soil Brown, I am leaving for the marketplace. We are secluded here, but not invisible. Your stepmother may yet wish you dead and may send her servants here to slay you. Do not open the door to anyone but me." Soil Brown nodded and promised to remain hidden in the safety of the house.

But no sooner had Nova left than a knock came at the door. "Oh," said Soil Brown. "My Nova must have left something behind." She opened the door and there found a wrinkled old crone dressed in tatters.

"Dear child," said the crone. "I have been selling delicious mangoes in the marketplace, and I have only one left. Let it go to one as beautiful as you."

Soil Brown remembered Nova's words and said, "I'm sorry, I must not let you in, for safety's sake."

"Silly child," said the crone. "What could be unsafe about a mango?" She quickly peeled the top half with a paring knife but was careful to hold the fruit by the skin, and not to touch the flesh.

The mango was bright gold and glistened in the sunlight. It looked just like the ones Soil Brown would eat in her father's house, from the tree her mother had planted. And truly, this mango was from the very same tree, and this crone was her mad stepmother in disguise. Soil Brown, however, sensed no danger despite Nova's warning.

"Very well, then," said Soil Brown. She took the mango from the crone and bit a small chunk from it, dripping juice onto the ground. Where the droplets fell, the grass immediately wilted and died, and likewise did Soil Brown fall to the ground and lie motionless.

The crone cried out in jubilation and threw off her rags and mask to reveal the exquisite beauty of the queen. She stared down at the girl's body and breathed in raspy heaves like a dog after a run. She waited for Soil Brown's skin to wither, her hair to dull, and her lips to shrivel, as had been the intended effect.

Yet Soil Brown remained whole and lovely as ever, despite lying unconscious on the ground, for her mother had watered the mango tree with her own tears of joy, and no fruit of that tree, no matter what toxins the evil queen added to it, would harm the girl.

The queen waited still longer, but Soil Brown's beauty did

not fade. Bitterly, she prodded the body with the ball of her foot and grunted her satisfaction that no life remained there. And then, one foot still resting on the body of her stepdaughter, the queen produced her phone from a pocket, took a photo of her own grinning face, and posted it online. "The excitement has given my cheeks extra color," she said to herself. "So much the better."

The queen left Soil Brown on the doorstep of Nova's house and rejoined her husband, who continued to grieve for his lost daughter.

When dusk came, Nova returned to her house and found the body of Soil Brown lying at the foot of the open door. "Goodness, Soil Brown," the giantess cried. "What have you done?" Nova listened at the girl's mouth for any sign of breath, and when none came, opened Soil Brown's jaw and saw a lump of mango in the back of her throat. Being a giantess, Nova easily overturned the girl and began shaking her to dislodge the fruit, but it did not fall out.

In desperation, she reached into Soil Brown's mouth with two fingers and tried to pinch the mango between them. Her fingers slipped right over it, and Nova's skin began to burn. Again and again she tried, and at last she managed to pull it out entirely. Soil Brown immediately awoke, and Nova's two fingers withered and fell from her hand.

"My Nova!" cried Soil Brown. "Forgive me, I did not listen to you. I opened the door for an old crone and took a bite of the mango she gave me."

"Surely this crone was sent by your mad stepmother, or else was your stepmother herself in disguise."

Soil Brown looked at the giantess' maimed hand in horror. "Is this the price you have paid to revive me?"

"My dear Soil Brown, it is as no price at all for the life of my friend."

The two embraced, and the kindly gaze of the giantess imbued Soil Brown with courage she had never known before. "Come," she said. "We will return to my father's house."

Nova looked worried. "Into the lion's den, where your stepmother will surely slay you?"

"Into my own home, where my father, my mother's tears, and you, my friend, will protect me."

And they set off at once for the house of Soil Brown's father, with the bearing of generals leading an army ten thousand strong.

Meanwhile, the queen hummed a tune as she waltzed about the house and said, "Phone of mine, in my hand, whose likeness is liked most in the land?"

"O my queen, fair and fine," spoke the phone, "Soil Brown is the one with the most likes online."

The queen was so startled that she dropped the phone to the floor. A large crack split its face, and slivers of glass flew in all directions. She dropped to her hands and knees and began swiping furiously at the screen, slicing her finger again and again so that when she had at last pulled up Soil Brown's photos, they were stained by smears of her own blood. The photo of Soil Brown with the giantess had been liked nearly one million times. It was far beyond any number her own photos had reached and was moving higher still with each passing moment.

"Curse Soil Brown!" cried the queen as she beat the floor with her fists. "If only my servant had followed my orders and killed her." She was in such a rage that she did not notice her words had been overheard.

Soil Brown's father stood in the doorway looking murderous. "Wicked woman," he said, "what have you done?"

The queen's rage gave way suddenly to sorrow. "For all I have done, I have accomplished nothing." She sobbed in ugly spasms, dripping tears and mucus to the floor.

"Where is my daughter?"

"She resides in a house in the forest, alongside a giantess."

At once Soil Brown's father called for his servants and bade them tie the queen's hands. "Call the police immediately, and get this vile disgrace out of my house," he said. As they prepared the queen, he raced outside and toward the forest, but no sooner had he left the grounds than the giantess appeared with Soil Brown close beside her.

"Soil Brown!" he cried, running forward.

Soil Brown embraced her father, and the two wept with the joy of their reunion.

"Father, this is my friend and savior, Nova, who revived me from my stepmother's poison."

Soil Brown's father took the giantess' hand and hugged it warmly, gazing up at her. "I thank you with all my heart, dear Nova. You are as another daughter to me and shall be welcome in my home now and forever."

"And what of my stepmother?" said Soil Brown.

Her father's eyes darkened. "Come," he said through clenched teeth.

The queen was sitting on the front steps of the house, servants on either side of her holding the ropes that tied her wrists. Her eyes found Soil Brown and narrowed. Deep wrinkles appeared in her brow. Her nose and mouth, once adored for their proportion and symmetry, contorted into a hideous snarl.

"Such ugliness," breathed Nova.

Soil Brown looked on with a mixture of pity and relief as the police arrived and the servants led her stepmother away from the house. The giantess squeezed her hand tenderly, and Soil Brown was grateful for her.

But as the queen passed under the mango tree, whose great height reflected her predecessor's love and warmth and pride in Soil Brown, a high branch of the tree broke away with a loud crack. Heavy with the weight of ripe mangoes, it hurtled to the earth with such force that when it crashed upon the queen, she buckled in an instant, dead.

From that day, Soil Brown, her father, and Nova lived together as a family. The townsfolk came to know the giantess as a gentle and selfless friend, and Soil Brown a caring and courageous young woman. Vanity no longer reigned in the house. Envy and ugliness were forever replaced by friendship and kindness, and all did live happily the rest of their days.

The Stone Frog

A RETELLING OF THE METAL PIG
JEANETTE WEASKUS

he war chief awoke from a dream of several hundred dogs flying through the air at great speed, so that very morning, he went to see the holy man to decipher the meaning of this dream. The trip took the better part of a day, and the chief, not wanting to be alone, took his son and his nephew along for company. The cousins were very much like twins, and so where one went, the other was also to be found. The horseback ride went along pleasantly enough, with plenty of laughter amongst the three, horseracing to certain points along the way, and stopping for lunch halfway through the trip. They arrived where the holy man lived in time for the evening meal.

Now, it was in those old Indian days that all the animals who had thus angered Coyote and had been turned to stone for their transgressions would come alive at night. Children were therefore not allowed outside after dark, lest one of those stone animals might take them away.

Near the holy man's camp was Miss Frog, who had been turned to stone when she mistreated her husband, Badger—Coyote's best friend. The children who lived in the camp were not allowed to play near Miss Frog, but the next day, the camp children took the war chief's boys over to see the great rock.

The cousin jumped atop Miss Frog and straddled her like a horse. Her back was covered in moss, still wet from the morning dew. He clutched at her head to keep from slipping down her wet back and, in doing so, covered her eyes with his hands. She thought it was nighttime and immediately came to life, jumping toward the riverbank. The boy let out a war whoop at the novel experience of riding a giant stone frog. His cousin, not wanting to let him have all the fun, also jumped onto the frog.

The frog sped along at terrific speed, for it was large in size and very strong from being made of basalt. They flew through the air, laughing and hanging onto her back with all their strength. At last, they came to a stop before a large buffalo-hide tipi, which Miss Frog told them was Coyote's lodge. She told them to go inside and look at all of Coyote's treasures, and if they should find her beaded purse, then could they get it back for her? It had once belonged to her great-grandmother frog.

The boys went inside and saw that the tipi had a great many painted rawhide parfleches containing war shirts made in the designs of all the surrounding Indian tribes. The boys looked through the collection until each found a good Nez Perce-style shirt to wear. Coyote's weapon arsenal was an almost endless array of war clubs, bows, arrows, knives, and spears. The boys took a club and some flints, before proceeding on to a variety of beaded items, including bags, gloves, saddles, moccasins, and knife sheaths. They found a beaded bag with an image of two frogs, which they thought to be the one requested by Miss Frog. They took it. After seeing all the marvels of Coyote's lodge, the boys emerged and jumped back onto Miss Frog, covering her eyes so that she could move once again.

"Take us back to the holy man's camp," said the war chief's son, and that is where she leapt.

The taller boy kept her eyes covered and told her they had her bag. This they gave to her and both threw their arms around her neck and thanked her for the wonderful ride to Coyote's lodge. When she put her beaded bag into her pocket, Miss Frog also took out two opals to give to these boys who had returned her purse that had been taken by Coyote. The opals were a mighty gift, as the very large ones could render their owner invisible. The boy removed his hands from her eyes, and she returned to sleep for the day.

Just as the children were returning to camp for the midday meal, the war chief came upon his boys, and they began the ride home. Along the way, he relayed to them that the dog dream meant that there would be a time when all of the people would run in a pack together away from a great danger and toward safety. The boys told him of their trip on Miss Frog, and the old chief bellowed with laughter at the thought of his boys riding that stone frog all the way to Coyote's lodge and looting the specific items that would turn them into great warriors.

Although there were a great many kinds of treasures in Coyote's lodge, the boys only took weaponry for themselves. Through the years, they practiced with the clubs, made arrows for the flints, and became accomplished marksmen. With the magic of the war items taken from Coyote's lodge that day, these two boys grew into the greatest leaders of the Nez Perce Tribe. History knows the eldest of the boys who covered Miss Frog's eyes as Chief Joseph and the younger, fun-loving cousin as Ollokut. These two would later become known as brilliant military strategists who led hundreds out of harm from General Howard's advancing troops during the Nez Perce War of 1877.

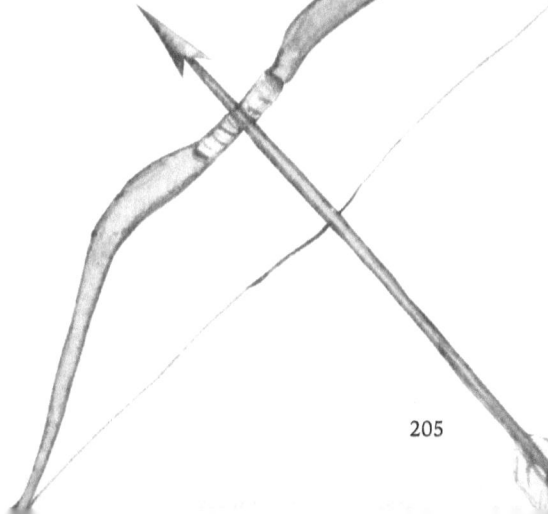

Dalia's Story

A RETELLING OF SUN, MOON, & TALIA
SIMONE-MARIE FEIGENBAUM

y name is Dalia, and I was once the princess of the Seven Kingdoms of Northern Africa. My father was the High King, and I his only heir. I was raised as a warrior—taught to ride, to fight, to lead. My duty would be to take over for my father upon his death; I must not have any weaknesses.

Unfortunately, when I was fifteen, I developed one: an extreme allergy to wheat. I could not consume even a little without becoming gravely ill. It came upon suddenly, and our wise men were at a loss as to the cause, or to the cure. It was therefore decided that until and unless I found a way to control my allergy, I would no longer be heir. This was unacceptable to me. I had worked so hard to prove myself as a warrior and a leader; I would not let a simple allergy stop me.

I decided that the best way to rid myself of the allergy would be to build a tolerance to it. I sneaked into the kitchen to steal bundles of wheat. I ate the smallest bits possible, which still led to vomiting and fevers, but I persisted. I refused to have as my weakness something as foolish and common as wheat. I suffered through weeks of this treatment, but to no avail. In fact, my allergy seemed to grow worse—the bare skin that touched the wheat was cracked, red, and raw. I wore long sleeves and gloves, even during the sweltering heat of day, to hide the damage I had done.

I became desperate. I stalked the markets, looking for something that might offer a cure, anything. The old women in the stalls had nothing to offer me, and the drinks and potions purchased on the black market were mere snake oil.

While I was buried in my task, Father was preparing for war. A ruler of one of the seven kingdoms, a man named Adatuma, was planning a mutiny. He had convinced two of the other kingdoms to join him in his quest to topple my father. Father had rallied three of the kingdoms, and the castle was now bustling with activity.

I was forbidden in the stateroom, but I was allowed to wander the grounds in my armor and observe the preparations. It was a warriors' carnival: blacksmiths clanging out weapons and armor, food being gathered and prepared, horses being trained for battle. I watched the pen where the soldiers practiced. The smell and sound of swords and strength were intoxicating. As I watched, I spied a weak link in the form of a boy, not much older than myself. Tall and gangly, he was unable to keep up with the other soldiers.

"You, there!" I called. "Boy!"

He stood straight and peered over the crowd to where I stood by the gate. I gestured him closer. He ambled to me and bowed deeply.

"Yes, Your Highness?" he said.

"Where are you from? Who trained you?"

"I am from the Fourth Kingdom. I am a farmer's son, and his third one at that. I was never trained or expected to do more than protect the fields from wolves." A flush rose in his dark cheeks, and he hung his head in shame. "I know I am a failure, Your Highness. I wanted to fight, but I'm afraid I have brought shame to my family and my kingdom."

I considered the boy before me and sighed. "What is your name?"

"Edgard, Your Highness."

"All right, Edgard, I will train you myself. Get your things, and follow me." I grabbed a sword and a shield for myself and led him to an open field behind the palace, beside the lake. I faced him and entered fighting stance. "I can teach you basic skills; there's no time for more than that. If you can master basic sword work, though, you should be fine. Just avoid running headlong into battle."

Edgard grinned. "I'm no fool, Your Highness."

"Very well. Let's see what you can do."

The boy was pitiful. Excellent in terms of brute strength, but not the least bit graceful or fierce—he could easily pick up and swing the heavy sword, but more often than not, swung himself around with it.

"Standing! Standing!" I said. "Know where your feet are! Don't lose your footing!"

I was smaller by far than any opponent he would face, but faster, and just as well trained. After three days, he could check me; after five, he defeated me. Just in time, as the troops were mobilizing.

"You're as trained as I can make you. You will do fine."

We met for the last time near the stables. Men led the horses and wagons, preparing to ride out that afternoon.

"I brought you something," he said. He pulled out from his pocket a small brown package tied neatly with string. "It's from my mother. It's *halva*. I know it's your favorite dessert, so I wanted you to have it, to thank you for your help."

I took the little package and smiled. "Thank you, Edgard. Your parents should be proud."

The horns sounded. It was time to leave. He ran from the stable to join the other men. I slipped the gift into my pocket and went to join my father on the platform before the palace.

"Where have you been?" a maid hissed at me as she adjusted my shawls.

"Telling the soldiers goodbye."

I went up the steps to stand next to my father and the other rulers, gleaming in the bright sun in their armor.

"Men, as you know," the High King said, "there has been a mutiny within our seven kingdoms. This cannot be allowed to stand. Adatuma has already taken two of our kingdoms in his mad quest for power. Next could be any one of your homes. Today, we stand and fight, men, for our homes and for our families. Today, you shall rise!"

A wave of cheers rose over the crowd. The men mounted their steeds. As Father left the stage with the other leaders, I stepped forward.

"Men," I said, "may God grant you a swift return, and a swift end to our enemies. Your Princess commends you."

Another cheer as the leaders joined their troops and rode off, those of us left behind waving flags and shouting them onward.

There was nothing to do once they'd gone. I did not have to rule in Father's absence; that job fell to Father's advisor. I had nothing but busy work to occupy my evening. When night fell, I put down my sewing to get ready for bed. As I removed my dress, Edgard's package fell out of my pocket. I picked it up and opened it. A little cube of halva lay in my hand. He was right—I did love halva. This looked a little less crumbly than usual but smelled so good, and I couldn't resist. I took a bite and savored the sweet, nutty taste.

Immediately, my throat swelled. This wasn't nut butter—this was wheat! I sank to the floor, clutching my throat. Where was the servant bell? Where did I put that damned bell? I spied it on the dresser and reached for it, but only grasped air as the room went dark, and my body hit the cold, stone floor.

I woke confused and in pain. My throat ached, and my stomach throbbed. I tried to sit up and was rewarded with a stabbing pain and a sharp cry.

Cry?

I leaned on my elbows as best as I could and looked around

me. The cry had come from around my thighs. Lying curled between them were two infants. I sat up sharply, ignoring the pain, and stared at them. Two infants, a boy and a girl, curled against my bloody legs on bloody sheets. My stomach lurched. Where had they come from?

The last thing I remembered was getting ready for bed and then—the halva! I'd passed out, but I certainly wasn't pregnant then, which meant … I blanched and backed away from them. Where was I, anyway? The bed I lay on was the only furniture in the circular stone room. There was a single window set high on the wall, and a heavy-looking wooden door. I had no memory of this room, nor of how I might have possibly ended up there. The only thing I could think was that whoever had fathered these children had dragged me to this room at some point to hide his crime. I had to have been there for months, so did anyone know I was there? I called out, but my voice was hoarse and raw. I carefully scooted to the edge of the bed and tried to stand. The second my body left the bed, I collapsed. My legs were weak, the muscles unused for so long.

I thought over my options. Calling for help was not going to work. Assuming I could crawl to the door, of which there was no guarantee I could, would I be able to open it? But if I stayed where I was, what if the man came back? No, I was going to have to try the door.

I crawled, painfully, slowly, to the door. I finally reached it and paused to listen for voices behind it. Hearing none, I struggled to stand, using the handle of the door to keep me steady. I leaned against the wall and pulled on the door as hard as I could. It opened, thankfully, and I peered into the hallway. I was in the palace, in an unused portion, judging by the amount of dust that coated the walls and floors and swirled in the beams of sunlight streaming in through the windows.

Using the wall as a crutch, I made my way to the nearest window and gasped upon looking through it. My kingdom, my beautiful kingdom, was destroyed, crops and homes burned to the ground, the people either fled or dead. I sank onto the windowsill and stared out at the devastation that was once my home. Lost in thought, I didn't hear the dust-muffled footsteps until they were right behind me.

I whirled around to see the tallest man I had ever seen, looming over me and grinning broadly. I stood quickly to move into a battle stance, but my legs betrayed me, and I fell. The man lifted me gently, still smiling.

"Princess! You've awoken! How wonderful! We've been so worried!"

I peered closely at him. I had never seen him before, but he somehow seemed so familiar. He certainly wasn't from our kingdom, but I couldn't place him.

"But what are you doing wandering the halls? You should be resting!"

I shook my head. "Father—I have to see Father."

He grinned even broader. "Of course, Princess. But first, let's get you back to bed." He moved to pick me up.

I stepped back. "No, thank you. I'd like to see him now, please."

His smile became a dangerous smirk. "I think, *Princess*, that you had better get to bed."

I struggled to back further away, but he grabbed my wrist tightly. "Who are you? Where is my father? Let me go this instant!"

He scooped me up easily and threw me over his shoulder. He carried me back to the room and dropped me unceremoniously on the hard stone floor. "Your father is dead, *Princess*," he sneered. "This palace is mine now."

All at once, it hit me. I did know him; how could I have forgotten? I had seen his insufferable face at countless balls with that father of his. He was Abejide, Adatuma's son. The palace was his? But how? The war ... Father ... what had happened?

He laughed at the confusion written on my face. "The palace is mine," he repeated. "And everything in it is mine. And how wonderful a gift that turned out to be from the High King of the Seven Kingdoms: an empty and decrepit palace, hiding such a lovely precious jewel." He stepped closer to me. I tried to scoot away, but he placed a heavy booted foot on the hem of my nightgown. "You belong to me, Princess, and I will use you as I choose." He kneeled down, replacing his boot with his knee, and covered me with his body until everything went black.

When I came-to, I was lying back on the bed. He was towering over me again, peering snidely at the babies mewling pathetically by the foot of the bed.

"Well, my happy little family, I'm afraid I must go." He strode to the door and pulled it shut behind him, locking it from the outside. "I'll be sending someone shortly to make sure your little escape attempt doesn't happen again," he said through the door.

As I listened to his boots clicking down the hallway, I burst into tears. This stupid allergy! I wish it had killed me. At least then, I wouldn't be locked in this room with these children. I glanced over at them, still crying weakly. I sighed. They had nothing to do with any of this, the poor things. It wasn't their fault their father was a monster. And above all else, they were still my own flesh. I scooped them carefully into my lap and used the edge of the sheet to clean them. The girl had my eyes, and the boy my nose and pointed chin. I pulled down my nightgown.

"Let's see if you can milk." I lifted the girl to my breast, and she latched on quickly and sucked greedily. I smiled down at her. "A strong girl, like your mother." I scooped up the boy and held him to the opposite breast. He hesitated a moment before latching on. "Cautious, like your grandfather."

Oh, Father … what had happened? You prepared so well for that war—how could you have lost? How could Adatuma now be king? When the children had drunk their fill, I lay them gently back on the bed, before curling up and sobbing myself to sleep.

For three days, the door unlocked every evening, and Abejide brought me a chunk of bread, some water, and a pot. He didn't attack me again and mostly left the children and me to our own devices. Unsure of the make of the bread—and unwilling to ask and therefore to reveal my weakness—I was slowly starving. I hated to be that weak, unable to protect my children or myself. I wanted to move, to exercise my limbs, but I could barely lift my head. I prayed for death, as it seemed the only way out of the hell I was living.

On the fourth day, there was a knock at the door in the early afternoon. "I'm coming in now, Miss." The door opened to reveal a small woman wearing a blue headscarf and dress. She carried a tray of food.

I curled suspiciously in the farthest corner of the bed with my children and glared at her. "Who are you?" I asked hoarsely.

She gave a thin smile. "Sorry, Miss. I'm Mariam. Abejide sent for me to watch over you, so he could return to his kingdom."

She crossed the room and brought me the tray. It was filled with food: some kind of bread and cheese and porridge. I stared greedily at the tray but made no move to touch it.

"Please, Miss. I know he hasn't given you much; he didn't take much with him when he left. I'm sorry for how long it took me to get here, but I've brought plenty with me, and he's arranged for more to be brought every week."

I narrowed my eyes. "Why? Why feed his prisoner?"

"To keep you plump and pretty, Miss," she sighed. "All of us servants know about you: fallen princess of the First Kingdom, the prince's new plaything. We've all heard the stories of you lying in the palace, sleeping as if dead, and we know why he makes so many trips out to this empty kingdom. Examining his holdings, indeed!"

I flushed with fury. "So, I am the fool of all the seven kingdoms, the prince's whore? God!" I struck at the wall next to me, injuring my hand and causing the children to cry. I clutched my hand to my breast and looked upward. "God ... how did this happen? This is all a nightmare!"

Mariam placed the tray on the floor and sat carefully on the bed beside me. She reached for my hand, and I reluctantly gave it to her. "Miss, no one thinks you're a fool. Some are angry and blame you for what's happened, but most sympathize." She placed my hand in my lap and picked up the tray. "Please, eat. When you're done, I'll run a nice bath for you, and I'll tell you everything you've missed."

I hesitantly reached for the tray. "Is—" I swallowed hard, hating to make myself vulnerable, but desperate after three days with no food. "Is any of this wheat?"

Mariam cocked her head. "Why?"

"I can't, um, have wheat. It makes me sick. It's what caused my, um, sleep."

Mariam breathed a sigh of either disappointment or relief, I couldn't tell. "Is that all? We'd all thought Adatuma'd poisoned you or something. That's certainly less dramatic."

I felt my face flush with shame and looked down at my hands.

Mariam chuckled. "No need for all that, Miss; we all have our weaknesses. I'm utterly useless come spring! Yours is just a little harder to manage, that's all." She looked over the tray. "The bread is made of corn, so that and the cheese are fine. The porridge is made of wheat today, but that can be made of corn, too. I'll send a message to the kitchens about your allergy when they send more food."

"Does Abejide know what they send me?"

"No. He doesn't concern himself with all that. He barely knows what comes out of there. As long as we make sure you eat, he doesn't care what we give you."

I hugged her gratefully. "Thank you so much, Mariam."

"Not a problem." She stood and smoothed her dress. "Just so you know, not all of us in the Fifth Kingdom supported Adatuma's quest, and almost none support him now. Most of us stayed loyal to your father and would do anything to see you returned to your proper place."

I smiled. "That means a lot to me. Thank you."

She took the children away to care for them while I ate. She returned shortly to take the tray, then led me out of the room down to the kitchen, allowing me to lean on her. "Sorry to have to give you your bath this way, Miss. The water to the palace has not been turned back on yet. I suspect the pipes are rusty. I'll send a message back with the first food delivery."

There was a large basin sitting in the kitchen, filled with steaming water. She must have filled it from the lake outside and then boiled it. I kissed her cheek.

"It's perfect, Mariam."

As she bathed me, she told me everything I'd missed in the long while I'd been asleep: "Like I said, we all assumed you'd been poisoned by Adatuma. When the news reached your father, he went crazy. You would've been proud, Miss, of how fiercely he fought for you. Unfortunately—" she paused to dump a cup of water over my head. "Unfortunately, he got reckless. The other leaders tried to talk sense into him, but he didn't listen. When they refused to send their own troops on his suicide missions, your father went himself. He fought valiantly, but well," she shrugged, "they don't call them suicide missions for nothing." She helped me out of the tub and wrapped a soft towel around me. She pulled a shift dress out of a trunk and glared distastefully at it. "He had me bring a bunch of these. He wants me to keep you pretty." She rolled her eyes. "I am sorry, Miss. I wouldn't wish this mess on anyone, let alone you. And you gotta wonder about that wife of his—she *has* to know. The whole damn castle knows! She can't possibly be that dense."

"He has a wife?"

"Mmmhmm." Mariam led me over to a chair once she'd gotten the shift on me. She sat me down and tugged at my tangled hair with a comb. "Cameela. She's a pretty thing, too, but cruel as a whip. That's probably why Adatuma chose her to wed his son. But Abedije ... he's not strong enough for her. With his father ailing, the castle is practically hers. He makes excuses to come out here all the time—" She stopped suddenly. "I'm sorry, Miss. You don't need to know all that."

"Maybe another time, Mariam. Tell me, what happened after the war?"

"Well, after your father died, all morale took a dive. Adatuma's forces smashed the other kingdoms easily and took them for his own. He destroyed the kingdoms that had opposed him, and the ones that didn't, well, they didn't fare much better, did they? He lied to them about wanting everyone to rule their own kingdoms, and only ever meant to replace your father as High King. We could've told anyone he'd do that; it's not like he was treating his own kingdom properly, was he? We were starving before, and it's only gotten worse." She shivered. "I dread the day that worthless boy takes over from his father." She finished the plaits in my hair and handed me a mirror. "There, now. Don't you feel better?"

I gazed into the mirror and frowned. I looked lovely—Mariam had done a wonderful job—but it was all for him. I pushed the mirror away and rested my head in my hands. "There's no way out of this, is there?"

"Sorry, Miss, I think not. I'm under strict orders not even to let you outside. I know it's terrible, but on the bright side, he can only come up here every few weeks or so before that wife of his gets suspicious. He's already got servants coming here once a week now; he's gonna have to be more careful. If we're lucky, we'll almost never see him."

That that was the only bright spot seemed impossibly depressing. I stood with difficulty. "If you don't mind, I think I'd like to lie down for a bit."

"As you wish, Miss."

To my surprise, instead of leading me back up the stairs to the room I'd been locked in, she led me to my old bedroom. Everything was just as I'd left it—even the sewing still sitting on the chair.

"That room upstairs was disgusting. I figured you and the little ones would be far more comfortable here."

Next to my bed was a little cradle, and in it, my clean and smiling babies. I hobbled over to sit on the bed and scooped them up. "You know, I've been so miserable, I never even named them." I smiled down at them. "You two are the only lights in my life, so I will call you Suleiman and Sahar." They snuggled against me and yawned. I laid them down on the bed and lay down beside them.

"I'll come back when your supper's ready, Miss." Mariam whispered as she left the room.

I curled against my children and fell deep asleep.

Exactly as Miriam said, Abejide didn't come back for nearly a month. In that time, between Mariam's cooking and daily walks around the castle, I had grown much stronger. I was nowhere near my former strength, but even a little was better than nothing. The day he returned, Mariam came rushing into my room.

"Miss! Miss! Wake up! Abejide's on his way! I can see the horses from the tower windows. He'll be here shortly!" She picked up the children's cradle and moved it to a room down the hall. She came back in, rubbed me down with oils, and changed my dress. She twisted ribbons into my hair, shaking her head as she did so. "I'm so sorry about this, Miss, but orders are orders."

I nodded grimly. "I understand. You are only doing your duty."

She opened her mouth as if to speak, then closed it and finished doing my hair. When it was done, she held my hands tightly. "Remember: be strong, for your children."

I nodded and allowed her to lead me downstairs. Abejide burst through the front doors just as we entered the main hall. He strode to me and lifted my hand to his lips.

"Ah, Princess Dalia! You are looking much better now, no? I knew I was right to entrust Mariam with my jewel!" He smiled at Mariam, and she returned it with a tight-lipped grimace that he ignored. "Is our lunch ready, Mariam?" he asked, gazing into my eyes.

I resisted the urge to sneer, and instead focused on keeping my face blank.

Mariam curtsied quickly. "Yes, Your Highness. Right this

way."

She started toward the main dining room. Abejide followed, leading me by the hand like a child. He pulled out a seat for me. I sat down sharply. Mariam brought bowls of stew and a platter of cornbread, then poured us glasses of wine. When she had excused herself, Abejide turned to me.

"I am sorry for how rude our last encounter was. Please forgive me. I went mad with the thought of my little treasure running away from me."

I took a sip of my wine and said nothing.

"And how lovely you are in your new dress with your hair all done! It's a shame I can only stay a few days."

I took a deep breath, willing my face to remain blank and resisting the urge to slap the smug little smirk right off his face. I busied myself with crumbling the cornbread into small pieces and adding them to my stew. When I glanced up again, he was complaining about the trials of being a ruler:

"—so lucky you don't have a kingdom to rule anymore, Dalia. It's *so* tedious! You wouldn't believe all the meetings and treaties I have to sit through every day. I pray Father lives, just so I never have to be the one in charge!" He suddenly pushed aside the glasses of wine and reached for my hands across the table. "Come, let's go upstairs." He led me up to my bedroom and gently pushed me down on the bed. "Are you ready to be mine, my love?"

I held my head high. "I will never be yours, Abejide. No matter what tides may come, I will never belong to you."

His eyes widened, and he laughed heartily. "So! She can speak! Well, Princess Dalia, you are already mine. You may submit to me or not, but I will continue to use you as I wish."

He pinned me down onto the mattress and kissed me. I pressed my knees together hard, but he forced them apart. I kept my teeth gritted tight to keep from screaming in pain as he took me, and I merely lay there when he was through.

"There, now," he said, as he pulled himself together. "You see how much easier things can be when we do them my way?"

He laughed again and left the room.

Mariam rushed in to find me curled in pain on the bed. "Maybe you should just go along with it, Miss. He's only going to keep forcing you if you don't."

"Let him force me," I replied through gritted teeth. "Let him see that Princess Dalia of the First Kingdom will not wilt before him. As God is my witness, I swear: I will never bow to him."

He stayed two more days, attempting to entice me and failing, becoming angry, and attacking me. By the time he left, I was sore and covered in bruises but did not feel that I had lost. I asked Mariam if I was allowed to enter my old training room.

She shrugged her shoulders. "If it's not locked, I suppose you're allowed."

The room turned out to be unlocked, though the weapons were all gone. Abejide had clearly found them in his exploring of the castle and had taken them to ensure I couldn't use them to escape. No matter. I spent hours in that room, slowly gaining back some of my former strength. My muscles were still so weak, though, stiff and frail from months of disuse. I could barely walk, and it took ages just to get to that point. In that time, Abejide had come back several times to repeat the actions of his first visit. His visits were coming further apart, though, and one day Mariam came worriedly into my room after a food delivery.

"The man who drove the cart says Cameela saw him leaving the castle with all the food. She asked where he was going, and he said he was under orders from Abejide to tell no one. He says she let him go without further questions, but he thinks he might have been followed here."

"Isn't that good? Abejide will have to stop coming here, and then we can all leave!"

Mariam chewed a finger nervously. "I dunno, Miss. Cameela is a cruel woman and jealous to boot. If she suspects that Abejide is keeping a mistress here, there's no telling what she'll do."

I nodded grimly. "I understand. We will just have to be ready for whatever happens."

Abejide didn't arrive that month. The next month, Mariam came to get me at the sight of horses in the distance. When we came down into the hall, it wasn't Abejide waiting for us but a dozen castle guards. One of them grabbed Mariam and pulled her outside. I heard screams and then a horrifying silence.

"Mariam!" I cried.

Two guards stormed upstairs. I started to run after them, but two others grabbed my arms and held me back. The guards returned holding Suleiman and Sahar.

"No! Let me go! Let go of my children!"

I struggled against their arms, but they held me fast. Another guard appeared and grabbed my legs, and the three of them carried me out to a waiting flatbed cart layered with straw. They bound my hands and feet and tossed me into the cart. The two guards joined me, holding my screaming infants.

"I say we kill them. She's gonna do it, anyway," one guard said.

"No," said the other. "She said to bring them back alive."

I screamed as I struggled against my bonds, and one of the guards stuck a piece of cloth in my mouth and tied it.

"At least one of them will be quiet now."

The horses attached to the cart lurched forward. I peered through the slats in the wood and caught one last glimpse of my palace before we turned a corner, and it disappeared.

After four days of travel, we finally arrived at the Fifth Kingdom. Even through my hunger and exhaustion, I was stunned. I had not expected this level of devastation. Everywhere around me, people were sick and dying. The land was arid and dry, with nothing growing. As we drove through the kingdom, dust kicked into the cart, stinging my eyes and nose, making it nearly impossible to breathe with the gag still in my mouth.

The cart drove through an entrance that led down beneath the castle into somewhere cold and clammy. The horses finally pulled to a stop, and the door on the cart opened. I was lifted out and placed on the hard stone floor of a cell. My children were placed beside me and my gag and bindings removed. I bit one of the guards nearest to me, and he slapped me hard enough to knock me over. The cell door slammed shut. I crawled to where they'd placed my children. The babies were hungry, but otherwise unharmed. I sat and nursed them while I assessed the new situation.

I was in a cell under Adatuma's castle. The guards had said that Cameela was going to kill us, or at least my children. But they hadn't killed us outright, the way they did Mariam; Cameela had requested us alive, so maybe there was a possibility of reasoning with her? I put the children down, pulled up my dress, and searched for ways to escape. The bars were solid, and there wasn't even a window in the cell. My only possible hope would be making a run for it when someone eventually opened the cell, but that wasn't feasible with the children. I would have to await my audience with Cameela and hope she could be made to see sense.

It was hours before anyone came, and when they did, it was not Cameela. A young man wearing a chef's apron made his way toward our cell, carrying a hatchet, and it hit me like a weight what Cameela intended. I grabbed my children and placed them in a corner of the cell, hoping the darkness and their blankets would conceal them. I stood tall in the center of the cell, my head high, and awaited whatever would come. The chef unlocked the cell door and stepped inside, hanging his head. He looked up when he reached me and gasped.

"Princess?" he breathed.

"Edgard?" I could hardly believe it. The boy I'd trained to kill had been sent to kill me.

He dropped the hatchet and slowly approached me. "Is it … is it really you?"

I nodded.

He lunged forward and hugged me. "God, I thought you were dead! And they said they'd found halva in your hand, and someone must've poisoned you, and I've just been so guilty, and oh, my God, you're okay!"

I hugged him back. "I'm fine, Edgard. It wasn't your fault. I have an allergy to wheat."

"An allergy to— Oh god! I never would've given you that if I'd known! I'm so sorry! I've caused you so much trouble, and all you did was try to help me."

I patted his back gently. "You meant well. I should've asked before I accepted it from you. I didn't realize your kingdom made it differently. It was my fault for not being diligent." A small cry came from the corner, and I glanced over nervously.

"What was that?" he asked.

I sighed and went to pick up the children. "These are my children. You know Abejide has been sneaking over to my kingdom for over a year now. This is the product of those visits." I sighed at the look on his face. "It's a very long story for another time. Princess Cameela sent you down here, didn't she? What were her intentions?"

He kicked nervously at the floor. "She sent me to kill you and your children. She wants to serve your heart and liver for dinner tonight."

The blood drained from my face, and I swallowed hard. I'd heard she was cruel, but that … I turned to Edgard with pleading eyes. "Edgard, you have to help us. Please."

He chewed his lip in thought. He owed me. "Okay, I have a plan." He pulled a bit of twine from his pocket and loosely tied my hands. He wrapped the children tightly in their blankets and picked up his ax. "All right. Follow me." He led me out of the cell and back through the entrance to the dungeon. He nodded to the guards at the door and held up his ax. "Princess' orders."

They nodded and allowed us to pass. He led me around to

the back of the castle, where the servants' quarters were. He walked over to the side of one of the small wooden houses and leaned his ax against the door. He reached for the rope handle on a door in the ground and opened a cellar.

"Sorry to lead you from one cellar to another," he said, as he carefully climbed down the ladder with the children. "Though, I assure you that mine is much safer." He untied my hands and handed the babies to me.

"What are you going to do about the princess' orders?"

"Well, I doubt she's ever actually eaten anyone before, so I doubt she'll know the difference if I kill a few goats instead."

I hugged my children tightly, tears in my eyes. "I really can't thank you enough for this, Edgard."

"It's the least I can do after all the trouble I've caused." He climbed back up the ladder and shut the cellar door.

I sat in the dark with Suleiman and Sahar, rocking them and praying they'd remain quiet. Hours later, Edgard returned, visibly shaking.

"What's happened?" I asked.

"Abejide, he ... he killed Cameela."

"What?"

"She had the dinner I'd made served to him and waited until he'd finished every bite. Then she laughed and told him she'd fed him his whore and bastards, and he just ... lost it. He pulled his sword out, leaped across the table, and *schiiick!*" He made a sharp gesture at his neck. "Off with her head!"

I gaped at him in disbelief. "Abejide? The man who had to sneak out to avoid her wrath?"

"Right? I mean, he's nasty when he's angry, but that ..." He shook his head. "Well, I guess you can go up to the castle now."

I glanced down. "I'd really rather not."

"Why not? Those are his, aren't they?" He gestured at the twins.

"Technically, but—" I sighed. "I was unconscious for months, Edgard. How old do you think they are? How do you think they got here?"

His eyes widened. "You mean he—" He slid down the wall to the floor. "That bastard." He held his cupped hands against his mouth. "That whole family is disgusting and rotten. Do you know where my family is? Our farm? Adatuma had it burned to the ground and my family thrown in jail. I haven't heard from them in months. They could be dead for all I know. He keeps me and others here to revel in how broken we are. I just … I can't take it anymore."

I looked down at this boy, not much older than I. He'd lost a family, too, to this kingdom. Adatuma's greed had ruined enough lives. It was time to put an end to this.

"Edgard, does this castle have quails on the grounds?"

"Er … yeah, they're the king's favorites."

"Good. Here's what I need you to do: Go find a field of hemlock, and allow a quail to eat the seeds. Kill the quail, and feed it to the king for dinner. Do not allow Abejide to eat any of it. I have something else in store for him."

"Princess? Are you suggesting we kill the royal—?"

"They have caused enough pain, Edgard. They have destroyed our families and ruined my honor. It is time for them to pay. I am not as strong as I once was, so I need you to help me. Can you do that, Edgard? Can I count on you?"

Edgard hesitated, then nodded.

"Thank you, Edgard."

I stayed down in the cellar with the twins for a little over a week while Edgard prepared the quail. On the ninth day, the sound of trumpets came from above, and Edgard came running down the ladder.

"The king is dead! Abejide is the new king!"

I nodded. "Next step, Edgard, I need you to get me a knife, and a fresh dress. See if you can sneak me one of Cameela's, the loveliest one you can find. I'll also need a mirror."

He nodded and left to bring me what I needed. When he

returned, he held the children and turned to face the wall as I changed. I had to admit, Cameela'd had wonderful taste in dresses. The one Edgard brought me was a deep blue and covered in jewels. I slipped the knife he brought me into a hidden pocket in the dress. I fixed my hair in the mirror and turned to face him.

"It is time. Keep the children here with you. If I succeed, I'll come get you. If I fail, bring them somewhere safe." I kissed his cheek. "Thank you for all of your help, Edgard."

I climbed out of the cellar and walked slowly to the castle doors, focusing on standing tall and letting no one know how painful each step was. I made it to the doors and strode past the guards. None of them recognized me or said a word. I made my way into the main hall where the coronation was taking place. Especially in light of all the dust and poverty outside, the inside of the castle was positively hideous. Gold and marble covered every surface. Abejide stood on a balcony overlooking the hall, having a crown placed on his head.

"As God is my witness, I will forever rule this kingdom in as kind and graceful a manner as my father ever did." He beamed out over the crowd who only stared blankly back. He turned to leave the hall.

I hurried to follow him into his chamber. I waited in the hall for his advisors to leave, then stepped quietly into the room. "One can only hope you'd be as wonderful a leader as your father, Your Highness."

He turned and stared at me in shock and delight. "Dalia? But you ... I thought you were—"

"I am alive and well, Your Highness, no thanks to your wife." I stepped closer to him. "Well? Haven't you got anything to say to me?"

He grinned. "Oh, my darling! I knew you'd love me, eventually!" He ran to embrace me.

I pulled my knife from its hidden pocket. "I will never love you," I hissed into his ear. I drove the knife down between his shoulder blades, causing him to scream and pull away from me.

I drew him closer and stabbed him again and again. "This is what happens when you toy with my honor."

I jabbed the knife into his throat and pushed him away from me. As he lay on the floor, gasping around the knife in his neck, I turned and left the room. I walked, stone-faced and covered in blood, past his stunned advisors. I glared down the guards who moved to stop me.

"If you take another step closer, I will not hesitate to kill you, too."

They stepped back in shock, and I continued out of the palace. I walked around the side to Edgard's little house and knocked on the door. He came out carrying the twins, and I took them in my arms.

"I'm going home. Would you like to accompany me?"

Edgard thought for a moment, then shook his head. "I'd like to find out where my family is first. I'll come once I know."

I nodded and hugged him quickly. "Thank you for all your help. You are always welcome in my kingdom."

Edgard led me to the stables and helped me connect a set of horses to a carriage. "Good luck, Princess."

"Good luck, Edgard."

It took months to track down the former members of my kingdom, and even longer to get the land to some semblance of what it was before. Crops matured and flourished again. Houses and families grew. Edgard came to live in my land, along with his mother and brothers. His father, sadly, had not survived the jail. I dissolved the seven kingdoms and have not taken my father's place as High King. I merely rule my own kingdom, and trust the other rulers to rule their own, as they wish. My allergy is still severe, but far more manageable. I've learned to be careful about what I eat and whom I allow to cook for me. My weakness does not make me any worse of a leader, or of a mother. I have grown stronger because of it, and I am grateful for it.

Yzabella

A RETELLING OF CINDERELLA
SAMANTHA GUZMÁN

he sun barely sits in the orange-streaked sky, and I am on my hands and knees, scrubbing the bathroom tub. Mellow R&B music fills my ears while bleach burns the inside of my nostrils. Typical Saturday morning for me, all cleaning, all the time. Until I have to make a full Dominican breakfast—*mangu, cebollas, salchichón, huevo frito, queso frito, y aguacate*—for everyone in the house except myself. The fragrant grease I use to fry everything clears the biting scent of bleach from my head. When I'm done, my stepmother, Mariela, and her two daughters, Estephania and Alma, slowly clog their hearts of stone with the dangerously delicious meal while I enjoy my cinnamon and brown sugar oatmeal and sit out on the fire escape watching over the stirring neighborhood.

I gaze at the summer sun, now high up in the clear sky, painting Spanish Harlem with an azure light. I remove my earbuds and listen to the *bachata* music blast from the bodega downstairs, the rattling gates of the other shops opening, and the kids squealing with excitement as their parents take them to the park. The morning breeze swirls around me and kisses the sweat from my forehead. I close my eyes and hold on to the moment.

The clatter of plates thrown into the sink yanks me back to reality, robbing me of my tiny bit of peace.

"Yzabella!" my stepmother shrieks from inside the apartment. "Stop daydreaming and come clean these dishes. Your *cocola* ass don't need no more sun."

Goosebumps prickle and rise across my bronze skin, warning me to haul back inside before she bellows again. I climb through the window and leave it ajar, letting out the fatty odor.

Mariela heads to the bathroom to get ready for a day of nothingness. Estephania and Alma stretch out on the living room couch (aka my bed), scrolling through their phones while I wash *their* dishes.

"Oh. Em. Gee!" Alma screeches. Her scrawny frame jumps up from the couch. "He's really coming!"

I lean back and peer out the kitchen to see what she's hollering about, while still scrubbing an oily plate.

"Nova is gonna be in Spanish Harlem tonight," Alma continues. "He's hosting a block party right down the street to find 'a girl with a *beautiful voice*' to be in his next video." Her bony knees bounce with excitement.

My hands tremble at the thought. The biggest *bachata* singer in the country will be just a block away. There's a lightness in my chest, and my fingers go numb at the thought of seeing him in person. I jolt out of my daze when the frothy plate slips from my hands. White ceramic shatters across the teal linoleum floor, creating a constellation of jagged stars.

Mariela shoots out of the bathroom wrapped in a pink towel. Her hair is set in big rollers, and her face is covered with green glop. "What's going on?" she asks, looking right at me.

I roll my eyes and sweep the shards into a pile. Alma repeats the announcement.

Within minutes, the neighborhood buzzes with the news of the block party. I watch from the window, dumping the ceramic into the trash, as girls rush from their buildings and disperse into different beauty and clothing shops. They all want to be the one Nova chooses.

"We gotta get you girls ready." My neck snaps around to Mariela's words. She looks human again, somewhat, in her dark-blue jeggings, highlighting her curvaceous figure, lime-green camisole, and matching *chanceltas*.

Excitement flutters inside of me like butterflies. I drop the broom in the corner and rush beside my stepsisters in the living room.

Mariela knits her heavily drawn-on eyebrows at me. "I wasn't referring to *you*, and besides you have chores to finish." She points to different spots of the house. Alma and Estephania snicker.

"But I'll be done way before the party starts," I say.

"*Mija, no!*" Mariela spits, waving that same finger at me. "You're not going."

"It's not like he's gonna choose some *prieta* for his music video, no matter how good you *think* you can sing," Estephania says with a nasally gurgle. "Y'all are usually shaking it in the back somewhere."

Morena. Prieta. Negrita. Sweet terms of endearment become weapons, laced in deep-rooted hate, to cut me down.

"And, after your chores, I need you to pick up my dry cleaning from Mama Luz before she closes." Mariela grabs a yellow slip from the refrigerator and hands it to me.

The three of them disappear into the back room while I'm left to finish cleaning.

"*Nova has to pick me*," I hear Alma say, "I have the best figure in the house, and I can carry a li'l tune."

I cringe at her bloodcurdling attempt to sing and block it out with my earbuds. "Neither of them can even sing. Why would he pick them?" I say to myself as I wipe down the kitchen counter. Estephania's comments hover over my head like a dark cloud raining a painful truth. "She's right. They wouldn't pick me," I say, looking down at the dark skin my mother left behind. "No matter how good I may sound."

After an hour of vigorous cleaning, I head out to the dry cleaners. Groups of snickering girls pour out of every shop in the neighborhood, carrying dozens of shopping bags. Everyone and their mother is getting ready for this party, and I am stuck running errands.

Outside of the shop, two cats—one orange and one black—lie at the feet of a tiny woman sitting on a plastic crate eating a bowl of what smells like *sancocho* soup. Her tawny, wrinkled face curves up to a smile when I stop in front of her.

"*Hola*, Mama Luz?" I ask. "I'm here to pick up." I fish the receipt from my pocket and hold it out toward her.

Paying the receipt no mind, Mama Luz slowly rises from the crate. A bell on the corner of the door jingles as she teeters her way inside the store. The top of her red headwrap and her shoulders are all I can see behind the counter. "You going to the party?" she asks in a thick Dominican accent. She steps up onto a stool and waves through the garment bags. The gears creak behind the crinkling plastic.

I remove my earbuds. "Nope."

"*¿Por qué no?* Don't you want to?"

"I do, but—" I shrug. "Girls like me aren't leading ladies, and besides, I really don't have anything nice to wear."

"Who told you that nonsense?" she says in a high-pitched tone. She stops and pulls out a plastic garment bag longer than herself. She lays it across the countertop and steps down. "*Para ti.*"

"For me?" I scrunch my face. I examine the beautiful white flare minidress with a lace chest. "This *definitely* isn't mine," I say, almost laughing.

Mama Luz pushes the dress toward me. "*Si*, trust me." She smiles and winks.

Her two cats come from behind the counter, each pushing a silver heel covered in dazzling crystals beside my feet.

"Girls like you intimidate the others," Mama Luz says, raising her hand to my throat. "Show them how incredible you are, *mija.*"

I cock my head, purse my lips, and grab the dress and shoes. "And the other stuff?" I ask, referring to Mariela's clothes.

"*Ayyy,*" she waves, annoyed, then disappears under the counter. She pops back up with a medium brown bag holding a couple of folded garments inside.

"*Pero,* have the shoes back by midnight."

"Why? Are they gonna turn into glass slippers?" I chuckle.

"No. They're my niece's, and I close at midnight," she says. "I don't need her nagging."

Without another question, I sprint back home, carrying the gown over my shoulder, the straps of the heels looped through my fingers, and Mariela's bag in my other hand. Thankfully, the three of them are still in the back getting ready. I take Mariela's clothes out before they wrinkle and hang them on the empty clothing rack outside her bedroom door. My ear catches the hard knocks of their cheap heels. They're almost ready. I tuck the dress and heels Mama Luz gave me away in the back of the living room closet behind old coats. At the click of the door, I grab the broom and sweep the imaginary dust.

Alma and Estephania wobble into the living room. I can't stop my eyes from popping out at their absurd makeovers. Alma wears a pink tube dress that clings to her skinny form, highlighting every bone in her body. Her hair is in two ponytails with spiral curls, dazzling with pink glitter. Estephania stands next to her looking like a Christmas ornament dipped in burgundy velvet and silver glitter. Her long, black hair flows down her back to her square behind. I stand fixed and speechless. Mariela struts in behind them wearing a skintight denim jumpsuit and highlighter-yellow pumps.

"Don't they look incredible?" Mariela says, beaming.

Incredibly hideous, I think as I nod with a smile.

The three of them grab their color-coordinated purses and head to the door.

"We'll be back in a few hours. Go in the back and straighten up," Mariela says, then slams the door behind her.

The sound of music and excitement fills the block. I peek out the window and watch the festivities begin. People flood the streets. An entire high-tech stage is constructed between *Cuchifritos* and the barbershop. Local restaurants—Spanish, West Indian, and even some Asian—have tables set up with intoxicating dishes.

My eyes shoot to the cable-box clock. It's 5:25 p.m. The competition starts at six. I run into my stepsisters' room (my old room). My stomach knots at the pigsty they left behind that feels almost purposeful. Taking a breath, I race around the room, hopping over shoeboxes and clothing bags, and pick up tacky dresses, spiky heels, and gaudy cosmetics. I move with determination to clean up everything so neat, they can't complain. Thirty-two minutes later, I'm done. A new record.

Without stopping, I jump into a hot shower to wash away the day and refresh. When I turn off the water, the off-pitched voices of girls who never sang a day in their lives threaten to shatter all the windows on the block and run off the stray animals.

Quickly, I shake my head, air-drying my curly 'fro, and change into the dress from Mama Luz. Other than the prickly tag in the back, it's a perfect fit. I leave the heels by the door and run to a mirror to give myself a onceover. Water droplets glisten in my larger-than-life hair, but my face is rather basic. I never had a want or need for makeup until now. Running back into the girls' room, I rummage carefully through the vanity I just finished organizing and find an untouched red lipstick. I smear it on and press my lips together. I glance again in the mirror, twisting my matte red lips into a frown. It would have to be enough.

I make sure everything is as it should be, even though I plan to be back home before they are. Satisfied, I hop into the dazzling two-inch heels and stumble out to the party.

The fragrant air reminds me I haven't eaten since breakfast, but I ignore my grumbling stomach. Mastering the heels, I squeeze through dozens of people munching on churros and empanadas, and follow the sound of Nova's voice on the speakers.

"Thanks, sweetheart, but we're going to have to pass." His voice grows crystal clear as he sits just a few feet in front of where I stand. He turns his head and whispers in the ear of the judge sitting next to him. Nova's lips curve into a sweet caramel smile before he turns back straight. My heart slams against my chest, fighting to get out. I can't tell if it's from nervousness or adoration.

I move to the back of the line of competitors, fidgeting to stop the annoying tickle in the back of my dress. It seems like an endless path to the stage. I only hope I can make it to the front, sing, and get back home in time.

The shrills of the singing girls are even worse closer up. No one has yet to make the cut.

Time passes until the familiar squeak of Alma's voice rings out and echoes through the buildings. People cover their ears and cringe as she does her best to sing one of Nova's love ballads.

"Oh, whoa, whoa, whoa," he interrupts her. "Sorry, but you cannot sing—at all. But … I'm sure you're good at other stuff, sweetheart."

Despite how nicely he lets her down, Alma scrunches her ruddy face and stomps off the stage, almost snapping her ankle before she makes it down the metal steps.

Estephania strolls on behind her sister. Her round face burns bright in fear—or a bad stomachache from too many churros. She belts out two notes in her nasally, hollow voice. Synchronized boos drive her off the stage faster than I ever seen her move. A chuckle escapes me, but I catch it with my hand.

I see Mariela at the end of the stairs with an arm around each tone-deaf daughter. They weep into her padded chest. Her mouth moves aggressively toward the judges.

I want to keep laughing, but panic sets in. What if they see me? Before I can decide to stay or leave, someone pulls me to the stage steps. My feet ignore my brain as I move to the center of the illuminated platform. A warm, single spotlight hovers over me.

Thousands of eyes watch me expectantly. My hand touches the microphone, and instantly my body freezes. I can't look left or right. Only center. I see Nova staring up at me with his perfect eyebrows. Behind him, I catch Mama Luz with her two cats. She smiles and winks at me. My body relaxes.

Before I know it, the words to Nova's hit song push up from my abdomen and out of my mouth, ten times louder than I ever allowed. Each word is laced with raw power and emotion, sourced straight from my heart. My thick hips sway to the melodic lyrics, and my feet catch a two-step. When I finish, the block is so quiet, all I hear is oil popping at Eliza's empanada stand. My heart inches its way into my stomach. I turn to make a beeline from the stage before they heckle me off, and I stumble out of one of the heels. I freeze when I catch Mariela's menacing eyes burning a hole into my dress.

A sharp clap pops in my ears. Then another. And another. Nova rises from his seat, clapping vigorously. The two judges beside him follow suit. Applause and cheers wave over the crowd so big, it drowns out my intense heartbeat and Mariela's screams.

YZABELLA! I read from her wide mouth, but I'm too overwhelmed to hear. I ignore her and stare at the adoring crowd.

Nova makes his way from the table to the stage and stands within inches of me. His woodsy aroma makes me want to faint even more than his presence.

"Wow, that was incredible. What's your name, beautiful?" he asks, grabbing my heel. It takes me a second to realize he's talking to me.

My lips graze the mic as I muffle my name.

"Yzabella," he repeats with a sweetness I never heard. "Well, Yzabella, I think you're the one. Your voice matches your incredible beauty."

My beauty? The beauty I was made ashamed of?

With the mic in one hand, he drops to a knee. "I would love

for you to be my leading lady." Then, he slips the shoe back onto my foot. "And we'll get you a dance instructor for better coordination," Nova chuckles.

The cheers around me sound miles away. It's like a fairytale, and for once I'm the girl at the center of it all. The words I want to say sit at the back of my dry throat. His eyes widen with every moment I don't respond. I feel the words inch their way up, closer and closer. Then, suddenly, my body lurches backward.

"No, she will not," Mariela says, digging her acrylic nails into my arm. *"No vas a ninguna parte."*

Nova frowns as he rises from the floor. "Excuse me?"

"I am her guardian, and she was not allowed to be here, *así que no.*"

Alma and Estephania stand behind their mother with pinched wet faces.

I swear I hear my heart ripping. As my feet move along with Mariela's pull, a light-and-dark blur races across the stage and circles around her feet. She lets go of me, trying to spot the unknown shapes whirling around her and her daughters. Mama Luz's cats. They growl and bounce between Mariela, Alma, and Estephania. The three of them scream and swing their arms clumsily, trying to scare the animals off, but the cats don't let up. The ladies run off the stage, screeching, pleading for help. People only laugh as they scamper into the crowd. Mama Luz grins before she turns and walks toward the shop with her cats following behind.

I turn back to Nova, who appears both confused and amused. His hand finds mine, and he repeats the question I swear I'm imagining. With my shoulders back and my chin held high, I open my mouth like I did when I sang, and let my voice come out.

"I would love to be your leading lady."

Nova throws his arms around me, engulfing me deeper in his heavenly aroma. Cheers from the crowd arise once again, even louder than the first time. The uncomfortable prick in my back returns as he squeezes, not allowing me to sink fully into the hug. When he lets go, I reach under my arm, feeling for the discomfort. I pull out a small, folded notecard and open it. My breath hitches as I read the unexpected words:

My darling, Yzabella. I hope this dress makes you feel like the queen that you are, and that your mother was to me. I had Mama Luz fix it up for a special day in your future. Whether I'm there or not, I want you to enjoy every minute of it because you deserve it, mi bella negra. Papí.

Both my throat and eyes tingle. Knowing that my late father anticipated this day for me warms my heart. He always saw the beauty and worthiness in me that I never did. With everything that was taken from me by my stepmother and stepsisters, this moment replaces it all. I look into the bright eyes of my future staring back at me. Never did I believe in happily ever after until today.

The Forbidden Room

A RETELLING OF BLUEBEARD
TRAVIS TYLER MADDEN

enjamin had always been fascinated by the concept of doors. As a field slave, he had never known doors. Doors were not, and never had been, a part of his life. Nor did he ever expect them to be. A door meant having the ability to keep someone out, or something in. And you did not have possessions when you were a possession.

Doors were a part of the big house, though. The world Benjamin could see but could not enter. The world just to the side of his own. The world he never thought he would be a part of.

Until now.

Steven, a crotchety old house-slave who walked with a stoop but refused to use a cane, helped Benjamin dress. (His name wasn't really Steven, but Benjamin didn't know what name he was born with. Just as he couldn't remember the name he, himself, was born with. All he knew was that it wasn't Benjamin; that was a white man's name.) Steven was the best-dressed slave Benjamin had ever seen, always impeccable in his suit, and now Benjamin was impeccable just like him.

When he was dressed, Benjamin felt like a completely different person. The suit was tight, and it was hot. The collar stood up and crowded Benjamin's newly shaven neck and cheeks. So many folds and tucks and buttons. He never liked his old rags—no shoes, pants multiple sizes too big that he'd cinched with a rope belt, and a torso covering that could barely be called a shirt anymore—but he couldn't believe anyone actually enjoyed dressing like this.

Just a few hours ago, Benjamin had been out in the fields. He'd panicked when he heard his name called from the direction of the big house, but he knew better than to lollygag. Steven was the field slaves' only point of contact with the big house, and from the porch the stooped man shouted and waved Benjamin over. Benjamin came slowly, tentatively, remembering the years of being told not to go anywhere near the big house, the implications of what would happen if he should. He'd been whipped before, only once, for accidentally breaking eggs. He wanted to tell himself that it would never happen again, but he knew better than to promise himself something like that.

When Benjamin asked what he could help with, Steven looked sad, like something was weighing on him. It was there for a flicker before he sucked it up, and his face returned to normal.

"Benny, you gonna come be in the big house now."

There was an agonizingly long moment of silence, where Benjamin simply stood there, waiting for Steven to tell him what he really wanted from him. Eventually, Benjamin simply asked, "What?"

"You heard me, boy. You gonna come live in the big house now. Master's orders."

Benjamin started to sweat, and not from the Georgia heat. Live in the big house? That ... that wasn't the way things worked. You either worked the house or the fields, not both. You didn't switch. At least not that Benjamin had ever heard of.

That wasn't the way things worked.

And yet here he was. With Steven tightening his tie. Inside the big house. What was the explanation for it? Why had he suddenly been called up?

"All right," Steven said, smoothing down the front of Benjamin's jacket. "Miss Margaret is outside waiting for you. Are you ready?"

"Wait, wha—"

But they were already on the move. The bathroom door was opening, and Steven was right behind him, and Benjamin was suddenly out in the hall, face to face with a tall woman in a magnificent blue gown. She had long, golden curls, and her skin was pale as a ghost's.

Benjamin had never been this close to one of the masters of the house before. He was panicking, and he knew it.

"Benjamin," Steven lightly whacked him on the shoulder, "say hello to Miss Margaret."

"Hello, Miss Margaret." Benjamin did what he knew he ought to in the presence of someone like Miss Margaret—kept his head low and his eyes lower, averted from her. He was distracted by a strawberry perfume Miss Margaret wore, and when she stepped closer and he got a better whiff, was temporarily overcome with the thought of her spritzing it on her neck and breast.

"Lift your eyes and look at me, sweetheart."

What was happening? Someone like Benjamin wasn't supposed to look directly on someone like Miss Margaret. Of course, the men and boys in the fields all sneaked glances upon her or any other woman with the safety of distance. At night, out of earshot, they joked in hushed tones. Aware that, though they had never seen one, there were mulatto children out there, they wondered about the carnal prowess of white women. Benjamin heard another slave once say the lighter the skin the nastier the woman, yessir, and everyone else laughed. Benjamin guessed that because they wanted to keep ahold of that laughter, no one ever questioned how he claimed to know that.

But this close?

He heard Miss Margaret's voice. "Benjamin." And then she grasped his chin in her hand.

There was lightning on Miss Margaret's fingertips, a power—or rather a power imbalance—that connected her to Benjamin. Terror sent acid surging through his veins and up out of his stomach, and he was sure Miss Margaret could see the sweat break on his temples. He struggled not to retch and could swear the entire house could hear his knees knocking together.

It wasn't supposed to be like this. Only hours ago, Benjamin had been out in the fields. Only moments ago, he'd been bathing, and for the first time in something that was not a lake or river. He wasn't sure he liked it. You were supposed to keep all the water in that little tub? The door was closed when Benjamin was bathing, and again he'd marveled at the fact that there were places people could go to shut out the rest of the world entirely.

He wished he had a door right now.

Miss Margaret's fingers clenched tighter on Benjamin's chin. He looked at her. He had no idea what to do with his hands, so he frantically gripped the tails of his coat.

Objectively, Miss Margaret was a very pretty woman, but Benjamin could barely move past the fear taking control of his body. Her hair was long and golden, wavy. Freckles dotted her cheeks, and her eyes were a vibrant spring green. Benjamin noticed a thickness to her, one he could see in her cheeks and upper arms, feel in her fingers, and he became envious of the food that must be served in the big house. Was any of that going to be his now that he worked here?

Miss Margaret let go of his chin and said softly, "It's very nice to meet you, Benjamin." Her voice was breathy, calm. Like how Benjamin would have expected the spring breeze to sound, could it talk. What was this that he was feeling, this lure toward Miss Margaret? Was it just the big house and its illusion of comforts? Benjamin's head was spinning too fast to think.

After a couple false starts, he finally said, "It's very nice to meet you, Miss Margaret."

"There."

She smiled, but there was something about it Benjamin did not like, could not identify. Her teeth were much better than any Benjamin had ever seen, and she still had all of them, and yet something told him it was not a smile of friendship. What was it, then?

"That wasn't so hard, was it?" She let go of him. "Now, Benjamin, Steven and I are going to give you a tour of the house, tell you about some of your responsibilities. Okay?"

Responsibilities? His responsibilities were supposed to be outside. *He* was supposed to be outside. None of this made sense to him. Benjamin was young. He was strong. Someone like he was supposed to be doing field work. Weren't they? He was the kind of slave who was supposed to help push a wagon out of the mud, like he had last week. Not serving food to the masters. Benjamin wanted to ask why him, why he was here, but he knew better than to ask questions of white people. Especially white women. Especially white masters.

It took a moment for Benjamin to find his voice again. "O-okay, Miss Margaret."

"Good boy," she said, and again gave Benjamin that smile that made him uncomfortable in some way he could not define.

Miss Margaret and Steven showed him the entrance room and the reception room (Benjamin didn't know why those were not just one room, but he didn't ask), the library and the study (the same applied to those). All of them had doors. They were all open, of course, in the middle of the day, allowing house slaves to head from room to room to tidy up, to transition from one place to another. Benjamin couldn't believe how many doors there were.

They passed other slaves, women in pretty dresses—but not as regal as Miss Margaret's—and men dressed in suits similar to Steven and Benjamin, none of whom acknowledged them except to step out of their way and bow as they passed.

Miss Margaret said, "Steven, now I think it's time to show Benjamin the most important part of the house, don't you?"

Benjamin almost missed it. If he'd blinked, he would have. Steven's reaction was nearly imperceptible, just a flicker of fear on his face before his default expression returned. Eyes widening, a slight puff of his cheeks, and then he was back to being Steven again. Just like the look he gave Benjamin outside.

They took Benjamin to the black door.

He followed Miss Margaret and Steven downstairs, past the kitchen, and into the basement, where Steven needed to light a lamp so they could see. They moved past enormous selections of ancient wines and stacked boxes, across a dirt floor, weaved around and between the foundations of the house. The darkness made Benjamin think of ghost stories told at the cooking fire, of prisoners and madmen, spirits roaming the earth, hunting for flesh. Some of the slaves said that spirits neglected to follow them over from Africa, but that America had its own ghosts to worry about.

When they finally stopped, it was at an enormous door in a stone wall.

"This," said Miss Margaret, "is the most important door of the house. It's the one you need to know the most about."

The door looked like it belonged to a house other than this one. Some old, decrepit, haunted place. It was black, and Benjamin could not tell if it were painted that way or if perhaps it had been burned. The design carved into it was horrifying: an old man, but he was crawling around on all fours like a beast. In fact, he appeared to be changing into one; the nails on his toes had turned into animal claws, and some sort of scales or fur crept along his legs and across his torso. Benjamin couldn't tell whether the look on his face were that of horror, pain, or madness. Maybe some combination of all three. The man's beard and long hair dragged along the ground beneath him, and the light of Steven's lamp cast rippling shadows over the door carving so that the crawling figure appeared to move and wriggle.

Benjamin only noticed it because of the lamplight, but he could see a thick line of what appeared to be salt on the floor right in front of the black door, stretching from end to end of the threshold.

"What is it?" Benjamin asked, trying to hide his disgust. He hoped Miss Margaret didn't want him to be in awe of the door.

"You don't recognize him?" Miss Margaret asked with a slight *tsk.* "Oh, Benjamin, I thought you people knew your *Bible.*"

Bible, Benjamin thought quickly, *Bible, Bible.* Who in the *Bible* turned into an animal? If that was indeed what was happening here.

Miss Margaret giggled. "Oh, give him a hint, Steven."

Steven said, "Starts with an *N.*"

"An *N,*" Benjamin echoed. And then, quieter, almost to himself, "Nebuchadnezzar." He remembered, of course. The Book of Jeremiah told Benjamin about when Nebuchadnezzar laid siege to Jerusalem. It called him the "destroyer of nations." He remembered where the Book of Daniel had Daniel interpreting Nebuchadnezzar's dreams. It was not Benjamin's favorite part of the *Bible,* if he was being honest, but he did not say that aloud. Benjamin much preferred the stories of heroes like Noah and David.

Miss Margaret purred. "Nebuchadnezzar," she said. "That's a smart boy."

For a moment, Benjamin thought she would reach out and stroke him gently, like one would a good dog, but Miss Margaret kept her hands to herself. Benjamin was only aware of his tension after he unclenched.

Miss Margaret said, "I knew we picked right when we invited you up to the big house. Now, Benjamin. I want you to pay very close attention to me."

She wanted such close attention that she turned, looked him straight on. Benjamin could again smell whatever strawberry scent Miss Margaret covered herself with, and it made the bottom of his stomach drop out. It stirred something inside him, the same thing that awoke when he saw the sweat running down the arms and the backs of the girls in the fields. He wanted to back away, knew this wasn't right, this proximity, this familiarity. They were too close. But something inside him said that to back away would offend Miss Margaret. Something told him she wouldn't like that. Why was she doing this? Why was she so close?

"Are you paying attention?" Miss Margaret asked.

In the humidity of the basement, Benjamin could see a single bead of sweat roll off Miss Margaret's neck. It traveled down her collarbone, and she moved in such a way to show it to him as it slipped between her breasts.

Stop it, Benjamin told himself. What are you talking about? What are you doing? Don't look there. He told himself it was only because he hadn't been with a woman in years. Such a long time would make anyone stupid.

"Yes, Miss Margaret," Benjamin said, not taking his eyes off hers, "I'm paying attention."

"Good boy," she said.

She held out her hand toward Steven without taking her eyes off Benjamin. Steven, apparently knowing exactly what this signal meant, reached into his jacket and pulled out a large ring of keys. He put them gently into Miss Margaret's hand, and then she put the keys into Benjamin's.

She said, "You have a key to every door in the house. Every door. Including this one." She gestured to the Nebuchadnezzar door. "But you are never to go through it."

Benjamin didn't ask why. With what was carved into the door itself, he had no inclination to see what was beyond. He merely clutched the keys as if they were a talisman. At the very least, they were something to do with his hands.

Miss Margaret said, "I want to make sure you understand fully, Benjamin. No one except the Master or myself is allowed beyond this door. Not anyone. Not even Steven."

Behind her, Steven was silent, but nodded.

"I understand, Miss Margaret."

She stared Benjamin right in the eyes for a long time, undoubtedly to see if there were any lie or misunderstanding. Benjamin knew that she would find none, but what she would find was fear. Questions. Why did he have the key to this door if he was not allowed to enter it? Why was the door carved in such a way? What was actually behind it? Why tell him about it if he couldn't go in? Why was he here at all? If he was so strong, why wasn't he back out in the fields?

In that silence, Benjamin thought he heard something stirring beyond the door, something shuffling, moving. Was it in his own head, or did he hear the sound of grunting? Of loud chewing? There was a sound like a tree branch breaking, and Benjamin spoke so that he would hear something other than those terrible noises.

"I understand, Miss Margaret."

Miss Margaret smiled and stood back. When she spoke again, her voice was as bright and happy as before, as if this door had never existed. "I believe you, Benjamin," she said. "Come now. We have the whole rest of the house to visit."

Benjamin quickly learned to serve the big house, but his mind never truly left the basement, the black door, and what he heard beyond it. He felt tethered to it. Benjamin dusted furniture and thought about the black door. He washed dishes and thought about the black door. He followed Steven's orders and thought about the black door. It never left his mind, always lingered back there, ready to pounce, like the crouching Nebuchadnezzar. He became more and more certain that there was something alive behind it.

While Benjamin was uncomfortable in his suit, he was glad to be inside, out of the heat. The big house was not easier work, exactly, but it was different work. He was away from the physical exhaustion of field work, even if it was replaced with mental exhaustion. There was something simpler about field work, though. Fix this, tend to that. In the big house, he felt pressure, that any mistake he made would be instantly witnessed and punished. But Benjamin made no mistakes. Even with the black door on his mind, he listened and obeyed, did everything he was told.

One of his daily duties was to bring Miss Margaret her meals. She ate afternoon snacks or took tea wherever she pleased, but her big meals were always alone in the lavish dining room. She often asked Benjamin to stay with her. He did not sit down, of course, but waited silently at the edge of the room in case she asked for anything from him. Occasionally, Miss Margaret spoke to him. Sometimes she did not. When she did, she asked him how he was liking it in the big house. A couple times she asked him to sing for her, and she seemed to appreciate it even though he didn't think his voice was very good. All he knew were religious hymns and fieldwork songs.

The more time Benjamin spent inside the big house, the more he realized he was constantly by Miss Margaret's side. Almost all of his duties were related to her. Benjamin often found Miss Margaret staring at him out of the corner of her eye, enraptured. Like he was the first black man she'd ever seen. Miss Margaret came physically closer and closer to Benjamin in a familiarity he found exceedingly strange. Stranger still was that it was never commented upon.

About the only job Benjamin had that took him away from Miss Margaret was to bring food to the Master. And that brought him to the black door.

His instructions were always the same: Take the prepared tray to the black door in the basement, place the tray on the small table just to the side of the door, knock three times, immediately turn and come back upstairs. Do not wait for the door to open. Do not wait for any sort of confirmation from the Master. Benjamin did this dozens of times, for breakfast, lunch, and dinner, and there was never an issue.

Until there was.

Until, as he was leaving, the black door opened. Benjamin was almost gone, almost up the stairs and back to the main level. He turned at the sound of swinging hinges. There was a man standing there. A man looking straight at Benjamin.

Was this the Master? The shape was small, but not just because it was hunched, or because distance made it tiny. The man looked sickly, like he hadn't had food in weeks. He didn't wear the clothes that Benjamin thought the master of the house should wear, nothing like the regal garments Miss Margaret wore. This figure was dressed worse than the slaves outside. A tattered blue blanket was draped around his shoulders and over his head like a hood. Beneath it, Benjamin could see rags, bandages. Beneath the shadow of the hood, Benjamin could see a long, blue beard draping down to the man's chest.

The man stood there, watching him, and Benjamin could feel the man's stare all over his skin, could feel it burrowing into him. He didn't know how to explain the stare, but he didn't feel it was entirely malicious. It reminded him of the time a wolf had made its way into the fields, and the creature had simply stared at Benjamin from a distance. Sizing him up. Studying him. Like it had not decided yet whether or not he were to become prey.

Still, Benjamin moved as fast as he could back to the kitchen without actually running.

Benjamin waited until Steven and he were alone to ask if the Master was ill. The old house slave was helping Benjamin with his vest and tie—Benjamin could still not get it quite right—when he told Benjamin not to ask questions. Steven tied Benjamin's tie just a little tighter than usual, and Benjamin wondered if that cinching was a small punishment for asking something out of bounds.

"But I saw him," Benjamin whispered. They were in a separate dressing room. Again, behind a closed door, so that it was only the two of them. Benjamin still had not gotten used to such a concept.

"You hush," Steven said, and whistled a hand in front of Benjamin's face without actually hitting him. "Don't ask questions. Just do what you told."

"The Master's not ..." Benjamin felt silly even thinking it, "a ghost ... is he?" He'd heard a ghost story once, when he was small. He remembered little of it other than the spooky noises the storytelling slave made. Afterward, an old woman whose name Benjamin could no longer remember—she'd long since been sold off—went around the circle, bopping the men on the heads for frightening the young ones.

"Oh, you hush, boy," Steven grumbled. "Ghosts ain't covered in bandages, Benjamin."

Not that there was no such thing as ghosts, but that they weren't covered in bandages.

Benjamin didn't say anything back, but he knew he never actually described to Steven what it was he saw down by the black door.

When Benjamin stood on the porch by Miss Margaret as she sipped her afternoon tea, she suddenly said, "I heard you were inquiring about the Master."

It took everything in Benjamin's power to remain completely and utterly still. And yet on the inside he cursed Steven for undoubtedly ratting on him.

"It's okay," Miss Margaret said.

She looked at him. Benjamin could see it out of the corner of his eye. He knew better than to look directly back at her, but then Miss Margaret's hand was on his sleeve. She tugged him once, lightly, just enough to get his attention, and Benjamin turned his face to her.

"Don't worry, Benjamin," she continued. Her eyes were soft. "It's okay for you to look at me." Everything Miss Margaret was doing went directly against everything Benjamin had ever known about slave-masters. She said, "It's perfectly okay to be inquisitive. Steven is too hard on you sometimes. In my opinion."

Too hard? What was happening?

Miss Margaret said, "I know how you people talk. So, word was bound to get around eventually, and I'd rather address fact than unsubstantiated rumor. Yes, Benjamin. Unfortunately, the Master is rather ill."

Benjamin gulped and tried not to let Miss Margaret see.

She said, "That's why we brought you into the big house. I chose you personally, Benjamin. Did you know that?"

He shook his head. He was too terrified to say anything. His brain chugged in place and refused to move, like a stubborn locomotive without enough fuel.

"Do you know why I picked you?"

Again, Benjamin shook his head.

"Do you remember last week, when you helped push that wagon out of the mud?"

Benjamin remembered. One of the Master's new hands had gone into town for supplies, and in the rain on his way back, he'd gotten a two-horse team and the wagon stuck in some mud. Benjamin and four other field slaves had been pulled off their normal duties to free the horses and the wagon, while the hands all stood back and smoked cigarettes under a tree and shouted orders. It had taken the slaves over an hour, the mud sucking at their feet and the rain coming down and the wind blowing, making it worse, but they'd managed to free the wagon without losing any cargo or harming the horses.

The hand who'd gotten the team stuck in the first place was given a nice bonus.

"I ... I remember," Benjamin said slowly.

"I was watching you that whole time. I remember seeing you help the horses out, seeing you free the wagon. I knew I needed someone strong like that. To help here, with the Master ill." It looked to Benjamin like she wanted to say more, like she wanted to tell him something. But all she said was, "With the Master ill, Benjamin, I need someone strong like you here in the big house."

And then she said nothing, simply stared out over the property, and Benjamin guessed their conversation was over.

It was beyond anything Benjamin had ever heard—ever even imagined—for a white woman to volunteer information to an inquisitive slave. And it was that unknown quantity that terrified him the most.

Benjamin tried to find some sense of normalcy in his new routine, but he was constantly reminded that none of this was normal. Every time he brought Miss Margaret food, he thought that he wasn't supposed to be in the big house. Every time he stood with her out on the porch, he thought that out in the fields was where he was supposed to be. Every time Benjamin brought the Master his tray, he thought that underground was not a place *anybody* should be. And on the day he went downstairs and found the black door yawning open at the end of the hall, Benjamin told himself it all had to be some sort of terrible dream.

The black door was actually open.

Benjamin ground to a halt when he noticed it, the tray of food in his hands. He was never supposed to open the black door, never venture beyond, but Miss Margaret never said what he should do if he ever found it open. It never even occurred to him as a possibility.

Maybe he should put the tray down right where he was. Maybe he should leave the tray halfway down the hall. Just close enough to where he could not see inside the room. Whatever he did, he knew he could not simply head back up. Not without delivering the Master his meal. Benjamin did not know the specific consequences of that, but whatever they were, they could not be good.

He thought, *Just head over and drop it*. That'll be all right. Just head over and put it down. Make a loud noise as you're coming. Maybe the Master, if he's inside, will close the door before you get too close. And then Benjamin thought that he could perhaps just close his eyes. The hallway was straight enough, the floor even enough. If he closed his eyes and walked straight ahead—

it looked to be about fifty paces—he could put the tray down outside the door, turn, and walk away.

Benjamin closed his eyes and found his way forward by slowly putting out one foot. He felt the ground with his toe, then put his foot down, repeated with the next. It made those fifty paces all the more agonizing, because he could hear something but not see anything. He wasn't sure what exactly he was hearing at first. Some sort of scuffling. Benjamin cleared his throat loudly. Coughed, even though he didn't need to. He dragged his feet. He whistled. Hoped any and all of it would let the Master—if he was indeed down there—know Benjamin was approaching.

But Benjamin did not hear the door close. No one spoke to him and told him to stop where he was. So, he kept going. Kept listening to that scuffling noise. As Benjamin came closer and closer, it became more defined. It sounded like cloth rustling. And on top of that rustling, he could hear something like muffled grunts, the sound of someone pushing, struggling. Like a violence.

And then all of a sudden it stopped.

The silence was worse than the noise. Infinitely worse. Benjamin felt as if he could feel someone standing in front of him, a face in front of his own, and when the fear became too much, he squinted open his eyes.

Just for a moment, he thought. I'll just do it for a moment. Just enough to see if I'm in danger. Just enough to know what's happening.

He wished he hadn't. Lord in heaven, he wished he hadn't.

Fifty paces had been too many. He was already inside the room beyond the black door; it was dimly lit, but Benjamin could see well enough. The space was large, but not spacious. A desk was pushed against the wall, on which Benjamin saw dozens of books and loose reams of paper featuring anatomical sketches of skulls. Old books spread their yellow pages wide open, and along one of their spines, Benjamin could see the letters P-H-R-E-N-O-L-O-G-Y, though he had no idea what that word meant. But worse, so infinitely worse than the strange books, was the old, rickety bed in the center of the room.

Onto which was strapped Miss Margaret.

A rag was in her mouth, knotted behind her head, and her limbs splayed in all directions. They, too, were tied, strapped to the edges of the bed. She wore nothing but underthings.

Benjamin dropped the tray of food, and it clattered at his feet. Whatever he was going to serve got all over his nice shoes. The noise crashed so loudly in the small room that Benjamin didn't hear the door shutting behind him. But he certainly heard the voice cut its way through the door's resounding echo.

"Do you like what you see, Benjamin?"

Benjamin turned around and saw the Master, a single, dripping candle in his grip, barring the exit. Only this time, the Master was without his bandages.

The man who stared Benjamin down looked like a monster. Some sort of demon. As animalistic as Nebuchadnezzar had become. The Master was shirtless and skinny, shot through with deceptive, wiry muscle. A thick beard draped down to his chest, and his eyes were bloodshot. But what frightened Benjamin the most was the Master's skin. At first, in the dankness of the basement, Benjamin thought it was a sickly gray, but as the candle-light crawled over it, he could see that it was a cold and steely blue, just like his beard.

The Master smiled. His voice was as cold as his skin. "We got you down here faster than the others."

Benjamin backed up until he could go no further; he bumped into the bed, chanced a brief look behind him toward Miss Margaret. Benjamin expected fear on her face, but what he found was something much worse. With fear, at least, they would have been in this situation together, but her expression was something Benjamin had never seen before, at least not on a person. He struggled, took a moment to recall where he'd seen such a focus, and what he came up with horrified him. He'd seen it when a cat cornered a mouse in the barn. It was the look of a predator, of someone who had complete and utter power, who had someone else right where she wanted him. Her hips slowly lifted up and down, and she breathed heavily. Her chest rose and fell in hungry anticipation.

Benjamin looked for an escape route, something besides the door in front of which the Master now stood, but there was nothing but stone in every direction. He saw only, on the other side of the bed, a small pocket of darkness. Something deeper than the shadow in the rest of the room. Surrounding it was another salt line. Benjamin was aware of it, distantly, before his head swiveled back to the immediate danger.

The Master sneered. "You people really do listen when you're told to do something. None of you has ever opened that door. Not a single one. So, we had to get a little inventive. Lure you in. Sound has always worked well, we've found. The sound of a woman, especially, to men who have not been with a woman in a long time. …" The Master smiled, as if that was all that needed to be said. And indeed, it was.

In his fear, Benjamin forgot all propriety, all pretense of how he was supposed to act in front of white people, let alone the masters of the house. He panicked, and his body told him to do something—anything—besides curl into a ball and surrender to whatever madness this was.

"W-w-what's happening?" Benjamin managed to ask.

The Master didn't come any closer, though there was not very much closer to come. From the bed, Miss Margaret looked on hungrily. Her hips were still bucking. Benjamin could hear her sucking in air past the gag.

When the Master spoke, his voice was not low, not angry. It was … happy. Like he was glad Benjamin could share in whatever horrific experience this was. "What's happening," he said, "is you've been chosen, Benjamin."

Chosen. Personally. If there ever was a doubt in Benjamin's mind that Miss Margaret was simply an innocent victim in this, it was gone now. Whatever was happening to him, it was because of her. Benjamin retreated further, so that the bed Miss Margaret occupied was between the Master and him. Benjamin briefly glanced behind himself, saw that salt line and the patch of darkness behind it. It looked like a hole. Like a well.

The Master stepped up to the bed, and while looking at Benjamin, untied Miss Margaret's right arm. She freed herself the rest of the way, removed the gag last, and let it drape around her neck. She licked her lips, looked from Benjamin to the Master and back again, perched on her hands and knees at the edge of the bed. She looked ready to pounce.

"It's okay, Benjamin," she breathed. "We're going to tell you why we chose you. We've found it goes a little better. The process is a little easier when you know. There's not as much ... spiritual resistance."

"What process?"

The Master took a single step forward. "I'm sure you know," he said, "that there are people from your continent who engage in certain ... dark, animalistic practices."

Benjamin swallowed. He wanted to back up, but he could not go any further. All that was behind him was the hole in the ground, the ring of salt surrounding it.

"It's been proven, you know," the Master said, nodding to the desk. "The science of phrenology. How the world's darker people are more susceptible to certain uncivilized urges. It's all there in the shape of your skull: the propensity for violence, the inbreeding. But especially the eating of flesh that is so popular among the indigenous peoples. In your dark continent, Benjamin, they say that such a thing allows someone to take another person's strength."

Benjamin wanted to ask them what they were talking about, what it was they intended to do, but his brain was frozen. He was unable to do anything: move, scream, cry, shout for help. All his functions were shut down. He could not even back away any further.

"But it doesn't last very long," the Master said. "Or, at least, not as long as I'd like it to." He looked at Miss Margaret, who was so close to the edge of the bed it looked as if she might tip right off.

She stared wide-eyed at Benjamin, and not just because of

the dark. "But bucks like you," she purred, "are young. And strong."

Benjamin remembered what Miss Margaret told him about watching him free the horses and wagon from the mud.

She lifted a hand and offered it out to him. "You last much longer. We want you to join us," she said, "to give the Master your strength." Her free hand caressed her hip, and Benjamin nearly retched at the fact that he once thought of her carnally. "The strength to be a proper husband to me."

Lord.

They wanted ... Benjamin couldn't even think it. Every time the thought came close to his mind, it grew spikes and stuck him. It was like trying to pick up a snake. He could not come at it from any direction without being bitten.

"You want to ..." Benjamin's head spun. He gripped the desk, so he didn't fall. If he fell, he knew, it was over. He would never leave this room. At least not in any way that he would want. In any way that was not a nightmare.

"We want you to become a part of us," Miss Margaret said. "You'll live on. Inside the Master. Inside me. Understand?"

Of course he understood. But she was really asking if he were okay with it. How could he *possibly* be okay with this? They were going to ... Benjamin couldn't even *think* it. He could only swallow the lump in his throat and say, "You want my power." That made it easier. Somehow. Not to acknowledge the true truth of what they wanted. The mechanics of how they would get his power hung unspoken. Benjamin would never be able to speak such words.

"Yes," said the Master.

Benjamin backed up further, felt his heel against the lip of the hole in the ground.

"Benjamin, *stop!*" Miss Margaret suddenly hissed, looking down at his foot.

But Benjamin hardly paid attention. All he could think was to get away. To run. There was nothing else except not letting this happen.

Miss Margaret reached for him. "Benjamin, *don't!*"

His foot scraped something. He nearly fell into the hole, caught himself on nothing other than muscle memory. He smelled salt kicked into the air, and then the Master's candle blew out, and everything went dark and quiet.

The room was silent for a long, long time, and Benjamin wondered if this were what death was like. Just nothingness. No, no, that couldn't be right. If this were truly death, he would not still be able to smell the smoke of the Master's candle, the salt behind him, the sickly smell of his own fear-sweat. Miss Margaret's perfume.

"H-h-hello?" Benjamin called into the dark.

And then there was a light. It was not the light of a fire, but something soft and blue. Benjamin thought it might have been the moon or starlight, but down here? In the deepest part of the house? That was impossible. Especially after it quickly increased in intensity. And took a form.

At first, it was nothing except a soft, pale hue, as if the Master had lit a strangely colored candle. But Benjamin could see both the Master and Miss Margaret illuminated in that steely light, and neither of them held it. They both stared up at the light, and for the first time Benjamin saw something submissive on their faces, saw that, although he did not quite know how, they had been stripped of their power. They flinched before the light, eyes wide and mouths agape, fear evident in their eyes.

The light swelled, became greater. Bigger, brighter, but not so much that Benjamin had to shield his eyes. He watched as it grew from a small orb into a recognizable shape, with translucent arms and legs, with eyes that glared a soft and yet terrifying judgment unlike anything Benjamin had ever seen.

It was a man. A black man. Benjamin didn't recognize him personally, but he certainly recognized a field slave when he saw one: the clothes that barely qualified as such, the thick, ropy muscles that could be seen through the rips in cloth, the callused hands and the scars of whippings.

And then there was another light. This one grew and swelled

much faster than the first, became yet another field slave staring down at the Master and Miss Margaret.

And then another. And another. And another.

Until the room was filled with the wraiths. So many that the basement would not have been able to contain them had they been flesh. So many that Benjamin had to view the Master and Miss Margaret, distorted and warped, through the floating legs and torsos of the ghosts. They were all men, most around Benjamin's age. All strong, all scarred, and all staring right at the Master and Miss Margaret.

One of those specters slowly turned away, toward Benjamin. It took all Benjamin had to look into the wraith's eyes, not to run screaming from the room. The ghost's lips moved, but Benjamin didn't hear him say anything.

"What?"

Again, it said something, but Benjamin thought he heard it this time. Far away, like from down a well. Echoing, never truly reaching Benjamin's ears. The ghost seemed to understand it was not being heard, and gestured behind Benjamin, to the patch of darkness in the corner of the room.

Benjamin turned and looked at it again and, in the light of the ghosts, could see that it was indeed a hole in the ground. It tunneled both horizontally and vertically away, and in the new, blue light, Benjamin could see what was inside it: a pile of bones. Human bones. He didn't know if he'd be able to tell what they were if he hadn't recognized the telltale shape of human skulls. Around the hole, the white line of salt had been broken. By his heel.

Benjamin looked back up at the ghost, nodded that he understood. He had freed them. The ghost nodded back at Benjamin, then turned with its spectral brethren to face the Master and Miss Margaret.

And then, finally, when there were no more eyes on Benjamin, he ran. He did what he was told, and left the door closed behind him.

The Mystery of the Worn-Out Shoes

A RETELLING OF TWELVE DANCING PRINCESSES
TORIE COMEAUX PLOWDEN

nce upon a time, in a beautiful and tropical land, there lived a large royal family. Queen Nia and King Jacob were blessed with a dozen sons and one daughter. The princess, the eldest of the children, was a somewhat reserved young woman. She had long legs and was much taller than her petite mother. She was very graceful, often being compared to a gazelle. Even her skin was the same tawny shade as a gazelle's coat. Princess Zoe was calm and measured, much like her father.

The twelve princes, however, were a rambunctious group. All of the boys were handsome and strong, brave and generous, loud and funny. The brothers were very close and were rarely found alone as they loved to be together. They were best friends.

All of them were tall, like their father. The color of their skin ranged from chestnut to bronze to a rich mahogany. Despite their differences in appearance, every single prince inherited his mother's bright smile.

The family's favorite pastime was dancing. Their royal balls were well-known throughout the seven neighboring kingdoms. These galas featured delicious food, lively music, and hours upon hours of dancing. Fast dances and slow dances, line dances, breakdancing, complicated waltzes, and simple two-steps. Almost every kind of dancing could be seen. Princesses from near and far flocked to the balls just for a chance to meet one of the twelve dancing princes.

The king and queen were kind rulers. Their realm was filled with beauty and laughter. Until the royal family encountered a particularly perplexing problem. One morning, the queen woke to find that her twelve sons had somehow each worn out a pair of shoes overnight. Very odd, indeed. When she asked her sons how this occurred, they were equally puzzled. This continued for an entire week. The king and queen interrogated the princes, yet the young men seemed genuinely confused. None could recall the events of the previous night. The parents couldn't detect any lies and were forced to believe their sons.

The king posted guards at the door of the princes' royal chamber after locking the princes in their room at night. Yet, each morning, the princes' beautiful, handmade shoes were completely ruined. Princess Zoe was concerned about her brothers. With every passing day, the boys seemed to be more and more despondent. They were obviously exhausted. They lost their appetites and barely ate at all. Each of her brothers swore he did not know what was happening.

Finally, the queen decided she'd had enough! How long could her sons go on like this? Their bright smiles dimmed. They lost weight. They were simply fading away. She had to do something! She issued a decree offering a handsome reward to anyone who could solve the mystery of the princes' worn-out shoes. Noblemen and lords came from great distances to find the answer to this riddle. None was successful.

And then a stranger came to town. This young woman was beautiful. Despite her youth, she had long, curly silver hair that glistened in the sunlight and swirled wildly around her face. Her skin was the color of cinnamon, and her eyes were a deep chocolate brown. Although she was lovely and had a commanding presence, she also had a gentleness about her that made people want to trust her.

"Greetings, Your Majesty," she said, as she bent into a deep, graceful curtsy. Her voice was like silk. "My name is Harmony, hailing from Elujah. I have traveled here for the opportunity to study the problem of the worn-out shoes." Elujah was one of the neighboring kingdoms. People in that land were rumored to be smart and shrewd. As the young woman straightened, she looked up shyly at the queen.

The queen offered her a big smile. "My dear, you are the first woman to take on this challenge. At least two dozen men, young and old, have tried … and failed. Let us women sit together and discuss the problem. I am hopeful *you* will be the one to find a solution."

The queen and Princess Zoe talked with Harmony over tea. They explained their recent woes. Harmony listened attentively, occasionally asking a clarifying question. She asked to see the princes' royal chamber. She explored it thoughtfully and thoroughly, peeking under their beds and poking into closets. After she was satisfied with her inspection, she turned to the queen.

"Highness," she said, as she dropped into another deep curtsy. "I am sorry for the distress this situation has caused to you. I will get to the bottom of this."

Later that night, the princes prepared themselves to retire for the evening. Harmony bid them goodnight and walked out of their bedroom chamber. But she had a plan. The usual guards were posted outside of the bedroom door. Harmony walked around a corner to put her plan into action. She closed her eyes and mumbled words unheard by the guards' ears. And then she disappeared.

Well, she didn't actually disappear. She was still standing just as she had been seconds before, except now she was invisible. Harmony was a witch. Descended from a long line of good witches, she used her powers to spread light and love. She would use her magic to help save the princes. Now that she was invisible, she went back to the princes' bedroom chamber, before the guards closed and bolted the door.

She sat down in a chair near the door and prepared to watch and wait. The princes each settled into his own bed and promptly went to sleep. About an hour later, she heard a small sound. She sat up straighter and looked around the darkened room, but she didn't see anything unusual. A few moments later, she heard the sound again. Was it coming from the largest closet? She stood without making any noise and took three steps forward. The closet door slowly creaked open. No one else in the room stirred. Then, a haunting melody, a song so beautiful it made her want to cry, came from the closet. Momentarily mesmerized, she listened. Her eyes widened when she saw each prince sit up in his bed. The princes got out of bed and stood. No one talked. No one smiled. They simply stood still. A moment later, the princes got dressed. As they formed a single-file line, Harmony realized they were entranced.

One by one, the princes walked into the closet. Harmony was confused. She had explored this closet earlier that day. Although it was large, it was completely ordinary. She walked in after the twelfth prince and saw a glimmering, swirling portal in the back of the closet. She watched as the last three princes stepped through the opening in the wall, then she followed.

She glanced around. She could not see anyone else, nor could she see any homes or manmade structures. She was alone with the princes in a forest. But this was not an ordinary forest. The trees were made of glittering sapphires. The dazed princes walked, oblivious of their surroundings but still moving purposefully toward an unknown destination.

Harmony murmured incantations of protection for each of the princes as they walked along through the unusual woods.

Passing the trees, she collected sapphires and put them into a pouch inside her dress pocket. Soon, she noticed the sapphire trees had given way to trees made of rubies. She marveled at the dazzling shades of red, while casting protection spells and gathering some rubies.

She felt as if they had been walking for hours, but she was sure it hadn't been nearly that long. Time moved differently in this place. Looming ahead were twelve large trees made of emeralds. These trees were by far the most beautiful, and she gathered several emeralds, as well. Just past the tree line, she saw a large castle. The air here seemed stale. Something felt very wrong, but Harmony couldn't pinpoint the cause of her anxiety. And then, she saw them.

Twelve lovely princesses stood in exquisite gowns on the castle lawn. Each princess wore ornate jewelry composed of sapphires or rubies or emeralds. Each tiara was so dazzling that it hurt to look at it. The dazed princes each walked toward a waiting, welcoming princess. The princesses' smiles were enchanting, but their eyes held contempt and anger. Did she see rage hiding in those eyes? Did she see the desire to harm the sleepwalking princes?

The castle doors flung themselves open. The princesses and princes walked into the castle and onto a dancefloor. The couples began to dance. Graceful and elegant, the couples moved together for hours and hours. The princes didn't stop to rest. They didn't drink any water. They didn't interact with each other. They only held their princesses and danced on.

A short time later, the couples left the dancefloor and exited the castle. The princesses accompanied the princes back through the forest and toward the portal. The poor young men still seemed unaware of their surroundings. The women accompanying them murmured sweet words to the princes, but the smiles on their faces were full of cruelty and malice.

Once they reached the clearing past the sapphire trees, the portal opened again. Twelve couples stood, each locked in an embrace. The princesses kissed their princes again and again, and the young men appeared reluctant to leave. The princesses released their princes. The princes turned and slowly walked through the portal, one by one.

As Harmony was waiting for her turn to walk through, she looked back at the lovely princesses. She gasped. Since the princes were no longer looking, the princesses had dropped their glamour spell. They were no longer elegant princesses. Harmony could see their real form. Their lovely noses had become sharp and beaklike. Their eyes were small and hard. They had large, gorgeous wings, and they were laughing. *Sirens*. The princes had been in the clutches of sirens all night.

"Don't worry, sisters," said one of the sirens with a sinister smile spreading across her lips. "One more night. Only one more. Tomorrow night, we shall capture the brothers, and they will be ours ever after."

Harmony leaped through the portal. The last thing she heard as it closed was the cackling of the siren sisters.

By the time Harmony exited the closet, the princes were removing their ruined shoes and climbing back into bed. It was dawn. Harmony was exhausted and afraid. She sank onto the floor as she realized the ramifications of what she'd seen and heard. How would she defeat a dozen sirens? She didn't know yet. But the one thing she did know was that she had to think of a way soon. She wasn't going to let them hurt the princes.

After getting a few hours of sleep, Harmony could think more clearly. She turned the dilemma around in her head, examining it from all angles, uncovering a smart course of action. She formulated a plan and spent the rest of the day gathering the items she needed and preparing herself to save the princes.

When night fell, she repeated her invisibility spell and sneaked into the royal chamber without being seen. The princes readied themselves for bed and soon were sleeping. She sprang into action, murmuring her incantations of protection over each sleeping prince.

An hour later, the closet door opened, and a haunting song poured into the royal chamber. Not a single prince stirred. She smiled to herself as she walked through the portal. She made additional preparations in the clearing, realizing that she didn't have much time. She knew that, when the princes didn't show at the castle, the sirens would come here to investigate. A few moments later, she heard footsteps. Then angry voices.

"Sisters, what went wrong?" The first siren came into view, disguised as a lovely girl in a pretty pale-pink gown. "This has never happened before."

The other princesses appeared, and each was lovelier than the last. Before they had a chance to understand fully what was happening, they heard a strong, fiery voice chanting words they couldn't understand. The princesses looked at one another and instinctively came together in a tight cluster, backs together, facing outward to confront this unknown threat. The sisters were clearly shaken. With quivering voices, several of them talked at once:

"Who's there?"

"What do you want?"

"Show yourself! Show. Yourself. Now!" seethed the sister who always took charge.

Harmony had never stopped her chanting. The wind rose, and at that moment, she chose to show herself. Her wild, silver curls flew in the wind she had created. Her chocolate eyes glowed with an inner fire, making them appear more orange than brown.

"What is this? A witch!" the leading princess said in a mocking voice. "Oh, dear, dear little witch. You are out of your element. In over your head, dear. You can't defeat us," she said, her voice dripping with sarcasm. She cackled and smiled at her sisters. "Sisters! Sisters, calm down. Let us show this witch who we really are. Now, we must sing."

They dropped the glamour and no longer looked like sweet little princesses. They revealed their true forms and reveled in it. The sirens smiled smugly at one another as they sang the haunting song that had helped them ensnare and seduce hundreds of men in the past. They sang the song that brought men to destruction.

Harmony continued her chanting. The fire in her eyes and the wind she generated kicked up significantly as she raised her voice louder than the sirens' song. The sirens sang louder and louder, coming to a thunderous crescendo. Lightning cracked from Harmony's hands. She lifted her arms. As the sirens sang, their voices floated out of their throats and rocketed toward Harmony. She drew a large jar from her cloak and uncorked it.

The sirens' eyes flashed with anger, and their faces contorted with rage. But there was nothing they could do. Their mouths remained opened in a silent scream. Their voices had already been collected in Harmony's jar, which she promptly corked.

"This is over," said Harmony. "You may not have the royal princes. Nor will you have anyone in your evil grasp ever again."

The sirens shivered violently as their bodies collapsed onto the ground and broke apart, becoming heaps of ash that blew away in Harmony's wind. She stepped through the portal once again, back into a room filled with sleeping princes.

Despite the late hour, Harmony rushed to the king's and queen's bedchamber. After being granted entry, she told the whole story. She pulled sapphires and rubies and emeralds out of her pockets as she talked about the forest. Finally, she held up her jar, which contained twelve glowing orbs of light—the sirens' voices.

"This is all that remains of those evil sisters," Harmony said.

The king and queen sat in astounded silence for a few moments. Then the king bellowed, "Through all of this, my sons just slept?"

"Yes, Majesty."

The queen said, "But even with your protection spells, I don't understand why the siren song had no more impact on my sons. How could they ignore that temptation after succumbing to it for weeks?"

Harmony smiled and said simply, "Earplugs."

The Devil's Advocate

A RETELLING OF THE CREATION MYTH
CHRISTIANA MCCLAIN

I don't usually take to telling no lies, but my great-granddaughter came strolling through my living room letting the screen door slam against the wall with her head hanging so low her chin might leave a dent in her chest. I'm sittin' in my brown corduroy chair tryna watch *Wheel of Fortune* and play *Candy Crush* on my tablet when she come place her head on my knee like my body was made for resting. Berry, now that's what I call her 'cause she as sweet as all that and dark as them, too, wipin' tears from her eyes and snifflin' real hard, and her chest is risin' up and down like it ain't enough air in the room for her. I do the thing I always do and ask her what's wrong. She start tellin' me 'bout some nappy-headed boy she been runnin' after who never takes the time to slow down for her. 'Course, I don't call him nappy-headed to her face 'cause she tell me black people ain't supposed to say that 'bout each other, say it's the white man got us hatin' our own hair. That's why her and all her friends done

abandoned perms, lookin' like Angela Davis only five shades darker.

Anyways, Berry get to talkin' 'bout this boy and this love like it's some big war. I done heard each of them, Berry and Shayla and NeNe, all plot from my black-leather couches on the best way to capture these men. Every move is calculated. They put on foundation thick as paste and eyeshadows painted blue and red all on their faces, remindin' me of the Indians from the Westerns her daddy and uncles watched when they was coming up. These young girls wait and hide in the places they know men will be just like soldiers in trenches, poppin' out at just the right time actin' like they had always been there. They turnin' themselves into spies, pretending to care 'bout something called mixtapes or highlight tapes or somebody named Lil Weezy, disguising themselves as the perfect woman. But the hidin' don't last long 'cause Berry always blows her cover asking questions she shouldn't, like why men always callin' women bitches and why women can't sleep around as much as men. And they both realize they two different type of people and love ain't enough. She waves the white flag and takes off her mask and returns home to me all wounded and beaten down with more tears and questions than the last time she was here.

I tell her like I always do, sit up and shut up. She pulls her head from my knee and turns to face me. I look down into her brown eyes and feel a heat in my chest remindin' me I been too harsh on her, even though in my ninety years of living, I done wiped away so many tears from faces that look like mine more times than I could count. She is the only great-granddaughter I got, and each time she heads out that door with her heart in her hand, I know she tryin' like I did, fightin' like I did, for someone to love me without restraint, like I was the answer to a endless prayer. And she asks me to tell her again, tell her why love hurts so bad and why it's so hard to find the right one. She wants me to remind her why she gotta keep tryin' even though it feel like she ain't ever gon' win. And I don't really take to tellin' many lies, but some lies ain't really lies, it's just people don't believe in them.

I start like I always do with the time before there was the heavens and the Earth and the humans made from dirt. When it was only God, his eight angels, and his daughter. Now the world ain't look like how it looks now. For one thing, everything was upside down. The skies was the ground, and they was purple, like the insides of grapes, and the grass was crunchy and twisted together like the stuff people shove inside Easter baskets. The moon and the sun was joined together, like a two-headed marble, all round and blue and orange.

Now my daddy told me that the angels was big ole giants way over three thousand feet, with skin the color of stone but still as warm as ours. He first told me 'bout all this when I was laying in my bed crying harder than I was breathin' after I caught Barbara Richardson kissing Isaiah Booker behind the schoolhouse, even though two days before, he had been kissing up and down my neck and whisperin' in my ear how much he loved me. My daddy said the angels had feathered wings the size of billboards and full of scales, but I think they was brown like me and Berry, so that's what I tell her.

God started with Lucifer first, makin' him the biggest with arms the size of eighteen-wheelers and wings that shook mountains each time they flapped. When Lucifer stood up for the first time and stretched out his limbs like a toddler wakin' from a nap, he knocked against the ground, and trees dropped, hitting his head. When he yawned and exhaled, makin' use of his lungs, the air from his body whipped up clouds like cotton candy fallin' to his feet. God was so pleased he set out to make more. He made Michael, this time with arms the size of mountains and wings like eighteen-wheelers, but he saw it was real hard for Michael to fly as fast as Lucifer. Then came Gabriel and Raphael, they was nearly perfect with wings and arms the same size. They could drink from the clouds when they was thirsty. They was always ringing them out when they got bored and floodin' the world when they felt like it. God rolled out Uriel, Raguel, Ramiel, and Simiel. They came out like printed copies, drinkin' up clouds, chewin' on trees, and spittin' out fire each time they breathed. Lucifer, being the oldest, coached them into existing without killing.

The eight angels carried on well enough. Arguing only when someone spent more time with God than the other. Berry always say the angels got more daddy issues than the whole black community put together, and then some. Always fighting for his attention, tryna please God as much as they could. God started hidin' from them just to get a little piece of quiet. He had loved his children but was tired of how much they loved him back. One day, God got so fed up with the angels that he snapped his fingers and took away their voices. Just like that, eight giants sat rockin' back and forth like tantrum-throwin' children. While they was busy tryna scream without voices, God leaned back, coughed two times, and he hacked Arini right into the world. And I know for sho' she looked like us because my daddy told me so. For one thing, she was way over one thousand feet tall. She had hair that fell like ropes to her feet, skin a color like copper, big lips, a big ole nose, and brown eyes big as airplanes.

The angels quit they crying and watched her take form. She opened her eyes, and they circled around her, mouthing the word sister with smiles wide as football fields, tryna reach out and touch, as God shooed away their hands. He said quickly she ain't their sister—yes, she was his child just like them, but this one belonged to him.

Arini looked around her, from angel to angel and then finally to God. Her chest started heavin', and she placed her hands around her neck. Lucifer rushed to her side, slappin' her back harder and harder until a sunflower fell from her mouth and landed in Lucifer's hands. He held it up to God, who grinned and placed it above Arini's ear. God grabbed her by the hand and led her away with the angels foldin' their wings in on themselves like dogs with tails between their legs.

It carried on like that for some time, with God keeping Arini all to himself and seein' the angels less and less. Seem like the angels was crying forever and ever, makin' the oceans out of their salty tears, each wave coming from the hiccups and pauses they took to breathe in air. God only remembered them when Arini asked 'bout the crying. He decided it be all right for Arini to have some friends.

God got to taking them all out for flying once a day, to stretch their wings, only Arini couldn't fly, and she got tired of waiting at the hem of God's sparkling white garment and tapping on his legs tryna beg for a set of wings. He'd shake her off and remind her she ain't like the rest of them; she was made to be grounded and to be with him. And see this how come I know Arini was the same color as Berry, made of the same type of woman 'cause she ain't listen to a word he said and took to surviving the best way she knew how, and she wasn't just fightin' her father, she was fightin' God. Arini was from the flesh of him. Unlike the angels, she could create. So, she pulled from the skin behind her ears and made these three big-bellied animals with pointy tails that was way over three hundred feet long. She called them her babies, even though they flapped scale-studded wings and had horns shaped like shark teeth on their snakelike heads. They nostrils was so big they could inhale any angel within five hundred feet of them.

The angels was terrified and jealous of Arini. When they disobeyed God, he took from their height and stole their voices, but Arini never suffered nothing. He would just shake his head and smile at her cleverness.

It was never clear if it was Ramiel or Uriel or Gabriel or Michael or Simiel that did it. And Berry always stop me to chime in, that it was never clear if it was Raphael or Raguel, either, 'cause I always forget 'bout them two. But one day, Arini fell from her babies, and they all screeched like nails against a board and started flapping their wings tryna save her but was caught in nets like fish in the sea. Arini landed on top of the sun, forever separating it from the moon and burning herself so bad, God had to shed tears for her skin to heal. Lucifer was the one who peeled her from the sun, takin' the pieces of her burnt skin from the star and throwin' them over his shoulder. He placed Arini inside one of his wings and she sobbed the whole way to God. All the angels was put in chains, except Lucifer.

God never did put the sun and the moon back together, and they been chasin' after each other ever since, always missing each other or passing right by without enough time to reach out and touch. That was the first day that passed. And God told the angels, with thunder in his voice, that if any angel so much as touched Arini, he'll kill them all without even blinking. They was to stay away from her.

But Arini trusted Lucifer and took to slipping away from God just to sneak a peek at him. She would hide behind the stumps of trees when Lucifer walked. And when he took to flying, she hid in the nostrils of her flying babies. Lucifer caught on to his stalker and started to talk real loud, knowin' she could hear him, and droppin' presents like crumbs for her as he traveled. One time he yanked down a flower from the ground and squeezed it 'til a nectar dripped down the stem, and he wrote with it like a pen, spelling out her name, then flying away quickly. When she was tryna read it, he snuck up behind her and grabbed her with his wings, shooting down into the sky like a rocket. She crawled up his back and placed her hands on his shoulders like they was handlebars. She gripped him tight as he turned and flipped and dipped. She felt the heat of her cheek against the curve of his neck, as the air blew so hard, her mouth kept opening like the tops of parachutes. And Berry always throws her head back sighing all loud, like this the first time she ever heard this, and she make me repeat the part 'bout the name, the neck, and the parachutes until I tell her to shut up and stop interrupting me, so I can gon' head and finish.

When Lucifer brought her home that night, Arini pretended she got lost, and Lucifer was the one that found her. The worry formin' on God's brows disappeared, and his face softened as he looked down at his first son. He was pleased. Lucifer pushed his luck and convinced God that since Arini ain't like the rest of them, she needed someplace to call her own, she couldn't sleep curled up like a fetus inside God's ear forever.

Before God could even disagree and any of the other angels got up, Lucifer built her a palace. He plucked from the scales on his wings, pickin' them off with his nails. They fell beneath his feet, and he stretched and stacked them into walls. He stripped the brown skin from the back of his knees and snatched the yellow from the sun, rollin' the mixture in his hands and holdin' it down against the rays until it melded into a hard ole thing like gold. He did this several times and used them like columns to hold up the place. Picking up clouds from the ground, stroking them and fluffing them, makin' them the perfect bed. He even cradled tubs of water in his big ole hands, bring them to the middle of her floors, mumbling to himself how Arini just got to have her own water. Arini saw what he had done, and she was pleased.

She was lounging on her cloudy bed, letting her hair lay on the ground, watching Lucifer as he kicked the columns making sho' they was stable when she started to wonder if Lucifer tasted as good as he looked. She called him to her. She was motioning with her hands and drawin' him in with a smile. He put one foot 'fore the other, only stopping once both legs was intertwined with hers, and he found his head deep into her neck. Her fingertips traced secret notes down his arms, down his chest, and down his legs. Each time she touched him, his wings fluttered, and when he ran his fingers through her hair, stars fell from her scalp and tumbled down into the sky. The two of them was rollin' into each other like magnets and rollin' away from each other like being close hurt and rollin' all over the palace, lusting hard and breathing harder.

But God was already on his way to the palace. Arini had been gone from him too long, he was anxious to see his favorite child, and he stumbled on them as they was knottin' themselves together like snakes. And every time I get to this part, Berry get real still and real silent like she was Arini and Lucifer, who stiffened when they saw God and stopped.

Arini untangled herself from Lucifer and walked to her father, looking up at him, hoping for a little piece of mercy and understanding. He reached out his hand, and she flinched, relaxing only as he cupped both hands around her face. He leaned his head to the side, seeing his most prized possession for the first time with her own will. He got to squeezing and squeezing until her head caved in on itself, with her eyes and nose and mouth mixing in together and sliding down her body. God kept on squeezing, and Arini kept on shrinking. When she was almost gone, he scooped her into his hands, takin' his index finger and smearing her in his palms, like a child playing with drying paste.

Lucifer sank to his knees. He opened his mouth to let out a cry, but nothing never came out, just a gust of wind that shook the palace like a twister. Just as he was letting out air, God summoned the other angels and sicced them on Lucifer like rabid dogs. They came at Lucifer with blood streaming where tears should have been and claws instead of nails.

Lucifer grabbed Ramiel and Uriel, smashing their heads into each other. They heads clashed together, splitting their skulls into halves. Lucifer dug his nails into Ramiel's head, peeling the skin from his face, revealing the white meat like wet potatoes, letting the pieces fall to the ground. He jabbed his nails into his brother's cracked head and pulled his head apart, holding it in two pieces. Uriel laid on the palace floor clutching his head and shouting in pain, crawling toward God. Lucifer grabbed Uriel's head and ripped it from the rest of his body. He tucked Uriel's head underneath his right arm like a basketball, dragging the rest of his brothers by their wings, starting a mound of dead bodies. Each angel that stepped to him ended up as a pile of limbs stacked on top of each other with blood spilling out of the palace and into the sky, mixin' the red with the blue.

He threw his slain brothers at his father's feet and eyed God's hands as tears rolled down his cheeks. God held Arini in his hands and smiled down at Lucifer. Lucifer started to yell up at him, talmbout God better let Arini go and he better bring her back to him right now and he better do it quick, or he'll kill him with his bare hands. And even though there ain't no killing God and they both knew that, once the words was said, it was like

Lucifer had already killed God.

God picked up his foot and stomped on Lucifer, not enough to kill him, but just enough to stamp out all the fire that was burning in his chest. And the next time Lucifer woke up, he was in the very palace he built for Arini. Only it had bars instead of columns and pits of fire instead of water. The palace rocked and shook, swooshing Lucifer from side to side. It wasn't 'til he steadied himself by holding onto the bars that he realized he was hanging from God's ear like a diamond earring.

He looked down from where he was and saw that the world was empty, there was only darkness and his father. God was standing still, drenching in darkness, listening as his first son wept for a world that no longer existed. He got this feeling like maybe he been too hard on Lucifer and maybe Arini was right to love him. Plus, he can't help that he a jealous god. So, he decided to level with his son.

The first day, God asked Lucifer for a apology, and Lucifer flat-out refused, so God decided he better start all over and maybe that would bring his son around. So, he made light for the world. The second day, God asked him if he was sorry for stealing his only begotten daughter, and Lucifer shook his head, so God made the sky, this time right side up. On the third day, God tried to bargain with Lucifer, said if he promise to never do it again, he'd let him out. After all, he was the only child he had left. But Lucifer remembered a time when Arini's hair tickled the inside of his wings, and he said he ain't promising him nothing. So, God made the heavens and the Earth and the oceans. By time the fourth day rolled around, God demanded a apology for Lucifer's disobedience, but Lucifer was balled up in a corner thinking 'bout Arini and the clouds, and he wasn't really listening, so God put back the sun and the moon and the stars. And by the fifth day, Lucifer cried and cried so much God ain't even get the chance to ask him nothing, so out of boredom, he just made the fishes and the birds and other sea creatures. On the sixth day, God told Lucifer this was his last chance, he better apologize and promise never to do it again, but Lucifer just asked for Arini instead, sayin' that if he can't have her, he rather have nothing.

God just got so angry, he snatched Lucifer from his ear. He lifted up his tongue and dug around his mouth scooping out the ashes that used to be Arini. Lucifer heard her whimpering after all this time. He started pulling on the bars and shouting for Arini as God lifted his hands and sprinkled her onto the ground the way people season food. Then God lifted the dirt, the clay, and the pieces of Arini, and made people.

He turned to Lucifer and said, if Arini can't belong to me and she can't belong to you, she gon' belong to the world. Lucifer backed away from the bars and started huffing and puffing, with his eyes turning black. He reached behind himself, pulling from the ends of his wings and ripped them off his back, slowly and mercilessly. Lucifer ain't ever really fall from heaven; he climbed down taking all the fire and resentment with him. And on the seventh day, they both wept.

Lucifer made a home out of darkness, collecting angels who disobeyed God and turning them into demons. And when Adam and Eve went into that garden, he sent his children in after them, slithering around to destroy all that God had made. Lucifer been testing mankind ever since, snatching up souls before they can ever make it into heaven.

One day, God got off his throne and traveled down into hell just to pay his only son a visit. Hell ain't look nothing like he thought it would, none of the flaming fire or rotting flesh, just a cave the color of blue crystals and a pile of bodies with gaping holes in their chest almost as tall as Lucifer. In the center of the cave floating like a swarm of fireflies was a orb yellow as pineapples, twisting and spinning around itself like a ball of lightning. The closer God got, the louder the whimpering got. It sounded like Arini.

Lucifer came from behind the floating flesh and eyed his father. His eyes was black, and he had scratches and bruises all over his chest from the bodies tryna fight him from tearing through their hearts. He placed another small piece of light into the floating orb and smiled. As he put the piece there, the orb bounced and made a soft moan. Lucifer vowed to rebuild everything God destroyed, even if it would take him millions of years, even if it means stealing every human's soul, he would have Arini back in his arms.

God stood there rubbing his hands together thinking 'bout destroying his only son and starting all over for the third time, but he was getting old and getting tired. So, he just gave the world Jesus instead. I guess he figure only a person made of light and obedience could snuff out Lucifer.

Berry rolls her eyes, saying it don't make no sense to her 'cause as far as she can tell, Lucifer still gon' strong and Jesus done returned to glory. I tell her like my daddy told me, Jesus already did his part and now we gotta do ours. I say to her, with my daddy's voice echoing so loud in my head it's like he sittin' right in this room with us, that love ain't only 'bout the findin', it's really all in the tryin'. I reason with her, the same way my daddy did with me, and his mama did with him, and somebody probably had to do with her, that if the sun and the moon ain't givin' up on finding each other, why should we? Her breathing done slowed down and her chin ain't hanging into her chest no more. She get to nodding her head again, like she done eighteen times before.

And Berry do like she always do and tell me she gon' ask God to have mercy on Lucifer. She say she gone pray that he gives that piece of her soul to Lucifer, so he can get closer to having Arini back. This love warrior of mine, with a wish to send pieces of herself to hell, then places a small kiss on my knee. She puts her head there, too, because my body was made for her resting, and I run my fingers through her hair that feels the way clouds look to me, and I ask God for a little piece of mercy for Lucifer, too. I pick up my tablet and return to *Candy Crush* and *Wheel of Fortune* and my only great-granddaughter until she runs out the door, and I gotta use these words to revive her again.

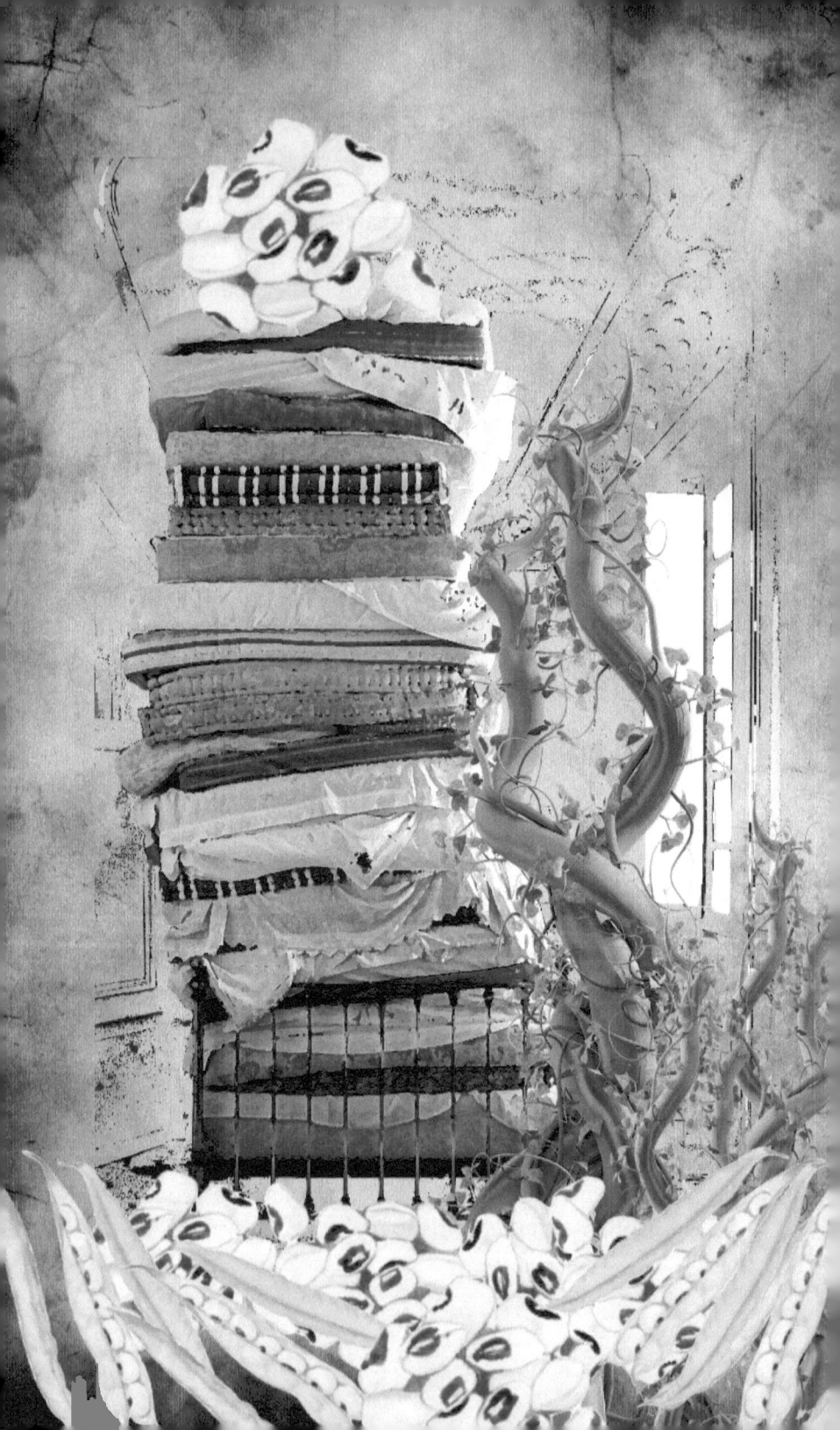

Once Raised

A RETELLING OF The Princess & the Pea
Monique Hayes

 t came as no surprise to the multi-hued multi-tude of Magnolia that Queen Melba was rather blunt whenever she pointed out that one never sees brown in rainbows. Of course, she meant the shade of rich chocolate or deep earth or solid tree trunks. She didn't value any color darker than tan, often balking at the beauty of twilight clouds. Thus, the people of Magnolia simply shrugged off her removal of the black-eyed pea crop from the royal fields.

"Such a poor and depressing crop," criticized Melba. "Plus, the pea's unattractive black eyes ruin my appetite."

Nobody told farmer Lennie that she should share the queen's opinion, except her mother, Petal. "There's an old Southern say-ing," recalled Petal, hiding her patched gloves in her pockets. "Peas for pennies, greens for dollars, and cornbread for gold. People used to cook each for prosperity. But no respectable peo-ple desire pennies or eat black-eyed peas anymore."

Lennie glanced at the withered collards on the castle grounds. These dry plants would fail to yield any dollars or com-pliments.

"Look how soot-colored you're getting behind the ears,"

remarked Petal. "You bend down too much."

With her lip curled, Lennie leaned down to rip a weed threatening the plant closest to her.

"Honestly, Carolinda," said Petal, stepping back from the flying dirt.

Lennie shifted her basket full of cultivated peas. "I prefer Daddy's nickname."

Her father, though uneducated, predicted the weather perfectly. Lander always knew when the last spring frost was visiting to lay claim to the black-eyed peas. It was a cold and hungry caller who sought to get a feast before the summer holiday. Lander waited, with Lennie sitting beside him at the window, until the soil was warm and rich. Then they would tread through the field next to their farmhouse and spread the seeds into rows. Months later, the protected seeds would spring into plants, the leaves kissing Lander's cheeks like Lennie used to do before last winter took him.

"There's still time for Queen Melba to change her mind," insisted Lennie. "While greens may bring prosperity, so do black-eyed peas, and they last for years if stored properly. If I can convince her, this famine won't remain in Magnolia."

"You're not going to call Prince Kamal inept again?" cried Petal.

Lennie shuddered as she spied several larvae devouring one of the more promising collard leaves. "If everyone sees a tree's tall, why mention that it's tall?" With a smirk, Lennie pressed on to the palace.

Petal released an agitated squeal. "Don't you ruin our first audience with the queen!"

"Was he not put in charge of the harvest this year?" asked Lennie. "Now it's June with nary an edible plant. I could've done better, but they wouldn't hire a female."

"He's off seeking a bride, a noble cause," said Petal.

"His bride will die if there's no food," said Lennie. "And his latest prospects could definitely use a meal." She nodded toward the door of the yellow-tinted palace, the golden walls much thicker than the dozens of young, well-bred women preening outside the entrance. Lennie stared at their spotless and dainty slippers, their coiffed curls lined with pearls, and their tight satin gowns.

"Kamal must be here today!" said Petal. "Here. Let's do something about your chapped lips." Petal grabbed her daughter's cheeks, then searched in her hand-purse for fruit-scented ointment.

"I'm here on business," said Lennie, moving back.

"You can be serious with peach-smelling lips," said Petal. "Oh, fine. Be an old maid."

Lennie barely heard her mother as an intimidating roar of thunder rolled over the area. The majority of the prince's prospects covered their heads with lace-trimmed gloves, and three of them pounded on the door with flower-patterned fans.

"We're going to drown!" cried a girl with rosebuds around the crown of her head.

"I won't be soaked, either!" said Petal, taking Lennie's hand.

Their valiant sprint to the palace still left them soggy. While a guard gave in to the panicked princesses' pleas, Petal and Lennie were delayed at the door. The guard reappeared a few minutes later. His bright buttons were as shiny as the glistening peas in Lennie's basket. He snorted at the visible vegetables.

"Your kingdom?" asked the guard.

"This one," replied Lennie, raising her eyebrows before Petal elbowed her. Lennie curtsied with her wet ebony hair falling into her eyes. "Sir," she added.

"You'll come with me for the teacup test," said the guard. "We'll … discard these."

"But they're a gift for Her Majesty!" said Lennie.

He took the basket from Lennie roughly, and ushered her mother toward an adjoining room. Lennie attempted to retrieve the peas until Petal stood in her way.

"Let the legumes go, sweetheart," whispered Petal. "If Kamal's smitten with you, you can have all the pesky pods you want as his bride. Make sure to stand in the most flattering light."

"Princess attendants to the kitchen, please," ordered the guard.

After a wink to Lennie, Petal followed the guard into the other room. Lennie glanced at the trails of raindrops dripping down her apron. She typically found relief in the rain after a hard day's work in the field, but now she appeared as if she'd traipsed through three floods. How could she converse with Queen Melba in such a state? Yet, she was fully aware that another audience with the queen might take weeks, especially if there were a royal wedding. Lennie glanced at her sodden burgundy sleeves and red cotton stockings in the foyer's luminous wall-to-ceiling mirrors.

"I look like a robin fresh out of a birdbath," she sighed.

The guard returned and motioned to a room to Lennie's left. When she entered the Grand Hall, decorative fans dipped to reveal the princesses' painted and open mouths. Fingers lifted demurely to adjust curls that weren't sopping like Lennie's plastered locks. Their tiaras were so blinding that Lennie had to blink. Her gaze then swept over the red marble floor, the ivory columns, and the foreboding throne with crimson velvet cushions. The guard guided Lennie to a spot between a petite woman with bluebells around her collar and a snickering girl whose gown was trimmed with sunflowers.

"You're not going to pass, dear," muttered the girl in sunflowers. "Somebody should've told you before you traveled here."

Lennie chuckled. "Are they going to make us walk with teacups on our heads?"

"The test is only a rumor, Tia," said the princess in bluebells. "According to the king's final declaration, the choice is ultimately up to Kamal."

"She's going to weed out the undesirables, Desiray," said Tia, smoothing out sunflower petals. "If you noticed, there's not a shade darker than sepia in this hall."

Desiray brushed Lennie's arm. "Ignore her."

"I'm from here, and I'm just here to talk peas," said Lennie, righting her shoulders.

"No wonder they're looking outside the kingdom for a match," whispered Tia to her neighbor before the hall doors burst open.

Lennie almost slipped on the floor while trying to get her first real glimpse of Queen Melba. Though Lennie'd seen the stone-faced monarch at harvest festivals two years ago, the queen had been only a speck for Lennie to view from far away. Melba's features were lovelier up close, her skin as fine as china and light as lemon meringue. Her emerald-encrusted gown appeared to float as she walked past the row of ladies. Lennie shrank back when the queen's embroidered shoes padded past her.

Melba inched something out of her pocket. Lennie realized they were two teabags stuck together when the queen separated one from the other.

"Step forward when I pass by you," said Melba. "It may not be so obvious. These will help."

She snapped her fingers, which sent sudden chills down Lennie's back. The guard hurried to Melba with a cup of steaming water. Melba placed the two bags into the cup and stood there a full minute. Lennie heard multiple intakes of breath and saw a few glances in her direction. Melba took in each of her guests and walked straight to Tia. Tia moved out of the line and grinned widely. Melba's eyes veered from the steaming ginger liquid in the cup to Tia's face.

"You'll be in the corner bedroom, not too far from mine," said Melba.

"Thank you, Your Majesty," said Tia, returning to her place.

Lennie narrowed her eyes at the curve of Tia's ivory chin. Lennie's stomach roiled with the memory of the way Tia said "undesirable," and Lennie's ears, whose sooty edges had earned consternation from Petal, burned.

"I remember you," said Melba, her shadow falling onto Lennie's shivering frame.

Lennie's feet shuffled ahead of her before she could stop herself. She parted her wet hair to better see the ruler. "I interviewed for the lead gardener position in February."

"You're a commoner," said Melba.

Lennie rubbed her wet palms together, both the queen and she recoiling at the sucking sound it created. "Yes, I don't belong here," admitted Lennie. "But if I could have a second of your time—"

"Take heart, gentle girl," interrupted Melba.

"Oh, I can wait to talk once you're finished with your guests."

"I was a commoner, too," said Melba, ignoring Lennie's last statement. "A woman of humble origins. Perhaps you'll shine brighter than everyone else. Forward, if you would."

Though her legs were hesitant, Lennie stood across from Melba, the space between them the width of a cup of steaming tea. Melba removed the hot teabags and draped their strings over Lennie's ears with considerable care. Lennie gasped as the heated water trickled down her neck.

"No, you're not bright at all," said Melba.

Tia looked at two other fair-skinned girls knowingly.

Lennie gritted her teeth. "Are you done?"

"Are you?" said Melba. "First you want my son's position and then his hand? You're desperate or deceptive. I have no tolerance for either."

Without lowering her head, Lennie pried the bags away from her face. Melba beamed when Lennie tossed them to the floor. "Am I too deceptive?" asked Lennie. "Or too dark?"

"You pick," said Melba with a wave of her hand.

After evaluating the queen's expression, Lennie recalled the prolonged wait at the door and how no other princess attendants had stood outside the palace. "You wanted to embarrass me," said Lennie.

"I granted you an audience with me," said Melba. "Maybe now you'll know your place. Princess of the Pea."

"I came here to offer you a solution for your dying kingdom," said Lennie. "Keep the black-eyed pea crop. There's still enough time to produce enough for every family!"

Melba gestured around the room at their awestruck audience. "This is the solution for my kingdom. A union between your prince and a wealthy neighboring land. Not some soul food."

"That food's fed us for generations ... until you got haughty," said Lennie.

"Can't you see I have other rooms to assign?" said Melba. "Your damp hand-me-downs and diatribe were amusing for a while, but now you may go."

No direct command was needed. The guard grabbed hold of Lennie's wrist and drew her from the queen's sight. Lennie took in the view of fourteen forlorn females checking the tints of their thumbs as if they hadn't been attached to their hands forever.

It should come as no shock, except maybe to Melba, that the peas were devoured rather than discarded. The queen had no mastery over the mouths of the kitchen staff, and they chewed Lennie's gift liberally. The peas' forbidden nature made them more tantalizing, and it had been months since a bean had been eaten in Magnolia. Lennie, however, had no knowledge of this. She observed her empty basket near the carriage house when her knees hit the dusty ground. The guard slammed the door behind her before she stood up.

Lennie hated herself for tarrying and taking in the solemn fields. She shouldn't care about the cabbage worms consuming the pathetic plants or the improper spacing of the rows. But farming was in her blood, and no family deserved to starve. Lander had loved a full table with blessings from the soil—mustard greens, okra, black-eyed peas. Lennie kept his garden as best she could when he became ill, and when it was only Petal and she, those edible blessings were a balm to their souls.

She went to retrieve her basket, hoping to find her mother in the process, but a voice rooted her in place.

"Miss, would you mind holding this?"

A thin instrument made of metal with a wooden tip appeared under Lennie's nose. She recognized it as a crude version of a tool used to measure the soil's acidity. She failed to identify the man holding the object, though his amber eyes were piercing.

"The other gardeners went off to eat some remarkable peas someone brought," said the young man. "The cook can't stop talking about them."

Lennie beamed until she remembered her bedraggled appearance and examined his lavender silk tunic. She really didn't want to discuss produce with another person of rank today.

"I'm just going to take some measurements, if you'll place it in the soil, please," said the man.

"Very well," said Lennie. "Then I must go." After Lennie placed the instrument between some collard plants, the two of them lingered until the man asked her to pull out the device. The readings were grim, and Lennie winced. "Soil's not rich enough."

"That's what I feared," sighed the man. "I'll have to approach this academically. There are certain rainfall patterns to keep track of. My books on meteorology ..." He paced while a baffled Lennie watched him.

"You need an almanac, greenhorn," said Lennie, thrusting the instrument into his chest.

"Those wouldn't be in the palace library, though," said the man.

"But they would be at the market's bookstall," offered Lennie. "It helps you predict the weather? Ask the queen to give you enough coin for a copy. Maybe you'll fare better than I did when you ask her to listen to reason."

The young man smiled. "You don't think her own son can convince her?"

Lennie closed her eyes and yearned to sink below the too-dry soil. How could she uproot herself out of this trouble? "Forgive me, Prince Kamal," she mumbled and bowed her head.

"For telling the truth?" said Kamal. "Perhaps if someone told me earlier that I was clueless, we'd have an ample harvest. Can you be more honest with me?"

From the corner of her eye, Lennie spied Petal clapping her hands with glee near the kitchen door. Honestly, Lennie never wanted to disappear more than at that second.

"Why do you look like this?" he said.

"I got caught in the rain ... and then ... your mother threw me out."

"She's doing the test now?" asked Kamal, standing close to her side.

Though she wouldn't confess it out loud, she was delighted how her breath evened out to match his and how she felt less cold. "It was very cruel," she said.

"Then I owe you a kindness. Can I offer you food and lodging for the night?"

Lennie hugged herself, though the warmth of her skin was overwhelming. She grew faint when she saw him stare at her mahogany neck for the first time. She felt guilty for noticing, caring, and trying to read his thoughts. "I'd rather have a job," she said, shirking away from him.

"My job?" guessed Kamal.

She cursed herself for the smile that crossed her face. "If I'm being honest, yes," said Lennie. "Despite your intellect, your crops are clearly in need of assistance."

"And how can you assist us if you leave?"

"Fair point."

"It's settled, then," said Kamal.

They walked through the fields, Lennie looking at him occasionally as they tramped through the lifeless plants. Kamal was as fair as Melba, but he reminded her of fresh honeysuckle, alluring and sweet.

"She doesn't usually look like that, Your Highness!" called Petal, waving at them with the basket in her other hand.

"That's my mother," sighed Lennie.

Kamal smiled. "I have two guest rooms."

"Well," said Lennie. "I'm sure she'll want to see both."

It was truly alarming when the potential brides beheld the much maligned "Princess of the Pea" in the dining room. Her borrowed clothing was impressive, what with the royal crest of two doves carrying a laurel wreath on her silk jacket. The suitresses were certain her new outfit was provided by the prince, who remained beside her as the trumpets signaled Queen Melba's arrival.

"Son!" cried Melba, going to kiss Kamal immediately. She eased back, squinting her eyes. "Oh dear, these freckles. Don't let the sun mar your face."

"Aspiring botanists don't worry about that, Mother," said Kamal.

Lennie straightened her jacket, still not used to the luxurious fabric or her teal gown's corseted waist. Tia's objectionable looks caused Lennie more discomfort. Oblivious, Petal kept stroking the taffeta gown with dramatic effect, even though Lennie mouthed for her to stop.

"There's two more places at the table," said Melba. She stilled when she noticed the crest and the lady bearing it.

"I've asked Carolinda and her mother to stay with us," said Kamal.

Melba glowered at the doves like they were two scorpions poised to sting her, then put on a pained smile. "I'm sure she jumped at the opportunity," said Melba. "But I'm afraid I've given each girl a room already."

"They'll stay in Father's former rooms," said Kamal.

"That's not what your father bequeathed them to you for," said Melba, patting his cheek. "Besides, you know what happens tonight."

All of the princesses and Lennie exchanged confused glances. With a smirk, Melba fondled the collar of Lennie's jacket. The hairs on Lennie's arms prickled.

"Fine, because it won't matter," said Melba. "Everyone, dinner is served."

Lennie exhaled when Melba slipped into the seat at the head of the table. Lennie marveled at the glass ceiling of the dining room, the crystal goblets, and the revolving chandeliers. Still, she was certain that, if she lived here, she'd tire of them after a while and would run outside to view the unending sky with its radiant sunlight instead.

"Kamal, you're next to me," said Melba.

He went to sit in his own gilded chair, grinning at Lennie before he lowered himself onto the velvet cushion. Melba addressed her head waiter, and Lennie was thankful for the reprieve. She situated herself between her mother and Desiray, who had changed into an indigo blossom-lined dress.

"Nice gown," whispered Lennie.

"I'm representing several kingdoms," said Desiray.

Tia maneuvered her embroidered sunflowers under the table while taking her spot next to Desiray.

"With their own symbolic flowers," added Tia. "Yes, lovely little Des' parents own most of Louisiana. That's why her family's so mixed."

Desiray crumpled her napkin. "Nobody cares, Tia."

"Is this what royal children really talk about?" whispered Petal to Lennie.

Lennie scratched her forehead while the waiters ferried in plates of cooked pheasants, jasmine rice, chard, and French rolls. The smoke rising from the plates and the scent of the food turned Lennie's stomach. She was almost relieved when no dish was set in front of her.

"Carolinda, was it?" said Tia. "I'm mystified you made it back after the teacup test."

Petal looked puzzled herself. With the prince's constant attention and the rush to get ready, Lennie had neglected to tell her ecstatic mother everything.

"Never fear," said Lennie. "Matrimony isn't my purpose." She ignored her mother's loud groan.

"Good," said Tia, fetching her goblet. "Because the queen's purpose is to have light-skinned grandchildren."

"Tia!" Desiray said.

"The queen was raised that way, Desiray," defended Tia after taking a sip. "Once you're raised that way, you don't change your ways."

Shifting in her seat, Lennie gave Kamal a long stare. He cut his roll in half and blushed under her scrutiny.

"It's sad you think that's true," said Desiray.

"I have to," said Tia with reddened cheeks. "My father's banking on it. A marriage would strengthen our country's army."

Lennie pushed her plate aside. "What if your child did come out dark?"

"Right," said Desiray. "There's no guarantee."

Tia stabbed her pheasant with her fork. "I'd pity my baby."

Lennie's head throbbed, and she made to rise until Petal placed a soft hand on her leg. Something in her mother's tender face, an expression she didn't often see, enticed her not to move. "Mother?" Lennie said.

"That crack about your ears?" whispered Petal. "Your ears … they're just fine."

While the silverware clattered, Lennie's fingers looped through Petal's fingers, and it was Lennie's turn to blush when Kamal witnessed the kind gesture and smiled.

"Ah, I do believe someone's been missed!" said Melba. She rang a bell that sat next to her plate.

The anxious head waiter streamed in with one more covered dish. He put it in front of Lennie, then flew from their sight.

"Do enjoy," said Melba.

Lennie uncovered the dish, revealing black-eyed peas in the shape of a *P*. It was silent enough in the dining room to hear Kamal's deep moan.

"Those are the last in the late king's stock," said Melba. "Figured you'd appreciate them more than anyone."

Lennie blinked at their black centers and turned toward

Melba. "I'm just happy your kitchen staff enjoyed every single one of mine," said Lennie, recovering her fork.

Melba started. "Pardon?"

"Oh, don't worry," said Lennie before eating. "There's more where that came from."

It came as an unexpected delight when Lennie found Kamal waiting for her outside his father's largest guest room. Melba dismissed the young ladies shortly after dessert, complaining of a headache, with a fair amount of the females knowing Lennie's last statement was the cause.

"You ate your sherbet fast," said Lennie, playing with the ruffles on her gown's waist.

"I wanted to see you before you retired to your room," said Kamal. "Commend you for your wit."

"Well, I thank you for your generosity."

"Father's rooms have remained unused for months," shared Kamal. "It'll be nice to hear footsteps in them again. Farewell, Carolinda."

"Lennie," she said, "after lentils."

Kamal cocked his head to the side.

"My father was a farmer, and we were often on the fields together," explained Lennie. "Peas and beans were his specialty."

"Mother won't let me spend too much time out there."

"That explains the charmless collard greens," teased Lennie.

"Go easy on us," said Kamal. "We are going through a famine, you know. Then the rain came suddenly today, and you showed up." His bright gaze bore into her, and Lennie stopped fidgeting with her dress.

Their encounter was cut short by a cleared throat. Tia presented a vellum volume to Kamal, nearly bumping Lennie with the wide book. "*One Hundred of Georgia's Best Arboretums*," said Tia, reading the title aloud. "I go through it every night."

Lennie found that hard to imagine, noting the book's pristine pages when Kamal flipped through it.

"You may have it now," said Tia.

"Thank you, Princess Tia," Kamal said.

"Has anyone ever told you your face is the color of goldenrod?" Tia said. "It's such a majestic flower. Even with those pesky dark-purple stems." Her smile elongated.

Lennie bit her tongue.

"I think stems are beautiful," said Kamal.

Lennie stared at the book, no longer able to focus on anything else.

"Can I escort you to your room?" asked Tia hurriedly, turning the prince in the other direction.

"I suppose," he said.

While it troubled Lennie to watch, she lifted her head to see them walk into another corridor, inches apart. The appearance of Petal and Desiray laughing together and coming toward her eased the pain.

"You need to try those peas with some bacon and pork," advised Petal. "That was my Lander's favorite. Going to bed, girls."

Petal pushed through the bedroom door next to Lennie's room. With a gentle touch, Lennie indicated that Desiray should follow her into the king's quarters. The two girls entered the magnificent space, with a gold four-post bed as its centerpiece. Lennie was amazed when she first came into the room, but she was more astonished that Desiray didn't seem too impressed.

"You don't have many mattresses," observed Desiray. "Just the one?"

"That's all I need," said Lennie. "Listen, I wanted to thank you for being nice to us—"

"You don't understand."

"Understand what?"

"This means you're not being considered!" said Desiray. "The rest of the princesses' beds have multiple mattresses. It's another test. We're not sure what it means."

"After this afternoon, I can live without any more tests," assured Lennie.

Desiray sat on Lennie's lone mattress, apparently no longer appalled by it. "The teacup test is more common than people think," she said. "They did this paper bag test when I was younger. I had to be a brighter color than the bag, or I wouldn't go to finishing school."

"What kind of person does that?"

Desiray shrugged. "My mother insisted."

Flanking her, Lennie flicked a loose and fake indigo petal off Desiray's shoulder. The dress' decorations were more fragile than Lennie figured. How could these women thrive like this, constantly evaluated, in less than hospitable conditions? Kamal's kindness seemed like an impossibility, and she doubted it would last in an environment like this.

"I'm leaving tomorrow," said Lennie. "Never mind that mattress test. I'm a gardener."

"That the prince gawks at," said Desiray with a giggle.

"He's not the least bit appealing," said Lennie, and the lie was sour in her mouth.

"Heh," said Desiray, looking Lennie up and down. "I didn't know you liked him *that* much."

It came as a stunning realization that Lennie was torn about her decision to depart the palace in the morning. The hour neared midnight, yet she tossed and turned amid the soft lavender sheets and pricy pillows. A blaze roared in the fireplace, so she elected to sit up and stare at the flames instead.

Several knocks sounded on her door. She hoped it wasn't Kamal since she was certain that would challenge her resolve to leave. Petal pattered into the dimly lit room.

"There's so much space in mine," lamented Petal. "It's lonely."

"Come sit with me," said Lennie.

They positioned themselves on the side of the bed, their feet against the carpeted floor.

"It's quiet as a church in the hallway," said Petal. "The guards were saying they thought a girl would be up by now."

"Desiray mentioned mattresses?" said Lennie.

"Yes, something about peas under a stack of forty." She elbowed her daughter. "Girl, this place is crazy."

Both of them laughed behind their hands. Lennie had a sweeter realization, that they hadn't done that in a while.

"So, you won't be destroyed if we go back to the farm tomorrow?" said Lennie. "If I don't marry the prince?"

"Wasn't 'til I got here that I saw what you'd be marrying into," said Petal.

"And?"

Petal wrapped an arm around Lennie, leaning in close. "I know I don't always say the right words," whispered Petal. "That I've got bad beliefs I've carried over the years. Don't know about the queen, but I'm gonna grow. Just you watch."

Lennie kissed her mother's tear-stained cheek. She didn't have an opportunity to respond because the door burst wide open. A dozen guards stomped through, Lennie speechless as they brought in mattress after mattress.

Melba, curls atop her head instead of a crown, came in and yawned loudly. "Apologies," said Melba. "You were a bit of an afterthought."

"My daughter's not an afterthought!" said Petal, shooting upright.

Lennie patted Petal's back soothingly before approaching Melba. "Let me make this easy for you," said Lennie. "I'm not interested in marrying Kamal."

"He is interested, and that's all I care about," said Melba.

"With all due respect ...," began Lennie, then she steeled herself. "No, you haven't shown me any respect, so why bother? You are not embarrassing me anymore. Get these mattresses out of here!"

"Dear, you've made my night," said Melba, beaming as she smoothed down her nightgown.

A series of groans escaped the guards' mouths, but they

removed the mattresses one by one. Lennie and Melba stared at each other silently with each of the guards' labored steps until the men were done.

"Kamal will be fine," said Melba. "I believe he thinks of you as an exotic flower. Fun to study for a while, but not likely to survive in new surroundings."

Lennie stepped forward. "I can survive anywhere."

Melba's nose twitched, but her fingers were firm when they took a round object from her nightgown pocket. The pea in her palm was fresh and green, perhaps the most familiar item Lennie had seen since the black-eyed peas on her plate.

"A princess' skin is supposed to be so delicate that she should be able to feel this through a stack of mattresses," said Melba. "It's the test that got me out of my swampy little village and into the king's arms."

"All of your tests are ridiculous," Lennie said.

"Are they?" asked Melba. "When you walked in here, you knew you weren't good enough. You said you didn't belong. When I held that cup up to your face, you didn't protest. You never argued that you were as beautiful as the next girl."

Stinging sensations went down Lennie's neck and arms. She wanted to blame the uncomfortably stiff waist of her nightgown, but the cause was really the lack of a comeback. "You shouldn't … you shouldn't make girls feel like this."

"Go back to your farm, and you won't feel like this at all."

Melba left a scent of honeysuckle after she shut the door. The perfume made Lennie think of Kamal momentarily, but Lennie had never hated the smell more.

It shouldn't be too startling that Petal chose to stay with Lennie for the remainder of that night. She stroked her daughter's hair as Lennie trembled against expensive blankets, until Petal's hands slowed, and she fell asleep first. Lennie's head hurt from crying, but she couldn't lie still any longer. Dawn was breaking through the windows, and she had a letter to pen.

Lennie tiptoed past the dozing guards who must've been waiting up for any sign of a pea-disturbed princess. She saw no evidence that a candidate passed the test, and she smiled, imagining the queen's expression when she heard. Lennie wagered she'd select Tia regardless, based on the previous test.

The other bedroom that belonged to the king was large but had more study materials. Bookshelves lined three of the walls, with the late king's bed near a balcony window. Lennie briefly wondered why the window was open while she hurried to the desk. She realized she didn't have much time to write Kamal a note before breakfast.

When she dipped the quill into the inkstand and started to write, a shadow fell upon her sloped shoulders. She glanced up at Kamal, who she deduced had been on the balcony a moment before.

"The guard told me your mother didn't come back to her room," said Kamal.

"We thank you for your hospitality," said Lennie, "but I'm afraid we can't stay."

Kamal scanned her face and askew clothing, clearly pleased. "You didn't sleep last night."

"Not for the reasons you're thinking," said Lennie, locking eyes with him. "There were no mattresses. No peas." His face fell, and she tried not to care. She could leave now that she'd thanked him in person, and she didn't want to discuss his mother's final words with him.

"I was hoping you were tired because you were reading over the contract I left in your room," said Kamal. "It's rather long, and a lifechanging decision."

"Contract?" said Lennie, moving from the desk.

"To be the lead gardener," said Kamal. "Today, I'm supposed to accompany Mother to each of the girls' rooms. They were to reveal the peas with Mother explaining the test. When we got to your room last, I thought the three of us could go over the contract."

"I didn't look," confessed Lennie.

"I left dessert early to put it on the desk in your room," added Kamal.

He may very well be kind, thought Lennie. *But his home isn't kind.* "I can't work here," she said. "This palace is too ... picky."

"Lennie, I promise you I've never approved of my mother's tests."

"It's not just that!" cried Lennie. "Her thoughts ... their thoughts ... are so ingrained in this kingdom."

Kamal reached for her hand, but Lennie recoiled from his touch.

"You know it, too," she said, "so why are you putting me through this?" Lennie rubbed her cheeks, smearing her palms with tears. If she hadn't fretted about the crop or fallen for his flattering speech, none of this would've happened. She wouldn't hate herself. She wouldn't be showing him how delicate she was on a morning he were to be pledged to someone else.

"Because you're ingrained in my heart already," answered Kamal. "I want to be your partner on any soil."

The breeziness of his words was comforting. He sounded as sincere as when he'd invited Petal and her to the palace. Lennie shook her head anyway, again and again.

"We'll plant any crop you want," said Kamal. "I'll give you free rein if you reign alongside me."

"The queen wouldn't allow me to be your queen," said Lennie.

"Didn't anyone tell you the final choice is mine?"

"Desiray mentioned it, I think," recalled Lennie.

"Well, believe her."

Lennie's hand brushed his chest, and he held it there. Their hands intertwined, like a blossom linked to a stem.

"I'm not sure about being a wife or mother," confessed Lennie. "But I am good with fixing dry soil."

"I'd like to dry these first." He lifted his fingers to wipe the wet trails from beneath her eyes.

A sudden cry of frustration echoed from the hallway. "All of them slept well?"

Kamal winced. "Mother spent a fortune on those mattresses."

It was the most amazing moment of the day when the infant princess took her memorable step in the bountiful black-eyed pea field. Of course, Lennie had walked the good green earth for decades, but not her mahogany-colored daughter. Nobody told Princess Ivy that rainbows didn't have brown in them, at least not yet. Her first step enchanted the citizens of Magnolia at the harvest festival, and Petal was the first one to swoop in when Ivy tumbled.

Kamal retrieved his wriggling offspring while Lennie read her latest note from Ivy's godmother.

"Desiray's in Spain until her coronation," said Lennie.

"She's become a great ambassador," Kamal said.

"Her parents are pleased, even without a ring on her finger."

"As long as you're still pleased with yours," said Kamal, planting his lips on her mouth.

Ivy let out a loud cry, which the citizens of Magnolia weren't so enchanted by.

"Yes, Ivy," cooed Lennie. "Parents can't have public displays of affection. You're embarrassed by us already, aren't you?" Lennie took Ivy into her arms and bent down to fetch a very small basket. "Let's go pick peas."

"And what am I supposed to do?" asked Kamal.

"Try out your new instruments. They came in from Japan."

"Perhaps I shall," said Kamal as he wistfully walked off.

The black-eyed peas stretched out for acres. Lennie grinned at the luscious legumes and healthy leaves. Each segmented row enthralled her. Bags of peas filled three palace pantries, just in case Kamal's almanac-based weather predictions weren't correct. Her expertise, and their teamwork, had done wonders.

"We do belong," whispered Lennie to Ivy.

From a distance, Lennie spied a sallow figure, creases on the face under the crown. Lennie stepped over two rows to reach Melba, the latter holding a boat ticket.

"I don't understand why you're going abroad," Lennie said.

Melba sniffled, though nothing poured from her eyes. "Well, I don't understand why you're here. You disrupted everything. Your skin's not the only thing that's dark. You're—"

"His wife," said Lennie. "And you're her grandmother." She slowly pressed Ivy into Melba's arms. Lennie's heart sank when Melba's nose wrinkled, not from a sniffle, but because of a scowl. Lennie was quick to take back her daughter. "Enjoy Europe, Your Majesty."

Melba failed to speak until she saw Kamal racing between rows, taking measurements in the moist dirt. Lennie grinned when he sneezed above the plants.

"Kamal's gotten so much sun," said Melba. "It looks good on him."

Lennie was about to agree, that her husband was darker and lovely, but Melba was gone before Lennie could say it. She watched her mother-in-law move stoically through the fields until she faded from view.

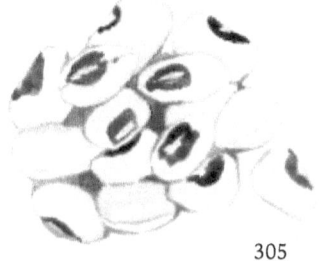

𝔓𝔦𝔭𝔢 𝔇𝔯𝔢𝔞𝔪𝔰

A RETELLING OF THE PIED PIPER OF HAMELIN
ASIA NICHOLS

apa was an exterminator. Correction: Not just *an* exterminator, but the best goddamn exterminator I ever saw in all my eleven years of living. Every morning, he left for work with his pipe, and he be gone all day, ridding Bay Area inner cities of annoying, sometimes-terrifying vermin. Papa called these jobs "hits," and hits were short and quick. Didn't nobody work harder than him. He worked so hard that a lot of times his pipe got really hot, pressed against his mouth, and that's why his lips, tongue, and fingers stayed cracked and blistered.

It wasn't special-looking or nothing, his pipe. It was four inches long and made of all glass. But it was made of all magic, too. The kind of magic that made people's problems disappear, and that's why Papa never let it out of his sight. That's why Papa loved his pipe more than he loved me.

He never let me play the pipe. I was his cook.

"Not everybody's cut out for cooking," Papa would say. "But you, baby girl, you got talent!"

And for a while, I was cool with cooking. But there comes a time in every girl's life when she needs something more meaningful. I was a big girl, and big girls need big jobs. I wanted to go with Papa on a hit. I wanted my turn to play the pipe. Problem was, Papa shared his pipe with no one. He said it was like sharing his own name.

"And all a man's got is his name," he'd say. "Without a name, he ain't worth a rat's ass!"

The Piper. That's what customers called him. Not only was his service top-notch, but it was the cheapest in the streets. Plus, it came with entertainment: pesticide-infused pipe music. See, I cooked the magic pesticides, but Papa said the "music" part was what got folks coming out the pockets because nobody was doing that but him, which made my job pretty unimportant, no matter how he tried to hype me up.

Anyway, I knew I needed to come correct when I propositioned him about his pipe. Or else he'd say I was being a pest and that I'd better shut up quick before I started to look like one. And then he'd have to exterminate me.

My chance came one night when Papa came home humming to himself. Papa was always happy after a hit, and that lasted anywhere from five to fifteen minutes before he got real weird and down on himself and sometimes on me, too, like I did something to let him down. But this time was different. Twenty minutes and counting, and he was still grinning and skinning. This was the night Papa said he got himself a hit in Marin County.

"Better see to that boil before it gets away from you," Papa said.

He had just come home and dropped a bag filled with food from a local Christian center, a few boxes of baking soda, and Chore Boys (the little round scrubber for super-dirty dishes) onto our kitchen table.

At this point, I might should mention the "home" wasn't exactly ours. It wasn't nobody's, really. More like it belonged to the public (in this case, the public of American Canyon). We'd find houses like this all the time. Not always in perfect condition —in this one, used rubbers littered the living room carpet, and the hallway toilet was overflowing with shit that had run out onto the floor because the water got shut off, but whoever was here before kept using it anyway. So, you see, I had to do some cleaning, but when something's free you can't really complain.

"Better cut down that burner, girl!" Papa said. "Just, go on, get it off the stove!"

"I know, I know." I got it off the stove.

He checked it. It was always the same. "What we calling this batch, anyway?" he said, settling in.

"I dunno," I said. "Can't we just call it magic pesticide? I'm tired of thinking of names."

"Don't nobody care what you tired of doing. We each got jobs to do—you ain't got to like yours, but you still got to get it done. We can stick with Killer High Note—that one's got musical style! Now, cheer up! I don't need you ruining my good mood."

"What you in such a good mood for, Papa?"

"Because they got rats in Marin, baby girl! Big, fat suburban rats!" he said.

"Ain't there a ton of places with rats?" I said. "What's so big about Marin?"

Papa reclined comfortably in the beat-up kitchen chair. "How about you stop asking questions and get to cooking, then I *might* just tell you what's so big about Marin."

With a spoon, I stirred the mixture of water, magic pesticide, and baking soda because baking soda's good for everything: cooking and cleaning and even toothpaste.

Papa said it started out as a leafy green plant, the magic pesticide, but by the time it got to me, it never did look like one. He'd get the plant from what's called a source (translation: sorcerer). First, he'd call up a man in Benicia who'd get it from another man in San Mateo who'd take a trip all the way down to Mexico to get it from a magic-sorcerer-man out there.

After going through all those hands, the magic would get to me practically dust. Like harmless, white-powered candy. But it's definitely *not* candy. It's seriously powerful extermination stuff. That's why it's got to be watered down some. Makes it last longer, too.

Finally, when the mixture finished boiling, I followed the steps from A to D.

A) Let it **air** off;

B) separate out hard **bits**;

C) **chop** them into tiny rocks and—voila!—magic pesticide was

D) pretty much **done**.

I knew Papa wouldn't give me the 411 about Marin until he was good and ready, so I kept up our daily routine and tried hard not to open my mouth about it.

Me and Papa then sat and bagged magic pesticide together, and this was our story time. Papa liked to boast about his greatest hits, aka all the extermination adventures he had *before*. And on this night, he was boasting up a storm. He boasted about the time he drowned a hundred million locusts in the Red Sea for a Hebrew god in the Middle East. You'd think working for a god's got benefits and that we'd be sitting pretty by now. But gods don't like giving credit where credit's due. That's why Christian centers be steady giving away stuff for free, to make up for God's fuckups. That's what Papa told me. That's why we never bothered with church.

He went on about the time he stopped three thousand drunken baboons from stealing food and stripping the thatched roofs off houses in the Groot Constania suburb of Capetown. Then there was the bazillion black birds that blotted out the skies every winter for the folks of La Grange, Kentucky. And how Kentuckians walked around with umbrellas to avoid getting shat on, and how a whole lot of them had the pinkeye.

"But the Asian Carp was the baddest bitch of them all!" said Papa. "Those flying fish shoot themselves out of the Mississippi River and directly at you. And they only ever did it when a boater came around. About a hundred pounds, they were, and could fly at least ten feet!"

Still waiting on Marin, I played along, although I'd heard these tales a thousand times. "So, what did you do, Papa?" I said. "I know you can't drown no fish."

"What did I do? Shiiit, I built a big barbecue pit on the shore, and when I played my pipe, they flung their fishy bodies right into the flames! Whole town ate carp for days!"

"Well, why you studying Marin so hard? You've been to so many places already?"

"Damn, baby girl, you got to pick up a paper," he said. "Educate yourself."

Maybe I could. If I wasn't always cooped up. Always cleaning and cooking.

"A hit like Marin is huge!" he said. "It'll pay me a fortune, put me back on the map!"

You see, in the mid-1980s, about the same time I came along, Papa got what's called a prior: where California policemen locked exterminators like him in giant cages for three years to teach them a lesson about carrying magic-pesticide. They claimed magic-pesticide was dangerous to people, too. (Not mine, though. Papa said the way I make mine is the most safest way there is.) Anyway, Papa didn't really like to talk about that time. Just that getting caged up set him back in a big way. Made the Bay Area forget who he was. Sometimes he'd forget who he was, too—I could tell. Sometimes he'd try to sneak magic pesticide into his pipe when he wasn't working, and I'd have to catch him.

"I'm through with these street-level jobs," he went on. "Your papa's about to be doing big things again. Real big things!"

California opened more cages since he was in one, so if you got a prior like Papa and get caught exterminating again, they'd put you in a cage forever. That's why Papa had to exterminate real secret-like, always looking over his shoulder, which made it harder for him to get ahead. And here's where I saw my chance.

"Papa?" I stood and straightened myself. "I'm a big girl, but so far I've done nothing but wait on you all day and cook, and I don't feel like that's contributing very much. What I'm trying to say is—" I took a deep, slow breath, "—I want my turn to play the pipe, please."

There was a long pause. Papa jammed another magic-pesticide rock in a bag. "I can't have my cook dirtying up her hands with my kind of work."

"But if you just let me try—"

"What did I say?"

"But Papa, I promise you, I swear—"

Suddenly, Papa gripped his chest like I had just put a curse on him. "Holy mother of— Look at you! Look at that fur growing on your face, and whiskers!"

I watched him carry on as he raised his pipe, pretending he was about to exterminate me.

"Listen," he said. "I don't need no giant pest to look after. A kid is okay, but not a pest."

"Okay, maybe I don't need to play *your* pipe," I said. I figured I'd already came this far. "But maybe I can get my own. I could be your helper. I'm just saying, if Marin got rats that big, then they need a lot of pesticide, right? Which means there's probably policemen, too, just waiting to catch you exterminating again, so they can lock you in a cage forever and—"

"I ain't getting caught," he said sharply. "So you can tone that shit right down."

Papa didn't say nothing after that, just glared at me. But I could tell he was thinking. So, I warmed up some of that charity food—two cans of Spaghetti Os—and put a bowl of that in his hands to help him out. A man can't think right on a empty stomach—that's what one of Papa's girlfriends used to say. She was not lying. Papa ate and about six minutes later …

"Stop staring and get some shuteye," he said. "Got yourself a long day tomorrow."

He didn't have to tell me twice. Without any food but not even hungry, I shot off to my pallet on the floor and got under the blanket. Except I couldn't sleep. Instead, I wondered all night what tomorrow might bring.

Now, Marin County was where all the filthy-rich white folks lived, but he only needed to focus on the one house we was going to, and let his business spread by word of mouth that way. When Papa broke it down for me, how filthy rich Marin was, I found it hard to believe a place like Marin even had rats.

"Hell, places like Marin's where rats get to feast!" Papa was stuffing a little pinch of Chore Boy down the pipe to keep the magic pesticide in the glass from touching his mouth. Getting ready for action. "Think about it, they eat steak, ribs, and scrimps all day. Can't nobody tell a rat like that nothing. And a rat like that for damn sure ain't skipping town. Not unless you get the best goddamn exterminator ever!"

"Exterminators," I said proudly. "You forgot the *s*. We're a family business now, remember?" I couldn't believe it—I was going with Papa for my first big hit!

Papa frowned. "Don't go bunching up your panties."

He made it clear that it wasn't my little speech that convinced him. Whatever. But it did get him to thinking about his new customer's location.

"Them some entitled knuckleheads up in the Marin," he said with a turned-up face. "Probably walk around in fur coats and shit."

I studied Papa's coat. It was falling apart by the left pocket. I'd have to hem that up.

"Probably think they can play me, too."

You see, it had occurred to Papa that the knuckleheads of Marin might try to rip him off. No, they weren't violent people, but they were used to getting what they wanted. And they could easily *want* to not pay Papa for his service and call the cops on him if he had a problem with it.

"Like in Hamelin?" I said.

"*Exactly* like that," he said.

Hamelin was one of Papa's *before* stories. When Hamelin's town mayor ripped him off, Papa went back and took care of it. When I asked him how, he just smirked, 'Let's just say the playgrounds was real quiet for a while.' He said he didn't want to have to break nobody's knees in Marin should they get all Hamelin-like on him. And he wouldn't have to.

"That's where you come in," he said.

He knelt down and picked through items in his bag, and I rubbed my hands together, thinking—this was it!—I was getting my exterminating gear. Thinking, after this, we'd be tight as a tick, him and me. What Papa pulled from that bag was no pipe, but a frilly pink cloth.

"Here," he flung it at me. "Put this on."

He told me the dress belonged to my mama. I always forget to mention her.

Mama ran away when I was four, so the story goes. See, while Papa was in the cage, she got behind on rent and lost control of herself and started tricking, meaning she made people appear and disappear for money like a magician. Once, she tried to make me disappear, too, and felt bad about it and told Papa when he called from the cage, and he cussed her out, and that's when Mama ran away. Left me with a friend. At the time, I was young, so most of her was a blur (sorry, I don't have adventures like Papa to tell), but I did remember Mama liked little clothes. So I wasn't surprised the dress fit.

"It's ugly, Papa."

"Come on out," he said. "Let me get a look at you."

I crept out from behind the wall so Papa could see me. I must have looked a hot mess, with my roughed-up knees, bare shoulders, and raggedy open-toe sandals. He walked over and hand-combed my Brillo hair. Then he licked his fingers and slicked down my eyebrows, too.

"You look like a girl."

"If you say so."

Satisfied with my looks, Papa instructed me on what I would do in the dress. "Now, once we get to Marin, all you got to do is stand back and let the people see you. But don't say a word! Don't you get to talking too much and telling all my business. Just nod your head and smile real polite, y'hear?"

According to Papa, my fancy looks should have these rich

people eating out the palm of my hand, which should reduce the chances of him getting played. That is to say, my being there would make them see him as a real person, not just an exterminator from the gutter.

Okay, so I didn't get my pipe. I should've tried harder, I know. But I got to thinking, maybe if I did a perfect job in Marin, Papa would let me move up in the ranks.

We caught a bunch of buses and ferries and got to Marin at the crack of dawn. The county itself felt unreal, like a place apart from the rest of the Bay Area. Rolling hills, cattle ranches, houseboats, roadhouses, and those great big old redwoods. There was no noise anywhere, except for one rat I saw scurrying across a cable line. Or was it a squirrel? The house we were going to stood alone, giant and gated, half-hidden behind a cluster of trees. Papa nodded at me and, at the same time, we straightened ourselves up. Then he rang a bell on the gates.

"Who is it?" said the waking voice of somebody inside.

"It is I, Mr. Piper, and for a certain sum, I'll rid your city of rats, leaving not-a-one!" Papa winked at me, then whispered, "You got to get poetic with rich folk."

"Who the fuck is this?" said the voice.

"Just open the door, man!" said Papa.

"Thank God!" said a woman's voice. "You're like a fucking savior!"

At once, the gates creaked open, and me and Papa went on inside. A narrow path from the gates to the front door cut across a lawn half the size of a football field. There were tables and chairs and colorful balloons all over, like somebody had a party. But people left whole pieces of food on their plates, so I figure the meal wasn't that good. As I studied the scene, I saw something running across the roof. Papa saw it, too. A white frecklefaced man opened the door.

"What's up, man," he said, and shook Papa's hand.

"Hey, I got my girl with me, so—"

"Oh, how cute!" A white girl poked her head out the door. "Come on in!"

We stepped inside the house. Immediately, I noticed there was a fur carpet on the floor in front of a furnace and, above that, the head of a deer with antlers mounted to the wall. A wall that seemed to go up and up and up and never end. But the house smelled bad, too.

"Let's just do this," said Papa. He turned to me. "You stay out here. I'll be right back."

Then he followed freckle-face into a back room. Soon as the door closed, the white girl from before rushed up to shake my hand. She had to be about ten years older than me.

"Hi, I'm Kate," she said. "What's your name?" She was all teeth and blond hair and wearing a paper crown.

I smiled, real polite.

"Don't you have a name?"

I wasn't saying nothing.

"Well, it's really nice meeting," She took my hand and headed for the kitchen. "Come on in here, and relax with us." She led me into the kitchen where another girl was pulling a tray out of the oven. "That's my friend, Ree."

"Hi," said Ree.

I waved. The kitchen was ten times better than in any public house we'd ever found.

"Would you like some brownies?" said Ree.

"Secret recipe," giggled another girl, who I didn't see sprawled out on the floor. "You got to taste it and try to guess."

"It's made with cocoa powder, rum-soaked raisins, vanilla. ..."

Ree kept on naming ingredients while she cut four pieces and laid them out separately. On one she put whipped cream, strawberries, and crushed walnuts. On the second, she put whipped cream, peaches, blueberries, and crushed walnuts, then jammed a candle in it. She handed that one to Kate. On the third, only strawberries and blueberries and slid it in the direction of the girl on the floor. Then she looked at me.

"Are you allergic to nuts?"

I didn't think so. I shook my head. She gave me the works. I lifted my cut of brownie to examine it as Ree lit the candle on Kate's brownie and personalized the happy birthday song:

Happy birthday to you,
Our friendship is true.
Happy birthday, dear sweet Katie.
Psst, your boyfriend I blew!

"Any many mooore!" said the girl on the floor.

Katie playfully shoved Ree, then they hugged for a long time, and fed each other brownies. White girls were so weird, I thought, as I put a big piece of my own brownie into my mouth.

"Daaaaamn girl," said Ree. "Slow down."

I waited and waited for Papa, wishing he'd hurry the hell up. But something wasn't right because, every now and then, I kept hearing Ree say: *damn girl, slow down.* She kept saying that to me, but I had long since finished eating.

Crazy thing was, Ree had been saying that very same thing for the past eight minutes! Like she was a broken talking doll or something. But what really shook me was, when I went to tell her to shut up, she wasn't even talking. Nobody was talking. That's when I realized something else strange: Whenever I looked at Ree, she just stood there leaning against the counter, nibbling, not talking. Whenever I looked at Kate, she just gleamed her teeth at me, nibbling, not talking. My legs were numb, but somehow I miraculously walked across the kitchen, stepping over the sprawled-out girl, to the stove and stared down at the shiny silver baking tray.

"What kind of crazy brownie is this?" I said.

"Take a big breath, girlie. It'll wear off."

"*What* will wear off?"

"Kate?" said Ree.

"Yeah."

"I'm like soooo seriously fucked up right now."

"Yeah."

"*What* will wear off?" I said again, though I wasn't really sure how many times I'd said it. I really hoped it wasn't as many times as Ree's damn-girl-slow-down, which was somehow still playing in my head like background music.

Curled into a ball, I waited and waited for Papa, wishing he'd hurry the hell up. Because, every now and then, I swore I heard Kate squeak or saw the girl on the floor scurry around the room on all fours searching for her brownie, which Kate or Ree or me had probably eaten. And *that's* what really tripped me out.

Behind me, a door opened and out came Papa and freckle-face, all buddy-buddy. That must've meant the man paid him up front, and that was good. *Now could we go?* No, he had to exterminate first. Right. I couldn't make out what he was saying, exactly, but I knew enough about his business to fill in the blanks. Papa took out his pipe and put it to his mouth—good!—so he was about to play the Killer High Note I made him.

Suddenly, all around me, there was a gentle rumbling sound that grew louder and louder. The cabinets shook, the ground beneath me quivered. With all the noise on the rooftop, you'd think it was a blizzard outside. Hundreds (if not thousands!) of rats, it must have been. Probably running every which way. Clumped together like that hairy gray carpet out in the living room. I looked over at Papa, excited to see the whole extermination process for the first time:

So, Papa played the pipe from *inside* the house. I didn't know he did that. But how come I didn't hear any music? Ah, must've worked like a dog whistle.

Then, I wondered if he was trying to be too fancy for these Marin folks because his entire head started to get all smoky like he'd lit his lips on fire. Like nothing I'd ever seen. *Easy, Papa, be easy.* I looked around to see if there was anything I could do to help with the actual exterminating part. I grabbed one of the bronze pots rattling on the rack that hung above the kitchen island.

"What is she doing?" said Ree.

"Hey, are you planning to cook something?" said Kate.

No, I was planning to pop as many rats as I could with this pan until I heard a crunch and they stopped moving—now, where *were* they?

"I like gumbo," said Kate. "Can you make gumbo?"

"Can you cook gumbo for Kate's birthday?" said Ree.

"No." I was climbing up on the counter to check cabinets. "I didn't come here to cook."

"Oh, but could you?" said Kate, pulling on my dress. "That would be super!"

"Stop touching me," I said. "Look, me and Papa are gonna take care of all your rats, then we'll be out of your hair."

"Rats?" said Ree.

"Did she say rats?" said the girl on the floor.

Kate shuddered. "Eek, I hate rats!"

"Norwegian rats, roof rats …" coming from the floor. "That's pretty much all we've got out here in paradise. Most of the time they keep to themselves."

"Oh my god, no they don't!" said Kate. "Me and mom found a rat in the garage the other day, hiding by the sedan. We called Orkin. Zapped that disgusting little fucker real quick."

"That's how you send a message," said Ree.

I was so confused.

"Ugh, you guys are so inhumane," said the girl on the floor.

"Rats are not humans, my dear," said Kate. "They are pests."

Then I was angry. "What are you are talking about?" I said. "My papa's the exterminator! He's out there right now exterminating your rats!"

"Oh, sweetie," said Ree. "Is that what you think?"

Kate put her hand to her mouth. "Oh my god, she does."

The girl on the floor sat up. "We have to tell her."

"Tell me what?"

"You tell her, Kate," said Ree.

"I said tell me *what*?" I searched their faces for answers.

"I want absolutely nothing to do with this," said Kate, walking away.

The other girls looked at each other, then at me.

"Your dad sells us drugs," blurted the girl on the floor.

"What?"

"He's in the other room getting high right now." As the girl lay back down, she added, "There, my good deed is done."

The noise stopped. The shaking stopped. It was like everything—all the people in the world, or just this house—fell quiet and still while I thought deeply about what I just heard. Why is it the one story that matters is the story nobody likes telling? The crazy part is, I knew, like, deep down in my bones of bones. I felt my eyes welling up. I wasn't gonna cry, though. I ran out the kitchen.

"Daaamn, girl," said Ree once again. "Slow down."

I stumbled out into the living room to confront Papa, who was lying on a stupid rug. The confrontation went something like this:

"You're in here getting high!"

"What's gotten into you?"

"There are no rats!"

"Yes, there was," said Papa. "I got rid of them, didn't I?"

Nameless, faceless people around the room chuckled.

"There is no such thing as magic pesticide. That pipe don't exterminate nothing!"

"Sure, it does." He twisted it around. "All I got to do is blow it until it catch."

More chuckles.

"You lied to me!"

He narrowed his eyes. "You need to tone that shit down."

I socked him in his shoulder. Hard.

He yanked me outside. "Look, baby girl, this ain't the time or place for—"

"Don't call me baby girl. Call me by my name." I shook my head. "You know, what? Doesn't matter what you call me." I ran out into the nice, clean streets of Marin.

Papa called after me, "Where the hell you think you're going?"

Where was I going? Couldn't tell you. What I did know was Papa didn't go to Kentucky or Capetown. Papa wasn't nobody's exterminator. Papa was a goddamn junkie! That man was getting high. Point blank. And I was helping him do it. How stupid could a girl be? How could I let Papa jerk me around all this time? Was any of it true? I didn't know. Didn't care. I was done. Eleven years of my life I was Papa's little fool, letting him use me up, hit by hit. That man wasn't playing the pipe. He was playing me! His own flesh and blood. But I was done being his cook, done being his partner, done being his daughter.

I was a big girl, and big girls don't get played.

I didn't know where I was going, to tell the truth. But I kept running until I saw signs for the 101, and I stood there on the side of the highway in my stupid little dress and stuck out my thumb to all the fancy cars passing me by. I didn't care where I was going, but I was gonna get out of there, out of the land of magic pipes and make-believe. To go somewhere real.

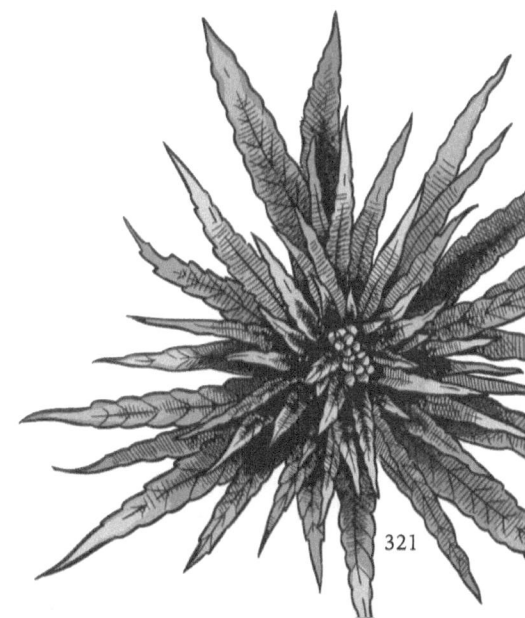

The Ruby Necklace

A RETELLING OF THE GOOSE GIRL
ANGELICA ESQUIVEL

nce upon a time, there was a nanny named Bonita. The family she worked for—a blond, blue-eyed couple and their blond, blue-eyed baby—invited her to join them on a trip to Cozumel, Mexico, so she could take care of the baby and guide them around. Bonita had never been to Mexico before, but she agreed to go because she needed the money and wanted to see Chichén Itzá, an old city containing a pyramid called El Castillo. She had only seen it in pictures and books. It was built by her ancestors, the Maya, a people she knew so little about.

Shortly after arriving at the resort, the couple left the baby with Bonita and went to drink by the pool. Zurie, the baby's mother, stopped on her way out the door to inform Bonita that there was a written list of every piece of jewelry Zurie brought with her, and it would be noticed if anything were missing. She also reminded Bonita to put sunscreen on the baby if they went outside. Bonita nodded mutely. She often pretended that she couldn't speak English to avoid a confrontation with Zurie. Bonita, however, had already looked in Zurie's jewelry box and had found nothing but bland pearl earrings. She wondered if these pearls were the kind slaves dived for, their blood staining the rocks along the sea.

Bonita was really curious about the smaller jewelry box Zurie kept with her at all times—it was identical to the large one: wooden and white, with ornate floral designs carved into the lid —but Zurie guarded this one obsessively. Bonita wasn't a thief, but she was determined to discover what Zurie had hidden inside the small jewelry box.

The next day, the four of them took a bus to Chichén Itzá. It was a long, bumpy ride. Bonita passed the time by looking out the window with the baby, pointing out greenery and goats and cows. Zurie passed the time by complaining about the malfunctioning air conditioner, about the likelihood of her getting food poisoning from eating local food, about how her husband didn't pay attention to her anymore.

She fell silent only when they reached Chichén Itzá. The city had seemed much smaller in pictures, but now El Castillo, the main attraction, loomed over Zurie like a Mayan warrior, eager to slice her heart out and sacrifice it to the gods. Bonita felt it, too, the ripple of angry energy. It was still rather than frantic, meted itself out methodically, steady in its pursuit of justice. The peak of the pyramid cut into the clouds, and Bonita's heart raced.

They climbed and were not even halfway up when Zurie started in again. "Bonita? I need some water."

Bonita noticed an unfamiliar glint across Zurie's neck. A ruby necklace. The jewel was tear-shaped and so shiny it seemed wet. Bonita was enchanted by the necklace, correctly assuming that it was what Zurie kept in the small jewelry box. Upon hearing Zurie's complaints, Bonita snapped back to duty and dug through the baby's diaper bag, looking for a bottle of water she was sure she'd packed.

"I'm thirsty!" Zurie said.

The husband took the baby from Bonita so she could search for the water. Zurie coughed, acting like she'd been without water for days rather than for one hour. She held her hand to her throat. She tumbled near the edge of a step, and there was a slinking sound as the ruby necklace fell from her throat and down the side of the ruins, clunking along the weathered stone.

"My necklace!" she screamed.

Her husband took the diaper bag from Bonita, who made her way down the side of El Castillo to retrieve the necklace.

"I don't want her to get it! You go instead. Here, give me the baby," Zurie commanded her husband.

Both Bonita and the husband ignored Zurie. The sun was too warm, the day was too long for her never-ending demands.

Bonita grumbled to herself and wiped sweat from her face as she walked back down the pyramid to find the necklace. She found it quickly—it was an ostentatious thing—and moved to put it in her pocket when she realized that her dress didn't have any. She decided to wear the necklace so her hands would be free for the climb. She heard a gasp from above as she clasped it around her neck. The necklace seized her, tightening along her collarbone, and Bonita was finally able to understand how Zurie had made it this far in life—white magic. Bonita touched the ruby and whispered quietly in a language she didn't know she knew, a language she had never heard before. She returned to the top of El Castillo.

Zurie stood defiantly with her husband, who still held the baby. "Give it back to me!" she said, looking as though she wanted to reach for the necklace but was too afraid.

"Alas, alas, if your husband knew, his loving heart would break in two," Bonita replied. In a wink of red light, she had traded places with Zurie.

Zurie looked down at herself, her tattered thrift-shop dress and stained sneakers. "What have you done?" she wailed. Her blond hair had darkened, her clothes had become worn. She desperately clutched at the tattered fabric.

Bonita grinned, her smile gleaming pearl-white. Zurie turned to her husband, but both the baby and he appeared to be frozen in time. Bonita walked over to them, removed the baby from his arms, and handed it to Zurie.

"You're the nanny now," Bonita said, "and if you tell anyone about this, I'll kill you." Then she murmured something to the necklace.

Zurie's eyes widened as she heard the necklace do something it had never done before: it whispered back.

A sigh of a voice, barely imperceptible, floated around Bonita. "It will know if you tell anyone. We'll both know. ¿Comprende?"

Zurie gave a weak nod.

Bonita placed her hand over the ruby pendant, and Zurie's husband and baby became animated once again.

Zurie thought her husband might recognize her, even if she did look like Bonita, but he didn't. He simply dumped the diaper bag on the ground next to her, expecting her to carry it, as well as a few souvenirs he had purchased for his parents—a ceramic lizard that was covered in a rainbow of swirls and spots, a pair of sugar-skull salt and pepper shakers. Even though she tried multiple times to catch her husband's eye, it was as though Zurie had become invisible. Her arms ached, and she longed to call out to him, but each time she was about to speak, Bonita would turn around, letting her newly blond hair fall in a curtain across her face, and narrow her eyes at Zurie.

Bonita enjoyed her new position. She ordered Zurie to fetch them water and complained that it was not cold enough. She next told Zurie to change the baby's diaper because the water probably made the baby soil it. When Zurie returned from the restrooms with the baby, Bonita scolded her for putting the diaper on too tightly. Zurie was able to hold back her anger until Bonita commanded her to take pictures of her with the baby and Zurie's husband, posing in front of various temples.

As Zurie tapped the red circle on her husband's phone, her eyes burned with hot tears. He had his arm wrapped around Bonita's waist. He looked at her adoringly, completely unaware that she was not the same person he had married. Or maybe he was aware, on some level—Zurie couldn't remember the last time he'd looked at her that way. She held the phone in front of her eyes so Bonita wouldn't be able to see her cry. She didn't want Bonita to see how easily she'd been broken.

Zurie finally got the opportunity to speak privately with her husband when they reached the resort. Bonita fell asleep quickly in the king-sized bed in the master suite, her hand wrapped around the ruby necklace to prevent Zurie from taking it.

Zurie's husband woke in the middle of the night and walked to the balcony to sneak a cigarette. Zurie startled him when she slid open the glass door and stepped outside.

"Can I bum one?" she asked, her eyes swollen and nose rosy from crying in her room.

"I thought you didn't smoke," he replied, handing her the pack. He cupped his hand around the cigarette as he lit it for her.

"I don't. Unless I'm stressed out." Zurie took a long drag and felt her chest tighten. She held her breath to avoid coughing.

"Being back in Mexico, that must be strange for you," he said, resting his elbows on the railing. Zurie noticed that his cheeks and the bridge of his nose were sunburned. She was still observing him from this new perspective, that of his not-wife, when he suddenly turned his attention to her. "Can I ask you to do me a favor, Bonita?"

"Well, that depends what it is." Zurie gulped. What kind of favors would her husband need to ask of Bonita?

"Can you tell me a story? It'll help me sleep better." He sat on one of the tan lounge chairs and looked at her expectantly. His cigarette was reaching its end.

Zurie opened her mouth to tell him about everything—the magic necklace, Bonita stealing her identity—before she remembered that she was forbidden from telling anyone. If she told another person, the necklace would tell Bonita, and Bonita would kill her. "I have a story," Zurie began, "but I promised I wouldn't tell it to anyone."

"Well, why don't you tell it to this potted plant? If someone happens to overhear, you can't help that, can you?" he said.

Zurie grinned. Her husband had always been clever. She could trust him to get her out of this. "Okay."

Zurie told the potted plant about the ruby necklace, which she had inherited from her grandmother who had inherited it from hers. Zurie said how she used the ruby's powers to get what she wanted, including her husband. She admitted that she hadn't been the best person, hadn't made the most moral decisions, but that didn't mean she deserved to have her necklace, her powers, and her identity stolen from her. As she finished her story, Zurie wept. Her husband came and put his arm around her. She leaned into him, inhaling the familiar, musky scent of his cologne, and some of her worry dissipated.

"We'll punish her for this. What do you think we should do?" he asked.

Zurie considered how to exact her revenge. "Let's abandon her here in Mexico. We'll take her documents, so she can't get back to the States," Zurie said.

"You don't think that's a bit drastic?"

"Oh, she'll be fine. She'll fit right in here," Zurie said, snickering to herself. Bonita was going to regret messing with her family.

"All right. Let me gather her documents, and we can leave in the morning. Just you, me, and the baby." Her husband gave her a quick peck on the forehead and patted her hair reassuringly, then went back to the master suite to gather their things.

"Just you, me, and the baby," Zurie repeated, letting the scarlet glow of her cigarette burn out on its own.

In the morning, Zurie woke alone in bed. She glanced at the clock: 11 a.m. The suite was eerily quiet. She thought that perhaps everyone had gone to the pool, but when she looked out over the balcony, they weren't there.

They weren't there. Zurie felt her heart leap, landing on the floor, where she saw it beat without a body. She bloomed. Her sweaty skin was florid and shining: garnets, rubies. Her vision tunneled into a red blur as though she had looked directly into the sun with her eyes closed, just to see the heat glowing through her lids. There was no one in the suite. All their suitcases were gone. Zurie was too shocked to do anything other than sit on the balcony, staring toward the water. He hadn't even left her a note.

She imagined this morning: her husband shaking Bonita awake, thinking it was Zurie. Him telling Bonita that the nanny was crazy, the two of them making fun of her. Them sneaking out, hand in hand, Zurie's baby on Bonita's hip, her necklace on Bonita's throat.

Zurie's hand shook. She gripped the balcony railing, anchoring herself, and knew: her husband and Bonita had laughed, their white teeth and skin reflecting the light, as they closed the front door behind them. As they abandoned Zurie without documents in a land that did not want her, a land she did not want.

Stronger Together

A RETELLING OF THE ANT & THE GRASSHOPPER
AZIZA SPHINX

e don't talk much about the first night that fire fell from the sky. Most perished, not expecting the collapse of everything around them. Those of us who saw the signs, who listened to the warnings, prepared. We gathered what we needed, meditated on the truth to come while stocking and sealing our refuge. Then we watched. And waited. For months, we carried on daily tasks, ever planning the escape to safety when the high-pitched sirens blared their song of the end.

I sat up in bed, the soft light of the levitating moon lamp in the corner casting an eerie orange glow over the sleeping faces of my family. My two sons and daughter, none more than the age of twelve, curled beneath my grandmother's handmade quilt. The buckwheat mattresses beneath them were designed to deter insect infestations inside the bunker. We carefully guarded our food supply against invasive intruders, unconvinced that what remained topside would support crop growth any time soon.

Vacating my bed, I followed the clanking of dishes past the two other bedrooms to the cordoned-off section we used as a kitchen. My wife hovered over a lone electric heating element, stirring a pot of what smelled like oatmeal with cinnamon and nutmeg. I smiled as she dropped in a handful of golden raisins, our treat for the day.

She kept a stash of items. Every other week she pulled from said stash, garnishing a meal with grated truffles or adding a sliced Twinkie as dessert. She did what she could to keep morale up, doting on the children, encouraging them to cover the walls with rainbows and sunshine, smiling faces and furry critters, the things left behind when the sky fell. We staved off cabin fever with photos of the outside. Of how we remembered it.

"Good morning, Ant," she said in that velvety voice that made the troubles of the world fade away.

Like with the others, formal names fell by the wayside in the confines of the bunker. The two other families who shared the space were appreciative of the sense of community that strengthened among us each day.

My arms slid around my wife's waist, her attention still focused on stirring breakfast, though she offered a shimmy of full hips into the comforts of my hold. "Morning, Fati," I said.

"You're going topside today, aren't you?"

The sadness in her tone cut deep. I understood her fear. The men decided it was best for us to take shifts, two at a time, once a week as necessary, to the top. We spent most of our topside time pumping out waste, checking the status of the solar panels, and scavenging for what we could. Last week showed promise, the air clearing, diminishing the need for the more expensive respirators, though we took them as backups. I'd missed that shift, which meant that I was on topside duty for the next two weeks.

"Yes," I said. "I have good news, though."

She switched off the burner and removed the pot as she scooted out of my grasp. "We're getting out of here?" she asked, placing the container on the metal stand next to the hand-carved slab of wood we used for a table.

It fit perfectly, dead-center in the room lined with buckets, chairs, and anything else we could find to sit on. We'd planned for our family. The five of us fit in the space with elbow room to spare. The plan had changed, however, when we watched our neighbors staring up into oblivion. I managed to save seven, ushering them into our bunker before the ground shook, warning me not to venture to the surface again.

I'd saved them, and in turn, saved us. Though it would cost us in provisions, we still had enough to go around, and the added mental stimulation others offered kept our minds fresh and off of the end of our world.

"Not that good of news," I said. I eased into the seat at the head of the table, a designation assigned to me by the others who avoided the responsibility of making the hard decisions regarding our lives. "Fagan reported the sky clearing. He's seen movement in the city."

"Movement?" she asked, excitedly.

"Yes. Lights and vehicles."

"But where are they getting gas? Do you think they are running generators? Are you all going there? Maybe they have food. ..."

I silenced her the best way I knew how—my lips on hers as I quelled the bubble of energy pouring from her. I drew back—breathless, as always. No other woman made me feel the way she made me feel, lost and complete all in the same breath.

She giggled, her fingers coming to rest over her kiss-swollen lips. "Sorry."

"Don't be. It's good to see you happy for a change."

She placed her hand on my cheek. "Long as we're together—you, me, the kids—I am happy."

"Still, I've missed your smile."

A throat clearing interrupted the intimate moment. The others filed in, having been aroused by the intoxicating aroma of the homecooked meal, and Fati busied herself filling their bowls with oatmeal. Everyone claimed a seat, settling in. Fati plopped bowls in front of them, the piping hot oatmeal tantalizing the senses. They waited until Fati served everyone and took her seat next to mine. More of a spiritual lot than a religious one, we gave thanks to the Universe and the powers-that-be for the meal and for protecting us through the night, then we dug in.

"So, the city today?" Sterling asked, before shoving a spoonful of oatmeal into the gaping hole he'd opened that had just ruined breakfast.

All eyes turned in my direction, waiting for an explanation to the question. Even the children's hands paused midway to their mouths at the possibility of others in the city. While we refused to believe we were the only survivors out there, none of us thought anyone in the city had survived. We'd watched as buildings burst into flames, collapsing upon impact from the giant flaming boulders raining down from the heavens. Plumes of smoke and screaming sirens, the last of my memories before the survival instinct kicked in, and my years of preparation forced my attention to the more important tasks at hand.

I sighed, setting my spoon hard on the table, then drawing my napkin from my lap. I planned a tactful response that would not raise their hopes too high, but would leave them with enough curiosity for wishful thinking. "Fagan has seen signs of others in the city."

"Like us?" my daughter said, wide-eyed and waiting.

"Maybe. We don't know their condition. I think we should remain cautious. The last thing we want to do is draw attention to our whereabouts. We have enough provisions to last at least a year. I'd like to keep our location a secret as long as possible."

"Are you really going?" Fati's question broke my heart, the risks weighing heavily upon her, knowing I might not return.

"While we are in a good place right now," I said, "eventually we will need to seek out others. For health reasons, if nothing else. We can't stay here forever."

"That sounds to me like you have a plan," Sterling said. While the others gawked at me like deer trapped in the trance of headlights, he'd already finished half his breakfast.

"I do. But this isn't breakfast talk."

We finished the meal in silence. The young ones stared into their bowls defeatedly. If they asked questions, they'd be met with the same answer: silence. I watched the adults ponder the possibilities, their spoons dragging through the cooling oatmeal, their appetites deserting them.

I finished my meal. I needed every ounce of strength for the journey ahead. Instead of waiting for Fati to gather my dishes, I scooped the rich-blue piece of porcelain from the table, placing it gently in the wash bin before giving her a curt nod and leaving the room.

Fagan joined me in the dust box, the closet between the central living space and the door to the outside. We stored our gear there, along with a change of clothes and wipes, a feeble attempt at reducing contamination from the dust, bacteria, and who knew what else from topside. At the end of the week, we'd fill a basin with pumped water, submerging our soiled garments. Then we'd spray them down with Fati's unique concoction that made us smell like women frolicking through a rainforest. Whether it worked or whether we'd just been lucky so far, not one of us had come down with anything. And since it appeared her home remedy did more good than harm, we humored her.

I donned my suit, curious why Fagan was joining me instead of Sterling. I waited until he was fully dressed and said, "Today is Sterling's day."

"That's true." His reply came across dry, like he was annoyed with my observation or at the fact that I dared question his presence.

"Is there something I need to know?" I asked.

"Nope. He needs to stay with his kids. He has more little ones than I do. Him not coming back has greater ramifications than me."

I gave him the onceover, unsure of how to perceive his sudden chivalrous gesture. Not that he hadn't spoken the truth. Sterling's kids were much younger—two and four, to be exact.

Young enough that they still needed their father. Fagan's and mine were closer to those independent years, their personalities already fully established. They could fend for themselves if it came down to it, so I guess the decision made sense.

"Care to share your plan?" he asked, taking a seat on the bench that stretched from one end of the room to the other.

"Pretty simple. Use the path through the neighborhood sticking close to the houses. Most of the ones heading toward the city are still standing." We'd scouted the area the first time out, getting a feel for what was left. The homes stood up well, most of them crafted from stone and cinderblock. Their roofs caved in, but the walls held steadfast.

He shot me an uneasy glance. "What then?"

I hadn't thought too far ahead. My plan comprised observation only. No contact until we evaluated the situation and reviewed our options. "We see what's out there and bring the information back."

"How far into the city are we going?"

I packed away my heavy-duty respirator, tucking two extra filters into my pack, just in case. He did the same, realizing I expected the worst. "We play it by ear," I said.

As we exited our bunker, I immediately stared into the sky, my mind not quite comprehending the sight. Blue. Not once had the sky been blue, not since the day before the heavens collapsed around us. A haze still hung over the city—the sky not the ocean blue I remember—but the smog was burning away, giving me hope that the surface would be safe soon.

I switched from the light respirator to a mask. Though the air was no longer heavy with the scent of burning flesh and chemicals, I chose not to tempt fate in going without something covering my nose and mouth.

We roamed the streets, sticking to the backroads while keeping an eye on the main thoroughfare. Our neighborhood sat a half-mile out from the city limits. When we had to commute, the preferred modes of transportation consisted of a shuttle bus, the bicycle path, or good old feet. I was thankful that I'd kept in shape.

We checked some houses as we made our way toward the city. A few appeared recently inhabited. Half-eaten, still-fresh fruit sat on the counter in one house, not an insect in sight. We found clean dishes and fresh-smelling linen in another, as if someone had gone about his daily chores—just as we did, to convince ourselves that the world as we knew it still existed, that we just needed to wait this out. But we saw no people nor any signs of forced entry. No sign that those who'd recently vacated the premises were dragged away against their will to be enslaved in the city. I noted the houses, filing the information in the back of my mind, to return should we need supplies.

The rumbling of motorcycle engines caught our attention when we exited the third house. We ducked behind the porch pillars. Around the corner, a motorcade escorted a dust-covered town car. Movement came from the house next to us. A young man in his twenties raced out to meet the vehicles before they moved away. His disheveled clothing and thinning hair made him look older than I was sure he was. Like us, he'd tried to wait it out. Apparently, he didn't have our survival instinct. He'd probably eaten the last of his food and was waiting for death.

A burly man in black pants and a red jacket bearing a familiar embroidered insignia climbed from his bike to meet the young man. The young man stumbled. The biker reached to steady him before the man careened face-first into the concrete sidewalk.

"How many?" the biker asked, his eyes scanning the area.

"J-just me," the man stuttered in response, exhaustion weighing his tongue.

"If you can work, you are welcome in the city."

"I can work. I just need food, and I can do whatever."

The window on the town car rolled down. A hand waved the young man over. A voice from the darkness of the vehicle said, "The work is hard, and there is a lot to be done."

"Anything, sir. Anything you need. Please."

A flick of the wrist and the biker led the man away. The window remained down. I felt eyes boring into my soul. Whoever hid in the shadows knew me. As an antelope plotting her escape from a leopard spotted in the brush, I waited—hoping he chose not to send those men after us. Then the window rolled up. The others pulled away, leaving the lone biker with the young man.

I eased back, pulling Fagan with me. We crouched behind the home. My eyes dropped to the disintegrated animal that once guarded this backyard.

"So, there are other survivors," Fagan said. He spoke the words to convince himself and me that maybe all wasn't lost. That if we reached out to those in the city, we could change our circumstances.

"So there are," I said.

His hand wrapped around my arm. "This changes everything."

Yes, we now knew there were others. But that didn't mean their circumstances were any better than our own. I shook him from the trance of possibilities. "We should head back."

He agreed. We retraced our steps, stopping to grab provisions from the houses we'd previously visited. We'd feast tonight then decide our next move.

Even with a full belly, sleep eluded me. No closer to a conclusion, the group agreed to sleep on the options and reconvene to discuss the situation in the morning. With plenty of supplies, a stable energy source, and clean water, time was an ally. I eased out of bed, navigating through the maze of beds and bodies, then slipping into the hallway. I peeked into each room as I made my way down the hall. The others were tucked into their beds, cuddled with their wives and children, the weight of the world playing on repeat in their dreams.

I, the unlucky one, with the ultimate responsibility for their lives, roamed the halls, playing the possibilities over and over in my head without the luxury of dreams. Too many unknowns made decisions difficult. The current situation in the city could be worse than our own. I needed more information. While what I was about to do went against my own rules that I'd established to maintain order, I had to know what was happening.

Slipping out of the compound unnoticed, I stalked through the darkness, taking a familiar path on the outskirts of the subdivision. When I reached the pile of bricks once composing the neighborhood welcome sign, I hunkered down. The city sat two blocks over, cold and quiet. A soft glow radiated from the central area, casting shadows over bits of buildings daring to remain standing against all odds. I assumed the glow came from the warehouse and factory district, where most of the area's food processing had occurred. Food was big business. Mom-and-pop restaurants with fresh delicacies to tempt the taste buds had once lined the streets. If even one of these buildings still stood, survivors would gravitate to the area.

I shifted my weight, prepared to sprint across the remaining open area, when a hand snatched me back. I landed hard on my bottom, not expecting the sudden downward momentum.

"What—"

A hand slapping over my mouth silenced me. Well, not so much the hand as the respirator crushing my nose and lips, rendering breathing difficult. My captor noticed my struggle. He released his hold on my face, but not on my arm. He gestured for my silence. I agreed. No one knew I was out there. Making noise endangered both of our lives.

He tugged me back, and I followed him into the house on the corner, the one with the least amount of damage. One wall had taken the brunt of the destruction, but the rest was intact. The curtains were closed, the lights out—not that I thought he had electricity. I followed behind him down a hallway. At the spot where a washer and dryer sat in the center of the hall, he pointed toward a room. I entered, and he closed the door behind us. Lights burst to life, and I noticed the hum of an electrical current over the silence of the night.

"You almost got yourself caught out there." The man removed his mask. I vaguely recognized his face. Maybe I'd seen him in passing.

"I was trying to sneak into the city."

"Can't do it topside." He held out his palm. "I'm Serino."

I shook his hand. "Anthony. But everyone calls me Ant."

"Good to know there are still a few survivors who haven't disappeared." He hopped up on the counter, resting his back against the wall.

"Disappeared?"

"Well, maybe *taken* is a better word. At least for the last of them."

I dropped my pack, removing my respirator and stuffing it into the bag. "By who?"

"Hopper, I suppose."

I paused, unsure I'd heard him right. "Hopper? As in G. Hopper, the meat distributor?"

"One and the same," he said with a shrug.

"How?"

"I'm guessing desperation. Masses of the unprepared flooded the city when they realized it was safe to come out of their homes. There were a few hundred of us then."

"And now?" I asked.

"A handful. We have twelve here, myself included."

I don't know why I trusted this guy, but my gut told me we shared the same philosophy. While the others saw their supplies dwindling, we were well stocked and prepared for the worst. "How'd you manage to survive?"

"Reinforced storm shelter. Been in a war or two. I've seen what happens when people feel they have nothing left. We pulled together when we saw the first flashes. Guess it was lucky it was the weekend. Would have been a much different outcome during working hours."

No denying the truth of his statement. "Have you been to the city?"

"Yeah." He shrugged. "Not pretty in there."

A heaviness filled the room, his somber mood spilling over to me. "I need to go there. See what's left. I'm good at salvaging."

"If you get caught, you're a goner."

"We saw a guy go there today. He looked pretty beat up. Not much hope. A town car with escorts stopped to help."

Serino shook his head. "If he can work, he'll be there until he's no longer useful. Then …"

I waited for him to continue. When he didn't, I dared to poke. "Then?"

"All I'll say is that everyone who's gone in there has never come back."

"Then how do you know what's going on in there?"

"Okay, maybe not everyone." A crooked smile inched across his lips. "But I didn't exactly prance in through the front door."

"You know another way in?"

"Many."

We gathered a few more supplies. Then, to my surprise, we dropped into the sewers, following the tunnels around the garden district straight into the heart of the city. We located a maintenance tunnel and came to the surface in the rear of a transportation wing a half-block east of the Hopper Corp factory. Serino jimmied a lock on one building, and we climbed the twelve stories, staying low to the roofline. On our bellies, he handed me a pair of night-vision goggles.

"There he is," I said.

The senior Hopper was at a window, staring over the two smaller buildings below him. The executive-office building stood at six floors, while the factory was a two-story structure. The warehouse was only one story but spanned several blocks. Small plumes of smoke billowed from the three vents atop the factory. It seemed inordinately bustling with activity.

"Look at him," Serino said, "standing there all smug."

Hopper donned an expensive suit and swirled the liquid in his glass.

"He does appear to be enjoying himself," I said.

"Yeah," Serino said, "while the rest of us scrounge for scraps or beg for a token morsel."

The foul smell of flesh and processed meat was potent. When

I finally recognized the shapes of what the laborers were pushing into the grinders, I nearly screamed. Serino covered my mouth at my gasp and shook his head. I didn't want to look back to the factory, but I couldn't glance away. The conveyor belt was piled with body parts. *Human* body parts.

I kept down the contents of my stomach, and we managed to hold our position for over an hour, watching and documenting the comings and goings of trucks, people and bodies being carted from one building to another. From what we could tell, the hotel two blocks west was where everyone slept who was still alive, and the factory was where they filled the machines with those too weak to keep working. As we prepared to depart, we noticed unusual movement in the penthouse of the executive building.

"What is he doing?" Serino asked.

I watched as two women entered the suite. "I think they're *ensuring* that they don't get sent to the grinders."

We didn't need to hang around to know what was about to transpire. I followed Serino down until we reached the lobby. The world rumbling forced us to stop and duck beneath the stairwell. Pieces of the building crashed down around us.

"Move!" Serino said.

He pushed me into a narrow space between the stairwell and the wall, then yanked me through a doorway, slamming the fire door behind us. When my eyes adjusted, I discovered we were in a tunnel with walls crafted of cinderblocks. We could still hear the world shifting around the outside, but only pockets of dust fell on us. Staying close to the walls, we made it to the sewers, retracing our path until we returned to Serino's house.

"Thanks for showing me the safe way in," I said. "It's almost daybreak. I'd better be getting back. There's ... a lot to think about."

He stashed his gear in a locked cabinet. "You guys got a radio? Cell towers are down."

"Yep. Ham."

"Good. Keep it on. I'll find you all later. What happened with the building wasn't a fluke. The city is unstable, and I fear an imminent collapse."

I turned in the doorway. "You think it's that bad?"

"I do." He leaned against the doorframe. "Those rumblings are becoming predictable. I'd say another week, and the city will collapse in on itself."

"What about all of those people?"

"What about them? Hopper's not going to warn them. Long as he's fed, he'll sit up in that penthouse having his way with anyone willing to throw themselves at him. He'll enjoy the spoils of others' labor until he either falls with the walls or escapes into the unknown with his hands washed of the whole situation."

I nodded despondently. The sky brightened, the sun inching over the horizon. I needed to move. "I'll wait for your communication. We're further out, so I'd appreciate any intel."

"The same on my end. We're stocked here and will probably grab as much as possible out of the city before it's all destroyed."

"Let's hope it doesn't come to that."

I spent the return journey going over the new information, pondering allies and adversaries and all the horror that I'd seen. I slipped back into the compound. The others were stirring, the whining of children echoing through the enclosed space. Dishes clanked in the kitchen as Fati prepared yet another meal. All I wanted to do was crawl into bed. Luckily, the path to our room sat clear, so I stripped and stumbled into bed without a second thought.

At some point, a warm hand caressing my leg drew me from a restless slumber. The worry lines across Fati's forehead reminded me of my disappearing act.

"I know what you're about to say." I rolled onto my back, pulling her down next to me.

"You had me worried."

I chuckled. "I had me worried, too. But I'm back, and safe."

She snuggled closer, her warm body molding to mine. "What did you find?"

"Some truth." I toyed with her hair. "We aren't the only survivors staying under the radar." She retreated from my grasp, but I held on tight. "In a neighborhood near the entrance of the city, I met up with another guy. Name's Serino. He says there are others with him."

She detected my change in mood. "What are you not telling me?"

I sighed, contemplating what and how much to reveal. I trusted Fati. And her judgment. And I knew I could tell her anything. Still, the last thing I wanted to do was frighten her with the gory scene I'd witnessed. "The city is different now."

"Well, I expected that."

"Not like this. Those who willingly enter the city do not leave."

"Hostages?"

"In a sense, yes. And Hopper is behind it."

She hmphed. "No surprises there."

"It gets worse. They are eating people." I paused for Fati's horrified gasp. "Serino says supplies are running low. The meat factory is still running, but Hopper and his goons have been leaving the city more often. Something must be up. They are searching for resources, and not in a good way."

"What are we to do?"

"Oh, there's more."

Fati turned on her side to face me. Her eyes narrowed. "How much more?"

"The city is unstable."

"War?" she said.

"No. On the verge of collapse. Physically. Whatever hit it has destroyed the infrastructure. The buildings are crumbling. I wouldn't risk going back in."

"Not even for supplies?"

She knew me so well. If I thought I could grab even a can of soup, I'd risk life and limb. Every morsel counted when we had mouths to feed, though we hadn't yet stooped to eating our neighbors.

The walls around us shook and interrupted the conversation. We shot up in bed. We dashed into the hallway. Fati ran in one direction to gather everyone into the central part of the compound. I ran to the storage room where we kept the ham radio.

I flipped on the contraption, scanning through the channels for a mayday request or an update on what was happening topside. Though we were underground, nothing muffled the echoing of booms. I prayed it wasn't bombs—that some entity hadn't discovered survivors and come to finish the job. I dared not consider the ramifications, the loss of life and other possibilities that fought to cloud my judgment.

"Ant!" a voice said. "Ant, come in!"

I stopped my channel surfing. The garbled message from Serino sent a wave of relief through my body. "This is Ant! Over."

"Thank God. How are you all holding up?"

I waited for the formal "over," then realized that Serino hadn't been trained in proper protocol for ham radio use. "We're hunkered down. Do you know what's going on up there? Over."

"The city is collapsing. I glimpsed the factory exploding and sinking before my video feed failed."

"Oh my God!" a voice said behind me.

I turned, not realizing Fati had entered the room. "Fati?" I called, but she dashed away. Knowing her, she'd make sure no one ventured this far down the hall. I'd have to remind myself to thank her later. "Any survivors?" I asked Serino, my heart sinking at the thought of all of those people we saw only hours ago.

"Not sure. Running through the previous feed to see if anyone got out. Just stay where you are. Give me a couple of hours. Keep the line open in case of emergency. Right now, as long as we stay in the bunkers, we should be safe."

I heard the sound of voices in the background. Realizing they were coming from his side, I relaxed. "Copy that. We'll rotate watch. If you need us, call."

"Got it."

"Over and out." I put the microphone down and stared at it.

The walls still shook, though the booming subsided. We remained busy, the children tending to small tasks, like wiping the falling dust from everything. We spread plastic over the bedding to reduce the need to wash or wallow in the mess. The women took inventory of supplies, the stocks of food, water, and necessities. They sat around the table, planning meals and schedules, not only to pass the time, but also to ration more than usual. We resorted to manual lighting, the hand-cranking radios and lanterns replacing the ones fed by solar power. We conserved the batteries for short bursts—mealtimes and such—when the need was most significant.

Fati handed me a plate with a cold sandwich, a handful of carrots, and a half-eaten snack cake.

"Dessert?" I asked, surprised at the luxury.

"Figured you could use the sugar boost." She forced a smile, her worry keeping it from reaching her eyes.

I pulled her closer and planted a wet kiss on her lips. "Thank you." I could tell a million questions sat on the tip of her tongue. "I'll let you know as soon as I hear something."

She nodded and tucked away her concerns, then left the room. I nibbled on my lunch/dinner, wondering how long we'd be trapped in this concrete heaven/hell. Yes, it offered safety—but from what? We couldn't stay here forever. Even with Fati's meal-planning, we'd eventually run out of food. Not to mention the cabin fever setting in. We needed to keep busy. Keep our minds fresh and on things other than whether or not we're going to die here.

"Ant. This is Serino. Do you copy?"

My stomach churned. My food threatened to come back up. "I'm here. Over."

"I've reviewed the tapes. Didn't see anyone come in or leave the city."

My heart sank. "Do you think they're all ..." I couldn't bring myself to say the word.

"Can't say till I get up there."

"You can't be serious." My hand slammed into the table as I stood.

"You only live once," Serino chuckled. "It's been quiet for nearly half an hour. I'm not going into the city. Just gonna check my video feeds. See if I can see where the damage is and repair what I can."

"But what if it wasn't just the factory. What if some nuclear bomb or something went off."

"Somebody's been watching too many end-of-the-world movies. I'll be fine. And if I'm not, someone here will let you know of my untimely demise. I need to get ready. If you don't hear from me by the end of the day—or should I say night—expect the worst."

I froze, torn between ordering him to stay where he was—as if I had any authority to do so—and wanting to join him. We needed information as much as he did. If the city was gone, and there were no survivors, then our plan to hunker down here made less sense. We could get what we could from the neighborhood. Load up a vehicle or two, and take our chances. The other option, stay here and die.

"I'm coming with you," I said, my mouth deciding for me.

"What?" Serino said.

Refusing to give him a chance to challenge my decision, I dropped the mic and dashed for the staging area. I ignored Sterling as I darted past.

"Ant?" I heard him calling my name, his footsteps following.

When I reached the staging room, I slammed the door shut and blocked it with a box. It was enough to give me a head start without permanently trapping anyone else in the compound. Suit secured, heavy mask in place, I pushed the hatch open. Dust filled the air outside, the sizzling and popping of transformers echoing in the distance. Aside from the added layer of smoke and smog, the neighborhood appeared untouched—a relief that gave us more options, at least for the short term.

I took my path through the alleyways, sticking close to the fences and houses, following the same pattern I'd previously used to make my way toward the city. I rounded the corner of a brick house. The front of it now sat in a pile in the yard, a victim of the blast from the city. A shadow darting through the trees drew my attention. I followed the dark speck for a block, hiding behind any object large enough to mask my presence. When the figure reached to reconnect the wires to a security camera, I realized who it was. I made my way closer. His back was to me, so I made a noise to get his attention. Pistol in hand, he swung around to face me.

"I told you I was coming," I said, through the muffling of the mask.

Serino either understood or recognized me. He lowered his weapon. "Give me a hand."

I had him by at least four inches, my reach much higher than his. I reconnected the wire and wrapped it with electrical tape. We repeated the process with four other cameras he'd either strategically placed around the neighborhood or hijacked in establishing his feed.

"I think that's all of them," he said. "I need to head back. See if I can reset my system and make sure everything is functioning." He smacked me on the back. "Told ya, old man, you worry too much."

A cough interrupted his chiding. On high alert, we both grabbed weapons. A machete in one hand, Serino wrangled a custom-modified, double-barrel, sawed-off shotgun from a holster hidden in the coat that covered his radiation suit. I easily managed a bump-stock rifle of my own, twice the size of his shotgun. The blasted thing took two hands to control, but I'd tested it a week before the sky fell, and I could handle its power.

We crouched, duck-waddling our way toward the sound of hacking. Our feet dragged through debris. I'm a lefty, so my weapon stayed out of Serino's way as he pressed his shoulder against the jagged bricks of a now one-story house.

When I looked over his shoulder, I couldn't believe my eyes. A figure stumbled through the billows of smoke coming from an overturned vehicle in the middle of the road.

"It can't be," I said. Of all the people to survive. No freaking way.

Serino glanced over his shoulder. "You seeing what I'm seeing?"

"Dead man walking?" I said, only half joking.

"Guess he had a plan C, too."

"You think he's alone?"

Lips pursed, Serino cocked his head and gave me side eye. "Has he ever been alone?"

I scanned the area, from the windows to the alleyways. I couldn't see much around the plume of smoke coming from the black town car we'd seen a day earlier. No other movement. No other shadows or figures moving from one hiding place to another. Just the portly man smudged with ash and covered in what I assumed was blood: Mr. Hopper.

The car exploded. Flames shot into the air. The boom startled Hopper as he staggered toward us. He tripped over his own feet to escape the rain of debris. He collapsed on the ground, his hand falling to his chest, fingers gripping the cloth as he hacked.

Tossing our safety to the wind, we holstered our weapons and raced across the lawn. The ground was covered with a thick layer of ash from the initial fallout. Serino retrieved a small first-aid kit while I rummaged through my bag for the spare respirator. I switched out the one I wore for the one from my pack and secured the new one in place against my mouth. Then I placed the other over the mouth of Hopper sprawled on the ground.

I stepped back and let Serino work. The meticulous routine he followed to check Hopper's body for injury told me Serino had once worked in the medical field. I focused on making sure no one sneaked up on us. I walked a circle around the two men, assessing threats from every angle. I still couldn't believe the gaping hole where the city once stood. Pillars of smoke rose to the skies. A flash occasionally raced across the empty space, the last of the transformers disconnecting from their power source.

"Do me a favor." Serino tossed me a set of keys with a remote on the ring. "Run over a block. Army-green stucco house. The remote opens the garage. There's an ambulance in there."

Ambulance? "Where are we taking him?"

"That's up to you. Your compound or mine. He'll survive, but I can patch him up better out of the elements."

I followed orders, risking capture by taking the main street. I found the house. The garage door lifted with ease. Once inside, I understood why: this house, too, ran on solar power. I assumed it belonged to Serino or to someone in his compound. I drove the ambulance back through a couple of overgrown lawns to avoid blocked streets. I doubt anyone minded much.

We loaded Mr. Hopper into the back. I made the call to bring him to my compound. I didn't know the full extent of Serino's medical setup, but I knew Sterling had enough medical training that—should something become infected—he'd chop off a limb without a second thought.

Drugged and under the watch of a guard, Mr. Hopper remained in our care for three days. Assured that Hopper had healed enough from his injuries, Serino, Sterling, and I waited for the last of the meds to wear off.

"Where am I?" Hopper managed in a haggard voice.

Fati offered him water, encouraging him to sip instead of gulp. "You're safe, Mr. Hopper."

"But where?"

"Does it really matter?" I asked.

"No. I suppose not," Hopper said. With Fati's help, he eased into a sitting position.

"What happened back there?" Serino asked Hopper gruffly.

"Don't know," Hopper said. "Was outside the gates when

the place went up in smoke."

Serino and Sterling shot me a glance. I didn't believe the man, either. I don't think any of us would have put it past him to have pressed the button.

A coughing fit started. Fati removed one pillow, so Hopper wasn't sitting so straight anymore. After another drink of water, Hopper said, "I suppose I should thank you for saving my life."

"You could. But we still have a lot of questions."

"I'm sure."

I didn't like the way he eyed my wife's chest. His tongue swiped across his lips. He caught me glaring at him, and he lowered his gaze to the plate of crackers and cheese on the folding table by his pallet.

"Is that for me?" he asked.

"If you think you can keep it down," Fati replied, placing a slice of cheese onto a cracker. She reached over to serve it to Hopper.

He grabbed her wrist. In one quick motion, he pulled her down, and his arm went around her neck. "Leave, or I kill her."

We all had weapons drawn now.

"You sure you want to do that?" I asked, calculating potential risks to Fati.

"You're right," he said. "Not yet."

He forced us all to the side of the bed, whispering something in Fati's ear. Her eyes widened, but whatever he'd said, she played along. She scooped a slice of cheese into her mouth, waiting for him to make his next move. I saw her throat move, the cheese morsel moving from her mouth down to her stomach. He swung her around, using her body as a buffer, and then his lips assaulted my wife's. A second later, blood ran down the sides of his mouth, a wet gurgle escaping parted lips. Fati rolled away. She spat out a chunk of his tongue along with a razorblade and wiped her mouth with the hem of her apron.

I eyed the empty syringe poking out of Hopper's side. He wasn't dead yet, but he would be soon enough. I closed the distance between us, leaned over, and whispered in his ear as intimately as he'd done to Fati: "Oh, Mr. Hopper. Don't you know how the story goes? You sat up in that penthouse of yours watching the rest of us scurry about, prepping for the end. And then, when it came, you took us hostage, surviving off the labors of others. Well, it stops here. Winter has come, and you have nothing left. Next time, maybe your kind will understand: the ants take care of themselves, while the grasshoppers leap headlong into an early grave."

Having spoken my piece, I walked away. We'd let him die, then leave him for whatever was left topside.

As I crossed the threshold, I heard Fati give the dying Hopper her last sentiment for him: "You could have lived with the ants. We didn't mind sharing. But you showed your true colors. Hope you don't end up an ant wherever it is you're going."

She joined me in the makeshift doorway, her fingers intertwining with mine. Like colonies of ants, we are and always will be stronger together.

Feathers

A RETELLING OF THE UGLY DUCKLING
RYAN PRIEST

By nature, ducks are really quite kind creatures and exceptionally accommodating. Innate to their character is a bend toward order, single-file lines, collective flight. They know how to get along, and they're very nurturing to their young and old.

Now, most of the ducks at Crown Hill Lake grew more light-colored, beige feathers than dark feathers. When Gregory hatched from his egg, however, his feathers were more dark than beige. Nobody knew how it happened. Other birds were known to sneak an egg or two into somebody else's nest from time to time.

That isn't to say the other ducks were necessarily cruel to him. Even when the other little ducklings, knowing no better, would tease poor Gregory, an older duck would step in and lightly chastise the little ducklings, using it as an opportunity to teach a lesson.

"Sweet little ducklings, you mustn't tease Gregory. Every bird is different, none better than the next. Gregory is not an ugly duckling, but a beautiful swan waiting to grow."

It was nice of them to say, but Gregory didn't feel like a beautiful swan.

As the ducklings grew older, they learned their lessons, the correct way to waddle, swimming and diving, how to quack properly. The lesson master, Ms. Mary Duck, went down the line demonstrating for each young duck. First, she'd make the appropriate quack and then call from the duckling, one of similar volume and pitch.

"Very good, my little duckling," she'd say, with a smile on her bill as she moved down the row.

Gregory waited at the end of the line nervously. This was going to be his first official quack, and he didn't want to mess it up. He lifted his head and took a deep breath, filling his body with air for the coming quack.

Ms. Mary finally made it to him. "Now, sweet Gregory, ducks quack, but swans honk. Let me hear your honk. Repeat after me." Ms. Mary uttered forth a loud, bellowing honk.

"Quack?" He was confused.

"No, Gregory, ducks quack. You need to honk."

His duckling friend Chris assured him, "It's okay, Gregory, you're lucky. I wish I could honk."

Later that day, the ducklings were practicing walking in line on the wet dirt at the edge of the lake, leaving little webbed footprints.

"Gregory, now you're a swan," Ms. Mary said, "and swans walk differently than ducks. Swans bob their heads more, like this, and they take wider steps, like this." Ms. Mary demonstrated. "Now, you try."

"But Ms. Mary," Gregory said, "I'm fine learning to walk like everyone else."

"Ducklings, every bird is different. It's these differences that make us beautiful. Can you imagine a lake in which all the birds looked alike, walked alike, sang the same song? It would be an awfully boring place."

"I wouldn't want to live there!" little duckling Hanna squeaked.

The other children didn't mind waiting while Ms. Mary went on with her swan-waddling lesson for Gregory. Ducks are really quite happy to accommodate.

That evening, as the sky dipped into a darker hue of blue, the little duckling class gathered together to display everything they'd learned for the adult ducks. They quacked, they waddled, all like good little Crown Hill ducklings should. The adults watched, tears in their black eyes, smiles on their bills—they could see themselves in these little ducklings, remember their own youths, so many seasons ago.

After the other ducklings performed, they made time for Gregory to exhibit his honking and his swan walk. At first, he stumbled and tripped. Chris laughed but was met with a sharp glance by Ms. Mary. As Gregory attempted a second time, all the ducks cheered and clapped for him. Unsure of himself, Gregory gave his impression of a waddling swan, and his honk was far more like a quack. He felt embarrassed. The minute he was done, he waddled away, with his feet together and his head down.

At bedtime, when Ms. Mary told the ducklings their nightly story, she told their favorite tale about the duck who steals a loaf of bread. In honor of Gregory, however, she changed the story to make the hero a swan instead of a duck, and she gave him an accent and a funny little walk that everyone in the class loved, except for sullen Gregory.

Sensing that something was not quite right with Gregory, the adult ducks convened and discussed how to make him feel better.

"It must be tough for him," Barnaby Duck said. "There's no other swans around for him to look up to. It's our own fault. We haven't done enough to make Crown Hill a welcoming place for all avian species."

The other ducks agreed and remonstrated themselves for always looking inward and not spending enough time outward. They decided that it wasn't enough for them to tell Gregory how to be a swan. They had to find actual swans for him. If he did not physically *see* other swans for himself, how was he to form the sense of self-image he'd need for adulthood?

The next day, Barnaby Duck and Ms. Mary Duck led the ducklings on their first fieldtrip out of Crown Hill. As they'd practiced, one after the other, single file, the ducks made their way across town and country, all the way down to Malarky Park, where swans were known to live.

Keeping their distance, the ducklings spent the day watching the swans. It was great entertainment. The swans walked so differently, spoke so differently. All the little ducklings could talk about on their long trip home was how creative and comical all the swans were. They, of course, took pains to assure that they were laughing *with* the swans and not *at* them. Nothing but complete respect.

"But the swans weren't laughing," Gregory pointed out.

"Gregory, why do swans wiggle their heads like this?" Hanna asked, as she mimicked the bobbing head movements the ducklings had seen earlier.

"I don't know why they were doing that," Gregory answered. He didn't know that, and he didn't know why the swans spoke so differently, or which word meant which, or anything else about them.

"I wish I were a swan," Chris said, happily putting his wing around Gregory. "You guys have such powerful wings and pretty feathers. Can I touch yours?"

Back home at Crown Hill, Gregory separated from the other ducklings. They couldn't quit talking about swans and asking him inane questions that he had no way of answering. Having seen real swans up close, he now felt more alone than ever. He walked through the tall grass, past the old log. The moon rose high overhead.

"Gregory Duck, is that you?" came a voice from inside the reeds. It was old, blind Lazlo Duck. He couldn't get around anymore and survived off the bread others brought him. Everyone knew this would be his last summer. "I could hear your sniffling across the lake. What is wrong?"

"Everyone says I'm this beautiful swan. But it feels like a lie. I don't feel like some beautiful swan at all."

"Of course you don't, because you're a duck."

"But my feathers are darker than all the other ducks. My whole life they've told me that means I'm something else. Something that's not a duck—no less valuable, but nevertheless, not a duck."

"That's the silliest thing I've ever heard. I don't care if your feathers are bright blue—that doesn't change a thing. In my five trips south, I've seen a lot of birds, met a lot of other ducks. We come in all shapes, sizes, and yes, even colors. I can hear it in your voice, smell the cattails on your down. I'm as sure you're a Crown Hill duck as I'm sure of anything."

"I think you're right," Gregory said, relieved. Even though Lazlo was blind, he was the first duck ever to see Gregory for what he really was. "But ..."

"What is it?" Lazlo asked, his white eyes forever in the darkness, but his other senses missing nothing.

"I get the feeling they don't want me to be a duck. They *want* me to be a swan. Not for me, but because it means something to them. A swan would add a little spice to the lake, allow them to see their community as more vibrant and diverse. It'd show all the other ducks, in all the other lakes, that Crown Hill wasn't stuck-up or insular. I feel like I'm disappointing them when I don't walk the way they expect me to, or when I quack instead of honk."

"Did you hatch for them, or did you break out of that egg for yourself?" Lazlo said. "Let them be disappointed. You are you, and that's what is special. Not the color of your feathers. You owe nothing to ducks who look like you or to ducks who don't. I know you're a duck, you know you're a duck, and anyone who expects something different out of you, just because of the color of your feathers, will never be able to see the magnificent duck that is underneath those feathers."

Gregory felt better. He waddled up and lay next to Lazlo, so they could share in each other's warmth. Gregory was glad to know that he wasn't a beautiful swan but in fact just a beautiful black duck.

The Hunter

A RETELLING OF LITTLE RED RIDING HOOD
ARIELLE K. JONES

n this evening, she wonders again if he will return.

It has become harder and harder to find comfort so deep in the woods, their home so hidden from the travelers' paths. She wonders if he's rock-a-byed a buck tonight, how the fight of antler, bone, and blade must've made quite the sound out there. Days have gone by, and after all her hours of fretting and bathing, she's found herself hearing footsteps near and far, hearing echoed howling as the windchimes gossip with autumn on the porch. Any sound outdoors or creak of wood within has her heartbeat tripping and catching on itself. Excitement and concern. He should be home by now.

Home is hanging herbs, is a bed meant for one but shared by two, is simple warmth, is hand-me-down curtains. The sun has been gone for some time, but she leaves the curtains open and busies herself at the crackle and murmur of the fireplace. It is a meager fire, only warm enough to maintain a face-to-face heat, like sharing a pillow. A fire is a poor substitute for a husband, like the blankets that she has been wearing to and from their bed as a makeshift robe.

While crouching to tend the heat, she lets the covers slip from her shoulders, bare-breasted and unblinking as she shifts the kindling. She rearranges the logs, and they tumble and collapse, little snaps of amber light breaking open in the hearth. She tracks the flickers as minutes pass, listens to the embers until her drying eyes become heavy, until they burn and water from sitting too long and too near the flame. Her attention wanes until she curls up naked on the floor, dragging the blankets back up around her.

A dream begins to begin when the front door thuds closed.

Her mind wakes before her body. Before her limbs rouse, she can tell by the drag of his footsteps that his journey back to her has not been interrupted by rest. He is usually more cautious than that. The hunter waits for her there at the room's edge, lets her untangle herself from the covers.

He fills the doorway like a living shadow, his features lit by the fire the same faint way that clouds appear in the afterglow of lightning. From what she can see, his hair looks as if the wind and night fog had fought over it, and the hair on his face is new across his cheeks and over his chin since a few days past. His time away has roughened him, and yet, relief flutters behind her lips forcing her to smile. Her husband is home, and with her face half hidden by her hair, hanging like moss, her eyes fasten to his in the dark.

"Wait," he says, voice crawling, grizzled and hushed and solid as he stays at the door. "Wait," he says, because he sees, can tell from where he stands, that her heart's beating in her like a jarred bee, and her legs aren't quite untangled yet.

She ignores the warning and tries to stand anyway, would skip the step of standing and just run to him if she could. She needs him to know that she's been home, just waiting.

Needles sting and race throughout her waking legs the moment she teeters. It happens faster than she can comprehend, not the tingling pain, but the fact that he is there, hands spread and bound to her bare waist like bark to a tree. The exhale of his hitched breath strokes itself warm across her scalp. Her name had never been so delicate before. She doesn't even wait until she's steady before she tiptoes onto his boots, slipping only once on the leather as she fits to him like flame, lips smiling onto the stubble of his jaw, fingers finding crevices to burn awake. Her fingers crawl into the collar of his cold coat searching their way up the soft spine stairs of his nape, seeking solace there.

Her stomach snatches back with a chill when she is pressed so close that his coat buttons push into her skin in a skipping line. It's a temporary withdrawal. With her fingers embedded in his hair, the hunter's wife is not sure if she is trying to hold him, or trying to hold herself up. She starts to say so, but chest to chest she can tell that their hearts don't match. His rhythm is amiss.

Refusing to let go, she simply leans just enough away to see if she can find something foreign in his face since the last time they were together. Which troubles have ridden him home? He was always such a tranquil thing in her arms, so docile and grave. But now, now he's looking at her the way a doe does, eyes wet and slow to blink. There's bad news.

He gently lowers her from standing on his feet. She starts to grant him space, but the hunter keeps his hold and leans in so close that temple to temple she knows his words before he speaks them.

"Last night, I buried a girl and an old woman."

His voice is muted against her neck, the words catching in her thick hair like weak-winged flies. She can feel it through his skull when he clenches his jaw. His breathing short as his arms stay wrapped around her.

The hunter's wife releases her held breath and draws her grasp from his nape forward to cradle his face. It takes soft work, but he allows her to guide him into looking at her. Lightly, she smooths her thumbs over handfuls of coarse cheek.

Together, they stand within the flicker of the fireplace. She can feel the heat from his mournful mouth. She takes his with her own, only slightly less hungrily than she'd like. More softly than she'd like. Their lips move in the way that grass is grazed, slowly taken in piece by nuzzled piece.

She continues until she lifts her chin and places a kiss into the wrinkle of the bridge of his nose, saying, "Give me your hands."

He stiffens, winces when his wife reaches down to take his wrists so reverently. The hunter's wife knows better than to rush him when she can feel the desperate way his fingers are searching for safety, for shelter around her waist, and her heart aches at the way that they knead frantically into the muscle and bone of her sides. Eventually, he consents.

His nod is slight, and his hands go limp as she eases them up between and nestles them to her face like a rough bouquet. He cringes, but she kisses his hands, anyway.

"We fought," he says, and won't look at her. She doesn't ask, but he answers, "The wolf. I chased it around the house," he leans away from her touch and swallows, "around the bodies."

She could smell it then, the blood-muddied earth soaked into his skin. Her husband's hands, cold and filthy shovels with five fingers each. She can almost taste the flesh of what he'd been left to bury, can smell the girl's sweat from walking so long, can smell the grandmother's jams just beneath that.

The fire crackles behind them, and the hunter's wife says nothing. Instead, she lays her forehead to their clasped fingers as if praying for the both of them. She has never prayed, though. With her eyes lowered, she becomes aware of her nakedness. She ought to be cold, usually is when she is standing like this. His lips are brief on her brow.

He then steps away to remove his coat, so much like a weary animal leaving its den. She follows him and takes the coat from his hands so that she can hang it. She has been waiting to do this.

"Let's go to bed," she says. And she can't see it, but she's sure he nods.

She follows him into the room. The moment he is seated, she wordlessly kneels before him. He protests, but she is already undoing the laces of his boots, methodically loosening each row of string before she disassembles the knot. The leaf litter and mud catching under her nails does not even distract her. She can sweep in the morning; there is other work to do.

With one hand taking an ankle and the other cradling his heel, she slides the boots from his feet. She peels off each sock. They roll away slow and clinging. He curls his toes the moment they hit the open air, and she smiles to herself, keeps it small enough for him not to notice. When she looks up, the hunter's hurting eyes surprise her.

"I wasn't fast enough, but I heard them yelling."

There is a wavering toward the end, a breaking of the last syllables. The shine of dampness easing slow as sap into the vague wrinkles near his eyes is hard to watch.

Hesitating only somewhat with the burden, she hoists both his legs up onto the mattress and the covers fall off of her. She is wordless when she sits astride him, settles her thighs on either side of him, and leans back against his raised knees. Upon straightening her back, her hair brushes his kneecaps through the fabric of his pants, and the breath he takes is fresh and uncertain. She tucks away a pinch of her dark hair behind her ears, the better to hear him with.

From this new vantage she still sees the shine of his eyes in the dark, and there is something humid in them. Her hands feel less steady on his chest as he stares at her face, letting the look wander heavily downward. She can feel it like water rolling over her cheeks, then her chin, then down her neck all the way to her navel where it thickens then roams, his eyes pouring back and forth over her sprawled legs.

And she should have been pleased under the worship of his regard, should feel eager when he reaches out and dapples his fingers into the hollow of her throat. He almost distracts her when he drags the heavy dry weight of his hand down from her neck and rests it between her breasts, lets it settle there like a stone to a riverbed. He is tempting when he applies pressure loaded enough that she can feel the echo of her heart through the center of his palm. She could have been pleased, but she knows him too well.

It is the restrained line of his mouth that damns her delight. She can tell that he isn't thinking of her.

The rumble of his voice buzzes in her fingertips, "It had me like this, pinned beneath its paws."

His heart has hastened its pace. It beats like a hammer swinging on a string, knocking back and forth between his spine and her hands on his chest. She considers her touch and can feel the scraped lines through his shirt. The claw marks will certainly scar.

Her head falls forward with her hair drenching his abdomen in black. She presses a kiss to him between her thumbs, just over his knocking heart. Her lips fail to leave his chest as they move. "Does it hurt?" she asks.

"Not severely," he answers, eyes still closed. The hunter sighs, and the inhale afterward brings in the pine scent of her hair with the hint of something floral or citrus clinging to her tresses even though the two of them own no garden.

"I'm sorry," she says, lays her forehead where her mouth had been, and lifts her hands from his wounds, pulls the pads of her fingers along his sides. She slips them down and traces where the pommels of their hips meet.

His words pause her. "There were silver scissors on the dresser. They were sharp."

She stills atop him, listening.

"Before it flew out the back door, I—"

She pulls back, supports herself with hands that sink into the pillow on either side of his neck. Her arms are pale pillars leading to the crown of her bent head, hair sinking heavy and draped across his chest, but he can see through a chance sliver that her eyes have fastened to the bedroom door. Her thighs are coiled.

"I'm tired," she mumbles and disentangles their legs, working not to meet his eyes.

But he knows her almost as well as she knows him and dislikes believing that she would have something to hide, not after everything they've been through. "Then lie down," he says.

He reaches up with knuckles grazing her neck as he sweeps the black mass of her hair over and behind her shoulders. She turns her head then from the direction of the door, not shrugging him off, but skips appraising his face to frown toward the window. The moonlight makes a perfect glowing square on the wood floor, and she wants so badly to be under that light again.

His voice shudders in her ribs like a rumble of thunder. "My grip wasn't as tight as it should have been on the scissors."

With fingers on the taut skin bridging her shoulders and her neck, he pulls her down. And she knows better than to fear her husband, but there is a pause.

"Before it bolted, I nicked it just between its shoulder blades, just too lightly."

He uses his blunt nails to trail a path down the knobs of her spine. By now, they both have noticed that the hunter's touch is not as gentle as when he had first come home. He is so close to apologizing but is struck speechless. His regret curdles and dries because of the texture that he finds square in the middle of the flesh of his wife's back.

A new scab, near the size of his thumb, clean and straight, freshly healed over. The hardened crumbs of it roll grainy then grow wet toward the middle.

"How did this happen?"

Instead of running like he can tell she wants to, she collapses into him concealing her face. Bit by bit, she seeps into him like a stain. Like a jar of preserves breaking on a cottage floor from a careless wag of a black tail. Like the warm flesh of fruit being flattened into a rug by the thoughtless weight of dirty paws.

"I love you." The words come out of her boldly.

The hunter says nothing, is still trying to find his breath. She looks up at him, and my, what big eyes she has.

They track his shaking hand, a finger still wet with the residue of her wound, as he reaches for her and moves the hair from her face. She sits stock still wondering where he'd cut if he wanted to make her easier to carry out of their home. In pieces or emptied as a pelt. He's looked at elk and rabbit and boar this way. Pleading seems like her only chance.

"Love, I never meant to." Her stare holds as she presses a kiss to his wrist. "They've been bringing the livestock inside, and you were taking so long."

She should be ready for the tug to her hair and the bite in his tone when he tells her, "You swore to me that you were above those beasts. You swore to me you were better than your brothers."

The pain stings her eyes, but she can't cry because then her vision will be blurred, so she blinks away the tears in her eyes, the better see him with, as they finish what they started in that grandmother's cabin.

The Fox Spirit

A RETELLING OF KUMIHO AND HULI JING
WEN WEN YANG

he legend is only partially true. I did bathe in the river, and the farmer did see me there in human-skin. I had hidden my fox-skin well. I am not the *huli jing* of the Western legend, whom they kidnapped, whose fox-skin they stole. One human poet called it devotion that she returned nightly to her husband. She was devoted to her fox-skin as one is devoted to one's hands.

When humans carved their way into the forest and turned trees into their homes, we determined some use for their village. Some of us can walk upright and sit in human-skin for hours in service to those who cannot. Madam Snake is too old to hunt rabbits. The ghosts want new clothes but cannot wait until the new year.

The farmer knew me from the market. This young man had shoulders as wide as his plow. He bought my herbs and tonics for aching muscles. I learned that he worked his land alone, that he considered it his because his grandfather had passed it down. I did not tell him that the land before his grandfather's time belonged to everyone, not just humans.

The humans had pasted wards across every threshold,

stopping weaker spirits from entering. Walking under the new wards felt like my bones were trying to erupt from my skin. Shamans had blessed these papers, but the magic came from the ink, made from the burned bones of spirits.

Nightly, I added a stroke to render the wards' magic impotent. One vengeful ghost had come through and chased her husband down their well. The humans thought grief had driven him to the same well where they had found his wife's broken body.

When he saw me at the river, I imitated a succubus' laughter. Water ran down my leg and caught the sunlight. I'd never seen a man disrobe so quickly. No wonder the Woman Spider never starved for mates and meals.

I remember the strength in his hands. I'd bandaged them with honey to prevent infection, once when his ox bit him. These hands had plastered wards across his wagon.

Afterward, when we were drying on the grass, he asked me to be his wife. Once seduced, would he remove the wards? Would he share his land with the demons who had lived there before his grandfather's time?

The sounds of men shouting in the distance startled us.

"It's the hunt," he said, searching for his pants. "There is a beast in the forest, luring men with a baby's cries. It eats our hearts and livers. But if *we* eat it, we will be immune to poison."

I escaped before he found his shirt.

The legend would have you believe an invader of our home could seduce a fox spirit into hiding her true nature. The poet laments that when he found her fox-skin, she abandoned him.

That night, I smeared every ward in the village with ash and pig's blood. I poured the blood onto the floor of my shop and splashed it across the walls. All of us who had lived in the village ran. We crossed paths with demons seeking to eat a holy man for immortality and tree spirits eager to water their roots with human blood.

Two new moons later, I had our son.

He has his father's shoulders, but we share the same fur. His is dark, soft as shadows. I've seen him sit in the inbetween-skin, pulling on his fox-skin and watching his reflection in the water. His human features melted into pointed ears and a bushy tail. Jagged tufts of white fur circle his right foreleg where a trap caught him when he was a cub. Each trap steals an acre of our safety while the humans hide behind their wards.

The legend ends with the human's forgiveness because the huli jing is his son's mother. I will not seek forgiveness. I will walk into the village in human-skin again and tear the wards down. My son will meet his father. I will ask the farmer if he would eat his son's flesh.

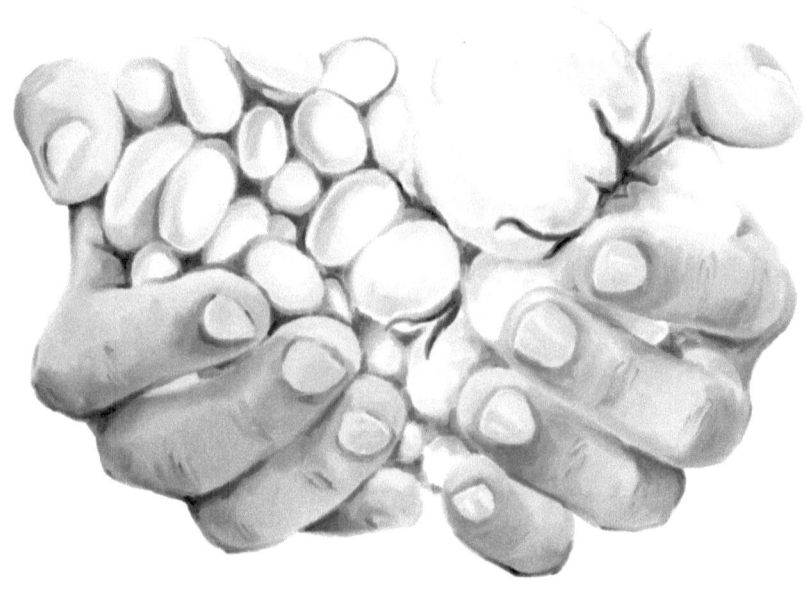

Author Biographies

ENEIDA ALCALDE
immigrated to the U.S. as a child, transplanting her Chilean-Puerto Rican roots into Pennsylvanian soil. Her stories and poems have appeared in several literary outlets, including the *SFWP Quarterly*, *Birdcoat Quarterly*, and *Magma Poetry*. Learn more about her at eneidapatricia.com, and follow her on Instagram and Twitter at @EneidaEscribe.

AZURE ARTHER
is a college professor in Dallas, Texas. Her work has appeared or is forthcoming in *Burningword Literary Journal*, *Aurealis*, *The Chaffey Review*, *Miracle Monocle*, and others. She has several obsessions, mainly good literature, both reading and writing it, teaching in Converses, and enjoying her time with her family.

SUH YOUNG CHOI
is an aspiring writer and student at the University of Washington, studying statistics and classics. Having spent most of her childhood in Arkansas, she now lives in Seattle. She enjoys drawing, wandering through secondhand bookstores, and attempting one-woman recreations of her favorite musicals.

ANGELICA ESQUIVEL
is a Xicana writer and embroidery artist. Her fiction and poetry have appeared in *Crab Orchard Review*, *Great Lakes Review*, and *Chestnut Review*. She is ever grateful for the existence of pens and paper, needles and thread.

SIMONE-MARIE FEIGENBAUM
is an ELA teacher currently teaching middle school in the Bronx. They live in Manhattan with their cat, Garnet, and way too many books. More of their work can be seen at shakespearetheatre.org, on *Button Poetry*'s Instagram page, and on their own Instagram page at @writemagick.

SAMANTHA GUZMÁN
is a native New Yorker of Afro-Caribbean/Latinx descent, who works as a designer by day and a passionate writer by subway commute, lunch, and night. Her goal as a writer is to capture the unique experiences of Black and Latinx people through a fictional and sometimes fantastical lens.

MONIQUE HAYES

received her MFA from the University of Maryland College Park. Her work has appeared in *Furious Gravity*, *Spark*, *Eastern Iowa Review*, and elsewhere. She's a VONA and Callaloo Fellow, and a recent Pushcart Prize nominee.

MELANIE HOBBS

is a writer of Malaysian-Indian descent. She lives in Perth, Western Australia, with her husband, two-year-old daughter, and dog, with another baby on the way. Melanie worked as a high school English teacher for ten years and is currently a full-time parent and writer of short fiction.

RIAZ JAHANGIR

is an engineer by training but a writer by calling. After a decade building software for corporations and various contraptions to amuse his children, Riaz now strives to build strange and wonderful new fictional worlds. Find him at riazjahangir.com.

ARIELLE K. JONES

is a QWOC from California's Central Valley. She earned her MFA from Fresno State University. A *Tin House* Summer Workshop alumna, Arielle has pieces with *The Rumpus*, *Blood Tree Lit*, *Blood Orange Review*, and other journals. Her work often portrays intimacy and underrepresented identities through taboos and fairytales.

MINA LI

is a Michigander through and through. She started getting into mermaids at the age of six and never really got out. She enjoys springtime walks, knitting everything from colorwork hats to lace shawls, and needs to try her hand at butternut squash soup.

KAITLYN LYNCH

is an actor, director, and author. You can read more of her work in *Litro Magazine* and anthologies published with Blood Song Books and Black Hare Press. With Turkish-Italian-Ashkenazi roots and a Christian upbringing, she has a unique cultural identity that shapes the voice of her writing. Find her at kaitlynlynch.com.

TRAVIS TYLER MADDEN

(they/their/theirs) is a graduate of Towson University's Professional Writing graduate program. They have been published by *Writer's Digest*, the Baltimore County Public Library, *Ligeia Magazine*, Paragon Press, and Castabout Literature. They currently work as a full-time writer for *Hunt a Killer*.

CHRISTIANA MCCLAIN

is a black writer from Houston, Texas. She graduated from Spelman College and is currently completing her MFA.

JAYET MOON

is a biomedical engineer and a history buff who has lived and worked in three continents and is currently a resident of Delaware. He likes historical fiction, detective fiction, wild blueberries, and buffalo sauce. He has obtained certifications in fiction writing from Wesleyan College and Delaware Community College.

DEBORAH D.E.E.P. MOUTON

is an internationally known writer, performer, artivist, and Poet Laureate of Houston, Texas. Formerly ranked the #2 Best Female Performance Poet in the World, a German translation of her Pushcart-nominated collection, *Newsworthy*, will be released in fall 2021. Read more at LiveLifeDeep.com.

ASIA NICHOLS

is a nomadic creator with roots in the Bay Area, California. She writes offbeat, fantastical stories appearing in *Betwixt Magazine* and in festivals for The Navigators Sci-Fi Theater, Pride Films and Plays, and others. Now in Mexico, Asia is working on an omnibus film subverting age-old fairytales.

BRIAN C. ORR

is a New York City-based writer, composer, and arts administrator. He often writes fiction based on his life driven by observational humor. He is a graduate of Carnegie Mellon University. He also writes short plays, which are compiled at his website, NoFsLeft.com.

EDWARDO PÉREZ

is driven by the belief that not every story has been told. He enjoys crafting speculative fiction in all its genres and engaging the unexpected point of view through an array of characters, evocative language, and poignant (often philosophical) narratives that speak to the spectrum of the human condition.

TORIE COMEAUX PLOWDEN

is a practicing physician, wife, and mother. She has a longstanding love of words and stories and recently rediscovered writing. She strives to tell stories with positive role models, allowing young African American children the opportunity to see themselves portrayed in fiction.

RYAN PRIEST
is an African American computer programmer who lives in Colorado. When he's not fighting for a paycheck, he's fighting for equality and never plans to stop until he gets it.

MONIQUE QUINTANA
is the author of *Cenote City* (Clash Books, 2019). Her work has been nominated for Best of the Net, Best Microfiction, and the Pushcart Prize. She has also been awarded residencies to Yaddo, The Mineral School, and Sundress Academy of the Arts. You can find her at moniquequintana.com.

AKILA RAYAPURAJU
is a student at Rutgers University with a strong love for capturing magic with words and for books that make you think. She is a writer and a budding scientist. Her dream is one day to add to the growing POC representation in literature.

DANAY ROBINSON
is a special-education teacher in Dallas, Texas. She fills her time writing and chasing stories in books, shows, and movies. She has a published short story in *Gravel Magazine*.

AZIZA SPHINX
sees the world through a canopy of weeping willows. Family matters—and not just blood, for those who take care of us are the truest. When the valleys of the journey summon, and the pen becomes mightier than the sword, this is the world Aziza Sphinx breathes for.

JEANETTE WEASKUS
is an enrolled member of the Nez Perce Tribe of Idaho and grew up listening to traditional Nez Perce tales along with studying many mythologies of the world. "The Metal Pig" was always one of her favorite fairytales, and she had great fun "Indianizing" it.

WEN WEN YANG
was born and raised in the Bronx, New York. She graduated from Barnard College, Columbia University with a degree in English and concentration in Creative Writing. She has two pieces, a fantasy short story and an essay, in the literary magazine *Grub Street*, Volume 70 (2021).

Acknowledgments

"The Empanada Man" was previously published in *Palabritas*.

"Soil Brown" was previously published in *Once upon a Time in Alexandria*.

"The Hunter" was previously published in *Blood Orange Review*.

"The Fox Spirit" was previously published in *So to Speak*.

Colophon & Permissions

The edition you are holding is the First Edition of this publication.

The cover title is set in Treasure Map Deadhand, created by Gem Fonts. The cover subtitle is set in Ailerons, created by The Hungry Jpeg. The back cover is set in Avenir, created by Adrian Frutiger. The Alternating Current Press logo is set in Portmanteau, created by JLH Fonts. Interior titles are set in DampfPlatz, created by Paul Lloyd. Interior subtitles are set in Old-Style Small Caps, created by HPLHS Prop Fonts. The drop caps are set in Goudy Initialen, created by Dieter Steffman. All other text is set in Iowan Old Style, created by John Downer. All fonts are used with permission; all rights reserved.

The Alternating Current lightbulb logo was created by Leah Angstman, ©2013, 2021 Alternating Current. The unicorn divider was created by Gordon Johnson.

The cover and all interior artwork was designed and compiled by Leah Angstman, using elements from the following artists and studios: VL Shop, Tribble Design, Liuba at BarvArt, Lizzie at Scarlet Heath Art, MyStocks, Catgo Digital, Olyamore, Dvarg Shop, Elena Dorosh, Old Continent Design, Tanya at Tanata Design, Busy May Studio, Microvector, Digitalartsi, Win Win Artlab, Marco Livolsi, Anastasia Sherbakova, Annalise Batista, Brigitte at Art Tower, Gerd Altmann, Susann Mielke, Bertrand, Evgeniias Art, Shuneika, Blanc and Graphic, PikePicture, Prawny, PrettySleepy Art, Schmidsi, VectorTatu, Victoria Borodinova, Evgeniia Grebneva Painting, Wolfgang Eckert, Parker West, Pete Linforth, Netkoff, Alexandra Koch, Le-Coq Design, Marcela Bolívar, Stefan Keller, Every Sun Sun, G Lady, Xamtiw, Sabina Z., Skyler H. at PixelHeart, Carla Burke, Svitlana Yanyeva, Astro Ann, Marcy Coate, Fox Studio, True Colors Original Hand-Drawn Artwork, Irina Koteneva, Joanne Marie, 愚木混株 CDD20, Piyapong Saydaung, Efes, JL G at Ractapopulous, R. Daudt, Ivan Pretorious, S. Bartels, Blitzmaerker, Tanin Graphic Design, Pablo Ariel Cañete, Enrique Meseguer, Graphobia, Tartila, Jazella, Watercolor Png Studio, Shannon Keyser at Old Market, Sasin Tipchai, While Baby Is Sleeping Design, Mete Humay, Gordon Johnson, Kalhh, b0red, Lisa Redfern. All images used with permission and full commercial licenses; all rights reserved.

All other material was created, designed, modified, or edited by Leah Angstman. All material is used with permission; all rights reserved.

OTHER WORKS FROM
Alternating Current Press

All of these books (and more) are available at
Alternating Current's website: press.alternatingcurrentarts.com.

alternatingcurrentarts.com

www.ingramcontent.com/pod-product-compliance
Lightning Source LLC
Chambersburg PA
CBHW030554020726
47494CB00005B/1606